Julia James lives in England and adores the peaceful verdant countryside and the wild shores of Cornwall. She also loves the Mediterranean—so rich in myth and history, with its sun-baked landscapes and olive groves, ancient ruins and azure seas. 'The perfect setting for romance!' she says. 'Rivalled only by the lush tropical heat of the Caribbean—palms swaying by a silver sand beach lapped by turquoise water… What more could lovers want?'

Maisey Yates is a *New York Times* bestselling author of over seventy-five romance novels. She has a coffee habit she has no interest in kicking, and a slight Pinterest addiction. She lives with her husband and children in the Pacific Northwest. When Maisey isn't writing, she can be found singing in the grocery store, shopping for shoes online and probably not doing dishes. Check out her website: maiseyyates.com.

D1322775

IRRESISTIBLE BARGAIN WITH THE GREEK

JULIA JAMES

HIS FORBIDDEN PREGNANT PRINCESS

MAISEY YATES

MILLS & BOON

First Published in Great Britain 2019
by Mills & Boon, an imprint of HarperCollins*Publishers*
1 London Bridge Street, London, SE1 9GF

Irresistible Bargain with the Greek © 2019 by Julia James

His Forbidden Pregnant Princess © 2019 by Maisey Yates

ISBN: 978-0-263-27357-1

MIX
Paper from
responsible sources
FSC‌ C007454

This book is produced from independently certified FSC™ paper
to ensure responsible forest management.
For more information visit www.harpercollins.co.uk/green.

Printed and bound in Spain
by CPI, Barcelona

IRRESISTIBLE BARGAIN WITH THE GREEK

JULIA JAMES

PROLOGUE

THE BEDROOM WAS still in shadow, the thick drapes masking the early dawn outside. On feet she could hardly drag forward Talia forced herself to the door. Every cell of her body screamed in silent protest, but she made herself do what she knew she had to do.

Leave.

Leave the man sleeping in the wide bed, the bare, lean-muscled torso that she had caressed in ecstasy exposed by the half-drawn cover.

Emotion stabbed her like a knife eviscerating her insides. To walk out on him—oh, dear God—to make herself walk out on the man who had swept her off her feet, who had taken her to a paradise she had never dreamt existed! The man who had offered her for such a pitifully few blissful hours the hope of something she had never known.

Escape—blissful, wondrous escape—from the prison in which she was trapped.

The prison to which she was returning now.

Because she could do nothing else.

As she turned the door handle as quietly as she could she could feel her phone vibrating yet again in her evening bag. It summoned her back home to the prison in which she had to live.

The knife twisted again. It mocked the wonders of the night she had just spent in this man's arms—how he had taken one look at her and with that single look she had known she would do what she had never done in all her life: give herself fully and rapturously to him without hesitation or doubt.

She had let him sweep her away from the party, their eyes only for each other, glorying in the sensual desire that had consumed her, that she had never known before in all her life. More—oh, surely more than only physical passion!

Another twist of the knife stabbed yet more achingly. There had been a connection between them as tangible as their bodies entwining in blazing passion in the night—something that had drawn them to each other. An ease in conversation, a natural communication that had brought smiling laughter bubbling up in her, a warmth and closeness that had been more than the physical union of their bodies...

The final twist of the knife almost made her cry out with the pain of it as she silently eased the bedroom door open, unable to tear her eyes from the man she would never see again.

Could never see again.

And now the anguish flooded through her veins, drowning her. She could never do what they had so ecstatically talked of in the long, long reaches of the night.

'Come with me!' he had said, his eyes alight. 'This night is only the start of what we shall have together! Come with me to the Caribbean—a thousand islands to explore! We'll see them all! And every single one will be for us! Come with me...'

She heard his voice, warm and vibrant, ringing in her head.

'Come with me!'

Her hand flew to her mouth to stifle the sob that rose in her throat. Impossible! It was impossible for her to go with him.

Impossible to do anything but what she was doing now.

Leaving him.

CHAPTER ONE

The previous evening

LUKE XENAKIS GLANCED up at the Victorian warehouse, converted now into highly fashionable loft apartments in the old London Docklands. He'd come here from the City, straight from that final meeting with his broker—the one that had taken him over ten long, punishing years to achieve. And now, at last—*Thee mou!*—at last he had done what he had set out to do.

Emotion speared through him, hard and vicious. Finally he was exerting his death-grip on his enemy's throat.

A life for a life.

His ancestors would have had no hesitation in making that bitter truth a literal one. Luke's mouth twisted as he entered the building. But in these more civilised days there had to be other ways to exert savage justice upon those who so deserved it. And now—tonight— that justice was finally being served upon his enemy.

Within twenty-four hours the man would be destroyed.

Wiped out financially. Ruined.

The twist in his mouth turned to a smile. A savage smile.

He headed up the echoing iron staircase to the topmost loft apartment, from which he could already hear the thump of pounding music, driving all other thoughts out of his head.

It was just what he wanted now.

The start of his new life…

Talia paused in the entrance lobby to the loft apartment, hesitant suddenly. Should she really dive into the party inside? Then she rallied her nerve.

I need this.

Tonight, at least, for the space of a few hours she would lose herself. Forget the pressures of her life—pressures that were increasing all the time, it seemed.

She sighed inwardly. She knew why. Her poor mother's nerves were more jagged than ever, and her father's perpetually short temper was even shorter these last few months. Why, Talia had no idea, and she didn't want to know. She spent all her energy trying to soothe her nervy mother and placate her tyrannical father so he would not turn on her mother.

It was wearying and stressful, but she had no option, she thought bitterly as she paused on the threshold of the party. No option but to go along with what her father wanted of her or it would be her mother who would pay the price of his vicious ill humour and displeasure.

So I have to go on being Natasha Grantham, ornamental daughter of the wildly successful property magnate Gerald Grantham, of Grantham Land. I have to be part of the image he puts out, along with his elegant, fashionable wife, his huge riverside mansion in the Thames Valley and this even more huge villa in Marbella. And the luxury apartments all over the world, the fleet of exorbitantly lavish cars, the yacht and the pri-

*vate jet. All of this so that others can envy his success
and wealth and achievement.*

It was all her father cared about—his success and
his image. Certainly not about his wife and daughter.

The pitiful thing, Talia thought bleakly, was that
whereas *she* was painfully aware of that bleak truth,
her mother persisted in believing the fiction that he was
devoted to them. She made endless excuses for him—
the pressure of work, the demands of his business, he
was doing it all for them. But Talia knew that her father
was devoted only to one person and one cause: himself.

She and her mother were merely possessions—props
to make him look good. Her mother, Maxine, was expected to be a glittering society hostess, and she was to
be the decorative dutiful daughter, working for him as
his interior designer, overseeing the refurbishment of
his property purchases as he directed, and available on
demand for the endless social functions he required her
to attend. In exchange she was allowed to live rent-free
in one of his many London flats, with an allowance to
cover her wardrobe expenses.

Talia's eyes shadowed again. The world saw her as a
pampered princess, her daddy's darling—but the reality
was brutally different. She was a pawn in the ruthless
power game at which her father excelled as he controlled every aspect of her life with an iron fist.

To get any time away from his demands was precious to her. Like tonight. On an impulse that was quite
unlike her, she'd taken up a casually worded invitation
from someone she knew in the world of interior design to come to this party. It was not her usual scene at
all. Typically, on the rare nights she had to herself, she
stayed in, or occasionally went to a concert or the the-
atre, either on her own or with a girlfriend.

JULIA JAMES   13

Never with a man.

She never dated. Only once had she indulged in an
affair, in her early twenties, but her father had ruthlessly used his influence to ruin the young man's career, and then told Talia what he had done. She had
learnt her lesson.

Now, at twenty-six, it was hard to accept that she
could never indulge in a relationship of her own choosing. All around her partygoers were mingling with each
other, dancing, flirting, hooking up. Restlessness filled
her.

How long can I endure my life as it is?

Never had the gilded cage she lived in seemed more
unbearable. Never had she felt so trapped, so stifled.
Never had she felt more desperate to escape.

And tonight, dear God, she *would* escape it. She
would immerse herself in the party and dance the night
away. Her mother was at the Thames-side mansion, her
father abroad—probably with one of his mistresses.

The longer he was away the better!

She took a breath, plunging forward. Through the
crush she could see, way across the huge room, beneath
the iron girder rafters of the loft apartment and the steel
columns dividing up the space, an area that had been
set up as a bar.

As she made her way towards it, squeezing past people, she could feel male eyes on her. It was a familiar
feeling—all her life she'd known that her glorious chest-
nut hair, tawny eyes, fine-boned features and flawless
skin were part and parcel of the image her father wanted
her to present to the world, reflecting well on himself
for having a beautiful ornamental daughter to show off.

Usually she dressed at his diktat, in suits and dresses
that were too fussy for her own taste. But tonight she

was defying his rules. She gave her head a little shake, feeling her long hair, loosened from its customary up-swept style, snaking lushly down over her bare back, framing her face. She'd used more make-up than she usually did, accentuating her eyes, her cheekbones, her rich red mouth.

The strapless dark burgundy dress she was wearing—shorter than she typically wore, and far more figure-hugging—had been an impulse purchase that afternoon, bought from a second-hand designer boutique she favoured because it helped her spend less of her allowance than her father realised, and little by little she could squirrel away some funds into a personal bank account he could not monitor. Just in case one day she could make a break for freedom…

She yanked her mind from that tantalising, though as yet hopeless dream, and focussed on reaching the bar. She could feel her hips sway as she stalked forward on vertiginous five-inch heels. Reaching the bar, she paused, resting her lavishly braceleted wrists on the downlit surface. She wanted a drink. Not to get drunk, but simply to signal to herself that tonight she was going to please herself. Let go a little. Lighten the endless crushing pressure of her life.

Live a little for herself, just for once.

'White wine spritzer, please,' she said, and smiled at the barman.

'And a sloe gin for me, please, while you're at it.'

The voice that had spoken behind her was deep and very slightly accented. She found herself half turning—and then stilled.

The man standing there was tall—easily six foot plus—and without her volition Talia felt her eyes widening in raw, female appreciation. It was an instinctive, visceral response to what she was seeing.

Dark hair, dark eyes, tough jaw, a blade of a nose and a sculpted mouth, wide shoulders, a broad chest, narrow hips, and long, long legs...

The man's gaze flicked from the barman to her, and an even more visceral reaction swept through her. In the assessing sweep of his eyes she saw instantly—felt tangibly—that he liked what he was seeing and was making no attempt to hide it. He let his dark gold-flecked eyes rest on her almost with a sense of entitlement, and she felt an answering quiver go through her that was shocking in its intensity.

It was as if he knew she would welcome his blatant approval of her appearance. As if he knew she would return it. As if he had no idea that she was Gerald Grantham's daughter, who was never free to follow her own impulses, whatever they might be. Whatever a man like this might incite in her...

She felt a strange quiver go through her, a flush of heat rush up her body—of which she had become suddenly, vividly aware beneath his dark assessing gaze. She was conscious of the swell of her breasts, the curve of her hips, the expanse of shoulders and throat exposed to his gaze and the wanton fall of lush hair down her naked back...

She felt her breath catch—half in shock at her own uncontrollable reaction, half in unstoppable response to the way this man was looking at her. She knew her pupils were dilating as part of her instant, overpowering reaction to his physical appeal, and there was nothing she could do to disguise it.

What is happening?

The words seared across her consciousness. This was

like nothing she had ever experienced! Not even with the one lover she had ever had.

She saw him complete his appraising sweep of her, and then he was reaching out a hand to close it around the ice-dewed tumbler being set down for him on the bar, raising it to his mouth in a leisurely fashion.

'To a suddenly more interesting evening,' he said, and tilted the tumbler at her.

The dark glint in his eye revealed his intentions and the tug at his mouth showed satisfaction.

For a second Talia felt something clench inside her—a kind of hollowing out that went right to the core of her and made it impossible for her to break the dark, binding hold of his eyes.

Oh, God, what has he done to make me react like this?

With a final effort she schooled her expression and, making no reply—which would have been impossible anyway, struck as she was with sudden breathlessness—reached for her wine glass, which was also now on the bar. Did her lifting of the glass make her hand tremble slightly? Or was it the after-effect of that assessing perusal?

She took a mouthful of her spritzer—a larger gulp than she'd intended. But she felt she needed it. Badly.

She realised the man was holding out his free hand towards her. He was wearing dark trousers and a white, deceptively simple shirt that she could tell was expensively tailored. It was open-necked, the cuffs turned back, exposing tanned, sinewy wrists, and he was sporting a watch she recognised as a luxury brand. Even the kind of people who frequented flashy, fashionable parties like this could not easily afford such a custom-made timepiece.

The dark eyes were resting on her still. The glint was gone, and now there was only speculation in his gaze.

'Luke,' he said, his hand still extended.

He was clearly waiting for her to respond in kind. And he seemed to have every confidence that she would.

As if of its own volition, she felt her hand take his. Felt the coolness of his fingers, the strength in them. A door seemed to be opening—a door that beckoned enticingly, alluringly.

'Talia.' She smiled.

Quite deliberately she used the name she had adopted as her own. Her father always called her Natasha, in place of her given name, Natalia, which was preferred by her mother. But 'Talia' was neither her father's dutiful imprisoned daughter nor her mother's protective guardian. 'Talia' was *herself*—and tonight... oh, tonight, on this brief, rare opportunity to *be* herself, it seemed fitting.

'Talia...'

She heard it echoed in a way that made it sound somehow more exotic, more sensual. His low voice had the trace of an accent in it, a timbre that seemed to set her vibrating at some subliminal level.

The dark glint of his eyes came her way again, and that knowing tug at his mouth. He took a considered mouthful from his glass, then set it back on the bar, letting his forearm rest on the surface. His stance altered, became relaxed.

But he wasn't relaxed. The thought flickered in her head. He was like a panther, trying not to startle its prey before it was ready to pounce.

'So, Talia, tell me about yourself.'

The invitation was casual, merely a gambit to continue the exchange. An exchange that was based, as she was so electrically aware, not on who they were but on the current that was running between them.

She paused a moment, taking another sip of wine. Should she go along with this, considering the powerful physical impact this man was having on her? *Because* of it?

Yet even as she hesitated, hovering between habitual caution and that intoxicating glimpse of freedom, she heard her own voice answer. 'I'm an interior designer,' she said.

Her voice was quite composed, she was glad to note, which was so at odds with what she was actually feeling as she sipped again at her spritzer. She saw him lift one questioning eyebrow towards the stark interior around them.

'This place, for example?' he asked.

She shook her head. 'No, this isn't my style at all!'

She glanced around the bare brick walls, the industrial RSJs exposed across the lofty roof space, the reclaimed floorboards and the spotlit modern art adorning walls.

Her eyes shadowed momentarily. Though this starkly modernist interior was not to her taste, it was true, her own style was not something she was ever allowed to express. Her father dictated exactly what he wanted her to do: produce flashy interiors that looked as if they cost a lot of money. And she was expected to produce them on a miniscule budget in order to maximise her father's profit on resale.

She hated everything she produced for her father.

No!

She would not think about her father now, nor about anything to do with the prison she lived in. Not when this amazing man was focusing on her, making her pulse quicken, making her eyes want only to gaze on him, drink him in…

'And what about you?' she heard herself asking, absorbing the way the planes of his face accentuated his looks, the way his dark eyes matched the sable of his hair—absorbing everything about him…*everything*…

He gave a slight shrug. 'Investments,' he replied.

He had said the word carelessly, but there was something in the timbre of his voice that was edged like a blade. Talia's eyes flickered uncertainly.

'You must be good at it,' she observed, her eyes slipping to the custom-made watch around his lean wrist.

He saw her glance at it. 'A present to myself today,' he said dryly.

'A very nice one!' Talia murmured, even more dryly. 'Is it your birthday?'

'Better,' he replied, taking another mouthful of his drink. 'I've just achieved something I've worked towards for more than ten years, and it's going to be a sweet, sweet moment.'

There was that same edge to his voice again, but it was more intense now. Almost…unnerving.

Not a man to cross.

'You sound very driven,' she heard herself say.

His expression stilled. 'Driven? Oh, yes…' For a moment he seemed to be looking far away, then abruptly his gaze refocused on her. 'So, what brings you here tonight, Talia?'

The unsettling note in his voice had gone and now there was only…*invitation*. Invitation in the sweep of his lashes, the slight but distinct relaxing of his pose as he helped himself to another mouthful of his drink.

She shrugged. 'What brings anyone to a party?' she countered.

That sweep of his lashes came again, as if her answer amused him. 'Do you want me to answer that?' he challenged.

Unspoken between them was the answer already. The reason so many people went to parties was to see and be seen. And to hook up...

She gave a little shake of her head, dipping it slightly to take a sip from her glass. Then, as if the wine had emboldened her, she glanced back at him. 'Is that why you're here?'

This time his lashes did not sweep down. This time his gaze was level on her. 'Perhaps,' he murmured.

His gaze lingered, telling her just why he had said that. She felt heat flush through her. Heat she was not used to. Heat that might burn her.

This is going too fast! I should back away, mingle...

But he was speaking again, draining his glass and setting it back on the counter. His eyes washed over her, and as they did so all the caution in her evaporated. She felt her pulse surge, her cheeks flush, her lips part. A heady sense of freedom—of what that freedom might offer her—was vivid within her. What this man had she didn't know. She only knew that never, ever in her life had she encountered it or experienced the impact he was having on her.

And she could not—*would* not—resist it.

Whatever is happening, I want it to happen!

'But one thing I *am* certain of,' she heard him say, and there was that glint in his eye that told her just how certain he was, 'is that tonight calls for champagne!'

He turned to the barman and instantly two flutes were presented to them, sparkling gently. Talia took one, feeling again that heady surge in her veins.

'Is this a toast to your "sweet, sweet moment"?' she

asked, lifting her glass to him, a smile flashing in her
own eyes now, as they met his boldly.

For a second his hand stayed, and then he lifted his
own glass to her.

'To even more,' he said.

The message was unmistakable, and it told her just
what 'even more' would be.

And in her eyes was the answer she was giving
him...

Luke lay, one arm behind his head, the other around
Talia's slender waist. Her long hair swathed his chest
and her breath was warm on his shoulder as she slept
in his embrace. Sweet God, had there ever been a night
in his life like this?

It was a pointless question. No woman had ever been
like this one!

From the very first I knew it.

From that first moment of seeing her there, at the bar,
with her glorious hair tumbling down her bare back,
her spectacular figure sheathed in that clinging dark red
dress... And her face... Oh, her breathtaking beauty
was so dramatic, so stunning, it had stopped him in
his tracks.

Desire, instant and immediate, had fired in him—the
unmistakable primitive response of a man to a woman
who seared his consciousness. Whatever it was about
her, it was like a homing signal, drawing him right to
her.

Talia.

A woman he had known only a few short hours, but
who had turned his life upside down.

He felt his arm tighten possessively around her. He
had known right from the first instant that he wanted

her—that she, of all the women in the world, was the one who would mark for him the start of his new life.

My old life is done. I have accomplished what I had to do: the task that was set for me the day my father died from sorrow for what had been taken from him and the day my mother died of a broken heart.

His thoughts darkened, slicing back down the long punishing years to the moment when he'd vowed to avenge his parents, who had been stripped—cheated— of everything they'd held so precious.

The stress of it had killed his father, and the man who had done that had laughed in Luke's face when, at barely twenty years old, he'd stormed into his office, raging at him, only for the cursed man to light a fat cigar with his fat fingers and summon his goons to beat up Luke, his victim's son, and throw him out on the street.

And now he is destroyed. I've taken everything from him just as he took everything from my parents. They can finally rest in peace.

And he, too, could rest now—rest from the infinite pursuit of more and yet more money, so that he could forge the weapon that would finally bring down his enemy.

Now his whole life stretched ahead of him.

He had been wondering what he should do with it, but suddenly his expression changed, softened.

In the long years of amassing his fortune, closing the net on his enemy, he had had only fleeting affairs with women who had only wanted that. Affairs that had been merely a brief respite from the dark, driven purpose of his life. Affairs that had not lasted.

I wasn't free to do anything else.

But now his long, gruelling task was accomplished, and there was nothing to keep him from finding for himself a woman who could transform his life, who could join him as he journeyed towards the bright, sun-lit future that beckoned to him.

And he had found her! Instinct told him she was the one.

He drew her close, grazing her cheek with his mouth, feeling her stir in his arms. He felt a stirring in himself, too, of the desire that had burned between them—the desire that they had slaked with mutual urgency when they had left the party and he'd brought her back here to his hotel suite.

They had dined on food from room service and drunk yet more champagne. They had talked of he knew not what—except he knew that it had not been about themselves. It had been with ease and familiarity, and with a ready laughter that had seemed to spring natu-rally and spontaneously, as if they had known each for so much longer than a bare few hours.

And he had found her on the very night that he had finally avenged his parents by accomplishing his en-emy's total destruction. He had wanted this night to be special, so that it would mark the start of his new life—the life he'd never been able to claim for himself until now—and now he knew exactly how he wanted this wonderful new life to be.

It would be spent with this woman, and this woman alone…

He felt a shuddering wonder at having found her at such a moment. He grazed her cheek again, softly and sensuously, emotion filling him. She stirred again in her exhausted sleep of passion spent, her arm around his waist tightening instinctively. His mouth moved from her cheek to her parted lips, feathering their tender contours. He felt her waking, and as he trailed a hand over the sweet mound of her breast he felt her nipple crest beneath his palm and his arousal strengthened, quickening his responsive flesh. Desire surged in him and he knew that he wanted to possess her again—to be possessed again.

His kiss deepened and she responded to him, her eyes fluttering open, full of wonder and full of desire. Full of a hunger that he was only too happy to share and sate. His body moved over hers and he murmured her name, caressing her soft, slender body, parting her slackening thighs as her arms wound around his spine. She was whispering his name, drowning in his kisses...

This second time was as glorious as the first—each reaching their climax with a shuddering intensity that swept them away in the ultimate union, an absolute fusing of their bodies. And afterwards, hearts still thudding, breathing ragged, he held her against him, her body trembling in the aftermath of ecstasy.

With a hand that was not entirely steady he smoothed back her hair. He smiled at her, his eyes lambent. But there was a seriousness in his voice behind the smile. 'You know this can't just be one night?'

Her eyes searched his. 'How can it be anything else?'

Her voice was troubled, and he needed to set her mind at rest. 'Do you not see how special this is? This night is only the start of what we shall have together.' He swooped a sudden kiss upon her mouth. 'Come with me. Come with me today—straight away, this morning!'

For an instant that troubled look was in her eye, and then, as if consciously banished, it was gone.

'Where to?' she cried out, half in humour, half in an emotion he could not name.

'Anywhere we want. Name somewhere you want to go. Anywhere at all.'

She laughed now, catching his eagerness. 'The Caribbean!' she exclaimed. 'I've never been in all my life!'

'Done!' He gave an answering laugh. 'Now all you have to do is choose the island.' He rolled onto his back, wrapping one arm around her shoulders, the other across her flank. 'There are a thousand to choose from—we can explore them all!'

He heard her laugh again, and then he was cradling her cheek with his hand.

'Come with me.' His voice was different now. Serious. Intense. 'Come with me.'

His eyes met hers, held them. She was still gazing up at him, and the troubled look had found a home there once more.

Could she not believe that he was serious? That this was no idle banter?

He drifted his hand languorously across her silken flank and felt her stomach tauten at his sensuous touch. 'Let me persuade you,' he said huskily.

Emotion was welling up in him, as powerful as the desire building in him again. Words shaped in his mind.

I will not lose her—not now. I will not.

It was his last conscious thought as passion was rekindled between them, consuming all in its heat.

I will not lose her...

Luke stirred. Something was wrong. Very wrong. He reached out his arm, feeling only cold sheets. His eyes flared open, going immediately to the en suite bathroom door. It was standing open, no one inside. His eyes swept the room.

No Talia.

And no handbag, no shoes, no jacket, no dress. No discarded underwear slipped from her eager body as he'd taken her to his bed, to sate himself on her and change his life for ever...

No trace of her existence.

Except the note propped on the desk.

Face stark, he got up and walked towards it. Something was tightening around his guts, like a boa constrictor throwing its coils around him to crush the life from him.

Luke—I have to go. I didn't want to wake you.

That was it. Nothing else. For a long moment he just stared at it as the breath was crushed from his lungs. Then, wordlessly, he screwed it up and dropped it into the bin.

He walked into the en suite bathroom refusing to feel a single emotion.

CHAPTER TWO

TALIA SAT IN the back of the taxi, staring at her phone. It was signalling a low battery, and she was glad of it in a cowardly way. Her brain was not working properly. It seemed to be split in two, and neither side would connect with the other. She was still with Luke, folded against his body, dreaming of Caribbean islands.

Islands to escape to...islands to set me free...

Free from what her eyes were forcing into her head as she reread her mother's repeated pleading texts.

Darling, phone me! You must phone me. You absolutely must!

She could not face making the call. Yet fear was biting at her out of nowhere. Her mother had never sounded so desperate...

But before she phoned her she must get to her flat, set her phone to charge and then shower—wash Luke from her. And she must change into her day clothes—what she thought of as her prison clothes.

A shaft of anguish pierced her. She silenced it. She had to. There was no choice but to bury it way down deep. Her prison door had opened—but for a fleeting moment only. Now it was slammed shut again and that fear was biting at her.

Something was up. What could have made her mother so desperate?

The taxi driver pulled up at her apartment block and she paid him, clambering out on shaky limbs, bare feet crammed into high heels. She slipped the phone into her bag and hurried to the exterior doors of the block.

The doorman stepped towards her, holding up a hand. 'I'm sorry, Miss Grantham, but I've orders to prevent anyone entering,'

She stopped short. Stared blankly. 'Orders?' she echoed, her voice blank.

'Yes, miss,' he said. 'From the new owners.'

She tried to make sense of what he'd said. 'Someone's bought the block from Grantham's?' she said stupidly.

He shook his head, looking at her with a touch of sympathy. 'No, miss. Someone's bought Grantham's—what's left of it.'

Talia's mother flung herself at her.

'Oh, darling, thank God—thank *God* you're here! Oh, what is happening? How did this happen?'

She was hysterical, and Talia was on the verge of hysteria herself.

How she had got herself from central London to her parents' house she hardly knew. Her brain had simply ceased to function. Now, the only thing she could do, besides tightening her arms instinctively around her clingy, crying mother, was say, 'Where's Dad?'

Her mother threw back her head. Her hair was unstyled, her make-up absent—she looked years older than she did in the carefully presented image Talia was used to seeing.

'I can't contact him!' Hysteria was present in her voice still. 'I phone and phone and nothing happens! I can't even get through to his office—it rings out! Something's happened to him. I know it has. I know it!'

Gently, Talia set her mother aside. 'I have to find out what's going on,' she said.

There was a stricken note in her own voice, and she was not sure how she was still managing to function, but she knew that above all she needed to discover what had happened to her father's company. To her father...

Five minutes on the Internet later and she knew. It was blazoned all over the financial press.

Grantham Land goes under:
LX Holdings picks over the carcass!

She read the article in shock. Disbelief. Yet her disbelief was seared with the hideous knowledge that everything was true, whatever her desperate hope that it was not. Her father's company had gone under, collapsing under a mountain of hitherto concealed debts, and all remaining assets acquired by a new owner.

Like her mother—sobbing jerkily on the sofa while Talia hunched over her laptop—Talia tried to phone through to her father's office. The call rang out, unanswered. Unlike her mother, she then tried to find a number for the company that seemed to have bought what was left of Grantham Land, but LX Holdings did not seem to exist—certainly not in the UK.

She started to search for overseas companies, but realised how little she knew of corporate matters. The press didn't seem to know much either—the adjective employed in their articles to describe the acquiring company was 'secretive'.

As for where her father was… Talia knew with bleak certainty that filled her entirely that he had gone to earth. He would not easily be found. As to whether he would bother to get in touch with his wife and daughter…

Her mouth tightened to a whip-thin line. She turned her head towards her mother, huddled in a sodden mass of exhausted hysteria. Would her father care?

She knew the answer.

No, he would not. He had abandoned them to whatever would be the fallout from this debacle.

Fallout that, within a week, she would know to be catastrophic.

Luke sat in his office. Beyond the window he could see Lake Lucerne. He had deliberately chosen this place for his base because of its very quietness.

Throughout his entire career he had striven to draw as little attention to himself as possible. The financial press called his company 'secretive' and he liked it that way. Needed it that way. He'd needed to amass the fortune he'd required for his purpose as unobtrusively as possible.

His corporate structure was deliberately opaque, with shell companies, subsidiaries in several jurisdictions, and complex financial vehicles all designed with one purpose in mind: to amass money through careful, assiduous speculation and investment without anyone noticing, and then, once his fortune was sufficiently large, to hunt his enemy to destruction.

And now his enemy was defeated. Destroyed utterly. Wiped off the face of the earth—literally, it seemed. For, like the sewer rat he was, he'd gone to ground.

Luke had a pretty shrewd idea of where he'd gone, and it was not a place where he would feel safe. Those from whom his quarry had borrowed money in his final desperate attempts to stave off the ruin rushing upon him were not likely to be forgiving of the fact that he could not repay them at all.

He tore his mind away—that was not his concern. His concern was what to do with the rest of his life.

He felt his guts twist. His face hardened with a bleakness in his expression that he could not banish.

Weeks had passed since the night that had transformed his existence—when he had so rashly thought, for those brief hours, that he had started his new life, free at last from the punishing task he had set himself. He still could not accept what she had done—could not accept how totally, devastatingly wrong he had been about her.

I thought she felt as strongly as I did! I thought what was between us was as special to her—as mind-blowing, as amazing and as lasting—as it was to me. I thought we had started something that would change our lives.

That twist in his guts came again, like a rope knotting around his midriff. Well, he had thought wrong, hadn't he? That incredible night had meant nothing to her—nothing at all.

She walked away with barely a word—just that brutal note. How could I have got it so wrong? Got her so wrong?

In the punishing years since he'd set out to wreak vengeance upon the man who had driven his father to an early grave he'd had no time for relationships—only those fleeting affairs. Was that why he'd got this woman

Talia—the name echoed tormentingly in his head...
Talia—so wrong?

What do I know of women? Of how they can promise and deceive?

With a razored breath he reached jerkily for the file lying in front of him. He flicked it open, seeking distraction from his tormenting thoughts.

The photos inside mocked him, but he made himself stare at them—made himself read the accompanying detailed notes and scan down the complex figures set out in the financial analysis provided.

With an effort of mind he forced himself to focus. The rest of his life awaited him. He had better fill it somehow.

His acquisitions team were busy stripping what flesh remained on the carcass of his prey, disposing of any remaining assets for maximum profit—which they would do, he knew, with expert efficiency. He had left them to it. His goal had been to destroy his enemy, not make money out of his destruction. He had plenty more of the money that he'd amassed—enough to give him a life of luxury for as long as he lived. Now all he sought were ventures to invest in that would be for his own enjoyment. And this project, displayed in the photos in front of him, would do as well as anything else.

His mouth twisted and thoughts knifed in his head. The photos showed palm trees, an azure sea, the verdant greenery of the Caribbean.

I would have taken her there...

The thought left a hollowness in its wake, an emptiness that would not leave him.

Talia stared out of the window of the low-cost carrier's plane that was winging her to Spain. Dread filled her.

Her mother was at the Marbella villa, where Talia had taken her in those first nightmare days after her father's disappearance and financial ruin.

It had been painstakingly explained to her by the blank-faced lawyer who had summoned her to her father's former City HQ, where she'd been able to see through the glass door all the deserted offices being dismantled and stripped of their furnishings by burly men. Her father's ruin encompassed not only the corporate assets, but Gerald Grantham's personal assets too.

'Your father put everything he owned into the company—initially for tax advantages and latterly to shore up the accounts. Consequently...' the man had looked impassively at Talia, who had stared back at him white-faced '...it all now passes to the acquiring owner.' He'd paused, then said unblinkingly, 'Including, of course, the riverside mansion in the Thames Valley and all its contents.'

Talia had paled even more, as the man had gone on.

'Vacant possession is required by the end of the week.'

So she'd taken her mother to Spain, thanking heaven that the villa seemed to have been spared. It appeared to be owned by a different corporation—an offshore shell company her father had set up.

In Spain, she'd tried to sort out the pathetic remnants of what they had left—which was almost nothing. All their bank accounts had been frozen, and all the credit cards. Had it not been for Talia's secret personal account—the one she'd opened in defiance of her father's diktats—she would not even have been able to buy air tickets or food. Or to pay Maria, the only member of staff in Spain she'd been able to keep on. She needed Maria as her mother's only support when she went back to London to see if there was news about anything else she could salvage.

But it had turned out to be the reverse. Now, with dread mounting in her, she knew she would have to give her mother the worst news of all. The Marbella villa was being taken from them…

They had been given a fortnight to get out, and in that time Talia was going to have to find them somewhere else to live *and* keep her mother from collapsing totally. It would finish her, she knew, to lose the villa as well as everything else—as well as her husband. Which was a loss she simply could not and would not believe.

'He'll come back to us, darling!' Her mother's pitiful words rang in Talia's ears. 'He's just sorting things out, making it all right, and then everything will be back to normal again!'

Talia knew better. Her father was not coming back. He'd saved his own skin, leaving his wife and daughter to face utter ruin.

Her mother repeated her pathetic hopes again that evening, when Talia arrived at the palatial villa, its opulence mocking her. Talia said nothing, only hugged her mother, who seemed thinner than she had ever been, her face haggard. She looked ill and Maria, taking Talia aside, expressed concern for Maxine Grantham's health.

Talia could only shake her head, feeling dread inside her at the news she must tell her mother.

She let her mother chatter on in her staccato, nervy fashion, telling her how the pool needed to be cleaned, and how Maria *had* to have help because she couldn't cope with such a huge house on her own, and that she *must* get to Rafael, in Marbella town, who was the only person she trusted with her hair, because she couldn't possibly let her husband see her with such a rats' nest when he came back—as surely he would, very soon now.

Surely Talia must have heard from her father by now, she said. For she herself had not, and she was worried sick about him, because something dreadful must have happened for him not to be in touch...

Talia put up with it as best she could, saying soothing, meaningless things to her mother. As they sat down to eat the meal Maria had prepared Talia encouraged her mother to take more than the few meagre mouthfuls that was all she seemed to want. She had to force herself to eat, too, because above all she had to keep her strength up.

I've got to keep it together—I can't fall apart! I can't!

It was an invocation she had to repeat when, after dinner, she sat her mother down in the opulent drawing room and told her she must speak to her.

'LX Holdings has made a successful claim on the offshore company which...' she took a breath '...which owns this villa. Which means...'

She faltered. Her mother's complexion had turned the colour of whey.

Talia's voice was hollow as she made herself finish what she had to say. 'We have to move out. They're taking the villa from us as well.' Her voice broke. 'I'm so sorry, Mum. I'm so, so sorry—'

A cry broke from her mother, high and keening. And then, as if in slow motion, Talia saw her mother's expression change, her hand fly to her chest. Her whole body convulsed and she shook like a leaf.

'No! I can't! *I can't!* I can't lose this villa too! Not this too! I can't! Oh, God, I can't!'

There was desperation in her mother's voice, and then she collapsed into a sobbing, hysterical mess, clutching at Talia. But Maxine Grantham was beyond any kind of soothing…beyond anything except complete collapse.

Restlessly, Luke seized the file from his in-tray, flicked it open, and stared down at the photos it contained. He frowned. Was this really a project he should go ahead with? It would take a lot of investment, a lot of work, and the return was uncertain.

Yet there was something in the photos that called to him. The state of brutal ruination inflicted by nature that the photos showed echoed across the years. Not earthquake damage this time, as in his memories, but the terrifying force of wind destroying whatever stood in its path.

His thoughts were bitter. Taking on such a project halfway across the world would help him put out of his mind what kept trying to occupy it—the infernal memory he needed to banish.

She didn't want me—didn't want what I wanted. Didn't want anything about me.

He cut the endless loop that wanted to play and play inside his head and went back to staring at the photos, making himself read the notes compiled for him by his agent. He needed something to fill the emptiness inside him now that his enemy was destroyed and the burning ambition that had driven him all his adult life had been finally fulfilled.

The low ring of the phone on his desk interrupted his concentration and he reached for the handset absently. It was his PA, and her voice was uncertain.

'There is someone here, Mr Xenakis, who is asking

to see you. She has no appointment, and will not give her name, but she is very insistent. I told her it was impossible, but—'

Luke cut across her. He had no interest in whoever it was. 'Send her away,' he said curtly. 'Oh, and is my flight booked and the villa reservation made?'

'Yes, of course, Mr Xenakis, it is all done.'

'Good. Thank you.'

He dropped the phone down on the desk, but as he did so there was a loud noise by the door to the outer office and it was suddenly flung open. The voice of his PA was protesting vigorously in English, not the French in which she spoke to Luke.

His head shot up, anger spiking at the intrusion. But the emotion died instantly when he saw who was pushing through the open door, his PA behind her, trying to stop her.

She stopped dead.

For a second there was complete silence, even from his PA. Then Luke spoke.

'Leave us.'

But it was his PA he addressed. Not the woman who had forced herself into his office.

Not Talia.

Blankness filled Talia's mind, wiping out every turbid emotion that had been raging inside her head since she had left Marbella that morning. With Maria's help she'd got her wildly sobbing mother to bed and summoned her doctor. He'd prescribed a sedative, then taken Talia aside. He'd told her with a frown that such upset was not good for his patient, known to him already for her nervous attacks and for her weakened heart.

Talia had been appalled by the latter—her mother

had never told her. The doctor had also made it clear to her that he blamed the slimming pills she took constantly. They'd put a strain on her heart—now exacerbated by her hysterical collapse.

'She must have complete rest and quiet—and no further upset!' the doctor had told Talia sternly. 'Or the consequences could be most dangerous to her! Her heart cannot take any more stress of this nature!'

Talia had shown him out, his words mocking her with a cruelty that she could scarcely bear. *No further upset...*

She'd felt a beading of hysteria herself—they were about to be evicted from the last place that Talia had so desperately hoped might be salvaged from the debacle of her father's ruin and disappearance. How could she *possibly* avoid further upset?

Throughout the sleepless night that had followed, during which she had tossed and turned, her hands clenching convulsively as she'd gazed tensely at the darkened ceiling, it had become clear that only one option was left to her.

Before she'd told her mother, her bleak plan had been to use the fast-dwindling amount of money she'd secretly squirrelled away to rent a tiny flat, somewhere in a cheap part of the *costas*, and then get the first job she could find to bring in a salary, however meagre. Her mother would be appalled, but what else could she do?

But if she insisted on that now, after the doctor's grim warnings, she would be risking her mother's life by forcing her to leave the villa and abandoning all hope.

By morning, dull-eyed and heavy-hearted, and filled with a kind of numb, dreadful resignation, Talia had come to the only conclusion she could. After her bleak exchanges with the lawyers in London, when they'd told her she and her mother were penniless and homeless, she had finally tracked down the headquarters of the mysterious LX Holdings. A morning flight had brought her here.

And now, paralysed by shock and disbelief, she was standing in the doorway of the huge office she had forced her way into in sheer desperation.

It could not be—it could *not* be…

Luke? But how—? Why—?

Shocked words fell from her frozen lips. 'I don't understand—'

With a curt gesture he dismissed his PA who backed away, closing the door as she left. She saw him step towards her. Heard him speak.

'Talia…'

There was a hoarseness in his voice but his face was closed, filled with tension.

'Why did you come here? *How?*' The questions shot from him like bullets.

Talia felt her face work, but speaking was almost impossible. Two absolutely conflicting realities echoed in her head. Then slowly, as the hideous truth dawned on her, she made the connection—forced herself to make it.

'It can't be—*you* can't be…' Her voice was faint. Her face convulsed again. 'You *can't* be LX Holdings—'

She saw Luke's brows snap together, as if what she'd said made no sense. His mouth twisted. 'How did you find me?' he said. He looked at her. 'How did you know?' he demanded. He had said nothing of his identity to her that fateful night—no more had she told him hers. So how…?

'They…they told me. Your lawyers in London. When they spoke to me.'

Her voice was staccato, shock thinning her words. He was still staring back at her as if what she'd said made no sense at all. Her face worked again.

'I'm Natasha Grantham,' she said.

CHAPTER THREE

LUKE FELT THE world reel. He heard her words—how could he not?—but he felt only denial slice through him. No, he would *not* let her be that! *Anyone* but that!

She was speaking still, and he could still hear her— hear her and want only to silence her.

'I'm Gerald Grantham's daughter. You've taken everything he possessed. But…but I'm asking you not… not to take the Marbella villa as well. That…that's why I've come here.'

Her voice faltered and she fell silent.

He stilled, and now a new emotion filled him—one that was cold, like ice water.

'You are Gerald Grantham's daughter?' he repeated.

He had to be sure. In his head skimmed fractured memory from long years ago, when he'd first set himself to studying everything he could about the man he was going to destroy. Grantham had a daughter, yes, and a wife, too—always being trotted out at his side, dressed to the nines, glittering with jewellery, frequenting expensive venues, spending his ill-gotten money.

What had been the wife's name? Marcia? Marilyn? Something like that…

And the daughter?

He felt that ice water fill his veins, heard her faltering

voice echo in his pounding head, forced the connection through his brain. Natasha, she had said.

Logic clicked. Natasha. Wasn't that a diminutive of Natalia? Talia…?

Talia!

Savage emotion seared through him, but he quenched it with the ice-cold water in his veins. His eyes rested on hers but they were masked, letting nothing show in them. He saw her nod and lick her lips. Those full, passionate lips that had caressed his body in ecstasy.

And all along she had been the daughter of the man he had spent his adult life seeking to destroy…

The irony, as savage as the emotion shredding his brain right now, was unbearable. How could the woman who had burned across his life so incandescently, so briefly, turn out to be the daughter of Gerald Grantham?

He tore his mind away. Focussed only on the present. Ruthlessly he slammed control over himself, refused to let any part of the emotion tearing across him show. There was no expression in his eyes and his body was taut and tense.

'And you have come here wanting to keep the villa in Marbella?' He echoed her words, his voice as impassive as his face.

He saw her nod again, as if her neck were stiff.

For one long, endless moment he just looked at her, fighting for control as the shock of her identity rampaged through his consciousness. He studied her as she stood in front of him, her stance rigid, clearly as shocked as he, and hiding it a lot less well.

Deliberately he let himself take in everything about her. She was wearing a suit in dark aubergine, a designer number, though too fussily styled to show her to her best advantage. Her glorious hair was confined to a plait, her make-up was subdued, and he thought she looked thinner than when he had seen her at that party.

He considered what had caused that: the sudden poverty she'd been plunged into…the complete reversal of her circumstances… What a blow that must have been to her.

Talia Grantham.

The name was like a dead weight around his neck. Gerald Grantham's daughter—the gilded, pampered daughter of his enemy.

She was that all along and I didn't know.

The realisation, coming as it had out of the blue, was like a savage blow to his guts, doubling him up with the force of it.

And now she was here, in a designer outfit Gerald Grantham's money had bought for her, wanting to go on living in a palatial villa on an exclusive gated estate in the rich man's playground of Marbella. As if she had every right to do so. Every expectation that of *course* she could go on living there.

Gerald Grantham's daughter—taking the world for granted. Taking what she wanted just as her father had. Splashing his money on herself—money that had been bled from her father's victims.

He could feel another emotion beginning to mount in him. It was an emotion he knew well, that had fuelled the last ten years of his life: slow, low-burning, inexorable anger.

But he would not let it show. Instead he went back to his desk and threw himself into his chair, swinging to look directly at her. As he gazed at her, taking in her presence a bare few metres from him, yet another emotion rose in him, just as powerful as his anger.

It was the emotion that had first kicked through

every vein in his body as his eyes had rested on her at that fateful party. And it was instant, immediate, and impossible to deny. Impossible then and impossible now.

Thee mou, how beautiful she is!

It turned out nothing could change that—nothing! Not even the hideous discovery of who she really was and why she had come here.

Not to find me again—not to seek me out after abandoning me that morning, after that unforgettable night together. No, not for that—

Anger rose within him, cutting across the sudden overwhelming longing that was flooding through him as she stood before him, so incredibly, savagely beautiful. She was having exactly the same effect on him that she had had from his very first moment of seeing her, desiring her...

Turbid emotion filled him, mingling anger and desire, and it was a toxic, dangerous mix. It was impossible to subdue. It steered him now, formed the thoughts that swirled wildly in his head—thoughts he should not be having.

I should send her packing. I should tell her to get out of my office and get out of this villa she wants to keep for herself. I should have nothing more to do with her. She is my enemy's daughter and she walked out on me as if I were nothing to her.

He could hear the words in his head and knew what they were telling him. It was the only sane thing to do.

But the words that came out of his mouth were not those words. He lifted his hands, as if making an accommodating gesture. 'Very well,' he said. 'I don't see why not.'

Even as he spoke the words he regretted them. But he could not call them back—would not. Something was starting to burn within him—a slow fire he knew he should extinguish to prevent it rekindling the passion he felt for her.

At his words he saw her expression lighten. He smiled and went on. 'I am prepared to offer you a short-term lease—say three months—while you make alternative arrangements for your accommodation.'

He spoke briskly, in a businesslike fashion, watching her all the time.

He could see her eyes lighting up, see the visible relaxation of her stance at his reassuring agreement to what she'd come here wanting. She was getting what she wanted, despite what she had done to him.

His expression changed, becoming bland—deliberately, calculatingly so. 'I'll have a lease drawn up and rent set. I would think, given the size and location of the villa, something like thirty thousand euros a month should cover it.'

He watched her face whiten. Her reaction—such obvious outrage at his reply—made the anger inside him spear him again. But he would not let it show. Instead he smiled again, though it did not reach his eyes.

'In life, Ms Grantham,' he said, his voice silken, 'we cannot have what we cannot pay for.'

He pushed his chair back, the movement abrupt. He stood and gave a shrug of deliberate indifference.

'If you can't pay the rent you must vacate the villa,' he spelt out bluntly.

His eyes never left her, never showed any expression. Even though they wanted to sweep over her glorious body, concealed as it was beneath that fussy over-styled outfit she was wearing. It didn't suit her—however expensive it had been.

Absently, he wondered at its difference in style from

the simple yet stunning dress she'd worn at that party. He wrenched his thoughts away from where they must not go. His eyes from where they must not go either…

He saw her expression change, as if her own self-control was very near the edge. It must be a shock to her, he found himself thinking, bitterness infusing his every thought and his mouth thinning. Daddy's darling daughter, realising her pampered lifestyle was over, that her doting father was no longer there to grant her every whim and wish.

'No!'

He heard her cry out in protest at his brutal spelling out of the harsh truths of life, saw her face working.

'Everything else has gone—but not that…not the villa too!'

For a moment so fleeting that Luke thought he must have misheard there seemed to be real fear in her voice, real despair…real desolation. She was staring at him, her expression pinched, and he thought he caught something vulnerable in the way she stood there, as if life had dropped a weight on her that she could not shoulder.

He felt a different emotion rise within him—one that made him suddenly want to blurt out that of *course* she could stay in the damn villa, that he didn't give a damn about any rent. It made him want to surge to his feet, close the distance between them, take her into his arms and hold her close, to tell her he would make everything all right for her, all right for them both, that he never wanted to lose her again.

But then it was gone. She was only repeating what she'd said before, just more insistently. As if she was assuming, taking it for granted.

Of course she was Gerald Grantham's daughter, was she not? She had never had to think of paying for anything at all. A rich man's princess of a daughter, who got everything she wanted handed to her on a plate by an indulgent father.

'I absolutely *cannot* lose the villa! I just can't!' Her eyes flared suddenly, widening as her long lashes swept down.

His mouth tightened again at the declaration of entitlement in her words. Her protest should have been like a match to his anger, and yet it gave rise to a quite different emotion. It was an emotion he should not let himself be feeling, but his eyes, his senses, were hungry to revisit it.

Memory flooded over him. The last time his eyes had held her she had been lying naked in his arms, sated from passion, her skin like silk against his body, her hair a glorious swathe across his shoulders, her mouth pressed against the wall of his bare chest, her exhausted limbs tangled with his...

And yet when he'd awoken from the overpowering sleep that had claimed him she had been gone, vanished into thin air.

Only to reappear now, suddenly, seemingly out of nowhere.

I can't let her walk out on me again...

The words were inside his head and he knew he should wipe them away. He knew he should send her packing. He knew exactly what he should say to Gerald Grantham's daughter.

He knew it. But he could not say it. Not for all the will in his body and in mind.

Instead, as if he were possessed by a force he could not resist, he felt his muscles start to loosen, his shoulders ease back, and then he heard the words that came from his mouth. Words he knew with every rational part of his mind he should not be saying, but which were coming from a place inside him where reason held no sway. There was only an instinct as old as time itself and just as powerful.

Not to let her walk out on him again…

'Then perhaps,' he heard himself saying, 'we can come to an alternative arrangement…'

Talia stared at him. Her senses were reeling. She was floored…in shock…mesmerised.

She had thrust her way into this inner sanctum to which that snooty PA had been determined to bar her entry, and then, as she'd stared at the man jolting to his feet at her entry, she had realised just who it was who stood before her. It was impossible to recover from this truly unexpected outcome.

She could barely countenance the brutal demand he'd made of her to pay rent in order to stay on in their own home, though she did understand on a rational level that the villa was part of the spoils of his acquisition of what was left of her father's once mighty business empire.

She had tried to ignore the leap in her senses as her eyes had clung to him in the custom-tailored suit that sheathed his lean body, the dark tie with the discreet gold tie pin, the gold links at his cuffs, the leather strap of that exorbitantly expensive watch she'd noticed the night they'd met. Still, his long-limbed pose was lithe and it radiated power—the kind of power that came from wealth, the way her father's had.

Yet Luke—*Luke Xenakis*, she reminded herself forcibly, of XL Holdings—had pursued her father's ailing company with a power that had nothing to do with his wealth. A power that he could exert over her with a mere flick of those dark lidded eyes, a twist of that sensual mouth...

She felt herself almost swaying as memories assaulted her: his arms tightening around her, his mouth opening hers to his, his hands gliding over her body that had trembled at his silken touch...

With a silent groan she tore her mind away. What use were those memories here, in this austere office, with its views out over the glacial alpine lake and the jagged, snow-capped mountains soaring all around, as icy as the coldness in the eyes that had once burned with heat for her?

She felt something wither inside her under the cold indifference of his gaze, and knew she must banish from her memory the night she had spent with him, with this man she had given herself to so gloriously and so freely—the man who had thrown open the gate of her prison, offering her a beguiling glimpse of the freedom and bliss that could be hers.

As always, her prison doors had closed on her and were still shut. For now, as then, her first responsibility must be to her mother, to protect her from the catastrophe that had engulfed them with her father's ruin. She must protect her from blows she could not cope with yet, and soften the final blow of losing her last refuge from the bleak poverty she was going to have to face.

She knew she must not run from Luke in an effort to try to end the torment of seeing him again and feeling his coldness towards her, and nor should she throw herself at him to beg him to listen to *why* she'd had to leave him as she had, though she desperately wanted to do both. She must accept whatever he offered her if it helped protect her mother just a little longer.

She forced herself to focus on what he was saying, to try to make sense of it. 'What…what do you mean?'

She saw a veil come down over his eyes—another layer of inscrutable protection. He was so close to her and yet so infinitely far away. Something ached inside her at the distance between them now. With every instinct in her being she knew that he had not forgiven her for walking out on him that morning, leaving him after such a night as they had shared.

For a moment she wanted to cry out, to tell him *why* she had left like that, to try and make him understand that her life had never been hers to live as she wanted.

That it still wasn't.

Whatever 'alternative arrangement' Luke had in mind, she'd have to go along with it—if it was the only way to let her mother go on living at the villa she had no choice. She had to buy the time that she so desperately needed to get her mother to face the brutal truth of how they had to live now—time to find a cheap place to move to, to get herself a job and earn money for the food they were going to eat from now on…

Her tired mind fogged as she made herself listen to what he was saying.

'I may have a job for you.'

She frowned.

'You told me you were an interior designer,' he went on. 'Are you only residential or do you have commercial experience?'

She blinked, remembering instantly the conversation they'd had, brief though it had been, as they'd introduced themselves to each other.

But we left out the most important information.

She gave a slight nod, swallowing with a dry throat.

'Very well. In that case, I'm embarking on a new

business venture—a potential refurbishment project—
your skills might come in useful to me. If so...' he was
watching her speculatively through those veiled lashes
of his '... I would accept your work in lieu of rent—if
that is agreeable to you.'

Talia stared. The hope that had flared so pathetically
briefly when he had first said there would be no problem in her staying on at the villa—before naming his
price for that—sparked into life again.

'Yes! Yes, of course—'

The words were out of her mouth before she could
stop them. The fact she would be working for the man
who had brought down her father, who now owned everything that he had once possessed, was irrelevant.

She saw him sit back, cross one leg over the other and
steeple his long fingers— fingers that had once trailed
through her loosened hair and skimmed the contours
of her naked body...

She dragged her mind away and stifled the inner
voice that was telling her she was insane even to *think*
of working for a man she had spent such a night with
and who was now regarding her as nothing more than
an employee.

*But I have no choice in the matter. If he is offering
me a job I have to take it—I have to! If it lets Mum stay
on in the villa... If it buys me time...*

She swallowed again. 'When...when do I start?'

She watched him smooth a hand over his thigh in
a controlled, leisurely fashion, his eyes never leaving
her, revealing nothing of what might be behind that
leaden gaze.

'I'm flying out at the end of the week. Meet me at
Heathrow,' he informed her.

Consternation filled Talia's face. 'Flying out? Where?'

'The Caribbean. I'll be there a fortnight—so will you.'

Violently, she shook her head. *A fortnight?* 'I couldn't! Impossible!'

It would be impossible to spend two weeks with Luke—and in the very place they had fantasised about that night together. About running away to a sun-drenched tropical island, a palm-fringed beach, with no cares or responsibilities or prison doors to stop her...

The cruelty of it mocked her. Mocked her with the torment of the prospect of having to be with him again as he was now—so cold, so distant...

She saw him shrug again—a gesture of indifference. And that was all he felt for her now, she knew.

'In which case be out of the Marbella villa next week.'

Talia shut her eyes as if she could shut out the reality of this situation. How could she turn down this offer he was making her? She couldn't. She had no choice.

Luke was speaking again. 'You can have twenty-four hours to make your decision. Phone my PA when you've made it.'

He uncrossed his legs, extending them under the wide mahogany desk, and reached for his keypad. Talia swallowed. It was a signal that she was being dismissed.

Numbly, she walked from the office.

Behind her, Luke lifted his gaze as she walked out. She could not have spelt out more clearly how repugnant she found the notion of spending time with him.

Memory stabbed at him again of how they had talked on that amazing, unforgettable night together, sated with passion, wound in each other's arms. Talked of taking off to the Caribbean together...

But it had never happened, had it? She had never had

the slightest intention of going anywhere with him, of spending a single further night with him.

She used me—and left me. Had what she wanted of me and walked out.

As the door closed behind her his face darkened. Was he clinically insane to have offered her a job? Actually invited her to go with him to the place that mocked him in his taunting memories? Why the hell had he done it?

Answers stirred in the deep recesses of his mind but he silenced them. They were too dangerous to acknowledge.

CHAPTER FOUR

CAREFULLY, TALIA SAT herself down in the wide leather first-class seat on the plane, feeling tense and strained. Luke had taken the window seat and had immediately snapped open his laptop. He was taking as little notice of her as he had when she'd joined him in the First-Class Lounge, where he had merely glanced at her and nodded briefly.

Inside her chest she could feel her heart thudding. Seeing him again, even knowing who he was and what he had done, was still an ordeal.

But it's an ordeal I'm going to have to bear. I have to bear it just as I have to bear everything else. Because I don't have any choice in the matter.

She didn't—and she knew she didn't. She had known all through that gruelling twenty-four hours Luke had allowed her to make her decision that there was only one answer she could give. She had to take his job offer. If it was the only way to stop herself and her mother being summarily evicted from the Marbella villa she had to take it. That was all there was to it.

And when she'd broken the news to her mother she had only felt that decision reinforced.

As she fastened her seat belt she deliberately made herself remember the expression on her mother's face when, on her return from Switzerland, she'd sat down on her mother's bed and told her that they could stay on in the villa for the time being. As her mother's fearful and haggard face had lit with relief Talia had gone on to tell her the exciting news that she'd been offered an interior design job. The only downside was that it would take her to the Caribbean for a fortnight.

Her mother's expression had faltered momentarily, then she had rallied. 'You mustn't worry about me a bit! Maria will look after me while you're away. And it's just what you need—a chance to use your talents! I'm sure you'll have a lovely time—it won't be *all* work, will it? Oh, I do envy you!' Maxine Grantham's eyes had softened. 'It's *such* a romantic place, the Caribbean! Of course your father never liked it...'

Her voice had wavered for a moment, and then she'd become momentarily reminiscent.

'I had a boyfriend once, you know, when I was a teenager. He talked of sailing to every island there—' She had broken off, then made her tone suddenly hopeful. 'Oh, my darling, perhaps you'll meet someone special there! Oh, that would be *too* wonderful! To be romanced beneath a tropical moon!'

Talia had changed the subject, but she'd not been able to banish her mother's words from her head.

'Romanced beneath a tropical moon...'

Memory had struck her again—but they were memories of what had never happened. She had never flown off with Luke that morning after their searing night together—never fled with him as she had so longed to do.

She had felt her thoughts shift and rearrange themselves. If she took this job with him, flew to the Caribbean… Hope, like a beguiling spirit, had welled within her. Was it possible? Could it be possible…?

Could I have a second chance with him? Dare I hope for the romantic escape we should have had?

She had felt hope strengthen, take wings. Longing had filled her.

Yet now, as she sat beside him on the plane, only anguish filled her. Her mother's words mocked her. Indeed, her own longings were mocking her.

At her side, Luke was focussed on his laptop, a faint frown of concentration between his eyes, clearly not paying the slightest heed to her presence. She felt the anguish stab at her. She knew she must subdue these dangerous, forbidden thoughts that came unbidden, but they were impossible to banish—especially the one thought that lingered, with a temptation that she felt clinging to her like a fine mesh of gold.

What if being in the Caribbean with Luke could bring them together again? What if what had happened after that party could happen again? What if he turned to her now and, instead of cold indifference, she saw in his eyes the warmth she longed for…?

'Champagne, madam?'

A stewardess was hovering with pre-flight drinks. With a start, Talia shook her head, taking an orange juice instead. Luke merely waved the tray away, not even looking up. That ache of anguish came again, silencing the pointless flare of hope that had fluttered so uselessly just a second ago.

With a silent sigh, she reached for her paperback, wanting her thoughts silenced, wanting to be diverted by something—anything that might get her through what lay ahead.

Hope was impossible—only torment was certain. Torment and regret.

I threw it away. I threw away my chance of seizing the happiness he promised me. And I walked out back to my prison.

The print in the paperback hazed and blurred. But what use was it for her to weep for what she had done? She had had to do it—nothing else had been possible.

Bleakly, she went on reading, numbing herself as best she could through the long flight. Luke barely spoke to her, and she was grateful—and yet his silence hammered nail after nail into her, showing her just how great was the distance between them.

No trace of intimacy. No trace of anything at all.

The same impersonal indifference continued once they had landed, and Talia spent the journey from the airport gazing out through the window of the chauffeur-driven car they'd climbed into.

The lush green of the island entranced her, along with the vivid glow of the setting sun, and when, after forty minutes or so, the car wound its way along a paved drive to draw up at a large house, she was happy to get out and gaze around her, feeling the humid warmth engulf her like a soft cashmere shawl after the chill of the climate-controlled car interior.

'Oh, this is beautiful!' she could not stop herself exclaiming as she gazed around at the lush gardens, with splashes of vivid colour from the tropical flowers all about.

She got no acknowledgement from Luke, who was striding indoors, so she followed him in. She'd wondered if they were heading for a hotel, but this was clearly a private villa. The large atrium-style hall reached up to high rafters, a reception room opened beyond, and there was a mahogany staircase sweeping upstairs. Staff appeared out of nowhere, murmuring in an island lilt, taking their suitcases upstairs, and Talia's bulky portfolio case and art kit.

She hesitated, not knowing what she should do, and Luke, striding towards a door at the side of the hall, turned his head.

'We'll be dining in an hour. Don't keep me waiting.'

It was all he said before he disappeared into a room in which Talia could glimpse a desk and IT equipment. He shut the door behind him with a decisive click.

With a sigh, Talia followed the luggage upstairs.

Bleakness filled her, and a weariness that came not only from the long flight. It went much deeper than that…

I've lost him—lost him for ever… And I must abandon any hope of winning him back.

She had to accept what Luke was making so chillingly clear—he had no interest in her any longer. Not as the woman she'd been at that party. There could be no second chance.

Wearily, she showered and started to get ready. A maid had unpacked for her, and as Talia selected a dress to wear she deliberately chose one her father had approved of. He had always wanted her to wear only fussy, over-styled clothes, and this knee-length dress in a pastel shade of pale blue did not suit her—but it would signal to Luke that she was well aware she was no longer of any personal interest to him. From now on she must remember that she was here only to work. Nothing more than that.

A tightness clutched around her heart, but there was nothing she could do about it.

He doesn't want me any more.

That was the truth—bleak, unvarnished—and she had to face it.

Luke sat at the head of the long table in the villa's dining room, his gaze focusing down the table to where Talia was sitting, immobile and expressionless. His face tightened. Inside him he felt the emotions he'd become all too familiar with, scything inside him. How could he still find her so beautiful?

Just as she had that day in his office in Lucerne, she looked nothing like the way she had at that party—there was no wanton wildness about her at all, no tightly sheathed body, no exposed shoulders and bare arms, no swaying walk from five-inch heels.

Now, she was dressed for the evening, in a knee-length cocktail dress that was high-necked and long-sleeved—as if, he thought with an illogical spurt of anger, she were deliberately hiding her figure from him. Her hair was caught in the same plain coil at the back of her head that it had been in on the flight, and she had not put on any make-up, let alone jewellery.

A thought flickered in his mind. *Maybe there wasn't any jewellery left for her to wear...*

After all, she couldn't even afford to pay rent on a single one of Gerald Grantham's many properties. There probably wasn't much jewellery these days.

She would be feeling the lack of it.

His eyes flickered over her, unconsciously changing her concealing gown to something much more to his taste. Something that would show her voluptuous cleavage, ripe for adornment with something glittering and expensive.

He tore his mind away. She wasn't here to look alluring. That was the last thing he should want her to do. It had been hard enough to have her sitting beside him hour after hour on the flight over and make himself blank her presence. It had been next to impossible not to turn his head and drink in that beauty that had caught his breath as it did again now, even when she was wearing the unflattering dress. But he must not yield to such a dangerous temptation.

She's here to work, to earn the right to go on living in a villa she can no longer afford.

It was time to remind her of that. Even more, to remind himself.

The staff were setting plates in front of them and pouring wine as Luke spoke. 'I'll be visiting the site first thing tomorrow morning,' he said abruptly, lifting his fork and starting to eat. He was hungry after the change in time zone and it was past midnight on his body clock. 'Because of the heat and the jet lag we'll make an early start.'

He saw her swallow and take a drink from her glass. 'Where is the site?' she asked. 'And what kind of property is it?'

It seemed to be an effort for her to speak, and that annoyed him. Why *she* should be radiating tension on all frequencies was beyond him. She was the one who'd rejected him. It had been *her* choice to leave, not his.

It was pointless to wonder, yet again, whether he was clinically insane to have brought her out here with him. He'd oscillated continuously in the twenty-four hours he'd given her to make her mind up, between cancelling his impulsive offer and raising the stakes on it. When she'd walked up to him in the airport lounge he'd felt that toxic mix of emotion writhe in him again, and he'd been plunged into confusion once more.

It filled him still, but he was hammering it down, refusing to face it. He *had* been insane to bring her here—truly mad to subject himself to her presence—but it was too late to change his mind. She was here and he would have to deal with it. Whatever strength of mind it took, he had to make this Caribbean project work and then get on with the rest of his life.

I can make myself indifferent to her. I can expose myself to her presence and get her out of my damn system.

His jaw set. That was what he must focus on. This time *he* would set the finish date: she'd stay here for a fortnight, work solidly to pay her rent, and would leave when he dismissed her. This time *he* would call the shots—not her.

And by the time she left—had been dismissed by him—he would have worked her out of his system. She would mean nothing to him and he would watch her being despatched from his life, on his terms, with all the indifference he was currently trying to present to her. But by then it would be genuine indifference—not the feigned, deliberate impassivity he was treating her with now.

He answered her finally, in the same clipped tone of voice he'd used for all their brief exchanges so far.

'It's a hotel in the south of the island, where the Caribbean coastline meets the Atlantic. It's where the hurricanes hit if they reach this far. As they did last year.'

She'd started to eat, but looked up as he spoke.

He went on dryly. 'Don't worry, we're out of hurricane season now. But last year the tip of the island was struck by a particularly vicious one—climate change is, as you probably know, fuelling their force and their frequency. The area we're visiting got a hammering.'

'Is the hotel still worth refurbishing?' she asked frowningly.

'That's what I'm checking out,' he said. Dryness had turned to terseness.

She was speaking again, her voice diffident, as if she were unsure whether to speak at all, and that irritated him more.

'How badly damaged is it?' she asked.

'The external construction has borne up well—it was built to resist wind shear. But the interior has been blasted totally. It needs complete renovation.'

For the first time there was a spark of animation in her face, lightening her features. 'What do you have in mind?' she asked.

Luke's mouth thinned. 'Surprise me,' he said flatly.

He was aware that he was supressing a stab of emotion he did not want to allow admittance. That the spark of animation in her expression which had brightened her eyes, giving her a glow for the first since she'd joined him in the airport lounge, had kicked at something inside him. For a few seconds she had looked as she had that first evening—with her eyes alight, responding to him, desiring him…

He repelled the memory. No point remembering that night, however much it hammered in his brain. It was over. Done. It wasn't coming back.

She was replying. 'I have to work to the client's brief,' she said tightly. There was no animation in her reply to his crushing rebuff.

Her father, the only client she'd been allowed to have, had been exacting in his briefs, and she had learnt long ago not to challenge him on what he wanted, or even suggest any modifications. Her father had not wanted creative input—he'd wanted docile compliance. She had produced only what he'd wanted, whatever her own opinions.

'Well, my brief to you is to come up with your own ideas,' Luke said indifferently.

Talia subsided, focussing once more on her meal. From the far end of the table Luke watched her close down again as she continued eating, and he said nothing more to her. She looked tired, he realised, and he felt the same way himself, jet lag having settled in.

When coffee arrived, Luke addressed her again. 'We'll make an early start for the site visit tomorrow morning before the day heats up too much. Wear suitable clothing—shoes for walking, not posing.' He paused, wanting to make the point clear. 'Remember you are here to WORK, Talia, if you want to stay on at the villa in Marbella.'

He saw her tense at the sharpness of his reminder, and something more. Had that been *fear* he'd just seen flash in her eyes? But why should it? He almost asked the question, his expression softening instinctively. Then that blank-eyed look was back in her face, expressing only tiredness.

'Finish your coffee and go to bed,' he instructed.

She did not need to be told twice. Draining her cup, she made her escape, heels clicking on the tiled floor. Luke watched her hurry out and that now familiar jab of anger came again.

She couldn't wait to get away from him, could she?

It wasn't the first time she hadn't been able to wait to get away from him, was it?

The memory only reinforced his determination to use her presence in order to become indifferent to her.

But what if it makes you want her more...?

* * *

Talia stared around her at the scene of devastation. There were palm trees felled by the hundred-mile-an-hour winds that had uprooted them like matchsticks, and the ground was strewn with branches and vegetation, including seaweed and sand from the beach.

The hotel itself looked as if it had been blasted. Roof tiles lay smashed on the ground, window frames were hanging loose, mosquito screens falling off. She was glad that she was wearing strong rubber-soled shoes and long olive green trousers. There was shattered glass in places, too, and thick palm fronds with sharp edges.

Silently, Luke handed her a hard hat, donning one himself.

'Take care,' was all he said to her as he headed indoors.

He'd taken little notice of her on the way here—this time in a high-wheeled four-by-four—just as he had the previous day. It was as if he were blanking her deliberately, and she could do nothing but accept it—and respond in kind. She was grateful, if nothing else, that she was able to mirror his obvious indifference to her. He was treating her as someone he'd hired to do a job of work for him. Nothing personal...nothing intimate.

There was a heaviness inside her that was not just tiredness or jet lag. It had been so stupid of her to have any idiotic hope that Luke might be willing to make a fresh start with her. No, whatever they'd had was over. All that was important now was earning the rent to keep her mother at the villa at Marbella. The doctor's warning meant she could not risk her mother's health—she was too fragile, in body and mind. And her dangerously weakened heart—

She sheered her mind away, felt anguish slicing through her with a painful jagged edge.

She had lost all claim to anything personal with Luke. That was all over now—brief as it had been. She'd walked out on him. Now all she was to him was a temporary employee. And that was what she had to remember. She was here to sell her interior design skills in exchange for rent, that was all.

Keep it professional. He doesn't want anything else than that. He's made that brutally clear.

As she trailed after him, picking her way through the debris, and then stepped inside the building, she heard herself gasp in shock and dismay at the ravages within. Furniture was overturned, curtains were hanging off their rails, crockery was smashed, and there was a fetid smell of hot, humid, overpowering damp. The place had clearly been drenched, both by the pounding rain and the storm-surge of the sea, and even in the months since the hurricane it had not dried out.

She followed Luke across the huge atrium, her heart sinking at the destruction all around her, stepping carefully through the debris on the floor—bits of furniture, shards of crockery, shreds of curtains, wind-strewn sand—gritty under the soles of her shoes. Dismay filled her. How could anyone think to make something of this place again? Surely the wreckage was complete and it was impossible to restore?

All she wanted to do was get out of there as fast as she could. There was nothing worth saving. The whole place was rotting.

Gingerly, watching every step she took across the littered broken flooring, trying not to inhale the gagging smell of damp and decay, she made her way towards the arching curve of the far side of the atrium where it opened onto the gardens—or what had once been the gardens.

Avoiding a louvered ceiling-height shutter, hanging from its hinges, she stepped out onto the terrace beyond, lifting her eyes and blinking in the bright light after the odoriferous gloom of the interior.

And her breath caught again, her eyes widening in amazement.

The garden might be strewn with palm trees, and vegetation had been hurled across the paths and lawns, but in this lush climate Nature had reclaimed her domain, throwing out vines and foliage to soften the fallen trunks, and vivid blossoms, crimson and white and vermillion pink, to festoon the emerald greenery. And beyond—oh, beyond glistened the brilliance of the azure sea, dazzling in the hot sun. The whole scene was radiant with light and vivid colour.

'It's *fantastic*!' she breathed in wonder.

She could see in an instant why the hotel had been built here, right at the sea's edge, fringed with sand so silver she could barely look at it in the bright sunlight. The contrast with the rank, ruined interior could not have been greater. Talia could feel her spirits lift, her face light up with pleasure at the sight.

'Not bad, is it?' Luke had stepped up beside her. His voice was dry and he was gazing around.

She turned to him. There had been something in his voice, in its very understatedness, that made her exclaim, 'I can see why you want it! It's worth any price!'

His eyes came to rest on her and she could see that for a second, just the barest second, he reeled. But then his gaze shuttered and she could tell that he was deliberately blanking her again.

'I don't get sentimental over projects,' he said tersely.

'That doesn't make me money. What makes me money is buying something at a good price and adding value. That's the opportunity here. The company that owns it wants shot of it, and if I can get it at the right price, and get the refurb costings right, it *will* make me money. That's all I'm interested in.'

How sad, Talia thought. What a shame that this place would be all about money. Where was his heart? Where was his soul? Where was the man she'd spent that incredible night with? The one who had lit up her whole world with his ideas, his passion, his determination?

'Even at the lowest possible cost a refurb will be expensive. More so than a new build because of the clearance costs.'

He glanced at her again. 'Go around the place—and watch your step. Meet me back here in forty-five minutes. Don't keep me waiting.'

He strode off, heading down to the shore, already on his phone.

Talia watched him go, watched his assured, powerful stride carving through the debris in the devastated gardens. There was a heaviness inside her. His blunt words had had a bleak familiarity to them. She knew that attitude, all right. It was her father's. Minimum cost, maximum profit. That was all he'd cared about, too.

It was chilling to see it echoed in Luke.

Then, with a little shake of her head, as if to clear all such thoughts from it, she went back inside and started her tour.

She fished out her notebook from her tote and started to jot things down—rough measurements to begin with, and then a sketchy layout of the ground floor guest areas as she walked, watching her step, through the desolate rooms.

As she did so her mood changed. She wasn't quite plunged automatically into professional mode, but she did find that, despite the desolation and destruction, the same lifting of her spirits was hitting her as when she'd seen the vista of the sea beyond the gardens.

If she looked past the devastation and ruin to the structure of the building she could see that this was, indeed, a beautiful space. With imagination and enthusiasm it could be made impressive again.

Ideas started to flow and her pen moved faster over the paper. She turned pages one after the other, and took copious photos on her phone of rooms and vistas.

She headed upstairs, ideas still pouring through her, a sense of excitement filling her. For the first time she was being given an opportunity to use her own creativity, to craft her own vision! Being allowed to give her ideas full rein and not have them ignored and dismissed by her father was a liberation.

Time flew by, and only when she saw Luke waiting for her down in the desolate atrium, with a dark expression on his face, did her mood crash again.

'When I say forty-five minutes that is what I mean,' he informed her tightly.

Talia's apology died on her lips.

'I've got some letters to dictate to you,' he continued. 'While you're here you might as well do some secretarial work for me, as well. We'll do it in the car.'

'Er... I don't take dictation,' she said. It wasn't a refusal, only a description of her secretarial limits.

'Tough,' he said.

She stared after him, her heart sinking. His mood was black, that was obvious, and she could only assume it was because the state of the hotel was worse than he'd realised.

As for acting as his secretary, well… She sighed inwardly. If that was what he wanted she would do her best. After all, to have stayed on at the villa paying rent would have cost her a fortune—whatever work she did here for him he was therefore entitled to, even if it wasn't what she was trained for.

So she did the best she could, taking down his dictation as he drove. But not only did the SUV jolting over the potholed roads make it difficult to write, but the complex legalese and financial figures he dictated at high speed tested her meagre abilities to the limit. The fact that she was only exacerbating his bad mood by asking him to slow down or repeat himself was patently visible.

By the time they finally arrived back at the villa there was a headache around her skull like a steel band in full swing.

Luke turned to her. 'There's a government minister I have to see. Those letters need to be typed up this afternoon. There's an office set up in the villa somewhere—the staff will show you.'

Talia nodded dumbly, heading up to her room to shower and change. Was this distant, terse man really the same man as the one she had encountered that fateful evening at the party? How could he be?

She felt her throat catch and hurried into the bathroom. Beneath the flow of water, she was only too conscious of her nakedness—a nakedness she had so briefly gloried in with the man who now looked right through her…

Memories rushed back into her head of when his gaze upon her had not been cold, nor indifferent. But these were memories she did not want and could not afford. She sighed grimly. She couldn't afford much at all.

Enveloping herself tightly in a bath towel, she emerged, steeling herself. What did it matter if Luke now looked right through her and gave her orders and instructions as if nothing had ever happened between them? It would simply remind her of what she shouldn't forget, even for a moment. That she was here for one purpose only—to work as he directed, so that her mother could have some reprieve from the loss of the final piece of her stricken life to which she was still so desperately clinging.

A knock sounded at the door and she went to open it. One of the soft-footed maids came in with a lunch tray, carrying it through to the balcony, on which a little table and chair had been set up under an awning. Talia threw on a sundress, and followed her.

She felt her spirits lift again in the heat and brightness after the dim cool of the air-conditioned bedroom.

Thanking the maid, she felt suddenly hungry and fell to eating. She'd hardly had time for breakfast—which had been served up here in her room—before she'd been informed that Mr Xenakis was waiting for her, and jet lag had also confused her hunger cues. Now they were fully restored, and she ate with relish the food that had been provided for her: chicken salad, cane juice, and fresh fruit.

As she ate, she gazed out at the vista. And such a vista! Now, for the first time, she could really appreciate where she was.

The villa was set on a slope, high above the sea, which was several miles away across lush countryside, and the beautiful gardens she'd seen from the carriage sweep were wrapped around the back as well.

Was that…? Ah, yes. Her eyes lit up. There was a large turquoise pool, glinting at the rear of the villa.

And as she gazed in delighted appreciation she knew, instinctively, that the colour palette for her design ideas was right in front of her: the deep cobalt sea, the turquoise pool, the emerald vegetation, the vivid crimson of the bougainvillea and fragrant frangipani. All would be called upon.

Enthusiasm fired her, and she longed to make a start on her colour boards and sketch out the vision that danced inside her head. Her ideas began to fizz and bubble in her imagination.

But that was not what she'd been instructed to do this afternoon. There were Luke's letters to type up first.

The office she was shown into by the stately butler—whose name, he informed her upon enquiry, was Fernando—was chilled with air-conditioning and had no outside light coming in. The windows were high set, with venetian blinds over them. An array of high-tech equipment hummed to one side, and a huge PC sat on the desk.

She took her place in front of it and got out her notebook. She sighed, hoping she would be able to decipher what she'd scrawled so hectically.

It proved hard going, and she knew, with a sinking heart, that she was making a poor fist of it. She did her best, all the same, though she was painstakingly slow, not being able to touch-type, and found the keyboard complicated to operate when it came to tabulating the many figures Luke had thrown at her.

Finally, she was done, though there were gaps and queries in every letter and attachment. She could only hope that Luke would make allowances for the fact that she was not a trained secretary and they had been going over a bumpy road while she was trying to write it all down.

The headache, which had cleared over lunch in the fresh air, was now back with a vengeance. With a final sigh of abject relief, she closed down the word processing software and got up, her back stiff and sore from hours of hunching over the keyboard.

Then her face brightened.

The pool! She would freshen up with a dip—that, surely, would clear her head and loosen her stiff limbs. And she would ask the Fernando if she could have a coffee, and a long juice drink.

A handful of minutes later she was plunging head-first into blissfully warm water, joyfully dipping her head under the water to feel her hair stream wetly down her back. Her spirits soared. Oh, this was joyous! She splashed around, frolicking like a child, delighting in the diamond sprays of water catching the late-after-noon sunshine, then pushed off the side, plunging in a duck-dive to the tiled bottom of the pool, dappled with sunlight. Then:

'What the *hell* do you think you're doing?'

CHAPTER FIVE

THE STENTORIAN VOICE halted Talia mid-plunge and she floundered back up. Her eyes went to the edge of the pool as she brushed the strands of wet hair from her face.

Luke was standing there, glowering down at her. Talia blenched, grabbing the edge of the pool to steady herself. 'I… I wanted a swim,' she said.

She didn't try to make her voice sound defiant—let alone entitled—but Luke seemed to take it that way. She could tell by the instant darkening of his eyes.

'May I remind you,' he bit out, and the sarcasm was blatant in his clipped words, 'that you are here to work. This is *not* a holiday for you!'

She saw him breathe in sharply, lips pressing in a thin line.

Talia opened her mouth to tell him she knew that, and understood it only too clearly, but he forestalled her attempt at self-defence.

'What's happened to those letters I left you to type up?' he demanded.

'I… I've done them. That's why I thought it would be OK to have a swim,' she said falteringly.

Clumsily, she hurried to get out of the pool, wading up the steps. As she emerged she was burningly conscious that, even though she was wearing a plain one-piece suit, it was clinging to her body, exposing every curve and a lot of bare leg. She seized a towel and wound it round her body while her wet hair streamed water down her back.

His eyes were on her, she could tell, and she felt colour flare out across her cheeks as she dipped her head, squeezing water out of her long hair. She hoped he would go, so she could escape up to her room, but he was not done with her yet.

'My PA said she's received nothing,' he retorted.

She looked confused. 'You didn't say anything about sending them anywhere. And I don't have any contact details.'

He cut across her. 'It will have to be done *now*.' His mouth tightened. 'Get changed and meet me in the office.'

He strode off before she could make any reply, and disappeared indoors. Hurriedly, Talia ran up to her room. The bad mood that had encompassed him as they'd left the hotel was clearly still clinging to him, and when she joined him again, as quickly as she could, she saw with a sinking heart that it had only worsened.

He was sitting at the computer, her work on the screen. At her entry he turned. 'This,' he said grimly, 'is a complete mess.'

He lifted a hand to indicate the screen, where one of his long, complicated letters was displayed. There were half-sentences in red, to show where she wasn't sure she'd taken down what he'd said correctly, and there were queries and question marks freely dispersed throughout.

Talia pressed her hands together. 'I told you,' she said, her voice as composed as she could make it—

which was not very much, 'I don't take dictation and it was hard to write in the car because of the bumpy road. You gave me very little time, and these letters deal with matters I'm not familiar with.' She swallowed. 'I did my best,' she said.

She could feel her throat constricting and sense tears building up behind her eyelashes. She was reminded of how once, when she was a novice designer, her father had given her instructions she hadn't been able to carry out. His anger had wiped the floor with her. She had cried, and he had been even angrier. But she wouldn't cry in front of Luke—she wouldn't!

Gritting her teeth, she blinked rapidly, taking the seat that Luke was now vacating with a bowed head. He positioned himself behind her, so he could read the screen as well, and she felt the closeness of his presence overpowering her.

'OK,' he said tersely. 'I'll give you the corrections.'

He did so, and her fingers stumbled on the keyboard, but she soldiered on, blinking away the haze in her eyes as she laboured over the intricate figures, the complicated tabulation they required, and then added headings for addresses and pagination as well.

It seemed to take for ever, and her head was aching again with the concentration and fumbling finger-work, but finally it seemed he was done. Done with the work and done with her. She hit 'send' on the set of documents, to the email address he'd dictated, and sat back, her hands falling nervously to her lap.

Behind her, Luke spoke in that remote, impersonal tone she was getting used to.

'You can clock off now. And you can have the evening to yourself—I'm dining out. Tomorrow, make a start on your initial design ideas. As for any more secretarial work…' his voice tightened. 'I'll use an agency.'

He walked out and, feeling crushed yet again, Talia slowly made her way upstairs to the sanctuary of her bedroom, lying for a long while flat on the bed, staring blankly at the ceiling.

The man she had once known so briefly, so incandescently, who had for a short few hours transformed the world for her, who had looked on her with passion and desire, had gone. Gone for ever.

A bleakness filled her. A sense of desolation. She felt her eyes haze over again, and this time she did not try and suppress her tears…her hopeless, flowing tears…

Luke was having dinner with one of the senior civil servants in the Department of Business Development, but he scarcely heard what the man was saying. His thoughts were elsewhere, circling round and round in his head like a vulture, and he could not banish them.

I can do this. I can do it and I will do it. I must. I will make myself immune to her and I absolutely will succeed!

But it was proving harder than he'd thought—damnably harder! Being with her again, tormented by all the memories of their unforgettable encounter, he'd felt his eyes constantly wanting to go to her, to drink her in.

It was bad enough when she was looking the way she had on the flight, or at dinner last night, and on the drive to the hotel site—so withdrawn and expressionless. But then—he felt emotion stab at him—at the hotel, when she'd walked out into the garden, her face and her eyes had come alive with delight and pleasure. The radiance in her expression! That brief moment of shared feeling with her.

He'd had to force himself to be terse, to stamp down on her enthusiasm, ramming home to her the fact that he was only interested in the profit he could make—that he did not get sentimental over projects.

Or sentimental about her, *either.*

That was the message he had to convey. His jaw tensed in recollection. And it was the only message he had allowed himself to convey when he'd come across her cavorting in the pool that afternoon. Harsh displeasure. Because if he hadn't—

I couldn't have coped with seeing her glorious figure, so nearly naked, that swimsuit clinging to her lush curves and slim waist.

So he'd made himself speak angrily to her—but the anger had been for himself, at his own weakness. His own vulnerability to her.

His hands tightened on his knife and fork as he made some abstracted reply to whatever had been said to him.

I will not be vulnerable to her—not again. Never again. I will not let myself desire her, or want her, or crave her. I brought her here only to teach myself how to be immune to her. How to feel indifferent as well as to pretend indifference. And I will succeed. I must succeed.

His host was speaking again, asking him about his plans, and he forced himself to focus. There was no point replaying the day in his head…no point letting his thoughts go to the villa, where Talia would be dining alone, going to bed alone…

He reached for his wine and knocked it back. He wanted to gain some strength from it but all he felt was tempted. Unbearably tempted by Talia…

Talia settled herself down at the table that Fernando and his staff had carried out onto her wide balcony, underneath a shady awning. A light breeze sifted off the sea far below, lifting the heat, and the awning took the blaze of the sun off her. Down in the gardens she could hear birdsong, and occasionally the voices of the villa's staff as they went about their work.

It was very peaceful.

It was a peace she was trying to find inside her own head—hard though it was. She had slept restlessly, neither comfortable with the air-conditioning nor without it, and had stepped out at one point onto the dark balcony to be enveloped in the balmy warmth of the night, to hear the incessant chirruping of the tree frogs all around her. The moon had sailed overhead and she'd felt her lungs tighten; she'd heard her mother's voice again, unbidden, talking about the joy of being romanced beneath a tropical moon...

She'd gone back indoors, the words ringing hollow in her head. Luke had returned quite late—she'd heard the car—and had, it seemed, retired immediately. She'd been in her bedroom, where the staff had served dinner—delicious, but lonely—after which she'd spent some time emailing her mother, doing her best to sound cheerful.

She'd told her mum about the site visit, the ideas she had come up with, and how excited she was about them; she'd explained that she would be working on them tomorrow, described the beautiful island, the hot weather, and reassured her that the jet lag was easing.

But that was all that was easing, because this morning had brought no sign of any thaw from Luke. She hadn't even set eyes on him. Breakfast had been served in her room, and when she had asked after Luke, somewhat tentatively, she had been informed that he would be out all day and he had instructed her to work from the villa.

So now she began to develop her ideas for the hotel refurbishment, reaching for her art paper, her paints and pencils. She got out her notebook with the rough floor plans and measurements, and loaded the copious photos she'd taken the day before onto her laptop.

As she scrolled through them she began to feel the same emotions building up in her that she had felt on site and at lunchtime yesterday. Enthusiasm started to fire in her. The hotel was in such a beautiful situation, its architecture so perfect for its shoreline position between the azure ocean and the emerald rainforest, how could she fail to want to see it restored to beauty? To rescue it from the decay and ruin it had been subjected to?

I'll make it beautiful again. I'll make it more beautiful than ever.

A thought ran through her head—one she clutched at. She would do it for Luke. For the man with whom she had spent that magical night. Not the man who was now treating her with such callous indifference.

He no longer wanted her, and was making it glaringly obvious that whatever had burned so brightly and yet so briefly between them was nothing more than dead ashes now, but still she would use whatever talent she possessed to show him how beautiful that sad, ruined place of devastation could be.

If her design talents were all he wanted of her now, those at least he would have.

With renewed determination, she got to work.

Luke strode back into the villa. He'd had a long day. Frustration was biting at him. He'd met with another bunch of civil servants and the site's owners in the morning—relatives, he knew, of the government Minister for Development—and the message he was getting from them was loud and clear. They wanted him to buy the site—but at a price he was in no way prepared to pay.

Meetings in the afternoon with the architect and the structural engineering firm he intended to use had indicated that the cost of restoration was going to be astronomical, and then he'd made another lengthy visit to the hotel.

He flexed his shoulders as he headed into the office to communicate with his PA in Lucerne. It was time for some tough negotiations to commence.

He relished the prospect.

What he did not relish was what he was about to do.

He settled himself at the desk and picked up the house phone. 'Fernando, please inform Ms Grantham that I require her company this evening. Tell her to be ready for six thirty—formal evening wear. It is a reception at the Minister for Development's residence, with dinner afterwards.'

He set down the phone, his expression flickering. Should he really do this? Should he really spend the evening with her? But how else was he going to make himself immune to her except by spending time with her? It had to be done.

I can do it. I will do it. I must do it.

It was a mantra he repeated to himself that evening, as they took their seats in the back of the chauffeured car that set off from the villa.

He'd said nothing to Talia as she'd joined him in the hall on the dot of half past six, just given her a brief nod of acknowledgement before heading out to the car. Now, as she sat beside him, assiduously looking out of the window instead of at him, he allowed himself a glance at her. Then he forced himself to really look at her. Forced himself to take in her profile and the soft swell of her breast, to catch the fragrance she was wearing. He *made* his senses endure it.

When they arrived, some twenty minutes later, at the lavish private residence of the government minister, they walked into the crowded interior past flambeaux flaring beside the portico. He did not offer Talia his arm—that was something he knew he could not endure—but he did endure the minister who, on seeing him arrive, strolled up to them with a genial smile on his face. He greeted Luke and clearly expected an introduction to the woman at his side.

'My...secretary,' Luke heard himself say.

What he'd intended by saying that was not to let the minister know that he was already progressing to interior design for the hotel. For that would reveal the extent of his interest in the purchase, thus weakening his bargaining position. But too late he realised that the note of hesitation in his description of Talia's role was fuelling an appreciative look from the minister, who was drawing a quite different conclusion.

'I wish *my* secretary were as beautiful as you, my dear.' The minister smiled at Talia, his gaze openly admiring.

Luke felt his hand clench. A primitive urge speared him—a desire to whisk Talia away from any man who cast such a look at her. And an even more primitive urge pierced him when he heard Talia give a light laugh at the compliment.

Then the minister was greeting another new arrival and Luke promptly clamped a hand over Talia's elbow, steering her away. He felt her wince at the tightness of his grip and let her go. A waiter glided up to them, bearing a drinks tray, and Luke took two glasses, handed one to Talia.

'I need to network,' he said. And then, before he could stop himself, he heard words fall from his lips which he instantly regretted but could not prevent, because of the dark thorn of jealousy that was driving him. 'Try *not* to flirt with every man here.'

He heard a low gasp from Talia but ignored it, moving forward to greet one of the minister's aides whom he'd met that afternoon.

Talia's lips pressed together. There had been no call for him to say such a thing to her.

What does he think I should have done? Told the minister whose approval he needs for his project that my looks have nothing to do with my professional competence?

She'd got through the moment in as graceful a fashion as she could, having had long experience of such comments and heavy-handed admiration in her years of endless hateful socialising at her father's side.

Feeling awkward in the extreme—as she had from the moment she'd climbed into the car beside Luke, with the atmosphere between them more distant than ever—all she could do now was fall automatically into the routine that she was familiar with at functions like this: murmuring anodyne greetings, keeping quietly at Luke's side as she had at her father's.

Her father had required her to be merely ornamental. Was that why Luke had brought her here?

Her mouth thinned painfully. It certainly was not for the pleasure of her company, that was for sure! She was punishingly aware, and it made her feel horribly constrained herself, that he'd not spoken a word to her except that totally unfair comment just now, which had stung her to the quick. And he was broadcasting on every frequency the fact that he had no interest whatsoever in her being with him.

So why had he stipulated that he required her presence?

As she did what was presumably her duty at his side—being his 'plus one' for the evening—it started to dawn on her why he might have insisted she come with him tonight.

Did he want to keep other women at bay? Was that it? Because it was clear, now that she paid attention to it, that he was being eyed up—covertly *and* not so covertly—by female eyes all around. Her mouth thinned painfully again. She couldn't blame them for gazing at him. *All* women would take one look and crave him.

The way I do.

She pushed the bleak, hopeless thought out of her head, letting the familiar anguish fill her instead. She had had her chance with Luke and had walked out on it. Although it had been for reasons way beyond her control at the time, the result had been the same—she had left when she had desperately wanted to stay, and her lack of courage in that moment had spoiled everything.

He doesn't want me any more. There's nothing left of what there was. Nothing at all...

She sighed. All that was between them now was the fact that, for some reason she really didn't understand, he had brought her here to do a job. She must be grateful for that. Grateful that he'd heard her plea not to be evicted from the Marbella villa immediately. Grateful for the generous terms he'd offered. And that generosity was undeniable, she knew. What she would have been paid for her interior design skills wasn't even close to three months' market rate rent on the villa.

No wonder he wanted her to do every extra he cared to chuck at her, she thought bitterly. From being his secretary—however useless he thought her—to accompanying him to glitzy networking events like this, the purpose of which, she could only suppose, was to shield him from a horde of eager females waiting for their opportunity to pounce.

He seemed to be making methodical progress around the room, selecting various individuals to talk to, and from his conversation it was clear to Talia that for him this was simply an extended business meeting. She didn't follow most of it, confining herself to shadowing him meekly and being mindful not to 'flirt'—as he had so sneeringly and so unfairly put it. She stayed as modest and docile as she could, while trying not to appear dull or boring.

It was more of a skill than she knew Luke would credit, and it had been learned from years beside her father.

The thought was bleak, bringing home to her just how little she meant to Luke. Less than little.

'Right, we can leave now.'

His voice interrupted her painful cogitations. She felt her elbow gripped again—in that tight, commanding hold that steered her purposefully in any direction he wanted. They were soon crossing the large room, pausing only for Luke to shake hands several times and make his farewells as they left. Dutifully, Talia, too, murmured her goodbyes, bestowed civil smiles, and then, finally, they were outside in the warm night air, before the chill of the air-conditioned car enveloped her.

Luke threw himself in beside her, leaning forward to instruct the driver.

Talia heard him give the name of the island's most famous hotel.

Now what?

It was dinner. As docilely as she had at the minister's cocktail party, Talia walked in beside Luke, the skirts of her evening gown swishing around her legs. She was grateful she'd packed it, having not been sure just what she should bring with her. It was a world away, she thought with a pang, from the tightly sheathing dark red dress she'd worn at the party where she'd met Luke. This, like all her evening gowns, had been chosen to suit her father's taste—fussier and more embellished than she would have liked. But her father had wanted her to look expensive, to show the world how wealthy he was.

Her eyes shadowed. That life had gone for ever, and now she was picking her way across the bomb site that was all she and her mother had left. She was trying to protect her mother as best she could, whatever it took. Including being here like this with Luke.

It was a mockery—oh, *such* a mockery—of the way they'd been that magical evening at the party! The coldness of his manner burned her, as if she'd swallowed bitter acid.

With that sourness in her throat, she took her seat at the table reserved for them, quietly accepted the menu and started to peruse it. Why had Luke brought her here? If her role as minder—keeping females from pestering him—was no longer necessary, he could easily have sent her back to the villa. But, whatever his purpose in bringing her here, she just had to cope with it, however painful.

She stole a glance at him. He was absorbed in the

menu, and then the wine list, his expression closed. The waiter came to pour water, bestow a basket of rolls upon the table, and then he stood and waited for their orders. She gave hers, smiling up at the young waiter, whose face split into a wide, answering smile as he repeated her order in his lilting Caribbean accent. She heard Luke give his order in the terse tone that was becoming grimly familiar to Talia. Then the waiter nodded and headed off.

'Try not to flirt with the waiting staff, either.'

Talia's snapped her head towards Luke, eyes widening. 'I *wasn't*!' she said, breathless with indignation.

'He couldn't take his eyes off you,' came his reply. His eyes narrowed. 'No man can.'

He glanced towards another table nearby, where two men were openly casting their eyes in Talia's direction. He couldn't blame them. Even in that unflattering evening gown of hers she was the most beautiful woman in the room. His jaw tightened, and he felt the scythe of emotion scissoring within him yet again. She'd been the most beautiful woman at the cocktail party and she was the most beautiful woman here.

The most beautiful woman anywhere she goes...

His eyes swept back to her. She'd dipped her head at his words, that wash of colour he'd seen before when he'd spoken sharply to her flushing across her sculpted cheeks.

It made him angry. But it was an anger that came from deep within. An anger that was *in* himself—*at* himself. He could feel his gaze drinking her in, absorbing the way the long lashes of her tawny eyes dusted the delicate curve of her cheek, how her rich mouth trembled, how the sweep of her hair exposed the graceful line of her throat...

Desire flooded him. Longing…

He cut it off, refusing to acknowledge it. He told himself yet again that the only reason he had brought her with him tonight was to inure himself to her, and that he must succeed in doing so.

To stop himself looking at her again, he beckoned the sommelier to the table, immersing himself in a discussion of wines. Yet he was still burningly conscious that across the table from him Talia's slender fingers were pulling a soft roll to pieces. Her head was still dipped, her eyes averted from him.

He chose the requisite wine, busied himself with its tasting and approval, then dismissed the sommelier and turned his attention back to Talia. He wanted to find something in her to criticise, something to bolster his determination to make himself immune to her.

His eyes alighted on her gown. He frowned. It really did nothing to accentuate her stunning beauty—and, whilst he knew he should be pleased, he heard himself say, his tone critical, 'Is that dress by the same designer as the dress you wore at the villa?'

She started, as if she hadn't expected him to talk to her. 'Er…yes,' she answered. Her expression was wary.

'It doesn't suit you,' he said bluntly. His eyes flicked over her dismissively, and he saw that flush of colour run out over her cheeks again. 'It's far too fussy and over-embellished.' Before he could stop himself, he added, 'Nothing like what you were wearing at that party—'

As the words left his lips he cursed himself. The last thing he needed to do was remind himself of that night.

But Talia was only dipping her head again, saying in a pinched voice, 'My father liked this kind of style. He said it was very feminine. It was the way he liked me to look.'

Luke's expression tightened. So she'd dressed to please her doting father? That shouldn't surprise him—after all, it was Gerald Grantham who'd bankrolled her luxury lifestyle.

Abruptly, he changed the subject. He shouldn't give a damn *what* her dress was like—the less flattering to her the better, as far as he was concerned!

'So, what progress have you made on your design ideas?' he put to her as their first course arrived.

She lifted her head again and took a steadying breath. 'I'm working on a colour palette at the moment. You told me to come up with my own ideas, but if you want me to run them past you, in case you don't like them—' she started.

He cut across her. 'When I hire professionals I don't expect to have to do their job for them,' he said brusquely.

She flushed, yet again, and said falteringly, 'That isn't what I meant. I just thought that if I'm coming up with some ideas you dislike from the off you might as well tell me now, so I can make it how you want.'

He took a draught from his wine glass. 'If I don't like them I won't use them,' he said. He set his glass back on the table. 'Tell me, what kind of commercial experience do you have? Anything I might have come across?'

She took a breath. 'I did all the interiors of my father's properties, but—'

She was going to say, *But please don't judge me on that work. I had to stick to my father's exacting brief, not use my own ideas.*

She never got a chance to finish. A frown had flashed across Luke's face, drawing his brows together darkly.

'You never told me that.'

He made it sound like an accusation, and Talia felt

herself flushing. 'You've never asked me anything about what I've done,' she started to protest in her own defence, wanting to let him know that the work she'd done for her father did *not* represent her creative skills.

But Luke was already speaking again, his frown deepening. 'What have you done for other clients?' he demanded.

She felt herself hesitating, but answered truthfully. 'Um…nothing. But—'

She tried to get out the fact that her father had not permitted her to work for anyone else but, as before, Luke cut right across her, his frown deeper again.

'Are you telling me that *all* your work has been for your father?'

The scathing note in his voice was unmistakable and Talia winced inwardly, knowing that if he'd seen any of the garish interiors she'd done for her father he would judge her by them—critically.

'Well?' Luke demanded, clearly wanting an answer.

She swallowed, nodding, and again tried to explain just why that was, and that the work did not represent what she was capable of stylistically. But Luke gave her no chance.

She heard him mutter something under his breath in Greek. It sounded disparaging, even though she hadn't a clue what it meant. Then he was eyeballing her again, his jaw set. Pointedly, he threw another question at her.

'So, what do you make of this place, then? From a professional point of view,' he asked her. His voice was sharp suddenly, his gaze pinning her. Challenging her.

She glanced around the opulent dining room, trying to gather her thoughts in what was becoming his blatant interrogation—and a hostile one at that. She felt wrong-footed, and tried to recover her composure.

'It's very…impressive,' she said.

She chose the word carefully. Personally, she thought the opulent gilded furnishings and décor out of place on a tropical island, but she did not wish to insult the famous designer whose hallmark was evident here.

Luke's eyes narrowed. 'And will you be attempting to emulate this style yourself?'

She looked at him uncertainly. His question had sounded sardonic, and she wasn't sure why.

'I would do my best, if that was what you wanted,' she replied neutrally.

It was the last thing she would choose herself—to impose this kind of overblown style on that devastated, hurricane-blasted hotel. It would be totally wrong for it.

She never got the chance to say so. He was nodding, his expression hardening. 'Ah, yes—just as you "did your best" typing up those letters so atrociously!'

She flushed at the derision in his voice. To her dismay, as when he'd been correcting her hopeless typing, pushing her harder and harder, she felt tears haze her eyes. She felt her throat tightening and tried to fight it in vain, blinking rapidly to try and clear the treacherous mist that was forming.

Unhappiness twisted inside her. Why was he getting at her over this? Why was he jabbing at her with everything he said? She dipped her head, taking another mouthful of her food, though it suddenly tasted like ashes in her mouth.

Luke's expression tightened. The revelation she'd made that the only design experience she actually had was courtesy of her father was damning. Totally damning! She obviously wasn't a professional interior designer in the least. She was nothing but a dabbling amateur—a rich man's daughter who'd clearly fancied the idea of interior design as something to while away the time between shopping and socialising.

Her doting father had indulged her and she had amused herself by producing interiors that were, without exception, in every property belonging to Grantham Land that he had seen since his acquisition, uniformly hideous! Flashy, ostentatious, and tasteless.

Luke's expression tightened even more. There wasn't a chance in hell she could come up with something that was of the slightest use to him.

But do I actually want to use anything she might produce anyway?

Would he really want anything to remind himself of her in his new hotel?

His eyes rested on her again as he faced up to the realisation. She'd dipped her head again, was mechanically eating her food, yet he could see that her expression was pinched. It irritated him. He didn't want her looking like that—looking as if he'd hurt her feelings by what he'd said to her. What he *wanted*, damn it, was to feel nothing about her at all!

But he wasn't succeeding, he wasn't succeeding at all.

'Talia—' Was his voice harsh? He didn't mean it to be, but it had come out that way.

Her head shot up and he saw, with that same spike of emotion that had made him not want to see her looking upset, that the pinched look was more pronounced than ever, that her lower lip was trembling, that there was a liquid haze over her eyes...

He dropped an oath in Greek. He was impatient. Angry. Angry at what he was fighting to crush back inside him.

'Don't try and make me feel sorry for you to get yourself an easier ride.' He was proud that his voice had come out flat rather than cutting. 'I offered you this job in good faith—and on extremely generous terms! The fact that you have financial woes is not my problem— so don't ask for any sympathy from me on that score.'

He wouldn't forget the hell her father had put his family through, or how he had watched them suffer before they died. Talia had lived like a pampered princess, while his own father had—

There was a sudden clatter as she dropped her knife and fork on her plate. He saw her expression change. Change totally. Suddenly she was angry, and her voice bit out as she cut across him.

'I am *not* asking for sympathy!' Her eyes flashed furiously. 'I am extremely grateful for your commission, and I am more than willing to do any ancillary work for that you may require. But I am *not* going to apologise for my failings as a secretary when I simply do not have the skills or training!'

She took a heaving breath, an audible intake, before plunging on, even more furiously.

'Nor is there *any* justification for you biting my head off every time I speak! And as for my behaviour—' her eyes flashed again '—I will *not* be subjected to your totally unwarranted accusations that I am flirting with *anyone*! You have absolutely *no* right to make *any* comments of that nature whatsoever. And if you can't tell the difference between civility and sexual come-ons, then that is *your* problem, not *mine*!'

Talia pushed her chair back, getting to her feet. Emotion was ripping her apart and she didn't care. She didn't care what she was saying or what the consequences

would be. She had *had* it with the man! She wasn't going
to take one more jibe, one more put-down! Not *one*!

'It is not part of my professional engagement to spend
my evenings with you—and this one is terminating
right *now*!'

Tossing her napkin onto her chair, she turned on her
heel, striding across the wide dining room, a red mist
in her vision. She had *had* it with the jibes, the accusations—the whole damn lot!

Emotion raged within her as she strode out into
the hotel lobby. Anger was uppermost—she had been
pushed beyond what any person could endure—but
there was so much more in her than anger.

She felt her chest tighten like a drum and her throat
constrict. There was a haze in front of her vision, as
well as the red mist of rage. She wanted out—oh, dear
God, she wanted out! And not just out of this overdone
hotel that screamed *Money! Money! Money! Money!*
in her face with every piece of over-decorated gilded
furniture and cream satin fabric and every ludicrously
over-the-top floral arrangement on every available marble surface.

She wanted *out* of this unbearable situation. To be
so close to Luke and yet as distant from him as the
stars was torture. And for him to be doing nothing but
taking pot-shots at her, criticising her and berating her
so that she could do nothing right—nothing at all… It
was as if he were a completely different person from
the one she'd thought she'd known—as if that raptur-
ous night she'd spent with him, when she'd had to tear
herself away from him with all the strength in her body
and soul, had never happened!

To think she had so stupidly, so pathetically hoped
that maybe she would have a second chance with him

to make up for having had to run out on him the way she had. What a fool to think they could recover the bliss they had found so briefly.

Misery consumed her, thick and choking in her lungs, as dense as the hot, humid air that hit her as she rushed out onto the forecourt. Blindly, she threw herself into the first taxi waiting there, summoned by a doorman who had hastened to open the door for her as she stumbled inside.

The taxi pulled off and she slumped back, numb to everything except an all-consuming misery.

CHAPTER SIX

LUKE JERKED HIS chair back, watching her rush from the dining room. For a moment he was simply frozen. Then, vaulting upright, he started after her.

But suddenly the maître d' was there, consternation on his face, expressing his concern, asking if everything was all right, if there was something wrong with the food, the wine, the service, the staff—

'No, nothing!' Luke exclaimed, wanting only to push past the man and catch up with Talia, who was disappearing across the lobby, heading for the huge glass doors beyond. 'My apologies!' he threw at the maître d', finally getting past him.

Then, in the lobby, he was delayed again, by a party arriving at the hotel who were filling up the entrance. By the time he emerged out onto the forecourt she was gone.

'Get my car!' he snapped at the doorman, who promptly got on his phone to the chauffeurs' station.

It seemed to take an age for the limo to appear. He couldn't complain—his driver would hardly have thought he would be leaving so soon after arriving.

He sank into the back of the car, cutting short the driver's apologies for the delay. 'It doesn't matter. Just get me back to the villa ASAP!'

Urgency possessed him. Urgency and a whole lot more.

Never had a car journey seemed longer, or more tormenting.

Never had emotion burned him to the quick like this, crying out the lie he was trying to cling to—the lie that was impossible to fool himself into believing any longer.

I can never be indifferent to her. I will never be immune to her.

The very words mocked him pitilessly, rendering to ashes all he had felt, all he had believed, since the woman with whom he had shared a life-changing night had left him with barely a word.

Talia clattered up the wide staircase, ignoring Fernando's stately greeting and his enquiry if there was anything she wanted.

Yes, to get out of here! Just get out! To get to the airport and on the first flight home.

But how could she? And where was 'home' now?

If she wanted to keep her poor stricken mother, so utterly unable to cope with the catastrophe that had torn her life apart, somewhere familiar and comfortable while she built up her strength, then she must stick this out. She had to go on enduring the torment of Luke being so horrible, so different from the man she'd spent that night with.

She was trapped here—hideously, unbearably trapped. Perhaps he would not even keep to their deal after her outburst in the restaurant.

Tears were choking her as she reached her bedroom, leaning back against the door in anguish, features contorted, consumed by the misery that encompassed her. She kicked off her shoes, struggled out of her evening

gown, her underwear, and enveloped herself in her ki-
mono-style robe. Finally she collapsed down onto the
dressing table stool and frantically unpinned her hair.
She brushed it with harsh, painful strokes, as if she
could brush out far more than the knots that tangled it.

Emotions raged within her, hot and heavy and choking, and she batted away the pointless tears. This wasn't
Luke! Not the man she'd known—the man she'd found
such incandescent, incredible bliss with. The man who
had taken her to a paradise she had never known existed.
The man who had wanted to whisk her away from the
misery of her life, to sweep her off in his arms to a tropical island, to a place that could be theirs and theirs alone.

The choking came in her throat again, suffocating
her with anguish. A cry rose within her. Oh, dear God,
the bitter irony of it. For she *was* here on a tropical island with him. One of the thousand islands in the Caribbean that they might have run away to...

Her face contorted with anguish again. Oh, she was
here on a beautiful, sun-kissed Caribbean island, all
right—but not with Luke. Or at least not with the man
she had thought he was. She was here with a hard-faced,
cruel-voiced stranger who only found fault with her.
A petty tyrant like her father, carping and dismissive.

Not Luke. It wasn't Luke at all.

*That man I knew so briefly, so wonderfully, is gone.
Gone and never coming back. Or perhaps that was
never the man he truly is in the first place. Perhaps
this Luke is the real him.*

A sob broke from her, but she stifled it, filled with
the misery that had possessed her ever since she had
realised that *he* was the man who had brought her father to ruin and then helped himself to the remnants
of his business.

In any case, he was supremely indifferent to her now.
It's as though he hates me!

Emotion blasted her once more.

And I hate him. I hate him for the way he is now. I hate him for his indifference, for his coldness, his anger, for his cruelty.

There was a sudden noise behind her. Her bedroom door was flung open and she saw the reason for her devastation reflected in the dressing table mirror.

She whirled around. 'Get out!'

She yelled it with all her strength but Luke did not obey. He strode up to her, dark purpose in his face.

With a smothered gasp of shock Talia lurched to her feet—and then he was in front of her. His eyes blazed with dark light while his hands reached for her, clamping around her upper arms. Heat burned through the thin silk of her sleeve. She reeled with the sensation of it—with his closeness. She could catch the scent of his aftershave, the scent of his body. Her senses were fully awake now, memories buffeting her like the wind on a tiny sailboat in the middle of a stormy sea.

She could not bear it. Could not endure it.

She yelled at him again. Her heart had started to pound, blood was surging in her veins. 'Let go of me! You've got no right! No right to barge in here and man-handle me! So get out—get *out*!'

There was fury in her voice. And desperation. How could he stride in here, looking the way he did? Tall, dark, and so, so dangerous.

He did not let her go. His face twisted, that dark light still blazing in his eyes, and it made her reel with the force of it. She felt faint at the intensity, and suddenly weak with what she dared not face.

She felt herself sway, and only the grip of his steel hands around her arms stayed her.

'Throw me out if you want...' The hoarseness in his voice made it low, like a growl, and it was filled with the same burning intensity that was in his eyes, pouring into hers. 'But not yet. *Not yet.*'

For one endless moment more his dark gaze burned into hers. And then he hauled her to him, his mouth swooping to hers.

The room disappeared. The world disappeared. Everything disappeared. She drowned in his kiss. It was unbearable to kiss him and unthinkable not to. Her hands flashed to his shoulders, grasping them tightly. Then, as suddenly as he had seized her, he relinquished her. He stepped back and gave a harsh, brief laugh that had no humour in it.

His eyes were still blazing down at her. She stared at him, breathless, heart pounding, mouth stung and pouting, stared at the naked passion in his kiss, lips parting helplessly, eyes aching.

'Do you see now why I've been so cruel to you? I've been trying to hold you at bay. I *had* to push you away...' The hoarseness was still in his voice. 'Because it was the only way—the only way to stop myself kissing you like that. It was my only protection.'

His hands fell away from her and she swayed in their absence. Blood was pounding in her ears and racing in her veins. She was dazed.

He gave that harsh, humourless laugh again. 'Tell me to go.' His voice had changed; his stance had changed. The darkness in his eyes had changed. 'Or tell me to stay...'

She could not move, could not speak. She could only stand there, knowing with a kind of fatal awareness that desire had leapt in her body as a kindled flame. That she could feel her breasts filling, peaking, heat flushing up inside her. They were all but declaring her answer to him.

His expression had changed, too, and what was in it now made Talia feel faint again, weak. She could not drag her eyes from him, could not move. She heard him speak again through the blood soaring in her veins.

'You see…' he said softly, and a taunt was there in his voice. But it was not directed at her, she knew, but at himself. 'You see how much protection from you I need.'

He reached a hand towards her as she stood there, so faint, so motionless. He drew one long finger down the length of her cheek, then let it fall away. It was the same casual gesture he had made when he had first touched her on that fateful evening.

She saw his eyes half close, long lashes dipping. She saw the planes of his face, the roughened edge of his jaw, the strong column of his throat, the sable feathering of his hair. She caught again his scent in her nostrils and felt weakness drain through her. This was insanity… madness. It could only be that, surely, after all that had passed between them? To let this happen all over again?

'I want you. I want you as much as I ever did from that very first moment I set eyes on you. It's that simple, Talia. So very, very simple.'

His mouth lowered to hers again, but this was no demanding kiss, no leap of hot, instant passion. This was slow and sensual and quite, quite deliberate, and it was meant to make her yield to him, to make it impossible for her to hear what every ounce of fading sense was telling her: that this was madness and insanity and she should put a stop to it immediately.

How could she resist? How could she pull away from that honeyed feathering of her lips by his? From the continued arousal of her senses and the blood pounding in her ears? She revelled in the deepening of his kiss as he opened her mouth to him, to taste the sweetness within…

She felt his hands splay around her waist, drawing her pliant form towards the strong pillar of his body. She felt the edges of her robe brush the smooth fabric of his tuxedo jacket, felt the delicate peaks of her breasts unfurl at the frisson, felt her blood bubble and fizz, her desire thicken. Of their own volition her hands lifted to his torso, sliding inside his jacket, feeling, with a leap of her senses, the hard-muscled wall of his chest beneath her fingers.

Her kiss intensified with his and she felt him quicken, the hands at her waist moulding her against him so that her hips were crushed against his. With a smothered gasp, though it should have come as no surprise, she realised his arousal was full and strong. It fed hers—sent heat flushing her core, sent her fingertips into spasm, as her mouth feasted on his and his on hers.

She moaned low in her throat and it was like a match to dry tinder.

He swept her up into his arms, strode to the bed, and lowered her down upon it. He shed his jacket, impatience in every gesture.

She lay there, her blood pounding and leaping in her veins. Desire surged in her limbs, flooding her in hot, hungry urgency. Oh, this was madness, insanity, but she didn't care. Could not care. She could only reach up her arms with a low laugh of delight, of wonder and glory.

This was happening. He was here again—with her—and he was all she wanted.

All she could ever want.

Everything else in the world fell away from her.

There was only Luke. Only his possession of her. Only that…

The dim light of dawn was filtering through the louvered shutters. Luke lay, sated, with Talia's soft, silken body in his arms. Idly, he curled a lock of her lush hair around his finger. She was half asleep, her rounded breasts crushed against his chest, her legs tangled with his. Warmth enfolded them both.

At some point in the night he'd turned off the air-conditioning, turned off the light over the dressing table, and let the warm tropical night embrace them as they lay in the wide bed.

A sense of rightness filled him. It was *right* that he had yielded, after all, to what he had been fighting so desperately, so uselessly…

He'd known it the instant she'd stormed away from him in the hotel restaurant. He'd known there was only one thing he wanted—only one thing he could do. And it was what he had wanted from the moment she'd walked into his office in Switzerland—what he had been denying himself.

He'd tried to steel himself against her by any means he could—he'd spoken to her harshly, treated her so distantly, so critically, and he'd tried for indifference with every ounce of his willpower. But his need for her had only grown, and he'd been able to maintain that impossible effort no longer.

He'd had to yield to what he had had wanted every minute of the day and the night.

To possess her again. To make her *his* once more.

After the night they had spent together, the passion

that had blazed between them, there was nothing else but what was between them. His finger released the silken tendril and drifted to the silk of her skin instead. He grazed it lightly along the line of her shoulder and felt her quiver at his touch, even in her drowsing. He bent his head, brushing her mouth with his, arousing her...

He wanted her again.

How long he would want her, now that he had her here with him, he did not know. Perhaps he would tire of her eventually. But he would not think about that. One thing he did know was that this time *she* would not be leaving *him*. He would make it impossible for her to want to do so. Not this time.

She had rejected him once but she would not do so again. While he desired her she would *crave* him—he would make very, very sure of that.

His hand smoothed over her flank, then her thigh, and eased inwards into the vee of her body...her quickening body... He heard her moan and gave a soft laugh, letting his fingers go where her slackening thighs told him she wanted them to go.

He heard her moan again and felt his own desire mount and harden. His body moved over hers, possessing her once more.

CHAPTER SEVEN

TALIA SIGHED LANGUOROUSLY and gave a rueful laugh. 'I feel so guilty! I really should be getting on with my designs!'

Luke reached for her hand. 'There's no rush,' he said lazily. 'I haven't even bought the site yet.'

Talia turned her head towards him. They were both relaxing on padded sun loungers, set beside the turquoise swimming pool beneath the shade of a wide parasol which protected them against the heat of the afternoon sun beating down on the lush gardens.

'You are going to buy it, though, aren't you?'

Was there urging in her tone? Whatever it was that had called to her in that sad, ruined place, she knew that she wanted it to be saved and restored, that it was important to bring it back to life again.

Luke squinted at her. 'Do you want me to?' he asked in the same lazy voice.

'Oh, yes!' she answered. 'It could be made *so* beautiful again!'

He nodded in assent. 'For a great deal of money, yes...' he agreed dryly. 'At the moment I'm still haggling over the price.' His tone sharpened slightly. 'The site owners are thinking I'm a rich foreign investor they can fleece for their own profit. *That*,' he said, and now there was a grim note in his voice, 'is their mistake.'

Talia glanced at him. It was unnerving to hear that change of tone, the hard, cold edge to it, and it sent a flicker of unease through her. She banished it, her expression softening. The Luke who had been so cold, so cruel and distant, had gone. He had vanished utterly and now—oh, now he was the man she remembered… the warm, passionate man who had swept her into his arms, showering her with kisses.

And, bliss beyond bliss, there was nothing to part them. She was here, with him, just as they'd dreamed of being—here in the sun-drenched Caribbean, in a tropical idyll to embrace them both. Before, it had been impossible—but now they could be together.

She felt emotion melt within her like warm honey and squeezed Luke's hand that was holding hers, just for the joy of knowing they lay hand in hand. He answered her gesture, lifting her hand to his mouth and kissing it softly, his eyes entwining with hers.

'I think we've had enough of the great outdoors for now, don't you?'

There was a husk in his voice, one that she was now thrillingly familiar with, and a speaking look in his dark, expressive eyes. He let his lips play over her hand, deliberately and sensuously exploring the tips of her fingers, softly biting at the mound of Venus below her thumb, brushing the delicate skin over her wrist.

She felt arousal beckon, her blood quicken, and her eyes clung to his. 'What did you have in mind?' she asked, her voice a soft tease.

He answered with a low laugh. 'Come inside and find out,' he challenged.

As he spoke, he swung his bare legs round and drew

her upright. He slid a hand warm from the sun around her slender waist.

'If the staff weren't around you could find out right here,' he taunted. His hand slid from her waist over her rounded bottom, shaping it lazily. His eyes glinted. 'Tomorrow,' he said, 'we go shopping. This one-piece suit has got to go—I want you in a bikini. Or in nothing at all.'

His voice was a growl of arousal now and Talia laughed, her eyes never leaving him. She ran a finger along the waistline of his trunks, letting it slip a little within, and laughed again at the sudden flexing of his muscles at her touch.

'That goes for me, too,' she answered. 'These trunks conceal far, *far* too much.'

Daringly, she started to ease her hand downwards—only for his lightning-fast grip to stay her.

'Don't!' he said, his voice dangerously taut.

It gave Talia a thrill of pleasure to know how very near to the edge of his control he was. Then, with a gasp, she was being hefted up into his arms.

He laughed in triumph and possession. 'Time to get you upstairs!' he exclaimed. 'Before I throw caution to the wind and ravish you here on the sun loungers!'

She snaked her arms around his neck, glorying in the strength of his body. 'Take me, I'm yours!' she cried with mock melodrama, laughing in return.

He strode indoors, carrying her as if she were a featherweight, sweeping her upstairs to take her and make her his—*all* his.

Luke leant forward against the deck railing on the yacht, gazing across to the shore.

Beside him, Talia gave a sigh of pleasurable appreciation. 'This is *so* gorgeous,' she breathed.

Luke laughed. 'It's a bit of a cliché, a sunset cruise, but definitely worth it!'

There was a soft footstep behind him and he turned. The steward was coming up to them, bearing a tray that held an ice bucket in which a bottle of champagne was nestling and two flutes. He set the tray down on a table near them, and the ice bucket in a stand, then took himself off. Luke reached for the champagne bottle and with a deft hand opened it, filled the flutes.

The rich light from the setting sun bathed them as the stately yacht creamed across the cobalt waters, and the distant shore was emerald-green and thick with vegetation. She gave another sigh of pleasure. Of radiant joy. How wonderful this was!

And all because of Luke.

She smiled now, taking the flute he was handing her, drinking him in. He was looking lean and relaxed, in an open-necked pale blue shirt, cuffs turned back, and tan chinos with deck shoes. He was elegant and absolutely edible.

She felt her stomach curl, knowing how much she wanted him, how much she needed him, how much she wished she could stay with him for ever.

A tiny flicker of uncertainty plucked at her. It had been nearly a week since they'd arrived on the island—nearly a week since Luke had claimed her for his own again. It had been the most blissful week in her entire life. But into her head came an echo of what he'd said to her back in his office in Lucerne, that day she'd had to seek him out and beg him for forbearance on evicting them straight away.

He wanted her to be here in the Caribbean for a fortnight. But what then? She didn't know. Could only hope. Hope against hope that being with her was as wonderful for him as being with him was to her. That with nothing to keep them apart now they could stay together…

She felt a longing surge within her—a longing never to be without him. Did he feel it, too? Did he want her in his life as she wanted him? She could only hope—hope with all her being.

'We need to celebrate.' Luke was raising his champagne flute.

Talia looked at him questioningly. He nodded across to the shoreline they were gliding past, and as they rounded a small cape a beach opened up before them, a crescent of silver sand littered with fallen palms, and at the far end were the wrecked remains of the building she had last seen from the land.

'Oh, it's the hotel site!' she exclaimed. 'There it is!'

'Indeed it is,' Luke said beside her. He raised his flute to hers. 'And now,' he said, and there was open satisfaction in his voice, 'it is *my* hotel site!'

She whipped her head round, her face lighting up. 'Oh, Luke, that's wonderful! You've actually bought it!'

'I drove a hard bargain,' he said, 'but, yes, it's mine now.' He glanced down at her. 'Are you glad?'

'Yes! I'm so, so pleased! It needed rescuing!'

He gave a laugh. 'You sound very sentimental about it.'

'And why not?' she countered. 'If you hadn't bought it what would have happened to it?'

'It would have been demolished, probably. Or left to rot totally.'

'Oh, that's awful. It deserves much better.'

He was silent a moment. Then, 'Yes, it does.'

There was something in his voice she hadn't heard before, and she looked at him curiously.

Then, abruptly, he clinked his glass against hers.

'So, drink up. Celebrate my latest acquisition.' His long lashes dropped over his dark, expressive eyes. 'It's almost as good as the first one I made earlier this week.'

She looked at him, not understanding.

He dipped his head and kissed her in a leisurely fashion. '*You've* been a wonderful acquisition,' he said softly.

She looked at him uncertainly. 'Is that what I am?' she asked. There was something in her voice and she wasn't sure what it was, knew only that she didn't want it to be there. Her eyes searched his but he was simply smiling down at her, appreciation in his open gaze.

'Drink up,' he said again, in a low voice. 'There's plenty more in the bottle. They'll be serving our sunset supper at any moment.' His voice changed, grew husky. 'And after that I have every intention of testing out the bed in the stateroom down below.'

And he kissed her again, in that leisurely, casually possessive fashion...

It was good to kiss her. So very good to feel that velvet mouth of hers open to his, to taste its sweetness, savour its honey. To arouse the passion that came as he deepened his kiss.

But not right now. That was for later. For now he drew back, taking another draught of champagne, gazing out in a proprietorial fashion over the property he'd signed the purchase contract for that afternoon. For now he wanted to savour the moment. He wanted to savour everything.

He had bought the ruined hotel at the price *he* had wanted to pay—not the one that had been anticipated from him. It had been a fair price—but a keen one. Restoration would be expensive, as he had told Talia, and it would be years before he would see payback on the investment. But it would be worth it—and not just from a financial point of view.

His gaze went across the water to the lush shoreline. Why had it called to him so much, that derelict building battered into ruin by Nature's formidable, pitiless forces?

But he didn't really have to ask why. He knew.

As he gazed across the water another shoreline came into his mind—one that was as familiar to him as the back of his hand. One that he had seen countless times from his boyhood dinghy, tacking back and forth across the bay. Finally tiring, or driven by hunger—or both— he'd head downwind to beach his craft on the sandy shore, where he would haul it out of the water and then lope back to the low-rise century-old building that had been his home. His parents' home. His grandparents' before them, and another generation before them, as well.

Villa Xenakis, which had become the Hotel Xenakis, was lovingly transformed by his parents into a small but gracious beachside hotel, filled with carefully garnered antiquities and family heirlooms.

It had been a bijou hotel, just right for the discerning traveller wending his way through the myriad islands of the Aegean, filled with charm, character, and heritage. There had been arched doorways set into thick walls, paved terraces edged with huge ceramic *pithoi*, tumbling with vibrant flowers—scarlet and white geraniums, crimson and yellow bougainvillea, glossy-leaved miniature olive trees.

Little stone fountains had cooled the air…shady pergolas had been wound all about with honeysuckle and jasmine. There had been the endless chirruping of cicadas and by day it had been hot, but then had come the starlit nights, the soft lapping of the sea by the water's edge…

He blinked and the view was gone. Reduced to ruins.

His face shadowed. Nature had struck with all its callous fury, just like the hurricane that had destroyed the hotel he had purchased. But it had been no wind that had destroyed his precious sanctuary. No, it had been an earthquake that had shaken his parents' hotel to its foundations, collapsing half the roof and the ceilings, shattering walls, turning the kitchens to rubble and the graceful archways to a heap of broken stone.

But it had not been the earthquake that had stolen his home from his parents and left them with nothing. That had been done not by the gods, or Nature, but by man. By one man.

He moved away from the rail, turning abruptly. He would not think of that—not now. He refused to think of the man who had stolen from his parents all they'd held most dear. He had got his revenge and that man was gone. Destroyed by his avenging hand.

'Luke?'

Talia's voice at his side was hesitant, her hand on his stiffened arm tentative. For a moment he looked down at her, at her upturned face. But it was not her face he beheld.

It was her father's.

His eyes darkened, but with an effort he cleared his expression.

It's not her fault—not her fault she's his daughter. I cannot blame her for being that.

He would not let it trouble him. Not now. Not when he had finally made her his.

He rested his eyes on her with appreciation in his

gaze. It was not just her beauty that drew him, incandescent though it was—it was so much else, as well. He tried to analyse it, and failed, and then he didn't care that he couldn't analyse it. All he knew was that he could spend time with her and never be bored or restless, that whatever they talked about the conversation flowed between them, easy and spontaneous, just as it had that very first evening they'd met.

He was enjoying this relaxed, easy-going time with her—enjoying the fact that he could put his arm around her shoulder and she would lean in, or take her hand and she would squeeze his and smile at him, a warm and wonderful smile. He took delight in simply watching her move, in listening to her voice, in simply being with her.

Whatever it is she does to me it is something that no other woman can.

It was a truth he accepted now. And all he wanted to do was celebrate that truth.

He had come a long way to reach this point in his life. He had avenged his parents, destroyed his enemy, and he had even—his smile was wry—stepped in to save that devastated hotel, as if in tribute to the lost pride and joy of his parents, the legacy he had never inherited.

And now he was ready for this time with Talia.

He tilted his flute to hers, hearing the crystal ring out softly. His eyes met her upturned gaze, warming as they did.

'To us,' he said. 'To our time together.'

And life felt very, very sweet.

Talia was working. She was out on the balcony of her bedroom—not that she slept there any longer, for after that first night with Luke she always shared his bed.

He was leaving her to work as she wanted, and she was glad.

Her eyes shadowed for a moment. Though he'd never referred to it again, it was clear that he judged her by the work she'd done for her father. But that fact only made her burn to show him that she was capable of better. And she was, she knew, for she was fizzing with unleashed creativity, inspired by the ruined majesty of the hotel, and she was rejoicing in it. She would make that sad, crumbling hotel come alive and show Luke just how beautiful it could be—in harmony with nature, as vivid and vibrant as its setting between the rainforest and the sea.

She worked on, busily and fruitfully, making the most of this time to herself, wanting to be as productive as she could be. Luke was away from the villa, interviewing architects, project managers, structural engineers—all the technical personnel who would be necessary to render the building sound again. Only when the empty shell was ready and waiting for her could her ideas start to take reality.

Once she had the artwork done, though, she wanted to head into the island's capital, to see what she would be able to source locally. She wanted to discover as much as she could about fabrics and designs that were in harmony with the island's heritage, its people, their culture. She'd already consulted Fernando and his wife, Julie, who was the housekeeper, and they had given her some good potential leads to follow up. In a small community like this one, there was so much untapped potential in local knowledge.

She felt her enthusiasm firing up a notch and it buzzed in her veins. She paused to look out across the vista, at the fabulous hillside view across the emerald-green landscape down to the azure sea. How beautiful it was! The whole world was beautiful—*her* world was beautiful. Her existence was blissful.

Because of Luke.

Luke had lit up her life and set her heart glowing with a fire that she could never quench—never wanted to quench. She sang his name in her head—more than just his name.

I'm in love with him.

As she gazed out over the vista before her she felt her breath catch as the realisation hit her. The truth of what she felt for him vibrated in her head as gloriously as his name! A rush of emotion fused through her. Of *course* she was in love with him! How could she not be? How could she not be in love with the man whose every touch thrilled her? Her expression softened with tenderness and recollection. The man with whom she felt so at ease.

That time of painful conflict between them had vanished. How had it ever existed, she wondered, when now the glow of warmth in his eyes never faded? How wonderful he was! How he made her smile, and laugh, made her feel carefree when he caught her to him and held her close, so close that she could feel the beat of his heart against hers!

Of course I'm in love with him! How could I not be?

She felt the rush of emotion come again, filling her being, and with it came another emotion, searing through her.

Hope.

Hope that if she was in love with him, then he might be in love with her.

Surely his passion for her, his ardour, cried out how much he felt—and not just in bed but all the time. The way he looked at her, took her hand, wound his arm around her, poured his gaze into hers, smiled at her, laughed with her… It was as if he could not get enough of her. And the way he nestled her against him, held her hand, meshed his fingers with hers, as if he would never let her go… Surely he felt the same?

She felt her breath catch again. A sigh of hope, of happiness, of sheer delight, escaped her as she breathed his name again.

In a dreamy-eyed reverie she reached for her colours again, more determined than ever to do her very best work for Luke.

A couple of hours later, a discreet cough behind her broke her concentration. It was Fernando, bringing a tray of tea for her, and she took a grateful break as the sun lowered to the horizon. Later she would ready herself for the evening. Luke was taking her out, and she wanted to dazzle him.

Julie had skilfully altered her evening gown for her, ridding it of all the frills and flounces. Its simple style had a sensual impact which she knew Luke would prefer.

Talia studied her appearance in the long mirror before heading downstairs for the evening, looking at her dramatic eye make-up and the long, loosened tresses of her hair tumbling over her shoulders.

She wished she could add some jewellery, but she had none. She'd never really had any, according to the lawyers who had brutally informed her that both her and her mother's jewellery were classed as a corporate asset, since her father had bought it with company funds and claimed it against tax.

Not, she thought with sudden bitterness, that it had been given to her by her father out of affection, but only because his daughter, like his wife, needed to be draped in expensive baubles to reflect his own success in life. They had been tokens of his wealth, not of his love.

She shook the memory from her, and forgot it completely in the glow of appreciation in Luke's eyes as she walked down the wide sweep of the staircase.

He closed in on her. 'Maybe we should postpone dinner,' he murmured, and the familiar husk in his voice sent a little thrill of arousal through Talia. Then he released her. 'No, I want to enjoy looking at you all evening and delay my gratification. The reward will come later.' His dark eyes glinted with open desire. 'And will be all the sweeter for it.'

He handed her into the waiting limo.

'Where are we going?' Talia asked.

He laughed. 'We're going to try the place you flounced out of and see if we can have a better time there tonight.'

Talia smiled. It was a certainty that they would enjoy the evening a million times more than the disastrous first time.

And so it proved.

This time Talia was as relaxed as she had been tense before. Now, as they took their places at their table, she gazed about the room with equanimity.

Luke followed her gaze. He frowned inwardly, remembering that first evening. when he had discovered how completely unqualified and inexperienced Talia was to undertake what he'd so rashly invited her here to do.

His expression softened. Well, he would come up with some tactful way of hiring a designer who *was* up to the task, and in the meantime, if it brought Talia pleasure to dabble with her colours and paints, imagining she was doing something useful with the time she was spending on dreaming up her designs, then he was happy to indulge her.

Just as her father had, he realised with another inward frown.

With a rich, doting father, Talia would have been allowed to imagine herself useful to her darling daddy, however hopeless she actually was. As witnessed by the dire interiors of all the Grantham properties. Tasteless, ostentatious, and 'cookie-cutter'—showing not a trace of flair or originality or style.

Impatiently, he cleared his unwelcome thoughts. His interest in Talia was not in her professional talents—or lack of them.

His expression softened and he reached for her hand across the table. 'Have I told you yet how incredibly delectable you look tonight?' he asked, a smile in his voice and his eyes. His gaze glanced over her. 'That dress is spectacular!' he breathed, his eyes lingering on the generous cleavage that it exposed.

Talia laughed. 'It's the same dress I wore that first time here. Julie altered it for me. I think it's a huge improvement, and if you do too then we're both pleased.'

Luke frowned. 'You shouldn't have had to do that. We'll go shopping tomorrow,' he announced decisively.

'Can we?' she asked eagerly. 'I really want to start checking out what I can source for the refurb here on the island. Fernando's been kind enough to make some suggestions as to shops I can look at, for fabrics and so on.'

'If that's what you want,' Luke agreed equably. It would do no harm, after all, and if it kept her happy then he would give her her head. 'But we'll try the boutiques first. There's an upmarket mall not far from here—you'll be able to find some of your usual designers there, I'm sure.'

She was looking at him uncertainly. 'I... I don't really think I should. I've got a wardrobe full of designer dresses at the Marbella villa. I didn't bring any of them with me because I thought I'd be here to work, and I wouldn't really need any evening wear.'

'Well, you do,' Luke replied decisively. 'Although...' his voice dropped, taking on a sensual twist '... I far prefer you with nothing on at all.'

The arrival of the service staff put paid to any further explication and he settled back to order. This time they would enjoy the Michelin-starred delights on the extensive menu—and the prestigious wine cellars. This time nothing would mar their evening.

Nor did it.

In the luxurious surroundings of the five-star hotel, both he and Talia enjoyed a leisurely meal and then, repairing to the terrace which overlooked the hotel's private beach, they settled down with liqueurs and coffee. What they talked about Luke couldn't remember—he knew only that conversation flowed easily, as it always did now.

Eventually they made a move. Luke's arm came around her shoulder and she nestled into his casual embrace. As they made their way back to the lobby, along a wide, marble-tiled concourse, Luke paused beside one of the several exclusive boutiques that lined each side.

'Want to look in?' He smiled. 'We could make a start on your new wardrobe.'

The store was still open, even at this late hour, for the hotel's patrons might wish to make purchases at any time. The window display sported several svelte evening gowns, all of which would have looked spectacular on Talia. But she shook her head.

'Way too late,' she said, and smiled.

Then her eye was caught by something. On a separate plinth in the window was a display of jewellery. She lingered another moment. One of the pieces—a showy diamond and pearl pendant—looked like the one her father had bestowed upon her for a birthday a few years ago. Her expression flickered.

'Does that take your fancy?' Luke asked in a genial tone.

'It's like one my father gave me,' she heard herself say. Then she cut herself short. She didn't want to think about it.

Her father had only ever presented jewellery to her when her mother was present, and Talia had had to exclaim in surprise and delight at his generosity. It would always elicit some comment from her mother about how wonderful her father was, how generous he was to them.

Talia shuddered at the hypocrisy of her response, at how her father had made her collude with his flattering image of himself lest her mother be upset. Her mother had always needed to go on believing in the fiction that they were a happy family, that hers was a happy marriage. She'd never been able to face the brutal truth of it.

'I think that would suit you better.'

Grateful for Luke's interruption of her troubled thoughts, Talia looked to where he was indicating a ruby bracelet, glittering under the spotlight highlighting the display.

'Oh, that is *beautiful*!' Talia exclaimed spontaneously, for the delicate array of rich red gems forming a continuous loop was indeed breathtakingly lovely in its stylish simplicity.

Then something else caught her eye. A watch—a man's watch, judging by its size and design—its face and casing almost completely obliterated with diamonds.

She giggled—she couldn't stop herself. 'Oh, Luke, do look!' She cast him a mischievous glance. 'Now, you *have* to admit that's a lot less dull than *your* boring watch!'

She touched with her finger the sombre, understated, formidably elegant—and ferociously expensive—custom-made watch that he always wore. Memory played at her—how she'd noticed it at that party, made some comment about it, and he had said it had been a reward for himself.

With an inner shiver she realised with hindsight just what the reason for that costly indulgence had been.

He had been celebrating taking over Grantham Land.

That inner shiver came again. Her father, too, had liked to celebrate any major kill he'd made in the marketplace. A new car—the latest model of whatever was the most expensive brand at the time—had been his favoured object of conspicuous display, his way of showing off his success to the world.

Again, she was grateful as Luke replied to her deliberately teasing comment.

'Diamonds would look better on you than me,' he said dryly. He squeezed her shoulder. 'Come on—stop drooling like a magpie!' His voice changed, grew husky. 'I want to get you home.'

He paused to drop a kiss on her mouth—lingering enough to let her know why he was so keen to get her home, just swift enough to keep it decent in public.

But as he bore her off across the lobby to get her into

the car, so he wouldn't have to care about public behaviour, he found himself glancing back at the display of glittering jewellery. So she liked the ruby bracelet?

A smile flickered around his mouth as he walked by her side.

Well, why not? He was in the mood to be indulgent.

CHAPTER EIGHT

'I'LL TAKE A swatch of this one, and this…and this. And
that one. And let's try that one as well.' Talia smiled as
the woman nodded, reaching for her scissors to cut the
strips of fabric that her customer had selected.

Talia got out her notebook, noting the fabric names
and colours, then checking the price per metre for each
of them and adding that too. She tapped the book in
satisfaction. There—that was a start. And it was looking promising.

She launched into a technical discussion with the
woman, of widths and weights and thread counts and
finishes. This was where she was in her element, and
she was loving it. Loving being able to get totally stuck
in to the next stage of turning her creative vision into
reality.

The saleswoman was enthusiastic—as well she might
be, Talia acknowledged, given the value of her custom
if Luke were to agree to her proposals.

*Oh, please let him like what I've come up with.
Please let him agree with my vision for the place! I so,
so want it to be beautiful and for him to love it like I do.*

She knew she had to be careful in her costings. Luke
had made it very clear he wanted value for money. Her
mouth tightened in grim memory. But she was used to

having to justify every pound she spent. Her father had always given her the tightest budget he could get away with, and there had never been any question that he would tolerate her exceeding it by so much as a penny.

She shook her head free of unpleasant memories. Her work here was completely different. This was a labour of love.

She smiled to herself. Thoughts fluttered deep inside, in a place she scarcely dared acknowledge. A labour of love, indeed—and not just for the sake of bringing back to vivid, vibrant life that sad, hurricane-blasted hotel.

It was for Luke's sake.

The man she loved.

Her smile became rueful. Out of love, she had let him do what she knew she shouldn't have that very morning.

As promised, he'd taken her to the upmarket shopping mall he'd mentioned, getting her to choose two more evening gowns, several sundresses, and a handful of ultra-brief bikinis and diaphanous wraps. She'd tried not to see the price tickets, for she knew she should not have let him buy such expensive things for her, but he had been insistent, and it had so obviously given him pleasure to do it.

So she'd squared her conscience by telling herself that she'd be wearing them for *him*, not for herself—that it would be to bring into his eyes that light of open appreciation that she so loved to see...the one that turned so swiftly to sensual desire.

She quivered with the little thrill that kicked in her pulse simply at the memory of how he could make her feel and how he made her respond. She gloried in it. It was like walking on air, floating in a haze of happiness. This was really happening to her; the man of her dreams was making her his own.

She all but skipped out of the shop, checking the time. Luke had left her to her own devices after they'd lunched at a beachfront restaurant, heading off for yet another meeting with architects and planning officials. But they were to meet for sundowner cocktails at a fashionable bar by the marina, and she quickened her step, for she still had more calls to make.

She was seeking out furniture, window treatments, bedding, and crockery—and then, if local suppliers didn't prove possible, a couple of import-expert companies to handle bringing goods in from abroad, all of which would require precise costings and copious paperwork. But she would include it all in what she presented to Luke—and hope that it would convince him to use her designs.

Multiple calls kept her busy, and by the time she reached the cocktail bar at the end of the afternoon Luke was already in the open-air lounge, looking sinfully relaxed, his long legs stretched out in front of him, a ferocious-looking margarita in his hand. He wore even more ferociously expensive sunglasses that made her go weak at the knees.

'Had fun?' he enquired lazily.

'Hugely!' She laughed, sitting herself down and ordering a fruit-based rum cocktail from the immediately attentive waiter. She fished inside one of her carrier bags. 'Do you want to see some of the materials I'm sampling?' she asked.

Luke waved his glass in negation. 'Not right now,' he said casually.

He didn't want to sound dismissive. She'd clearly had an enjoyable session—choosing colours and fabrics, or whatever it was she thought passed for work—but he didn't want his time wasted over something hopelessly amateurish, and he couldn't bear to have his infatuation with her diminished if she brought out tasteless designs. He wouldn't be able to lie and smile and pretend it was good work. If what she was going to produce was anything like what she'd done for her father's buildings then she had absolutely no eye for colour, style, or shape.

He'd eventually have to get around to hiring a professional designer and handing the work over to them to produce something suitable. However, he had no wish to hurt Talia's feelings, so he softened his rejection by laughing gently.

'And in return I promise not to tell *you* about how irritating I find planning officials!' He took another mouthful of his margarita. 'But from now on I'm leaving all that to the project manager I've appointed. He can cope with officialdom. Besides—'

He broke off. He'd been about to say that he wouldn't be spending much more time here on the island. Buying the hotel site had been an impulse, catching at something deep within him. But his business life was conducted in the financial centres of the world. That was where he'd made the fortune he'd had to make in order to forge the weapon he'd needed to bring down his enemy.

His fingers clenched over the stem of his cocktail glass and forcibly he made them relax again. Grantham was destroyed. And everything the man had once possessed was now his.

His eyes skimmed over the woman at his side, sipping delicately from the multi-coloured cocktail she'd been served.

Everything he had is mine now. Even his daughter.

His eyes were shadowed behind his sunglasses. He would have given a great deal for Talia *not* to be Gerald Grantham's daughter. His mouth tightened. But he would not blame her for what she could not help.

His eyes skimmed over her now. She was wearing one of the floaty, floral sundresses he'd bought for her that morning. It had been formidably expensive, though she hadn't even glanced at the price tag. Of course for Gerald Grantham's daughter price tags had never been of any concern.

But he would not blame her for that, either. It was what she was used to—of course she took it for granted. Why shouldn't she? It was the habit of a lifetime.

But not one she can afford any longer.

Unless, of course, there was another man to provide it for her.

The thought hung in his mind, but he knew what must come next.

It is what she will want—what she will expect. And if I want her I have to accept that.

He raised his cocktail to his lips, taking another mouthful. What they had was worth it—oh, more than worth it. He must accept her as she was—as he had done when he hadn't known she was Gerald Grantham's daughter.

His eyes rested on her again and instinctively he took her hand, feeling her fingers press his in return, watching her mouth parting in a fond smile at his gesture. His gaze softened in automatic response. Tonight—this very night—he would make his feelings for her clear.

And what her answer would be he already knew.

She will never leave me again. Never.

The certainty warmed in his eyes and he meshed his fingers with hers, entwining them together, sure in his possession of this most irresistible of women. So very, very special.

And tonight I will show her just how special she is. I will show her exactly what she means to me...

It was a good feeling.

Slowly, with deliberate control, Luke let his fingertips trail down the valley between the ripe orbs of Talia's lush breasts. His fingers splayed out across the slender softness of her body and then, with even more deliberate control, he slipped them between her thighs.

She gave a low moan of pleasure and he lowered his mouth to the crested peaks of her breasts, adoring each in turn as more moans came from her arching throat. His own arousal was complete, and he was ready—more than ready—for his possession of her. With the same absolute self-control he moved his body over hers.

Afterwards, as their heart rates slowed and their breathing eased in the exhausted torpor that had come to them, Luke settled her into the crook of his arm, feeling her body warm and drowsy against his, their limbs still tangled. Above them, the slow blades of the ceiling fan rotated lazily, cooling the ambient air, though not enough for him to need to reach for the coverlet which had slumped to the floor.

Lightly, his hand brushed the soft contours of her rounded hip, then trailed over her slender thigh. 'Do you realise,' he murmured, 'that we've been here on the island nearly two weeks?'

Did he feel her tense suddenly? If he did, he was glad of it. It gave him reason to continue. His life had changed utterly since Talia had walked into his office, and he wanted to keep it that way. He could not—*would* not—lose her again.

He dropped a soft kiss on her forehead, smiling. 'Tempting though it is, I can't stay here lotus-eating for ever,' he went on. 'I've got to the point now where I can leave the restoration of the hotel to the experts I've appointed, and it's time to pick up my life.'

He took a breath, his hand on her hip tightening slightly.

'So what do you say to coming with me to Hong Kong? Then on to Shanghai? I've got various matters I have to see to there—business matters—but after that...' his voice warmed '...maybe we could drop down to the South Seas and explore the islands there?'

He took another breath, and then he said what had been burning in him for days.

'I want you with me, Talia—wherever in the world I go. Will you come with me? Stay with me?'

He paused, levering himself up on his elbow, looking down at her. Waiting for her answer.

For a moment there was absolute silence. Then, with a cry, she flung her arms around him.

'Yes! Oh, yes. Oh, Luke, yes! Yes, yes, *yes*!'

Her voice was full of a joy that blazed like the sun, and Luke's heart felt suddenly whole for the first time he could remember.

Talia was floating on air. She was ten feet up, soaring with happiness. There were things she would have to sort out first—she knew that. Before she could take off for her very own personal paradise with Luke. But with Luke now committed to her she felt no apprehension about explaining to him about her poor mother, how she must ensure she was safely settled and secure in her future. Surely Luke would see that? Surely he would let her mother stay on in the Marbella villa for as long as she wanted, once she told him about her health condition?

She would take Luke to meet her when they were back from the Far East. Luke would reassure her, and she knew her mother would be overjoyed that her daughter had found love and happiness.

It's the happily-ever-after that I've always longed for!

All day she continued floating on air, even though she saw little of Luke. He'd incarcerated himself in his office, telling her he had work to get on with, but he had said they would celebrate that evening, and asked her to confer with Julie and Fernando to lay on a suitable celebratory feast for dinner.

Talia didn't mind that Luke was working, because she was, too. Gathering all the samples she'd collected the day before in the island's capital, she settled down on her bedroom balcony to produce her colour board, happily humming away to herself as she did so, referring back to her sketches and annotating everything with the costing notes she'd made and the calculations she'd run.

She was kept busy all day on the internet, researching for furniture, window treatments, and bed linens, and all the other myriad requirements that would be needed, whittling them down to a shortlist before she printed out photos and added copious notes and yet more costings.

As the sun was setting they shared a late swim in the pool—Luke vigorously ploughing up and down, Talia contenting herself with some gentle breaststroke. Then she left Luke to it while she headed back upstairs to get ready for the evening ahead.

She all but floated up the stairs. And back down again, some two hours later.

She had dressed with exceptional care, her heart

beating fit to burst, and knew that she looked as beautiful as it was possible for her to look.

Julie, emerging from the kitchens, clapped her hands, and Fernando smiled benignly and ushered her through to the terrace, where Luke was waiting for her.

For a moment he did not speak, and then he came up to her, reaching for her hands. 'How can you be so beautiful?' he breathed, his eyes warm upon her, lighting up her face, her eyes, her smile, like the moon and the stars.

She was wearing another of the new gowns he'd bought for her the day before, this one more formal than the one she'd worn the previous evening. It was in pale blue silk, with a very fine plissé texture, and it cupped her breasts almost like a strapless bikini top, then fell in graceful folds to her ankles.

He himself was in a tux, but he had slung his jacket and tie over a chair in the close warmth of the evening. He looked elegant, roguish, and—Talia gave a little gulp of sheer attraction—unbearably gorgeous...

He handed her to her seat at the table, which had been beautifully set by Julie, with scented flowers rioting all over, candles sheltered by glass containers, crystal and silver sparkling in their light. Beside the table champagne nestled in ice on a stand, already opened and smoking gently.

Luke hefted the bottle out, filled their glasses.

'To us,' he said. His gaze was lambent, rich with expression.

Much later, Talia rested her cheek against Luke's bare chest. Her heart rate was easing, her breathing slowing. Yet her whole body was still glowing, flushed with the aftermath of her physical ecstasy.

How can it be so incredible? Every time!

Wonder still filled her at what Luke could arouse in her—an explosion not just of the most intense pleasure possible, but of an intense joy that flowered in her heart.

She felt her soul soar, turning over and over in ecstasy.

I love him so much. How can I love him so much?

She did not know—only knew that she did. And that giving herself to him with all that she possessed, with all that she was, had transformed her life utterly and completely.

Did he love her?

The question was there—she had faced it, accepted she could have no answer yet. Perhaps he did, but did not yet realise it? Or perhaps he was still growing towards it? Letting it steal upon him as it had for her?

But he would come to love her—of that she was certain. Men took longer to realise their emotions—she knew that…everyone knew that. It was common knowledge. They told of their emotions in deeds, not words. And with everything Luke did, and the way he was with her, he demonstrated just how precious she was to him. After all, he'd asked her to travel with him, to *stay* with him…

She gave a sigh of happiness, wrapping her arm around his strong, lean waist. How gorgeous he was… how unutterably gorgeous. And how impossible it was, she thought, to be anything except blissfully, wonderfully happy! She and Luke were together. Building a life together—*always* together!

Nothing can part us now. Nothing.

The certainty of it filled her as she nestled into him, glowing with radiant happiness and love, revelling in

the warmth of his arm around her back, folding her to
him, and knowing with every fibre of her being how
absolutely perfect her happiness was. And how she gloried in it!

She gave another sigh of bliss and pure, perfect happiness, then felt his arm move and reach out past her;
heard the noise of his bedside table drawer sliding open.
Her eyes fluttered open as she felt Luke shift position,
drawing back so that he was half propped against the
pillows. She raised her head to meet his gaze, which
was drawing down towards her in the soft light from
the lamp.

'I have something for you,' he said, and his smile
was warm, his eyes warmer still.

He lifted the box he'd taken from the drawer, flick-
ing it open with his hand.

Talia gasped. She couldn't help it. Catching the lamp-
light, the ruby bracelet glittered with a crimson fire that
seemed to burst from the heart of each precious gem.

'For you,' said Luke. A half-smile tugged at his
mouth. 'I would have given it to you at dinner, but it
would not have matched that blue gown. But now...' his
mouth dipped to graze her shoulder '...it will suit you
perfectly. Just as you are.'

He lifted her hand, took the bracelet from its velvet
case and draped it around her slender wrist, fastening it.

'It fits you perfectly,' he said. He smiled again. 'I had
it delivered this afternoon. It's the one from the hotel
that you so admired. It's yours. Yours to keep.'

He kissed her mouth, sealing his gift to her. Then he
eased her body back against his. Her hand lay on his
chest, glittering with the bracelet's fiery gems. They
seemed to glow against her skin.

The bracelet had been expensive—overpriced, he knew—but then it was priced for a hotel concession, and the impulse buys that men like him would be likely to make when on holiday with a woman they desired and cherished. He hadn't cared about the mark-up—only wanted to bestow upon the woman he was going to take with him now wherever he went something she had shown she desired. To show her that he wanted to give her what she desired.

He heard her speak, and expected to hear an expression of delight. But it was not.

'Why...why have you given this to me?'

There was a note of incomprehension in her voice. Of doubt. He kissed her again. He wanted only to experience the joy of giving her something that showed her how precious she was to him.

'To make you beautiful for me!' he said lightly.

Then, knowing it was time to say more, he looked down at her, cupping her face with his hand. His voice would be serious now. He had to say what needed to be said—what had to be acknowledged if they were to continue together now.

'Talia, I know how difficult it has been for you since your world crashed about you. Losing your father...' His voice held an edge. 'I think we both know he isn't coming back. And even if he did—' that edge was harder now '—he would be penniless. No use to you at all. But whether or not he ever does show up again, nothing can take away how hugely traumatic this time has been for you. I understand that.'

He took a breath, knowing it was time to confront the unspoken truths that lay heavy between them. If they were to make a life together they had to be addressed and dealt with so they could move on together.

'You went from wealth to poverty overnight—the kind of poverty you were never equipped to deal with. You are the daughter of a very wealthy man, who doted on you and spoiled you, and I understand that the life you have been reduced to now is unimaginable for you. All your life you've been sheltered, as only the daughter of a rich man can be. And I know and I understand— truly I do, Talia—that your situation is something you find incredibly hard to accept. I want you to know that I don't blame you for that. You are not responsible for your upbringing, nor for taking for granted the way of life your father's wealth allowed you to have. It would be harsh of me—unfair of me—to judge you for that. You can't help being the way you are, for being *what* you are—a rich man's daughter who has had everything provided for her all her life. A life of luxury and ease. It's no wonder you don't understand how brutal and tough the world can be.'

His expression changed.

'That day you came to me at my offices in Lucerne, expecting me to give you what you wanted, I was tough on you. I didn't make allowances for you and I should have. But now I *do* make those allowances. And, just as it wasn't fair of me to expect you to be able to do sec- retarial work for me, so it wasn't fair of me to expect you to try and take on something as major as a com- plete hotel refit.'

He picked his words carefully, for he did not want to hurt her feelings.

'I realise that your father let you enjoy trying out your design ideas on his properties, and that he indulged you in this, but I would hate for you to spend any more time with your paints and fabrics, however much you've been enthusing over them.' He smiled at her with fond affection. 'The hotel is a major project—a huge amount of work will be involved—and I'll be hiring a firm of professionals at some point to take it on.'

He smiled again, trying to be tactful.

'You don't have to worry about it any more. Besides, you won't have time to do anything like that— not if you're going to be with me from now on. I'd far rather you spent all your time and energy on *me*!' he said lightly, keeping his tone humorous, so as not to upset her.

Then, in a more serious vein, having—he hoped— explained to her as gently as he could why she no longer had to feel she should work for him, he went on. This was the key message he needed her to absorb—the message that would reassure her, that would ensure she was never tempted to leave him again. This was where he would explain that he would provide all she could ever want or need or dream of.

He softened his voice and stroked her hair, gazing down into her wide, wide eyes. 'Because, Talia, from now on you won't have to face the world on your own.' He dropped a tender kiss on her lips. 'From now on you'll have me to look after you. To take care of you.' His fingers dropped to the glittering ruby bracelet around her wrist where it lay across his chest, tapping it gently. 'This is a token—proof of how much I want you, of how much I want to take care of you. You can trust me, Talia, because of *this*. That's what I want you to know.'

He lifted his hand away and traced the soft outline of her parted lips as she lay gazing up at him. He could not read her expression, but that did not trouble him. She would be taking in his words, finding in them the reassurance he wanted her to have. The knowledge that she was safe to commit herself to him as she had not dared to do before,

'You won't have to leave me again, Talia. I know you did that first night, because you were afraid. Afraid to risk coming with me because you might have been disappointed. I was a stranger—you knew nothing about me other than that we lit fires inside each other. So you went back to the safety and the security of your existing life.'

His expression changed.

'I was angry with you then. For walking out on me. For rejecting me. But since then—since our time together—I've come to terms with it. And now that your old life is gone, now that it's behind you, I acknowledge...' He paused, and when he spoke again there was a rueful quality to his voice. It was guarded, as well. 'I freely admit that my actions caused the destruction of your former life. Maybe you can accept this bracelet as...as recompense?' His voice warmed and he gazed lovingly upon her. 'As my promise to you that I will take care of you from now on.'

He trailed his finger along the glittering gems once again.

'Rubies are beautiful, but so many other gemstones would suit you, too!' He relaxed back against the pillows, his hand cupping her shoulder affectionately. 'Hong Kong is brilliant for jewellery,' he told her. 'And how about a Tahitian pearl necklace when we explore the South Seas? Would you like that? Hand-picked from oysters of our own choosing!'

Talia was looking at him. There was something strange about her expression, and in her voice when she spoke. 'Oysters die when you take the pearls to make a necklace from them.'

He gave a rueful laugh. It was an odd thing for her to say, to be sure, but he had a reply for it all the same. 'There's a price to be paid for everything in life, Talia. No one can escape it.'

'Yes, you're right,' she said quietly. She lifted the hand which was weighed down by the ribbon of rubies and shifted her gaze to look at it.

'Do you like it?' Luke asked softly. He knew she did, but he wanted to hear her say so.

'It's beautiful. Exquisite,' she acknowledged, though her tone was unexpectedly flat.

His hand tightened around her shoulder. 'And so are you, Talia. Beautiful. Exquisite.'

There was a husk in his voice, a quickening in his limbs. He felt arousal stir and begin to take him over. He started to kiss her, opening her soft mouth to his, letting his free hand drop to her breast, moulding it with his palm until it peaked between his scissoring fingers.

She gave a low moan in her throat—a sound that was so familiar to him now that it served to heighten his own arousal. He moved his body over hers, beginning his possession. He would lose himself to this woman, and for some reason that no longer frightened him. He *wanted* to lose himself to her, this beautiful woman. She might be the daughter of his enemy, but that was behind them now that he had cleared the air.

A tide of passion flooded through him as he felt the facets of the rubies brush against his shoulder when she lifted her hand to snake it around the nape of his neck. He could feel her surrender to the passion flooding through her as powerfully as it was through him. Her fingers meshed into his hair, shaping his skull, deepening her own kisses.

His last conscious thought was, *She will never leave me now. Never.*

Triumph filled him. Triumph and absolute certainty.

Yet when he woke at dawn she was gone.

CHAPTER NINE

TALIA CLIMBED OUT of the taxi which had brought her from the train station. Her journey back to Marbella had been long and arduous. It had begun with her creeping from the villa, catching the early-morning bus to the capital, then taking another bus to the airport.

She had been reluctant to waste her meagre resources on taxis, and for the same reason she'd bought the cheapest flight available, which had meant multiple changes at various airports before she'd finally landed in Malaga to take the coastal train to Marbella.

Tiredness ate at her—and, worse than tiredness, a desolation of the spirit such as she had never known. She had thought she'd felt desolation before, on that morning after the party when she'd forced herself to leave the man who had swept her off her feet.

But that had not been desolation like this.

She felt again that crushing, stifling feeling in her chest as she stepped inside the luxurious villa that was like a mocking ghost from a life that had ceased to exist.

Maria greeted her warmly, and with a grim effort Talia pasted a doggedly bright smile on her face. It was a smile that softened as she went out onto the terrace to find her mother relaxing in the shade, looking a hundred times healthier than when Talia had last set eyes on her.

'Mum—oh, you're looking *so* much better!' Relief flooded through Talia as she greeted her mother. It was the only good emotion she'd felt since—

She sheared her thoughts away. They had been agony for her all the way back here, and she could bear to think them no longer. Not now when she had to face her mother. When she had to hide the truth from her. When she had to hide what she had so nearly been reduced to. It had taken all her strength to reject Luke's promises and she could not bear to think about it.

'Well, I've Maria to thank for that.' Her mother smiled, encompassing the Spanish woman still beaming at Talia's return.

'I made sure she ate!' Maria pronounced.

'Oh, dear, I'm sure I've put on pounds!' Maxine Grantham admitted, as if that was a crime. But then, if her father had been here, for her mother to have gained even half a pound would indeed have been a crime.

'Do you think I want a fat wife?' he had berated her often enough, if he'd thought Maxine was looking anything less than fashionably stick-thin.

Talia's eyes darkened. As usual, her mother had done whatever it took to please the husband she was devoted to—including taking the slimming pills that had weakened her heart.

And what might I have done to please a man? The man I was devoted to until the veils were ripped from my eyes.

She sheared her mind away and silenced the pain inside.

'Well, it suits you—you look much healthier,' she said firmly to her mother, smiling brightly.

She would not let her mother think about her controlling husband. Instead she told her again how well she looked, and thanked Maria for her care of her.

Maria bustled off to make supper, refusing Talia's offer to help, leaving her to sit down beside her mother and enjoy the last of the evening sunshine. Low sunlight glinted on the pool beyond the terrace and bathed the garden in warmth.

'I'm so *glad* you're home, darling!' her mother exclaimed. 'Maria has been an angel, but I've missed you!' Her eyes lit up. 'Now, tell me—how did it go? Tell me all about it!'

Talia braced herself. She'd known her mother would ask questions—known she had to find something to say. Because it was the safest thing, she launched into a description of the island, knowing it would divert her mother. But as she rattled on pain and bitterness twisted inside her.

All the long journey home she'd kept hearing Luke's words to her. Words that had stripped from her the pathetic illusions she'd been building up. Words that had shown her—brutally and unambiguously—what he truly thought about her. Behind the smiles and the kisses and the passion there had always been this.

He had reduced her to the most abject and contemptible of human beings. He thought her a pampered doll, useless and worthless, totally talentless, amusing herself with pretending to be a designer. He thought she had a sky-high sense of entitlement and he believed she thought the world owed her not just a living but a deluxe lifestyle. The man she loved saw her as a spoiled princess, to be indulged and sheltered from life's vicissitudes, unable to cope with anything at all. A pet who had to be tossed bracelets and baubles to keep her happy, to make her feel valued and protected.

No! She couldn't bear to think of it! Couldn't bear to face what Luke truly thought of her.

She bit her lip to stop the emotional pain, making it physical instead.

'Darling, what is it?' Her mother's hand pressed on her arm. 'You look upset. Oh, darling girl, don't worry if you don't get the commission after all. It would be lovely if you did, but as soon as your father gets home we won't have to worry about anything like that any more. He'll be taking care of us again soon.'

Talia tensed, as if jerked on a wire.

'Mum, don't!' Her words were blurted out, harsh and angry.

Her mother looked hurt and shocked, and Talia tried to soften the impact. To hear her mother still mouthing such impossibilities, still believing in them, was galling. But it was more than that for Talia—her mother's words were an echo of Luke's promise.

Luke said he'd take care of me.

She hauled her mind away. She must not let herself hear those words in her head again. She had to banish him completely.

Pain and bitterness twisted again, and she cast about to find some way of replying to her mother's useless longing.

'Mum, he's not coming back. You mustn't think that's going to happen. You have to face the truth.'

Her mother's expression hadn't changed. 'No, darling. We mustn't give up on him. We mustn't give up hope. He's simply sorting things out. He's off somewhere, making everything right again. You'll see. He'll be home soon and everything will be back to normal— just the way it should be. We'll get back our lovely home by the river and—'

Something snapped inside Talia. She couldn't stop herself. The gruelling journey had left her dog-tired physically—but infinitely worse was the despairing bleakness inside her, which had left her at the very edge of self-control. And now it snapped like an elastic band that had been stretched tighter and tighter.

She leapt to her feet. 'Mum, stop it! Just *stop it*! Dad isn't coming back. He's left us here to cope with nothing. No money, no assets—nothing. Everything's gone—including this villa.'

'No, don't say that—please. I can't bear it.'

Her mother's face had contorted and Talia cursed herself for losing her rag the way she had. Her mother couldn't cope with the brutal reality into which her husband's ruin and disappearance had forced them.

'You told me you'd sorted it all out,' her mother rushed on now. 'That the villa is ours.'

Talia closed her eyes in weariness and dejection. 'Only for three months, Mum. Just to give us time to find somewhere else to live…for you to get strong enough to face the truth of what Dad's done.'

A moan came from her mother, and Talia's dismay at her rash outburst deepened. But it was too late to stop now.

'We have to be grateful we can stay on even for that long. It was the deal I agreed—I would do some initial design work in the Caribbean in exchange for three months here in the villa to get you well and strong. I struck a bargain with Luke Xenakis—the man who now owns everything that's left of Grantham Land.'

Her mother's expression changed and her hand flashed out to grasp Talia's arm. 'You've been working for *that man*? That dreadful man who stole your father's company from him!' she gasped, aghast.

Talia sighed heavily. 'He didn't steal it, Mum—he just took it over. That's the way these business deals happen—'

'He *ruined* your father!' Maxine shot back.

'No, Mum. Dad did that himself. He went under because he took out more and more unsupported loans. Luke Xenakis just bought up what was left—which is why he's ended up owning everything that once belonged to Dad's company.'

Her mother's face contorted again. 'I don't care what you say happened—he ruined your father! How could you agree to work for him? How *could* you?'

'I told you, Mum. It was the only way to get him to let us stay on here until you're strong enough to move.'

'I can't bear it!' Maxine wailed, wringing her hands. 'To be beholden to that dreadful man! I hope you gave him a piece of your mind for what he's done to us?'

Talia rubbed her forehead. No, she had not given Luke a piece of her mind. She had given him everything else, but not that.

I gave him everything willingly, gloriously—my body, my soul. I would have gone anywhere with him, done anything for him.

But, she thought bitterly, she had concocted a fantasy in which he loved her the way she loved him. In which he knew her, respected her, believed in her...

I gave him my stupid, worthless heart, and all he wanted was me between the sheets.

A sob broke from her. She couldn't stop it. Couldn't stop the one that came after, either, which tore like barbed wire through her throat, choked from her, desperate and despairing.

'Darling!' Her mother's voice was different now. 'Darling, what is it? Oh, my darling, what's the mat-

ter? Was it that dreadful man? What did he do to you!
Tell me, darling—tell me what he did to you.'

And, to Talia's mortification and tearful dismay, she
broke into uncontrollable sobs and told her mother just
how Luke Xenakis had broken her heart.

Luke was on his balcony. In his bedroom, his suitcase
was being packed. Rage scythed in him. More than
rage. Worse than rage. Blackness filled him, obliterat-
ing everything around.

She had done it to him again. She had walked out
on him. Just upped and gone without a word. Not even
a note this time.

But he hadn't needed a note to know the brutal truth.
She did not want him. *Still* did not want him. She had
rejected him—left him *again*.

His fists spasmed in the depths of his trouser pock-
ets, his face contorting.

*I did everything I could think of to make her happy.
Everything!*

This time he'd known who she was, *what* she was.
That first time, after the party, he'd taken her at face
value—had never dreamt in a million years that she
would be Grantham's daughter, that she would be a
pampered princess, the spoiled and indulged daughter
of his sworn enemy. This time he'd known just what
he needed to do to give her what she wanted, what she
expected so that she would stay.

But she'd still walked out on him. Still rejected him.

He felt pain like a whiplash across his shoulders.
Pain that was a thousand times worse than it had ever
been that first time.

How could she walk out on me? After all those nights

when we burned in each other's arms! After all those carefree days, the companionship, the togetherness?

But it had meant nothing to her—nothing at all!

Bitterness flowed in his veins like acid, etching into his flesh, consuming him from the inside out until he was nothing more than a hollow shell. Until there was nothing but raw pain to keep him upright.

Roughly, he turned away from the view he couldn't see, was blinded from seeing by his inner turmoil. He couldn't bear to see the azure pool where they had disported themselves, dazzling in the hot sunshine, the terrace they had lounged on, dined on, with candlelight catching her hair, the languorous warmth of the night like a caress…

He stalked indoors. He wanted out of here—as fast as he could.

'Are you done yet?' he demanded.

He didn't mean to sound curt, but impatience drove him. He was desperate to be on his way to the airport, to leave this place. He had to get to Hong Kong, then maybe Shanghai. He would do business there—profitable business. Because doing profitable business was what he did with his life, wasn't it? He made money. At first it had all been to bring down Grantham, but now it would be for its own sake. It was what he was good at, after all.

A sense of emptiness gaped in him. He'd achieved his goal—now what? What was he going to do with his life? What purpose was going to drive him now? There was nothing there for him. Nothing.

I thought I'd found what I was going to do with the rest of my life. And then she left me. Again.

Even though he'd been appalled to discover she was Grantham's daughter, dismayed by her taste in design, despite all that he'd come to terms with it. He'd made himself accept it because of the way he felt about her.

And she still rejected me.

Fernando was closing the lid of the large suitcase, fastening it securely. Then he straightened. 'What are your instructions in respect of the bracelet left in Miss Talia's room?' he enquired blandly.

Luke started. 'What do you mean?' he demanded. 'What bracelet?'

'I believe it is the one you had delivered yesterday,' Fernando elucidated.

Luke stared. 'The ruby bracelet?'

Fernando nodded in his stately fashion.

Luke frowned. 'She left it here?'

Again Fernando nodded.

Luke's face hardened. 'Send it on to her,' he said tersely.

He walked out of the bedroom, heading downstairs with a heavy tread. He had no idea why she'd left it— to make a point, perhaps? But what point? Why was *she* angry at *him*?

Perhaps it was insufficiently valuable?

His mouth twisted, his mood becoming blacker than black as he stalked out of the room, heading downstairs to the car waiting to take him to the airport. To take him anywhere in the world that was not this island where, for a brief space of time, he had thought he had found happiness.

What a fool he had been.

Well, never again. *Never again.*

Talia walked around the villa for the last time. It was empty now of all their possessions, right down to the kitchenware. Everything of value had been sold to raise some much-needed cash to tide them over. All Talia and her mother were taking with them were the bare necessities. It was all they could afford.

As she gazed about her Talia still could not believe what had happened since she had collapsed into desperate sobs on her mother's lap. When she'd finally stilled, the sorry tale told, her mother had been very quiet. At the edge of exhaustion—emotional, physical and mental—Talia had known, though she hadn't been able to face it, that she would have to cope with another complete collapse from her beleaguered mother.

Yet what had happened had been the complete opposite.

Maxine had finally patted her daughter's shoulder, and got to her feet. 'We,' she'd announced, 'are leaving. The moment we can. I will not stay for a day longer than it takes us to move out in *any* place owned by a man who has broken my daughter's heart. Nobody does that to my daughter. *Nobody!*'

That was all Maxine had said, but not all that she had done. She had conferred with Maria, returning to announce, with a straightening of her thin shoulders and an air of firm resolution, that Maria had come up with a *wonderful* solution to their dilemma.

'Her brother runs a café bar—not here in Marbella, down the coast in one of those tourist places. He needs someone to run it since he opened another one last month. And,' she continued triumphantly, 'it comes with an apartment above! We'll move in the minute we can.'

Talia had stared disbelievingly. This was not the mother she had known all her life. Nervy, brittle, and totally dependent on her daughter and husband.

'Mum, are you…are you sure you could cope?'

The change in lifestyle would be absolute. Terrifying, surely, for her mother?

Maxine's eyes had flashed. 'Yes,' she said simply. 'It's time—way beyond time—that I faced the truth about what has happened.'

Talia still couldn't believe the change in her mother, but she was abjectly grateful for it—and to Maria, who was giving them a way forward. It would be hard work, but right now—a choking sob tried to rise in her throat, but she pushed it back with determination—anything that blocked her mind from going where it kept trying to go was to be clung to with all her might.

Exhausting herself by running a café—waiting on tables, keeping it clean, doing everything except the cooking, which Maria's nephew was going to be doing—surely would leave her no time to think of Luke?

Please, God...

Luke flipped open the locks of his suitcase, intent on extracting a clean T-shirt to sleep in. Beyond the sound-proofed windows in this most prestigious hotel in Hong Kong the glittering skyline of the city was like jewels glistening against the night. It was a city with millions of inhabitants, but he had never felt more alone in his life.

Emptiness gaped all around him.

Being on his own had become a way of life for him. He'd spent ten years focussed on making money and hunting down his enemy. There had been neither the time nor the inclination for relationships. His affairs—if they could even be called that—had been fleeting... strangers who met and parted again, never finding anything to keep them together. For what woman would want to attach herself to a man as driven as he had been? As he had *had* to be in order to achieve what he had promised his parents he would do in their name?

But now that was all over. He was free—finally, blessedly free—to find someone to share his life with.

And I found her! I found her and wanted her and offered her everything I thought would make her want me too—

The cry came from deep within but he cut it off. There was no use listening to it. No use staring around this anonymous hotel bedroom and wanting, with a longing that was a physical pain in his gut, the one person who would make it the most wonderful place in the world for him.

She didn't want you. She left you.

He would force himself to stop wanting her. After all, she wasn't exactly the woman of his dreams, was she?

He knew what he was doing—that his mind was seeking ways to dull the pain by finding fault with Talia. But he forced himself to think of all the things that were wrong with her, to think about whose daughter she was, about what that had turned her into.

Do you really want to have a woman like that in your life? A hothouse flower unable to survive without the shelter of a man to provide her with the luxuries of life, to look after her and cosset her? A woman who's only ever played at life? Who's never had to hold down a job, earn a living, work for what she has? Who's never had to take any responsibility? A show pony living off her father's wealth? Who panicked and collapsed when she was faced with losing her luxury lifestyle?

The questions seared in his head but he would not answer them. Dared not.

All he wanted now was a shower, a shave, and then to drink himself to oblivion from the bar in the room.

Alcohol and sleep would silence the torment in his head. Because he was sure nothing else could.

He frowned. What the—?

On top of his neatly folded clothes was a large, stiff art folder. He stared angrily. Why on earth had *that* been packed? Talia's tasteless amateur daubs were the last thing he wanted to see!

Roughly, he yanked the portfolio out, flinging it onto the desk beside the suitcase stand. But he'd been careless in his aim, and as he fetched a clean white T-shirt the toilet bag in his hand caught the corner of the portfolio. It clattered to the floor, its contents spilling out. With an oath, he stooped to scoop it all up, glad the sheets had fallen face-down. All except one, which he had to reach for.

He straightened, holding the sketch in his hands. Staring. Frowning.

Shock went through him.

This was no amateur daub. Nor was it anything remotely like any of the interiors he'd seen at the Grantham Land properties.

This was *good*! The vision was immediate, impactful. The wide space of the hotel's atrium was just the way it had been before the storm, but brought back to life in startling relief. He went on staring, taking it all in.

The deep cobalt-blue-tiled floor and the emerald-green walls made one vast fresco, bringing the lush rainforest indoors, splashed with the vivid colours of tropical flowers, of birds darting through the foliage with rainbow plumage. The huge arched opening to the terrace framed the gardens leading out to the sea, as azure as the tiling was cobalt, blending the interior with the exterior, making it one seamless whole.

And in his mind's eye it was instantly real—he could see it, *feel* it. Feel just what a newly arrived guest would experience on entering the hotel. It would stop them in their tracks. There was no question this design had the total wow factor.

Mesmerised, he turned over the other sheets one by one, discovering what she had done for the restaurant, the bar, the bedrooms. All had been designed to have that same vivid, vibrant impact.

He spread them out on the desk, gazing down at them. Then he realised there was a transparent folder amongst them. Frowning again, he unfastened it to study its contents. There was an envelope of fabric swatches, each labelled carefully, and another envelope of downloaded illustrations from potential furniture, flooring, and fabric suppliers. And there, too, were multiple, neatly set out sheets—costings, prices, delivery schedules, names and contact details for suppliers and shippers, even notes about import licences and customs duties.

The information had been methodically researched and laid out, comprehensively covering all that would be required for him to make a decision on whether to go with her designs or not, and what it would cost him if he did. It was as thorough and as professional as her artistic vision was brilliant.

Numbly, he went on staring at Talia's work, his thoughts in chaos.

'Buenas tardes!' Talia smiled cheerfully at another customer arriving at the busy café.

She was glad it was busy because it gave her no time for thoughts of Luke. Run off her feet, she could keep her misery at bay. Only in the long reaches of the night, attempting to sleep on the settee in the sitting room of the tiny flat above the café, her mother in the single bedroom, would it devour her in muffled, useless sobs.

What use was crying? But that didn't stop her from doing it anyway.

Instead she must focus on her work: serving customers with drinks and relaying the dishes emerging from the kitchen, where Maria's nephew Pepe was in charge, and keeping an eye on her mother, who sat at a small desk off to one side and, to Talia's continuing astonishment, pored assiduously over the café's accounts.

'Darling, I'm good at accounts—you know I had to justify every penny I spent to your father!'

Talia did remember bleakly how her father had interrogated her own costings, brutally knocking off anything that he'd thought she'd overspent on, taking it out of the allowance he paid her instead of a salary.

But she shouldn't let herself think of that, because that made her remember how enthusiastically she'd worked out the costings for the ruined Caribbean hotel. Anguish tore at her—and not just for the waste of her efforts. For a reason so much more unendurable.

But endure it she must—and so she hurried back out to the pavement tables to take orders there.

The café was in a side street of this busy tourist town, with nothing to remind her of the showy glitz of Marbella and Puerto Banus. Which was why the logo on the side of a delivery van turning into the road caught her eye. It was that of an upmarket courier company she remembered from the days when expensive items had used to be routinely delivered to the Marbella villa.

The driver was getting out, looking uncertainly at the modest café. 'I am looking for Señorita Grantham,' he said to her, his voice doubtful. In his hand he held a small package.

Talia stared, then walked slowly forward. She took the package and signed for it with a confused frown. Her heart started to beat heavily, and on impulse she tore at the packaging. Then, as the tell-tale contents were revealed, confirmed by the glittering river of fire as she lifted the hinged lid of the box, she gave a cry of revulsion.

Slamming the lid back down, she dashed to the driver, who was climbing back into his van. *'Take it back!'* She thrust the package at him. 'I don't want it! Take it back!'

She whirled away, her heart slugging with a furious hammering. She bolted back inside the café, her face black with anger. Bleak with it.

That's all he ever thought I was: a silly, spoiled princess who wanted rubies from him.

The pain of it pierced her like a blade in her heart—her stupid, stupid heart.

Luke was in his office in Lucerne, sunlight bathing the high peaks visible from the windows. But he did not see them. His entire attention was focussed on what was being said to him on his phone.

'It was *refused*?' he snapped. 'And what the hell do you mean, the villa was empty? It can't have been!' He drew a sharp breath. 'Then where—?' He listened. *'What?* They were located *where*?'

He dropped the phone on to the huge mahogany desk, still staring, uncomprehending.

I told her she could stay another three months.

So why, when she had got exactly what she'd come begging for, would she have vacated the villa after all?

His frown deepened, lines indenting around his mouth grimly. And why the hell had she ended up in some dump of a café in a cut-price tourist town, waiting on tables?

Why leave the villa? Why end up in a dump instead? And why, above all, refuse the damn rubies I sent her?

That bracelet was worth thousands. To refuse it when she had been reduced to waiting on tables... It didn't make sense.

A space hollowed out inside him, as if a skewer had ground it from him.

But then, nothing about her made sense. Nothing at all.

Dimly, he became aware that his phone was ringing again, and he snatched it up. Only pre-screened calls came through on this line, so his PA must have cleared the caller. And when he answered it, he knew why. He listened with a gradual steeling of his body, his expression grim.

Then, as the call came to an end, he simply nodded. 'Good,' he said.

A single word. But in it was a wealth of meaning. More than ten years' worth of meaning.

He set the phone down again and crossed to the window. He looked out across the lake to the cold snow-topped mountains beyond. The same snow seemed to be around his heart, inside his lungs. Memories from long ago pierced him—and a single word in his own mother tongue. A single name.

Nemesis.

Over ten years it had taken, and it had turned him from a carefree young stripling, full of eagerness for life and all that it could offer, to what he was now—to what he had become. An agent of the dark, unforgiving goddess of vengeance. Nemesis.

Justice, he tried to tell himself. Justice was more noble than vengeance.

He turned away, walked back to his desk, and threw himself into his chair, pressing his hands over the arms, his face set in steel.

Remembering.

Remembering what Grantham had done to his family had always been a kind of absolution for whatever sins Luke had committed in his pursuit of the man and his ill-gotten riches. But now, as his dark and troubled thoughts finally sank from his consciousness, another thought came.

His expression changed.

She needs to know.

He took a sharp, incising breath.

And I need to know, too.

To know why Talia had not stayed on in the villa when she'd begged him for it. Why she had refused the rubies he'd sent her to wait on tables instead.

His mouth tightened to a thin line.

And why I thought she hadn't a shred of talent or professionalism when what she produced is blazing with it!

But there was one question above all that he had to have the answer to—whatever it took to find it.

Why did she leave me?

CHAPTER TEN

TALIA WAS MOPPING the café floor, chairs piled on the tables, before finally closing up for the night. Pepe had left, her mother had long gone to bed, and Talia was yawning, too, tired as ever from the long working day.

Her glance went to the café's large windows. A car had drawn up outside—a long, low, luxurious black car. A car that suddenly, urgently, caused her to abandon her mop and dash over to shut and bolt the café door.

Too late.

He was getting out of the car and striding across the pavement to her as she fumbled with the locks and bolts. He effortlessly pushed the door open before she could get there. Stepped inside.

'I need to talk to you.'

Luke's voice was terse, his face grim. He'd known she was at this café, but to see her with a mop and bucket, swabbing the floor, had been a shock for all that.

She backed away—an instinctive, automatic movement. Shock was crashing through her—and so much more than shock.

'Go away! Leave me alone!'

Talia's voice was high-pitched and she stepped back from him, clutching at a table as if for support. Her legs were suddenly weak, the blood was drumming in her veins, and faintness was dimming her vision.

I can't bear for Luke to see me here. I can't bear to see him at all.

He was speaking again, stepping forward.

She tried to push past him, but his words stopped her.

'*Listen* to me—please. I have something important to tell you.'

'I don't want to hear it!' she cried out in that same high-pitched voice, shaking her head violently.

He ignored her. He had to say this—whether she wanted to hear it or not.

'There is something you need to know.'

Was that hesitation? Uncertainty.

She stared at him. Her heart was still thumping like a hammer in her chest. He was looking at her with an expression in his face she did not recognise. She could not get her brain into gear because all her senses were firing, overloaded with the closeness of him that was causing her lungs to seize and her breath to come in short pants.

He was speaking and she surfaced, finally hearing his words. She heard them, but could not take them in.

'Talia—your father is dead.'

She seemed to sway as the words reached into her consciousness. With an oath, he caught her arms, holding her upright, supporting her weight as faintness swept over her. He gently pushed her back and down, into a chair he yanked off a table, setting it upright for her to sink into on legs that were suddenly cotton wool.

Thee mou, he should have told her more gently. But to see her again, to have her there in front of him… The physical reality of her presence was still impossible to believe. And that was without the changes he could see—her hair scraped back off her face in an untidy ponytail, not a trace of make-up, wearing only a white shirt and a black skirt with an apron around it, the discarded mop behind her.

She was working like a skivvy and his brain struggled to blend this with the spoiled little rich girl image he'd had of her for so long.

'How…how do you know?' Her voice was faint, her glistening eyes staring at the floor.

Luke hefted down another chair and sat himself on it. 'I've been searching for him,' he told her. 'Him disappearing as he did made it harder for me to complete the finer details of the takeover. And besides that—' He stopped.

Besides that I had to know what had happened to him…to the man I destroyed.

He took a breath. However bad this news for her, she had to give up on any hopes she might have that her father would come back to rescue her from a life of washing floors.

'How did he die?' She was still not looking at him, her voice remote.

'He…he fell from a hotel balcony in Istanbul.'

Her eyes lifted to stare at him. She had heard the hesitation in his voice.

'Fell?' She could feel her jaw tighten, to stop herself shaking.

Luke's lips pressed together thinly. 'An accident. That will be what the official report says. And it is best to keep to that.'

Her face contorted. 'Tell me the truth!' she demanded. Her eyes were like stones.

He took a heavy breath. If she wanted the grim truth, he would tell her. Why should she not know what her doting father had resorted to?

'Talia, in order to try and stave off financial ruin your father ended up borrowing money from some very unsavoury characters it was unwise not to repay.'

He didn't say more. Didn't need to. Whether Gerald Grantham had jumped or had been pushed, it came to the same thing.

He stood up. 'I didn't want you to hear it from the police—or read it in the newspapers first.'

She was looking at him, her expression masked. 'So you came to tell me in person?'

'Yes.' His own expression was as masked as hers, but inside him emotions were engaged in a savage dance.

'Well, you've told me, so now you can go.' Her voice was as expressionless as her face as she pushed herself to her feet.

Those emotions broke through the mask of his face. 'Talia, what the hell is going on? What on earth are you doing *here*?' He swept an arm around the café's interior.

Those stones were back in her eyes. 'That isn't your business, Luke. Nothing about me is your business.'

He took a step towards her, clasping her arms, emotions surging in him, hot and unbearable to endure. 'Talia, *talk* to me—please. You owe me that, surely? After all we had together—'

Violently, she threw off his hands. 'Don't *touch* me!' she cried.

And then suddenly, from behind the bar, where there was a door to the upstairs apartment, came another voice. 'Get away from my daughter!'

Talia whirled around. Maxine was standing there, clutching her dressing gown to her thin body, her eyes sparking with fury. Two spots of colour burned in her cheeks.

'Mum, it's OK. He's leaving. He's leaving right now.'

She turned back to Luke. 'Please go. Just go.' She spun back to her mother. 'Mum, please—it's OK. Go back upstairs. I'm just shutting up here. I'll be there in a minute. *Please!*'

But her mother was surging forward, bearing down on Luke where he stood, frozen.

'Get away from my daughter!' she cried again, her voice rising.

The cry was almost a shriek now, and Luke could see Talia's mother hyperventilating, her colour mounting. Then, horribly, with a strangulated gasp, she put a shaking hand to her chest. Clawing frantically, as if in hideous slow motion, Maxine collapsed.

'Mum!' Talia's voice was a scream, and then she was crouching down where her mother had folded, unconscious, onto the wet floor.

Luke pushed her aside. Talia gave another cry, but he thrust his mobile phone at her. 'Get an ambulance! *Now!*' he ordered.

Then he fell to work on her mother, lying mobile on the floor, seemingly lifeless.

He checked the pulse at her neck—*no pulse!*—then, ripping the lapels of the dressing gown aside, he found the end of her sternum and measured two fingers further up. He pressed one palm over the dorsum of his other hand and started a rhythmic pumping of Mrs Grantham's stricken heart as memory flooded through him.

Suffocating memory of knifing fear and horror.

'Is she going to make it?' Talia's stricken brain was trying to find the Spanish she needed. Whatever she'd said, the paramedics understood.

'We'll do our best,' they said, and then the ambulance launched forward, siren wailing, down the street.

Talia had no idea where the hospital was, and it seemed to take for ever to get there. But her mother was hanging on—just. The paramedics, when they'd arrived, had taken over CPR from Luke, applying defibrillation, then got her on to a stretcher, attached her to monitors. And now they were getting her where her mother's life might be saved.

And through that long, long night, as Talia sat by her mother's bedside in Intensive Care, the thread of life held still—though it was as frail as Talia's grip on her mother's hand was strong.

In the morning the cardiologist visited and carried out a careful examination. Her mother was to be kept under sedation, but it seemed, Talia was told, and she felt a relief so profound she was weak with it, that she would live. The CPR, instantly and correctly carried out, had saved her.

As Talia walked out into the reception area, numb with relief and exhaustion, Luke got up from a bench.

'How is she doing? They will tell me very little.'

Talia stared. 'Have you been here all night?'

He looked haggard. A thick growth furred his jaw and his eyes were sunken.

'What else could I do?' He took a breath. 'So, how is she?'

'She's pulling through,' she said, her voice hollow. 'She'll be kept in for some time, while she recovers from the operation, and then they want her to have some time in a convalescent home.'

'I'll arrange it,' Luke said.

Violently she shook her head. Her emotions were shot to pieces, in a thousand jagged fragments. 'Luke, this is none of your concern.'

She made to move past him. She had to get to the café to start work.

But her arm was caught.

'Talia, we need to talk—' Luke's breath caught. 'Especially now.'

She stared at him. Exhaustion, both of her body, from her long sleepless vigil by her mother's side, and her spirit from seeing Luke again, consumed her.

She shook her head wearily. She wanted to pull away from him, but she had no strength left. Numbly, she let him lead her out of the hospital and walked beside him, saying nothing, down to the sea front.

He sat her down on a bench on the promenade and then joined her. She moved away from him, to the end of the bench. It was an automatic gesture. To be here at all with him was hard to bear. To be close to him would be impossible.

Everything to do with him was impossible.

Impossible. Impossible. Impossible.

The word echoed in her head—useless and pointless.

He doesn't see who I really am so everything is impossible.

She couldn't look at him—could only stare out over the promenade. The beach below was starting to fill up, parasols unfurling, tourists settling in for another carefree day of their holidays.

'Why,' she heard Luke ask, his voice grim, 'did you never tell me about your mother?'

Talia glanced at him, and then away. 'What relevance does that have?'

'That,' he retorted, 'is what I want to know.'

'It doesn't have any relevance,' she said.

'Did you know her heart was weak?'

She looked at him again. 'Yes.' Her eyes went out to

the sea, so calm and still at this hour of the morning. 'It's why I wanted us to stay on at the Marbella villa for longer. She'd already been taken ill when I had to tell her we'd lost that, as well. She found it…difficult to cope.'

Her voice was stilted, reflecting her reluctance to speak. But she just didn't have the strength to oppose Luke right now. Exhaustion was uppermost in her mind. And an overwhelming level of emotion that she could not cope with. Not now.

She heard Luke swearing. It was in Greek, and it was low and vehement.

'And why,' he asked, 'did you not tell me that when you came to my offices to beg not to be evicted?'

Her head twisted. His voice was cold. Cold with anger. But anger was in her, too.

'Tell you *what*?' she spat. 'That the wife of the man you'd reduced to bankruptcy wasn't taking it too well? That she didn't like the fact that she wasn't going to have a lavish budget for topping up her designer wardrobe any longer? That she'd been reduced to nothing more than an eight-bedroom mansion with ten bathrooms, a swimming pool and a gourmet kitchen, on a millionaire's estate in Marbella, which she couldn't— oh, dear me, no—just *couldn't* bear to leave? Why didn't I tell you *that*?'

She saw his expression close at the violence of her tone.

'And what would you have done, Luke, if I'd told you all that? You'd have told me to get real. That our days of being pampered pets—her a queen and me a princess—were over! *I* knew that. But—' She stopped short.

She turned back to stare sightlessly over the Mediterranean Sea, dazzling in the sunlight, too bright to behold.

'But my mother couldn't face it. She was still clinging to hope. Still deluding herself with pointless illusions about my father sorting it all out and coming back to save us.'

And Mum's thoughts were as pointless as the illusions I wove about you, Luke—the illusions you tore to pieces when you made it clear what you thought of me.

She wrenched her mind away. What use was it to remember the illusions she'd so stupidly had about Luke? Clumsily, she got to her feet. She stood looking down at him where he sat, hands held loosely between his thighs. His head lifted. His expression was unreadable.

She gave a heavy sigh. It was all too much right now. Last night her mother had nearly died… And the man who had put the 'nearly' in that sentence was before her now. He deserved her gratitude, no matter how he had treated her.

'Luke, thank you. Thank you for what you did for my mother…' She took a difficult breath. 'At the café.'

He didn't say anything for a moment. Then, his expression bleak, he simply said, 'Don't thank me. If I hadn't turned up like that she probably wouldn't have collapsed.' Wearily, he lifted a hand to run it through his hair. He got to his feet. 'Talia—'

She shook her head violently. 'Luke, *no*! I can't take any more interrogation. I have to get back to the café. I have to start work.'

An oath broke from him. 'It's *absurd* that you should be working there!'

She lifted his hand from her arm, and even to touch him was unbearable. 'Luke, I *have* to go! I'm late. I have to open up the café.' She took a ragged breath and then said what it would cost her everything to say, but say it she must. 'I... I don't want to see you again. Please leave me alone.'

She didn't look at him. She could not. Instead, head bowed, she hurried from the promenade, diving into the narrow streets through which she could make her way towards the harbour and the café.

At the café, Maria's nephew was shocked at her news, and told Talia he'd get a friend to wait on the tables that evening and she must go to her mother. Gratefully, she conceded.

When she set off for the hospital at the end of the day she stopped off at the bank, checking to see if they could afford a week at a convalescent home to help her mother recover.

After that... Well, after that her mother would just have to recuperate in the apartment above the café. She sighed, but knew that anything else was out of the question. They just did not have the money for anything else.

Like a luscious but poisoned fruit, Luke's offer to pay her mother's nursing fees dangled in front of her. She thrust it aside.

I can't—I just can't. It would...

It would reduce her to what she would have become if she had stayed with him. What he thought she was— what he had always thought her—even when he'd held her in his arms. Pointless. Pathetic. A useless bauble.

She gave a muffled cry of pain and hurried into the hospital. It was no use to think of Luke or to agonise over what was in the past. No use at all. She must focus only on her mother—as she always had, all her life. And now, when she had come so close to losing her, her mother was more precious to her than ever.

A shiver went through her. In all her terror for her mother, and in all her personal anguish over seeing Luke again, she had hardly given the news Luke had brought her about her father a second thought. For a moment guilt went through her. Her father was dead—surely that should elicit some emotion from her? Some sense of grief?

Her face hardened. Her father had been nothing but a malign, controlling presence in her life. And in the life of her mother.

The life Luke saved!

Oh, she could tell herself that had Luke not come to the café as he had her mother might not have had her heart attack, but that did not take away the fact that it had been Luke's prompt action that had saved her.

Talia felt her heart constrict. For that she would be for ever grateful.

She was grateful too—abjectly so—that her mother, propped up on pillows, wired up to monitors and on a drip, could greet her with a weak smile. Talia hugged her carefully, closing her eyes in a silent prayer of thanks that she had not lost her.

But as she straightened her mother spoke in an agitated voice, one thin hand clutching at her daughter. 'Darling, that man! That dreadful man!'

Immediately Talia was soothing. 'Mum, he's gone, OK? He left. We won't be seeing him again.'

Even as she said the words she felt pain strike her. To have seen him again...to have had him so near...

Her mother's grip tightened. 'Darling, you mustn't go to him. Not after what you told me.'

Talia shook her head. 'He didn't come here to try and persuade me to go back to him,' she said heavily.

She paused, took a breath. She had to say this, and

maybe telling her mother here in a hospital, where there was a crash team on hand if necessary, might be the safest thing to do? Her mother had changed so much since they had left the villa in Marbella. She had become strong and determined. Perhaps she could take this final blow as well? Talia could only pray so.

She took her mother's hands, held them in hers. 'Mum, Luke Xenakis came to see me to tell me...' She took another breath, then told her mother the grim news.

For her mother's sake, she kept to the official report that it had been an accident. Whether her mother believed it or not she would not press to find out.

Her mother listened, then loosed her hands to pick at the bedclothes, her gaze turning inward. 'I think I've known all along he would never come home. You were right about it from the start, darling.' Her voice twisted, became infused with pain and regret. 'He never cared about us at all. Not really.'

She looked at Talia, her gaze troubled. 'Never give your love to someone who does not—who *cannot*—love you back.'

Slowly, her eyes filling with tears, Talia bent to kiss her mother's cheek. Only two words sounded in her head.

Too late.

Desolation filled her.

CHAPTER ELEVEN

LUKE SAT OUTSIDE the hospital in the car he'd hired, his eyes peeled for Talia. He knew she was visiting her mother because he'd checked at Reception. In his head burned the one desperate question he must ask her. Only one—and he had to get an answer to it. However many times she told him to leave her alone, he needed to know why.

His expression was stark, his eyes focussed only on the brightly lit hospital entrance. And then suddenly she was there, head bowed, shoulders hunched, walking away. He gunned the engine, drew up alongside her and vaulted from the car.

She started in shock.

'Let me give you a lift. Talia—please. You look dead on your feet!'

She made to walk on, but he took her arm, feeling her tense instantly. He yanked open the passenger door and for a moment thought she would resist. Then, as if running out of energy, she sank down inside with a weary sigh.

Luke resumed his seat, moving the car off into the traffic. 'How is your mother?' he asked.

He kept his voice neutral. It was an effort, but he did it. To have her so close again, to catch her scent, to feel her presence pressing upon him, was torment.

She sighed, not looking at him. 'Improving, but still weak.' She swallowed, taking a difficult breath. 'I... I told her about my father.'

Luke's expression tightened. 'It will be hard for her—hard for you, too.' He didn't say any more.

Talia didn't answer, only closed her eyes. A weariness so profound she could not fight it any longer was sweeping over her.

'Why are you still here, Luke?' she heard herself ask tightly. 'I told you I didn't want to see you again.'

She heard the engine change gear and felt the car swing round to the left, heading inland. Her eyes flew open. 'This isn't the way to the café!'

'I know.' Luke's voice was grim. 'I need to talk to you, Talia.'

'There's nothing to say!' she cried. 'Nothing I want to hear from you!'

In the intermittent lights of the street, his expression was as grim as his voice. 'But there's a lot I want to hear from *you*, Talia. And I am not leaving Spain until I have answers.'

He pressed the accelerator and the car shot forward, picking up speed. Talia realised they were leaving town, heading up into the hills inland. A knot was forming inside her, but there was nothing she could do. Wearily, she sank back into torpor. The desolation she had felt at her mother's warning twisted inside her like snakes writhing.

The road started to wind, gaining height, and the outline of a *mirador* opened up before them. Luke slewed the car towards it, cut the engine. Far below the lights of the town pierced the night. Far beyond the sea glimmered beneath the rising moon.

He turned towards Talia. She wasn't looking at him,

only straight ahead, her face unreadable in the dim light.

'I need to know, Talia, the answer to a very simple question.' His breath incised into his lungs. 'And you owe me an answer.' His jaw tightened and in his chest he felt his heart starting to thud heavily. 'Why did you leave me?'

Her head slewed round. Her face was expressionless. 'I didn't care for your offer, Luke.'

A frown flashed across his eyes. 'You prefer skivvying in a café?' There was open derision in his voice.

She gave no answer, and his expression twisted. Emotions were churning in him and he was fighting to keep them under control. He must not let them out—not until he had the answers he needed.

'I didn't care for your offer.'

Her words mocked him, echoing in his head.

So what offer did *she want?*

'And why waitressing?' he pushed. 'Why not interior design?' He paused, then said what he knew he had to say. 'You're good, Talia. *Really* good. I was wrong to think otherwise—your designs for the hotel are stunning, and I want to use them for the refurb.'

For a second—fleetingly—he thought he saw something move in her eyes, but then it was gone. The same closed, tight expression was back. He could see that her hands were clenched by her sides.

But *why*? None of this made sense—none of it!

The words broke from him suddenly. 'None of this makes *sense*, Talia! Waiting tables when you could be using your talents—'

Something flashed across her face as her head whipped round. 'Which talent are you referring to,

Luke? My interior design skills or being good enough in bed to be your mistress?'

'What?' Now the flash of black fire was in his eyes, not hers.

Her expression contorted and, like a dam shattering under impossible pressure, her self-control broke. She could take no more of this.

'You heard me. Tossing a ruby bracelet at me…telling me there was plenty more where that came from. What else did that make me but your *mistress*? Payment for services rendered.'

Luke's hands clenched over the steering wheel, an oath escaping him. 'That is *not* how I was thinking of you. I was simply trying to make it clear that I would look after you. That I understood—that I still *do* understand—just how hard it is for you without your father to look after you the way you're used to…the way he always did. That I would take his place—'

A noise came from her—a harsh, ugly sound that had shock in it and something more, too.

Horror.

Her eyes were sparking fury, her cheekbones stark against suddenly hollow cheeks as the breath was sucked out of her.

Emotion was running like a black tide in him now, and it was unstoppable. He heard himself speaking again. The words bitten from him, each one as sharp as a dagger.

'It's taken me a long time, Talia, to forgive you for walking out on me after that first night without a word of explanation. Not until I discovered whose daughter you were did I understand why you'd walked. It took me a while to work out what I had to offer you to get you to be mine—the same luxury lifestyle you got from your father. *That's* what you went running back to—why you left me. That was the choice you made, wasn't it?'

She slewed round towards him, the suddenness of her movement cutting across him, and in her face was a fury that was like a blow across his cheek.

'No, it was *not*! It was *not* the choice I made! The choice I made, Luke, was the choice I have had to make *all my life*!'

Her features convulsed, and her eyes were pinpoints of anger. They skewered him like daggers. Her hands were fisted and he saw her lift them and bring them down sharply, vehemently, on the dashboard.

'You keep talking on and on about how I was a pampered princess, Daddy's doted-on darling! Showered with designer clothes and jewellery, given some toy job to preen my inflated ego, given a free deluxe apartment to live in, a flash car to drive. Everything a spoiled little brat could ever want. Well, I *was*, Luke. Yes, I *was* a pampered princess. But I lived in a *cage*, Luke.' Suddenly her voice was not vehement, but hollow, bleak. 'In a cage that had bars of gold that my father had welded around me. And I hated it.'

His lips thinned. The black tide was still running.

'You could have walked out, Talia, at any time. Made your own way in the world. You're a talented designer— you could have done real work...work you could have been proud of. You've shown you can with your designs for the hotel. Why didn't you have the guts to leave your gilded cage?'

She could hear the condemnation in his voice and a deadly familiar hollowness opened inside her. She let her hands fall limply to her lap again and slumped back in the seat. She ran a weary hand over her eyes. Tiredness ate at her. It broke her heart to be here with Luke, who was as harsh and as utterly uncomprehending as everyone else. He saw her the same way everyone else did.

Right from the very moment she'd walked into his office—when they'd both realised the coincidental connection between them—he had treated her as so much *less* than the person she knew she could be. The person she was in her heart—the one she wanted to be, tried to be. The person she thought he had seen that one incredible night when they had first met and again in their Caribbean paradise.

But all that time on the island this is what he thought of me. I worked so hard on my designs and he didn't even look at them. He was just working out how to buy me, how to drape me in jewels and fly me in jets to exotic places so he could own me, control me, just like my father. I thought he was offering me freedom, but he was just building his own gilded cage around me.

He would not understand, and she hardly knew why she was bothering to say it—knew only that she might as well, because she was here, now, in this car with him, high above the Costas, looking down from afar. Below, in the town, her mother was in the hospital. In a day or so she would move her out to a nursing home, and then back to the tiny apartment above the café. And she would go on working—waiting on tables, mopping floors, and getting by.

Luke would be gone. Back to his own life—a rich man's life that had nothing to do with her—and she would never see him again.

'No, Luke, I didn't have the guts to leave—just as you say.' She heard herself sigh, defeat in every word. 'I only had the guts to stay.'

She didn't bother looking at him. What would be the point of that?

'I don't understand…'

There was an audible frown in his voice so now she did turn her head to look at him. A great weariness of spirit weighed her down.

She heard her voice answering him…weary, defeated. 'Luke, my father gave me everything, just like you said, but he made me pay for it. He made my mother pay, too. Oh, not in ways that anyone would notice, but we paid, all the same. We had to live our lives exactly as he wanted us to. We had to wear the clothes he wanted us to, live where he wanted, entertain the guests he wanted us to—had to be the ornaments in his hugely successful life that he wanted us to be. That was our purpose. To be his trophy wife and his trophy daughter.'

'And you were happy to do that.' Luke's voice was flat. Condemning still.

She could not make out his face, not in the dim light of the car's interior, but she knew it would have a closed, shuttered look on it. She should stop talking now, she knew, because he would not understand—could not understand. But she went on anyway.

'No.' A single word. And then. 'But my mother was.' She shut her eyes. 'No one will ever understand, Luke, what goes on in the head of someone who is in thrall to a man who wants only to control every aspect of her life. I tried so hard, so often, to get her to see what my father was, but she kept blinding herself to it. My father knew it—knew I would never succeed, however much I longed to.' Her voice became bitter. 'And that became his way of controlling me, too. Because if I ever did anything that displeased him he would take it out on my mother. And then tell me that was what he had done. Any anger he had at her, from which she would flinch, and then make up endless pathetic justifications to excuse it, would be *my* fault! And if there was any attempt by me to break free of my cage, to exert my own will, my mother would suffer. My life was spent trying to reassure her, to soothe her jagged nerves, to calm her and support her—to protect her. I could never break free while she would be the one to suffer for it. And it takes courage to bear that, Luke. More than you know.'

Her eyes flashed open suddenly.

'And then that one night, at that party, I dared to take a risk that I had taken only once before.' Her face hardened now, with bitter memory. 'The only time before I had ever dared have a romance of my own, my father meted out punishment for it. Oh, not to me—to the man. My father got him sacked from his job and ruined his reputation so he would never get another in the industry. And then he told me exactly what he'd done. So that I would never do it again. It was his way of controlling me.'

Her face was stark, her eyes bleak.

'Even as you talked of escaping to the Caribbean I knew I could never take off with you, Luke. I couldn't abandon my poor, helpless mother, and I couldn't risk my father doing to you what he'd done to that young man. I knew nothing about you. I had no idea who you were. I knew only that you sported a fancy watch and stayed in an expensive hotel. But that would not have been enough to protect you from my father. His reach was long—he was a powerful man, and very, very rich.'

She gave a laugh—a hollow laugh that had no humour in it.

'And all along—' She took a ragged breath. 'All along you were poised to take over Grantham Land. *That* was why I was deluged with desperate texts from my mother that morning! My father had disappeared off the face of the earth, and now, of course, I know why. Because you were about to finalise the acquisition of everything he possessed, reducing my mother and me to absolute penury. Penury that made me go begging to you, that made you think of me as you do.' Her voice twisted with a savage bite. 'That made you think that all I craved was to be your bejewelled and pampered bird in a cage.'

That hollow half-laugh broke from her again, then stopped abruptly. 'How ironic does life get, Luke? Tell me that. You've turned out to be just another rich, ruthless bastard like my father!'

She heard an oath escape him in his native Greek. Its tone was harsh, crude, and ugly, though she could not understand its meaning. Then he was hurling words at her, in Greek and then in English, his eyes burning with a savage fire.

'I am *nothing* like your father! *Nothing* like the man who killed *my* father!'

A razored intake of air seared Luke's lungs like a heated blade. Emotion convulsed in him. He rounded on her, staring at her, but it was not Talia he was seeing. His gaze was into the past.

He began to talk.

'My father owned a hotel—small, but beautiful. It had been his grandfather's house, right by the sea, a haven of peace and tranquillity set in olive groves on an island in the Aegean. To my parents it was everything and they loved it dearly, dedicated their lives to it. But…'

His voice grew shadowed. 'When I was a student, an earthquake hit and the hotel was badly damaged. They could not afford to restore it. So…' He paused. 'So when a wealthy investor—an Englishman—offered them financial help, they could not believe their good fortune.'

He paused again.

'My parents were simple people. Naive in many ways. Dangerously so, you could say. They trusted this eager, enthusiastic Englishman and signed the paperwork he set in front of them, believing they had years to repay their debt out of future hotel profits. It seemed a fair deal.'

He could see Talia's expression changing. He went on remorselessly.

'But your father did not believe in fair dealing. What he believed in was profit—made any way he could. And what he saw in my parents' place was not a small boutique hotel but the valuable land it stood on—shoreline, beachfront.' He paused yet again. 'Ripe for development.'

Luke's mouth twisted.

'You won't need me to spell out what was on the paperwork that my parents so gratefully signed—a contract giving your father total control over the rest of the land. It let him bring in chainsaws to demolish the olive groves, bulldozers to flatten the terrain, teams of construction workers to build a massive high-rise monstrosity of a hotel right beside my parents' hotel, dwarfing it, destroying all its charm, its beauty. It was ruined financially for ever. And then, when my parents were unable to repay any of the money he'd lent them, he simply foreclosed on them. He took everything from them. *Everything.*'

He realised his hands were still clenched around the wheel, as if moulded to it. Forcibly, he lifted his fingers away, flexing them. He looked away from her, out at the coastline far below.

'Do you know the reason I knew how to do CPR on your mother? Because I made myself learn.'

His voice had changed again, and in it was something that struck fear into Talia,

'I had to watch my own father collapse and die of a heart attack in front of my eyes because of what your father had done to him. Your father caused his death as surely as if he'd plunged a knife into his chest himself.'

His head snaked to face Talia.

'Your father was doomed the day I buried mine. I vowed to ruin him, to bring him down. And, yes, the night of that party was the very night I'd finally acquired the means to do so. After ten gruelling years of turning myself from student to tycoon, forcing myself to build the fortune I knew I'd need to destroy him, I finally acquired a sufficient shareholding to take over Grantham Land.'

For a long moment Talia was silent. Then she spoke with a heaviness that was crushing her. 'I walked back that morning into a cage that was no longer there. But I did not know it.'

He didn't answer. The silence between them stretched. Then, 'And if you *had* known it?'

His voice was so low she could scarcely hear it. She shut her eyes. They were hot suddenly, and burning, and she could not bear that either.

'What does it matter, Luke?'

The weariness was in her bones. To know that Luke had been as much a victim of her father as she had been, that he had wreaked havoc on his parents' lives as he had on so many other lives, could make no difference.

'What does it matter?' she said again. 'Any more than it matters why I walked out of the gilded cage *you* offered me in the Caribbean!'

Her hands convulsed in her lap.

'I thought I had been given a second chance out there on the island with you. I knew that wherever my father was he would not be coming back—and that meant my mother and I were penniless. But it also meant that I could take my chance of finding happiness.' Her voice was sad as she stared down at her hands. 'Discovering what you thought of me ripped that stupid illusion from me.'

She made herself look at him. Forced herself. It hurt to do so, and not just because of the pain that she was fighting to ignore pricking behind her eyes. It hurt to see the planes of his face, the hard edge of his jaw, the deep darkness of his eyes that had no expression in them at all as he met her gaze.

Something cried out inside her, but she tamped it down. 'I'm sorry, Luke,' she said, her voice still heavy. 'I'm sorry that I am the daughter of the man who did so much harm to you. I'm sorry I abandoned you that first morning after the party. I'm sorry I don't want to be your mistress. I'm sorry—'

She broke off. His hand had shot out and crushed down on hers, silencing her. Greek broke from him again, vehement and urgent.

'*Thee mou,* do you think I *wanted* you to be a pampered princess who expected a life of luxury? Corrupted by your father's wealth so that you'd crave it in any man you might choose to replace him with?' He took a ragged, scissored breath. 'Don't you *know* what I want? What I have wanted from the moment I set eyes on you?'

He closed his other hand around hers, lifting it to his cheek. His fingers were warm around hers but her hand lay still, as if paralysed. The same paralysis held her motionless, stilling the breath in her lungs, the set of her gaze on his face.

'I knew I shouldn't want you—not after you walked out on me that morning. Not after you revealed yourself as the daughter of my enemy. Not after you begged me to let you keep the villa in Marbella that I thought you felt entitled to. Not after I succumbed to the temptation to take you to the Caribbean, telling myself it was to make you work and earn the right to stay on in the villa.'

His voice grew heavy now—with self-condemnation.

'Not even when I told myself, as you lay in my arms, that I should make allowances for you being a hot-house creature who could not survive without luxury and someone to look after you all the time. I *knew* I shouldn't want a woman like that.'

He halted, and Talia felt his strong fingers spasm suddenly over her limp hand.

'But I did,' he said. 'God help me, I did.'

Abruptly he let her hand drop, turned away again. The cramped confines of the car were claustrophobic suddenly. On an impulse he could not control he threw open the door and vaulted out. He stood in the mild night air, with the moon sailing serenely overhead, the chorus of cicadas in the vegetation all around raucously audible. For him there was only the hectic beating of his heart. Like blows against his chest.

Grimness possessed him.

He had got her wrong. So, so wrong.

He heard her get out of the car as well and take a few steps over the gravel to stand beside him. He tensed at her approach. Heard her speak.

'And *I* knew,' she said, with strain in her voice, 'that I should not want a man who thought so ill of me…' She paused. 'But I did.' She paused again. 'I *do*.'

For the space of a heartbeat he did not move. Then slowly, infinitely slowly, he turned towards her.

'It cost me so much to leave you that first morning, Luke—after the party. But I had to do it for my mother's sake. And it cost me even more to leave you when I did on the island. But I had to do that for *my* sake. Because if I'd stayed it would have destroyed me—day by day, night by night. Knowing what you thought of me…what you believed me to be. What I would have become. A woman in love with a man who despised her.'

She made to turn away, but Luke stopped her with a hand on her arm.

'*What* did you say?'

He stepped towards her, and as Talia stared up at him she saw his expression change in the moonlight.

'You said,' he told her, and now there was something in his voice that went with the expression on his face, 'that you would have been "a woman in love"?'

Tears, hot and anguished, pricked her eyes now, breaking away from the control she'd pressed them back with.

'I shouldn't have said that, Luke. We have nothing else to say to each other now.'

'*Yes!* Yes, we *do*!' Luke's voice cut across hers. Vehement and urgent. 'After everything we have finally said to each other we haven't said the one thing that really matters.'

He took a breath, his eyes directed at hers.

'Right from the very first time I set eyes on you I knew, with every instinct in my body, that you were special. It had nothing whatsoever to do with the goal I had finally achieved, the destruction of the man who had destroyed my parents. I was finally free of that burden—finally free to choose how to live my life. Free to *choose*, Talia.' He took another breath, his eyes never leaving her for an instant, a heartbeat. 'Free to fall in love…'

He heard her give a little cry, but he could not stop. 'Had you come with me after our first night together I would have fallen in love with you then.'

He saw the tears spilling from her eyes, catching the moonlight, and then his arms were around her, drawing her to him. He felt his heart soar in his chest.

'Forgive me, I beg you,' he said, his arms tightening, 'for all the ill I thought of you. I will strive with all my strength to make amends for it—to be worthy of your love!'

He felt her arms tighten around him, clutching at him, felt her shoulders heave with sobs, and then he was cradling her tear-stained face with his hands, his eyes soft and cherishing. His mouth grazed hers in tender homage.

'Don't cry. Never cry again. I honour everything about you—your loving loyalty to your mother, your courage in sticking by her, not abandoning her to your father's wrath just to gain your own freedom. I honour you for the strength and courage you've shown in protecting her after your father's ruin, whatever the cost to you. And I honour, above all, the choice you made in leaving me—both that very first morning and when you left me in the Caribbean after I got it so, so wrong about you.'

'I was scared!' she cried, remembering her mother's words to her in the hospital. 'Scared I would repeat what she had done. That I would stay with a man who treated me with contempt—who never loved me.'

He kissed her again. 'Love me as I love you…and if you do then you will love me.'

His smile seemed to melt away the harsh words that had passed between them and turn her heart over.

'I love you to all the reaches of infinity.'

She broke into renewed sobbing and he let out a laugh, swirling her around in his arms, lifting her feet off the ground in the moonlight. Then he lowered her gently, tenderly, back to the ground.

'Weep all you want,' he said softly. 'For when you have done I never want you to weep again.'

He shut his eyes momentarily, filled with an emotion he could barely contain, and then they sprang open again as he put his arm around her and they turned together to face the view of the town, the coast and the horizon beyond. A great quietness settled over him...a peace of the heart.

'We're finally free,' he said quietly. 'Free of what your father did to both of us. Free to live our lives as we wish. Free to love as we wish. And even free,' he finished wryly, 'should we wish it, to avail ourselves of my suite at my hotel! It's a beautiful place up in the hills. An old Moorish fort with fabulous views over the coast.' His hand tightened over hers. 'Will you come with me? Stay with me this time?'

Her smile was all he needed to see. And the softening of her gaze with a light that outshone the moon.

'I'll never leave you again, Luke,' she said. *'Never.'*

It was a promise. A vow. To him, and to herself.

EPILOGUE

'SO, WHAT DO you think, Mum?'

Talia swept an arm around the circular atrium with its cobalt floor and its walls muralled in vivid emerald, with foliage and crimson flowers, wide arches opening to the glorious gardens beyond.

'You've got an incredibly talented daughter,' said Luke, and smiled, standing beside her.

Talia's mother clapped her hands. 'Oh, darling, it's *wonderful*!'

The man beside Maxine grinned. 'Pretty good, Talia.' He nodded. Then he glanced at Luke. 'When's the grand opening?'

Luke helped himself to Talia's hand. 'Right after our wedding,' he said. 'Until then we're keeping it private—just for family. Talia and I are going to test-drive the open-air chapel out on the promontory. Shall we go and take a look now?'

'Oh, Luke, yes!' Maxine cried. She cast a look at the man beside her. 'And maybe after you two have tied the knot,' she said lightly, 'Mike and I might try it out too!'

Talia's expression lit up. 'Oh, Mum! That would be *brilliant*!'

She cast a warm look at the man beside her mother. Easy-going, weather-beaten, with a piratical beard. He was dressed in cut-off denims and a striped top—the uniform of a seafaring yachtsman—and he was the very antithesis of her father.

She could not have been gladder of it. Already, in the nine months since she and Luke had gone to see her mother in the hospital and told her of their love for each other, her mother had bloomed. And then Mike, who had one day moored his boat off the hotel jetty, had taken one look at Maxine, who had been visiting the island, and recognised in her a teen romance from their youth and stayed to rekindle it.

Now, as the four of them made their way through the restored atrium out on to the terrace beyond, and then along the pristine pathways, there was no sign at all of the devastation that the hurricane had caused.

Talia felt her heart swell with happiness. She leant into Luke. 'How can I be so happy?' she breathed.

He smiled down at her, his eyes warm with love. 'Because you deserve it,' he told her, and dropped a kiss on her forehead.

He led her out on to a small grassy promontory, where a ring of palm trees swayed in the constant breeze, lifting the heat. A thatched open air chapel, with seating in front was set out there. They paused while Mike and Maxine caught them up, and then they all turned back to look at the hotel, fully restored now, after months of endless work.

Again, Talia felt her heart lift. 'We've made it *so* beautiful again!' she exclaimed.

'It deserves to be,' Luke said. He looked down at Talia again, squeezing her hand. 'And I know why I was so determined to save it.'

There was a thread of sadness in his voice that made Talia squeeze his hand in return, to comfort him.

'Because what is broken can be restored, with enough time and enough love—buildings, people, re-lationships...'

'You saved it for your parents' sake,' Talia said in a low voice. 'And I'm glad—*so* glad.'

Luke turned her gently towards him. 'Will you truly be happy, getting married here on this spot?'

Her eyes lifted to his, shining with the sun. 'How can you even ask?' she said. 'I would be happy mar-rying *you*, my darling, darling Luke, anywhere in the whole wide world! For you are my heart, Luke. My whole heart.'

He lowered his mouth to hers. Peace filled him. Peace, thankfulness and love. Always love. And love embraced him as he embraced the woman he loved... embraced them both for ever.

* * * * *

HIS FORBIDDEN PREGNANT PRINCESS

MAISEY YATES

To Nicole Helm.
Ask and you shall receive.
Dare and I shall deliver.
Can I make a children's cartoon a romance novel?
Yes. Yes, I can.

CHAPTER ONE

SHE WAS BENEATH him in every way. From her common blood to her objectively plain appearance—that years of designer clothing, professional treatments from the finest aestheticians and beauticians and the work of the best makeup artists money could buy had failed to transform into true beauty—from the way she carried herself, to the way she spoke.

The stepsister he had always seen as a particularly drab blot on the otherwise extravagant tapestry of the royal family of San Gennaro.

The stepsister he could hardly bear to share the same airspace with, let alone the same palace.

The stepsister he was now tasked with finding a suitable husband for.

The stepsister he wanted more than his next breath.

She was beneath him in every way. Except for the way he desired most.

And she never would be.

There were a thousand reasons. From the darkness in him, to the common blood in her. But the only reason that truly mattered was that she was his stepsister, and he was a king.

"You requested my presence, Luca?" Sophia asked,

looking up at him with a dampened light in her blue eyes that suggested she was suppressing some emotion or other. In all probability a deep dislike for having to deal with him.

But the feeling was mutual. And if he could endure such an indignity then Sophia—in all her borrowed glory—certainly could.

"I did. As you know, it was my father's final wish that you be well cared for, along with your mother. He wrote it into law that you are part of this family and are to be treated as a daughter of his blood would be."

Sophia looked down, her lashes dark on her pale cheek. She had visible freckles that never failed to vex him. Because he wanted to count them. Because sometimes, he wanted to kiss each one.

She should cover them with makeup as most women of her status did. She should have some care for the fact she was a princess.

But she did not.

Today she wore a simple shift that made her bare legs seem far too long and slender. It was an ungainly thing. She also wore nothing at all to cover them. She had on flat shoes, and not a single piece of jewelry. Her dark hair hung limp around her shoulders.

He could only hope she had not gone out in public that way.

"Yes," she said, finally. Then those dark eyes connected with his and he felt it like a lightning bolt straight down to his stomach. He should not. For every reason cataloged in his mind only a moment before. She was not beautiful. Not when compared to the elegant women who had graced his bed before her. Not when compared to nearly any other princess the world over.

But she captivated him. Had done from the moment he had met her. At first it was nothing more than feeling at turns invaded and intrigued by this alien creature that had come into his life. She had been twelve to his seventeen when their parents had married.

Sophia had possessed a public school education, not a single hint of deportment training and no real understanding of the hierarchy of the palace.

She had a tendency to speak out of turn, to trip over her feet and to treat him in an overly familiar manner.

Her mother was a warm, vivacious woman who had done much to restore his father's life, life that had drained away after the loss of his first wife. She was also a quick study, and did credit to the position of Queen of San Gennaro.

Sophia, on the other hand, seemed to resist her new role, and her new life. She continued to do so now. In little ways. Her bare legs, and her bare face, as an example.

His irritation with her had taken a sharp turn, twisting into something much more disturbing around the time she turned sixteen. That sense of being captivated, in the way one might be by a spider that has invaded one's room, shifted and became much more focused.

And there had been a moment, when he had found her breathless from running out in the garden like a schoolgirl when she had been the advanced age of seventeen, that everything had locked into place. That it had occurred to him that if he could only capture that insolent mouth of hers with his own she would finally yield. And he would no longer feel so desperately beguiled by her.

It had only gotten worse as the years had progressed.

And the idea of kissing her had perverted yet further into doing much, much more.

But it was not to be. Not ever.

As he had just told her, his father had decreed that she was family. As much as if they were blood.

And so he was putting an end to this once and for all.

"He asked me to take care of you in a very specific fashion," Luca continued. "And I feel that now that it has been six months since his passing, it is time for me to see those requests honored."

A crease appeared between her brows. "What request?"

"Specifically? The matter of your marriage, *sorellina*." Little sister. He called her that to remind himself.

"My marriage? Shouldn't we see to the matter of me getting asked to the movies first, Luca?"

"There is no need for such things, obviously. A woman in your position is hardly going to go to the movies. Rather, I have been poring over a list of suitable men who might be able to be brought in for consideration."

"You're choosing my husband?" she asked, her tone incredulous.

"I intend to present you with a manageably sized selection. I am not so arrogant that I would make the final choice for you."

Sophia let out a sharp, inelegant laugh. "Oh, no. You're only so arrogant that you would inform me I'm getting married, and that you have already started taking steps toward planning the wedding. Tell me, Luca, have you picked out my dress, as well?"

Of course he would be involved in approving that selection; if she thought otherwise she was delusional. "Not as yet," he said crisply.

"What happens if I refuse you?"

"You won't," he said, certainty going as deep as his bones.

He was the king now, and she could not refuse him. She would not. He would not allow it.

"Why wouldn't I?"

"You are welcome, of course, to make a mockery of the generosity that my father has shown to your mother and yourself. You are welcome, of course, to cause a rift between the two of us."

She crossed her arms, cocking one hip out to the side. "I could hardly cause a rift between the two of us, Luca. No matter what you might say, you have never behaved as a loving older brother to me."

"Perhaps it is because you have never been a sister to me," he said, his voice hard.

She would not understand what that meant. She would not understand why he had said it.

And indeed, the confusion on her face spoke to that.

"I don't have to do what you tell me to." She shook her head, that dark, glossy hair swirling around her shoulders. "Your father would hardly have forced me into a marriage I didn't want. He loved me. He wanted what was best for me."

"This was what he thought was best," Luca said. "I have documentation saying such. If you need to see it, I will have it sent to your quarters. Quarters that you inhabit, by the way, because my father cared so much for you. Because my father took an exceptional and un-heard-of step in this country and treated a child he did not father as his own. He is giving you what he would have given to a daughter. A daughter of his blood. Se-lecting your husband, ensuring it is a man of impeccable pedigree, is what he would have done for his child. You are welcome to reject it if you wish. But I would think very deeply about what that means."

Sophia didn't have to think deeply about what it meant. She could feel it. Her heart was pounding so hard she thought she might pass out; small tremors running beneath the surface of her skin. Heat and ice pricking at her cheeks.

Oh, she wasn't thinking of what this meant in the way that Luca had so imperiously demanded she do.

Luca.

Her beautiful, severe stepbrother who was much more king of a nation than he was family to her. Remote. Distant. His perfectly sculpted face only more desperately gorgeous to her now than it had been when she had met him at seventeen. He had been beautiful as a teenager. There was no question. But then, that angular bone structure had been overlaid by much softer skin, his coal-black eyes always formidable, but nothing quite so sharp as crushed obsidian as they were now. That soft skin, the skin of a boy, that was gone. Replaced by a more weathered texture. By rough, black whiskers that seemed ever present no matter how often he shaved his square jaw.

She had never in all of her life met a thing like him. A twelve-year-old girl, plucked up from obscurity, from a life of poverty and set down in this luxurious castle, had been utterly and completely at sea to begin with. And then there was *him*.

Everything in her had wanted to challenge him, to provoke a response from all of that granite strength, even then. Even before she had known why, or known what it meant that she craved his attention in whatever form it might come.

Gradually, it had all become clear.

And clearer still the first time she had gone to a ball and Luca had gone with another woman on his arm. That acrid, acidic curling sensation in her stomach could have only been one thing. Even at fourteen she had known that. Had known that the sweep of fever that had gone over her skin, that weak sensation that made it feel as though she was going to die, was jealousy. Jealousy because she wanted Luca to take her arm, wanted him to hold her close and dance with her.

Wanted to be the one he took back to his rooms and did all sorts of secret things with, things that she had not known about in great detail, but had yearned for all the same. Him. Everything to do with him.

As Luca had said not a moment before, he had never thought of her as a sister. He was never affectionate, never close or caring in a way that went beyond duty.

But she had never thought of him as a brother. She had thought of him in an entirely different fashion.

She *wanted* him.

And he was intent on marrying her off. As though it were nothing.

Not a single thing on earth could have spoken to the ambivalence that he felt toward her any stronger than this did.

He doesn't want you.

Of course he didn't. She wasn't a great beauty; she was well aware of that. She was also absolutely and completely wrong for him in every way.

She didn't excel at this royal existence the way that he did. He wore it just beneath his skin, as tailored and fitted to him as one of his bespoke suits. Born with it, as if his blood truly were a different color than that of the common people. As if he were a different creature entirely from the rest of the mere mortals.

She had done her best to put that royal mantle on, but much like every dress that had ever been made for her since coming to live at the palace, it wasn't quite right. Oh, they could measure it all to fit, but it was clear that she wasn't made for such things. That her exceedingly nonwaiflike figure was not for designer gowns and slinky handmade creations that would have hung fabulously off women who were more collar and hip bone than curves and love handles.

Oh, yes, she was well aware of how little she fit. And how impossible her feelings for Luca were.

And yet, they remained.

And knowing that nothing could ever happen with him, knowing it with deep certainty, had done nothing to excise it from her soul.

Did nothing to blunt the pain of this, of his words being ground into her chest like shards of glass.

Not only was he making it clear he didn't want her, he was also using the memory of his father—the only man she had ever known as a father—to entice her to agree.

He was right. King Magnus had given her everything. Had given her mother a new lease on life, a real life. Something beyond existence, beyond struggle, which they had been mired in for all of Sophia's life prior to her marriage to him.

He had met her when she was nothing more than a waitress at a royal event in the US, and had fallen deeply for her in the moment they met.

It was something out of a fairy tale, except there were two children to contend with. A child who had been terrified of being uprooted from her home in America and going to a foreign country to live in a fancy palace. And another child who had always clearly resented the invasion.

She had to give Luca credit for the fact that he seemed to have some measure of affection for her mother. He did not resent her presence in the way he resented Sophia's.

She had often thought that life for Luca would have been perfect if he would have gotten her mother and his father, and she had been left out of the equation entirely.

Well, he was trying to offload her now, so she supposed that was proven to be true enough.

"That isn't fair," she said, when she could finally regain her powers of speech.

Luca's impossibly dark eyes flickered up and met hers, and her stomach—traitorous fool—hollowed out in response. "It isn't fair? Sophia, I have always known that you were ungrateful for the position that you have found yourself in your life, but you have just confirmed it in a rather stunning way. You find it unfair that my father wished to see you cared for? You find it unfair that I wish to do the same?"

"You forget," she said, trying to regain her powers of thought. "I was not born into this life, Luca, I did not know people growing up who expected such things for their lives. I didn't expect such a thing for mine. I spent the first twelve years of my life in poverty. But with the idea that if I worked hard enough I might be able to make whatever I wanted of myself. And then we were sort of swept up in this tidal wave of luxury.

And strangely, I have found that though I have every resource at my disposal now, I cannot be what I want in the same way that I imagined I could when I was nothing but a poor child living in the United States."

"That's because you were a delusional child," Luca said, his tone not cruel in any way, but somehow all the more stinging for the calm with which he spoke. "You never had the power to be whatever you wanted back then, Sophia, because no one has that power. There are a certain number of things set out before you that you might accomplish. You certainly might have improved your station. I'm not denying that. But the sky was never the limit, sorely not. Neither is it now. However, your limit is much more comfortable, you will find, than it would have been then."

Her heart clenched tight, because she couldn't deny that what he was saying was true. Bastard. With the maturity of adulthood she could acknowledge that. That she had been naive at the time, and that she was, in fact, being ungrateful to a degree.

Hadn't her position in the palace provided her with the finest education she could have asked for? Hadn't she been given excellent opportunities? Chances to run charitable organizations that she believed in strongly, and that benefited all manner of children from different backgrounds.

No, as a princess, she would never truly have a profession, but with that came the release of pressure of earning money to pay bills.

Of figuring out where the road between what she dreamed of doing, and what would help her survive, met.

But the idea of marrying someone selected by her

stepbrother, who no more knew her than liked her, was not a simple thing.

And underneath that, the idea of marrying any man, touching any man, being intimate with any man, who wasn't Luca was an abomination unto her soul.

For it was only him. Luca and those eyes as hard as flint, that mouth that was often curled into a sneer in her direction, those large hands that were much rougher than any king's ever should have been. It was only him who made her want. Who made her ache with the deep well of unsatisfied desire. Only him.

Only ever him.

"I will be holding a ball," Luca said, his tone decisive. "And at that ball will be several men that I have personally curated for you."

"You make them sound like a collection of cheeses."

"Think of them however you like. If you prefer to think them as cheese, that's your own business."

Something burst inside her, some small portion of restraint that she had been only just barely holding on to since she had come into the throne room. "How do you know I like men, Luca? You've never asked."

Luca drew back slightly, a flicker in his dark eyes the only showing that she had surprised him at all.

"If it is not so," he said, his tone remote, "then I suggest you speak now."

"No," she responded, feeling deflated, as her momentary bit of rebellion fell flat on its face. "I'm not opposed to men."

"Well," he said, "one less bit of damage control I have to do."

"That would require damage control?"

"How many gay princesses do you know?" he asked.

"The upper echelons of society are ever conservative regardless of what they say. And here in this country it would be quite the scandal, I assure you. It is all fine to pay lip service to such things as equality, but appearances, tradition, are as important as ever."

"And I am already a break with tradition," she pointed out.

"Yes," he said, that tone heavy. "My father's actions in granting you the same rights as I have were unheard of. You are not his by blood, and in royal lines blood is everything. It is the only thing."

"I will go to the ball," she said, because there really was no point arguing with Luca once he had made pronouncements. But whatever happened after that... It would be her decision.

But she was too raw, too shocked, from this entire conversation to continue having a fight with him.

He wanted to marry her off to another man. He wanted her to be someone else's problem.

He felt nothing about doing it.

He did not want her.

He's your stepbrother, and even if he did he couldn't have you. As he just said, tradition is everything.

She squared her shoulders. "When is this blessed event?"

"In a couple weeks' time," he responded.

She blinked. "Oh. I'm not certain my mother will be back from France before then."

"She will be. I have already spoken with her."

That galled her. Like a lance through her chest. Her mother, of course, had no idea how Sophia felt about Luca. She told her mother everything. Everything except for that. Everything except for the completely forbidden lust she felt for her stepbrother. But even so, she couldn't believe that her mother had allowed Luca to have this conversation with her without at least giving her a call to warn her first.

"I told her not to tell you," Luca said as if he was reading her mind.

She sniffed. "Well. That is quite informative."

"Do not be indignant, *sorellina*," Luca said. "It is not becoming of a princess."

"Well, I've certainly never been overly becoming as princesses go," she said stiffly. "Why start now?"

"You had better start. You had better start so that all of this will work accordingly."

He looked her up and down. "We need to get you a new stylist."

"I use the same stylist as my mother," she said defensively.

"It doesn't work for you," he said, his tone cold.

And with a wave of his hand he dismissed her, and she was left somehow obeying him, her feet propelling her out of his royal chamber and into the hall.

She clutched her chest, gasping for breath, pain rolling through her.

The man she loved was going to marry her off to someone else. The man she loved was selecting from a pool of grooms for her to meet in two weeks' time.

The man she loved was her stepbrother. The man she loved was a king.

All of those things made it impossible for her to have him.

But she didn't have any idea how in the world she was supposed to stop wanting him.

CHAPTER TWO

"WHAT IS *THIS*?" The disdain in Sophia's tone when Luca presented her with a thick stack of files the following week was—in his estimation—a bit on the dramatic side.

"It is the list of possible husbands to invite to the upcoming ball. I feel strongly that an excess of five is just being spoiled for choice. Plus, you will not have time to dance with that many people. So I suggest you look it over, and find a way to pare them down."

"This is…" She looked up at him, her dark eyes furious. "These are dossiers of…*men*. Photos and personal profiles…"

"How else would you know if you're compatible?"

"Maybe meeting them and going out for dinner?" Sophia asked.

She crossed her arms, the motion pushing her rather abundant décolletage up over the neckline of the rather simple V-neck top she was wearing.

They really needed to get ahold of that new stylist and quickly. She was, as ever, a temptation to Luca, and to his sense of duty. But soon it would be over. Soon he would have his problematic stepsister married off, and then she would be safely out of his reach.

He could have found a woman to slake his lust on, and over the years he had done just that. After all, whatever was broken in him… Sophia should not have to suffer for it.

But during those time periods he had not been forced to cohabitate with Sophia. Always, when he had spent too much time with her, he had to detox, essentially. Find a slim blonde to remind himself that there were other sorts of women he found hot. Other women he might find desirable.

And then, when it was really bad, he gave up entirely on playing the opposite game and found himself a curvaceous brunette to pour his fantasies into. The end of that road was a morass of self-loathing and recrimination, but on many levels he was happy to end up there. He was comforted by it.

But this… Sharing space with her. As he had done since his father had died. No other woman would do. He couldn't find it in him to feel even a hint of desire for anyone else. And that was unacceptable. As all things to do with Sophia invariably were.

"You are not going on dinner dates," Luca said. "You are a princess. You are part of the royal family. And you are not setting up a Tinder profile in order to find yourself a husband."

"Why not?" she asked, her tone defiant. "Perhaps I want nothing more than to meet a very exciting IT guy who might swipe me right off my feet." He said nothing and she continued to stare at him. "Swipe. Swipe right. It's a dating app thing."

"That isn't funny in the least. As I said, you are part of this family." Perhaps if he repeated it enough, if he drilled it into both of them that they were family, his body would eventually begin to take it on board. "And as such, your standards of marriage must be the same as mine."

"Why aren't you looking for a wife yourself?" she asked.

"I will," Luca said. "In due time. But my father asked that I make your safety, your match, a priority."

He would marry, as duty required. But it would not be because of passion. And certainly not because of love. Duty was what drove him. The preservation of reputation, of the crown. If that crumbled, his whole life was nothing.

He would choose a suitable woman.

Sophia was far from suitable.

"What about the production of an heir?" Sophia lifted a brow. "Isn't that important?"

"Yes. But I am a man, and as such, I do not have the same issues with a biological clock your gender does."

"Right," she huffed. "Because men can continue to produce children up until the end of their days."

"Perhaps not without the aid of a blue pill, but certainly it is possible."

For a moment she only blinked up at him, a faint pink tinge coloring her cheeks. Then Sophia's lip curled. "I find this conversation distasteful."

"You brought up the production of heirs, not me."

She scowled, clearly having to take his point, and not liking it at all. "Well, let me look through the dossiers, then," she said, lifting her nose and peering at him down the slender ridge, perfecting that sort of lofty look that was nothing if not a put-on coming from Sophia.

Though, possibly not when directed at him.

"Erik Nilsson. Swedish nobility?"

"Yes," Luca responded. "He's very wealthy."

"How?"

"Family money, mostly. Though some of it is in sheep."

"His money is in sheep?" Sophia asked, her expression completely bland. "Well, that is interesting. And one would never want for sweaters."

"Indeed not," he said, a vicious turn of jealousy savaging his gut. Which was sadistic at best. To be jealous of a man whose fortune was tied up in sheep and who had the dubious honor of being a minor noble in some small village that wasn't part of the current century.

A man he had not expected his stepsister to show the slightest interest in. And yet, here she was.

"So he will have access to…wool. And such," Sophia said. "And…he's quite handsome. If you like tall and blond."

"Do you?" he asked.

"Very much," she said with a strange injection of conviction. "He's on the table." She set the folder aside. "Let us get on with the next candidate, shall we?"

"Here you are," he said, lifting up the next folder and holding it out toward her. "Ilya Kuznetsov."

She arched a brow. "Russian?"

He raised one in response. "Very."

Sophia wrinkled her nose. "Is his fortune in vodka and caviar?"

"I hate to disappoint you but it's in tech. So, quite close to that IT guy you were professing to have a burning desire for."

"I didn't say I had a burning desire for anyone," she pointed out, her delicate fingers tracing the edge of the file.

He couldn't help but imagine those same fingers stroking him.

If he believed in curses, he would believe he was under one.

"I don't know anything about computers," she continued, setting the folder off to the opposite side of the first one. "I prefer sheep."

She was infuriating. And baffling. "Not something you hear every day. Now, to the next one."

She set aside the next two. An Italian business mogul and a Greek tycoon. Neither one meeting up to some strange specification that she blathered on about in vague terms. Then she rejected an Argentine polo player, who was also nobility of some kind, on the basis of the fact that a quick Google search revealed him to be an inveterate womanizer.

"You're not much better," she said mournfully, looking up from her phone.

"Then it is a good thing that I am not in the files for consideration."

Something quite like shock flashed through her eyes, and her mouth dropped open. Color flooded her cheeks, irritation, anger.

"As if that would ever happen. As if I would *consider* you." She sniffed very loudly.

"As my sister, you could not," he bit out.

"Stepsister," she said, looking up at him from beneath her dark lashes.

His gut twisted, his body hardening for a moment before he gathered his control. The moment seemed to last an eternity. Stolen, removed from time. Nothing but those eyes boring holes through him, as though she could see right into him. As though she could see his every debauched thought.

Every dark, terrible thing in him.

But no, there was no way she could.

Or she would run and hide like a frightened mouse.

"In terms of legality, in terms of my father's will, you're my sister," he said. "Now, the next one."

She went through the folders until she had selected five, though she maintained that the Swedish candidate was top of her list.

It did not escape his notice that she had selected all men with lighter features. Diametrically opposed to his own rather dark appearance.

He should rejoice in that.

He found he did not.

"Then these are the invitations that will be sent out," he said. "And I will be reserving dances with each of the gentlemen."

"Dances?" She blinked. "Are we in a Regency romance novel? Am I going to have a card to keep track?"

"Don't be ridiculous. You can keep track of it in an app."

She barked out a laugh. "This is ridiculous. You're ridiculous."

"Perhaps," he said, "but if you can think of a better way to bring together the most eligible men in the world, I'm all ears."

"And what happens if I don't like any of them?"

"You're very excited about the sweaters."

"What if I don't like any of them?" she reiterated.

"I imagine something will work out."

"I'm serious," she said, her blue eyes blazing with

emotion. "I'm not marrying a man I don't like because you have some strange time frame you need to fulfill."

"Then we will keep looking."

"No," she said. "I promise that I will be fair, and I will give this a chance. But if it doesn't work, give me six months to make my own choice. If I can't find somebody that is suitable to me, and suitable to you, then I will let you choose."

"That was not part of the original bargain."

Six months more of her might just kill him.

"I don't care," Sophia said. "This isn't the Dark Ages, and you can't make me do what I don't want to. And you know it."

"Then you have a bargain. But you will have to put in serious effort. I am not wasting my time and resources."

"Well I'm not marrying a man just to suit you, Luca. I want to care for the man I marry. I want to like him, if I can't love him. I want to be able to talk to him. I want him to make me laugh."

Luca braced himself. Braced himself for her to start talking about passion. About wanting a man who would set her body on fire.

She didn't.

She had stopped at a man who made her laugh, and had not said she wanted a man who would make her come. He shouldn't think such thoughts. Shouldn't want to find out why that didn't seem to occur to her.

Why attraction didn't come into her lists of demands to be met.

It made him want to teach her. Didn't she understand? That physical desire *mattered*?

And if she didn't understand…

Some Swedish sheep farmer would be the one to teach her.

Luca gritted his teeth. "But do you need to want him, *sorellina*?"

He should not have asked the question. He shouldn't entertain these thoughts, and he certainly shouldn't give voice to them.

Cursed.

If he weren't a logical man, he would swear it.

"Want him?" she asked, tilting her head to the side.

"Yes," he bit out. "Want him. His hands on your body. His mouth on yours. Does it matter to you whether or not you want him inside you?"

He hadn't realized it, but he'd moved closer to her with each sentence. And now he was so near her he could smell her. That delicate, citrus scent that always rose above the more cloying floral or vanilla perfumes the women around the palace typically favored. A scent he was always assured he could pick out, regardless of who else was around. Always Sophia, rising above the rest.

"I… I…" Her cheeks blushed crimson, and then she stood, her nose colliding with his cheek before she wobbled backward. "I've only ever wanted one man like that." The words seemed to be stuck in her throat. "I never will again. I'm sure. And I refuse to discuss it. Least of all with you."

And then she turned and ran from the room.

CHAPTER THREE

SINCE MAKING A fool out of herself in front of Luca days earlier, Sophia had done her best to avoid him. It wasn't that difficult. Luca was always busy with affairs of state, and it was actually for the best. The problem was that every time she heard heavy, authoritative footsteps on the marble floors of the palace, her heart caught, and held its position as if it was waiting, waiting to bow down to its king.

She did not want Luca to be the king of her heart. Being King of San Gennaro was quite enough power for one man. But her heart didn't listen. It beat for Luca, it stopped for Luca, tripped over itself for Luca.

It was starting to feel like she was running an obstacle course every time she made any movement in the palace. One wherein Luca was the obstacle that she was trying desperately to avoid.

But she wanted to see him, too. That was the real conundrum. The fact that she wanted to both avoid him and be with him all the time. Foolish, because he wasn't even nice to her. He never had been. But still, he captivated her in ways that went beyond sanity.

And today there would be no more avoiding him as he had engaged the services of a new stylist to help her prepare for the ball. The ball wherein she was supposed to choose a husband.

Luca and those dossiers had enraged her. She had picked every man who was completely opposite to him, to spite herself, mostly.

She highly doubted that she would marry any of these men. But one thing she knew for certain was that she would not marry a man who was simply a pale carbon copy of her stepbrother. She would not choose a man who was tall, dark and handsome, who had that kind of authority about him that Luca possessed. Because it would simply be an effort at giving her body a consolation prize. And that was far too tragic, even for her.

She shouldn't be tragic, she mused as she wandered down the labyrinthine hall toward the salon where she was meeting the new stylist. She had been a commoner, and she had been raised up to become the princess of a country. She had been adopted by a king. A man who had loved her, and had loved her mother. Who had shown them both the kind of life that neither of them had ever dreamed possible.

But Luca. Always Luca.

It was as though her heart was intent on not being happy. As though it wanted to be tragic. In the same way that it had determined that Luca would be its owner.

In a palace, a life of luxury, and with that came a fervent, painful love for the one man she could never have.

And, he didn't like her.

Star-crossed lovers they were not. Because Luca could hardly stand to share the same space as she did. He thought she was silly, that much was apparent from their exchange yesterday. They were from completely different worlds. The man couldn't understand why she found it off-putting to be looking through file folders filled with profiles of men she had never met, trying to work out which one of them she could see herself marrying.

Although she supposed it wasn't entirely different from online dating.

No. She refused to pretend that any of this was reasonable. It wasn't.

She wondered if she would ever find someone who just wanted *her*. These men, who had agreed to come to the palace, would never have done so if she wasn't a princess.

It was the only reason her biological father had ever spoken to her. After he'd seen her mother in the media, marrying King Magnus.

King Magnus had loved her. But…he had only strived to love her because of her mother.

And Luca…

Well, nothing seemed to make Luca like her at all. Not status, or herself.

He was consistent, at least.

She took a deep breath, bracing herself for the sight of him. That was another problem with Luca. Too much exposure to him and her poor heart couldn't recover between moments. Not enough, and it always flung itself against her breastbone as though it were trying to escape. Trying to go to him. To be with him.

Her heart was foolish. And the rest of her body was worse.

She gathered herself up, drew in the deepest breath possible, hoping that the burning in her lungs would offset the rest of her physical response. That it might drown out the erratic tripping of her pulse.

Then, she pushed the door open.

And all the breath left her body in a rush.

There was no preparing for him. No matter how familiar she was with his face, with that imposing, muscular physique of his, it was like a shock to her system every time. Those dark eyes, eyes that she sometimes thought might see straight through her, but they couldn't. Because if they did, then he would know. He would know that she was not indifferent to him. He would know that her feelings toward him were in no way familial.

He would be disgusted by her.

It took her a while to notice that there was a woman standing next to him. The new stylist, presumably. It took her a while, because as far as she was concerned when Luca was in the room it was difficult to tell if anyone else was there at all.

"You must be Princess Sophia," the woman said. "I'm Elizabeth."

"Nice to meet you." Belatedly, she decided that she should try and curtsy or something, so she grabbed the edge of her sundress and bent forward slightly. She looked up and saw that Luca was watching her with a disapproving expression on his handsome face.

If she bowed down and called him King of the Universe he would disapprove. He was impossible.

"She needs something suitable for an upcoming event," Luca said. "She must look the best she ever has."

"I am confident that I can accomplish such. It is simply a matter of knowing what sort of energy Sophia should be projecting. All these colors that she's wearing now are far too drab. And from what I have seen in pictures and publications over the years, her overall color palette doesn't suit her. I have plans."

Suddenly, Sophia felt very much like she was being stared down by a hungry spider. And she was a fly caught in the web.

"Just leave it to me," she said, shooing at Luca.

"I must approve the selection," he said. Obviously not taking kindly at all to being shown the door in his own palace.

"You will approve," Elizabeth said, her tone stubborn. "You will see soon."

The rest of the afternoon was spent styling and plucking and scrubbing.

Sophia felt as though she had been exfoliated over every part of her body. This woman did not try to have her hair completely straightened, but rather, styled it into soft waves, which seemed to frame her face better, and also—so she said—would not revert halfway over the course of the evening. Which was the problem that Sophia usually had with her hairstyles. Her hair wasn't curly, but it was not board-straight, either, and it could not hold such a severe style for hours on end. It became unruly when she got all sweaty. And she supposed it was not a good thing to sweat when you were a princess, but she did.

Then there was the matter of the gown she chose. None of the navy blue, black or mossy-green colors that her mother's stylist favored. No, this gown was a brilliant fuchsia, strapless with a sweetheart neckline that did nothing at all to cover her breasts. It draped down from there, skimming her waist, her full hips. Rather than making her look large like some of the high-necked gowns that had been chosen for her before, or blocky like the ones that hit her in strange places at the waist, she actually looked…curvy and feminine.

Typically, she didn't show this much skin, but she had to admit it was much more flattering when you could see that she had cleavage, rather than a misshapen mono breast.

Her lipstick matched the dress, and her eye makeup was simple, just black winged liner. Her cheeks were a very bright pink, much brighter than she would have normally done, but all of it created a very sophisticated effect. And for the first time she thought maybe she looked like she belonged. Like maybe she was a princess. Not a girl being shoved into a mold she resolutely could not fit into, but one who'd had a mold created just for her.

"He will approve of this," Elizabeth said.

"You know he is my stepbrother," Sophia pointed out. "He doesn't need to approve of it in that way."

The very idea made her face hot. And that she wanted him to…that she wanted him to want her was the worst humiliation of all.

"I know," the woman said, giving her a look that was far too incisive. "But you wouldn't mind if he did."

Sophia sputtered. "I… He can't."

"That has nothing to do with what you feel. Or what you want."

Sophia felt like she had been opened up and examined. Like her skin had been peeled away, revealing her deepest and most desperate secrets. She hated it. But she didn't have time to marinate in it because suddenly, the door was opening, and Luca had returned. Obviously, Elizabeth had texted him to say that Sophia was ready.

But she wasn't ready. She wasn't ready to face him, not with the woman next to her knowing full well how Sophia felt about Luca. Because now she felt like it was written across her skin, across her forehead, so that it could clearly be read by the man himself.

Her earlier confidence melted away, and her skin began to heat as Luca stopped, his dark eyes assessing her slowly.

Her body tingled, her breasts feeling heavy, her nipples going tight as though his fingertips were grazing her skin. As if he was doing more than simply looking.

"It will do," he said, his tone as hard as his features.

Her throat felt prickly, and she swallowed hard, feeling foolish, her heart fluttering like a caged bird trying to escape. How could she feel so much when he looked at her, while he felt nothing for her at all? While he clearly saw her as an annoyance.

He didn't look impressed; he didn't look awed or surprised with what she had felt was a total transformation.

"I am glad that I reach at least the bottom of your very lofty standards, Your Majesty," she said stiffly. "I can only hope that a certain Swedish noble has a slightly more enthusiastic response."

"I said that it will do," he reiterated. "And it will. What more do you want from me, *sorellina*?"

"I spent the entire day receiving a makeover. I would have thought it would garner a response. But it seems as if I am destined to remain little more than wallpaper. It is okay. Some women are never going to be beautiful."

She grasped the flowing skirt of her dress with her fists and pushed past Luca, running out of the room, down the hall, running until her lungs burned. The sound of the heels she was wearing on the floor drowned out the sound of anything else, so it wasn't until she stopped that she heard heavy footsteps behind her. And she was unprepared for the large, strong hand that wrapped around her arm and spun her in the opposite direction. It was then she found herself gazing up into Luca's impossibly dark and imposing eyes.

"What is it you want from me?" he asked, his voice low and hard. Shot through with an intensity she had never heard in his voice before. "What do you want me to give you? What reaction would have been sufficient? In the absence of the one man you have ever wanted, what is it you expected *me* to give you? Do you want me to tell you that you're beautiful? Do you want me to tell you the curves would drive any man to distraction? That every man in that ballroom is going to imagine himself holding you in his arms? Feeling those luscious breasts pressed against his chest? Kissing those lips. Driving himself inside you? Is that what you want to hear? I can give you those words, Sophia, but they are pointless. I could tell you that any man who doesn't want you was a fool, but what is the point in saying those words? What could they possibly mean between the two of us?" He released his hold on her, and she stumbled backward. "Nothing. They mean nothing coming from me. It will always be nothing. It must be."

"Luca…"

"Do not speak to me." He straightened then, his expression going blank, his posture rigid. "It will do, Sophia. You will wear that dress the night of the ball. And you will find yourself a husband. I will see to that."

It wasn't until Luca turned and walked away, wasn't until he was out of her sight, that she dropped to her knees, her entire body shaking, her brain unwilling to try and figure out what had just passed between them. What those words had meant.

He said it could be nothing. It was nothing. She curled her fingers into fists, her nails digging into her skin.

It was nothing. It always would be.

She repeated those words to herself over and over again, and forced herself not to cry.

CHAPTER FOUR

HE HAD ACTED a fool the day that Sophia had received her makeover. He had… He had allowed his facade to crack. He had allowed her to reach beneath that rock wall that he had erected between himself and anyone who might get too close.

He never acted a fool. And he resented the fact that Sophia possessed the power to make him do so.

His entire life was about the crown. The country.

His mother had driven the importance of those things home before she died. In an exacting and painful manner. One that had made it clear it was not Luca who mattered, but San Gennaro. The royal name over the royal himself.

He had shaped himself around that concept.

But Sophia had looked…

Thankfully, it was time. The guests had all arrived for the ball, with Sophia scheduled to arrive fashionably late so as to draw as much attention as possible.

His attention had been fixed on her far too much in the past few days. Sadly, everything his body had suspected about her beauty had been confirmed with this recent makeover. This stylist had managed to uncover and harness the feminine power that had always been there. And she had put it on brilliant display. Those curves, not covered anymore, but flaunted, served up as if they were a rare delicacy that he wanted very much to consume.

And of course, other men were going to look at her this way. Other men were going to dance with her.

Another man was going to marry her. Take her to his bed.

It was the plan. It was his salvation. Resenting it now… Well, he was worse than a dog in the manger, so to speak. Much worse.

He made a fox and a hen house look tame. Of course, if he were the fox he would devour her. He would have no one and nothing to answer to.

He was not a fox. He was a king.

And he could not touch her. He *would* not. He would honor that final request his father had made. To keep her safe. To see her married to a suitable man.

He was not that man, and he never could be.

Even if their relationship wasn't as it was, he would not be for her. He might have been, once. But that possibility had been destroyed along with so many other things. He had very nearly been destroyed, too. But as he had set about to rebuild himself, he had made choices. Choices that would redeem the sins in the past. Not his sins to redeem. But that mattered little.

He was the one who had to live with the consequences. He was the one who had to rule a country with strength and unfailing wisdom.

And so, he had purposed he would.

But that did not make him the man for her.

Thank God the ball was happening now. Thank God this interminable nightmare was almost over.

She would choose one of the men in attendance tonight. He would be certain of that.

He stood at the back of the room, surveying the crowd of people. All of the women dressed in glorious ball gowns, none of whom would be able to hold a candle to Sophia, he knew. None of whom would be able to provide him with the distraction that he needed.

"This is quite lovely." He turned to see his stepmother standing beside him. She had been traveling abroad with friends for months, clearly needing time away to process the loss of her husband. Though she was back now, living in a small house on palace grounds.

It suited her, she said, to live close, but no longer in the palace.

She had lost a significant amount of weight since the death of his father, and she had not had much to lose on that petite frame of hers to begin with. She was elegant as ever, but there was a sadness about her.

She had truly loved his father. It was something that Luca had never doubted. Never had he imagined she was a commoner simply looking to better her station by marrying royalty. No, there had been real, sincere love in their marriage.

Something that Luca himself would never be able to obtain.

"Thank you," he said.

"And all of this is for Sophia?"

"Yes," he said. "It is as my father wished. He wanted to see her in a good marriage. And I have arranged to see that it is so."

"Yes," she said, nodding slowly. "But what does Sophia think?"

"She has agreed. In that, she has agreed to try to

find someone tonight. And if she does not, she has six months following to choose the man that she wishes. But I have confidence that one of the men tonight will attract her."

"I see," she said.

"You do not approve?"

"I married your father because I loved him. And one of the wonderful things that came with that marriage was money. With money came the kind of freedom that I never could have hoped Sophia to have if we had remained impoverished. I hate to see it curtailed."

"This is not curtailing her freedom. It is simply keeping with what is expected of those in our station. I have explained this to Sophia already."

"Yes, Luca. I have no doubt you have. You are very like your father in that you are confident that your way is always correct."

"My way is the best for a woman in her position. You must trust that I am the authority on this."

"You forget," his stepmother said, "I have been queen for a sizable amount of time. I did not just leave the village. So to speak."

"Perhaps not. But I was born into this. And you must understand that it is difficult to marry so far above your station. That is not an insult. But I know that it took a great deal for yourself and Sophia to adjust to the change. I know that Sophia still finds it difficult. Can you imagine if she married someone for whom this was foreign?"

"You make a very good point."

"This ball, this marriage, is not for my own amusement." It was for his salvation. However, he would leave that part unspoken.

Suddenly, the double doors to the ballroom opened, and all eyes turned to the entryway. There she was, a brilliant flash of fuchsia, her dark hair tumbling around her shoulders. She was even more beautiful than he had remembered. Golden curves on brilliant display, her skin gleaming in the light.

"Oh, my," her mother said.

"She got a new stylist," he said stiffly.

"Apparently."

Sophia descended the staircase slowly, and the moment one foot hit the bottom of the stair, her first suitor had already approached her. The Swede.

Sophia would probably be disappointed he didn't have a sheep on a leash to entertain her. Or a sweater.

"You do not approve of him?" his stepmother asked.

"Of course I approve of him. I approve of every man that I asked to come and be considered as a potential husband for Sophia."

"Then you might want to look less like you wish to dismember him."

"I am protective of her," he said, straightening and curling his hands into fists.

"If you say so."

He gritted his teeth. He did not like the idea that his stepmother of all people would find him transparent. He prided himself on his control, but Sophia tested it at every turn.

And so he told himself that the feeling roaring through him now was relief when the man took hold of Sophia and swept her around the dance floor.

The other man's hand rested perilously low on her waist, on the curve of her hip, and if he was to move his hand down and around her back he would be cup-

ping that lovely ass of hers. And that, Luca found unacceptable.

*He will not stop there if he marries her. He will touch
her everywhere. Taste her everywhere. She will belong to him.*

He gritted his teeth. That was the point. The point
was that she needed to belong to another man, so that
he could no longer harbor any fantasies of her.

As the song ended, another man approached Sophia,
and she began to dance with him. Another of her se-
lections.

Luca approached a woman wearing royal blue, and
asked her to dance. Kept himself busy, tried to focus on
the feel of her soft, feminine curves beneath his hands.
Because what did it matter if it was this woman, or another. What did it matter. Sex was sex. A woman's body
was a woman's body. He should be able to find enjoyment in it. He should not long for the woman in pink
across the room. The woman who was tacitly forbidden
to him. But he did.

The woman he held in his arms now might well have
been a cardboard cutout for all that she affected him.

But still, he continued to dance with her, knowing
that he should not. Knowing that dancing with any single woman this long would create gossip. He didn't even
know her name. He wouldn't ask for it. And tomorrow
he would not remember her face until he saw it printed
in the paper. She didn't matter.

Suddenly, Sophia extricated herself from her dance
partner's hold, excusing herself with a broad gesture as
she scurried across the ballroom.

"Excuse me," he said, releasing hold of his dance
partner, following after his stepsister.

Sophia wove through the crowd and made her way outside. He followed. But by the time he got out to the balcony, she was gone. He looked over the edge and saw a dark shape moving across the grass below. He could only barely make her out, the glow from the ballroom lights casting just enough gold onto the ground to highlight her moving shape. He swung his leg over the edge of the balcony and lowered himself down to the grass below, following the path that Sophia had no doubt taken.

He said nothing, his movements silent as he went after her. To what end, he didn't know. But then, he had no idea what she thought she was doing, either. It was foolish for her to leave the ball. And it was foolish for him to go after her. All of this was foolish. Everything with her. Always.

And yet, he couldn't escape her. That was the essential problem. She was unsuitable because of their connection. She was inescapable because of their connection. And for that reason, he had never been able to master it.

He could not have her; neither could he banish her from his life.

And here he was, chasing after her in a suit.

He was the king of a nation, stumbling in the dark after a woman.

Finally, she stopped, her pale shoulders shaking, highlighted by the light of the moon. He reached out, placing his hand on her bare skin. She jumped, turning to face him, her eyes glistening in the light. "Luca."

And suddenly, he knew exactly why he had gone after her. He knew exactly what the endgame was. Exactly why he was here.

"Sophia."

And then he wrapped her in his arms and finally did the one thing he had expressly forbidden himself from doing. He claimed her lips with his own.

CHAPTER FIVE

LUCA WAS KISSING HER. It was impossible. Utterly and completely impossible that this was happening. She was delusional. Dreaming. She had to be.

Luca *hated* her.

Luca saw himself as being so far above her that he would hardly deign to speak to her if they weren't re-lated by marriage.

He didn't want to kiss her. He didn't.

Except, with the little bit of brainpower that she had, she recalled that moment in the halls of the castle days ago. When she had gotten her makeover. He had grabbed hold of her arm and had told her he could not tell her how beautiful she was because it was pointless. Because nothing could come of it.

Did that mean he wished it could?

It had all felt like something too bright and too close then. Something she couldn't parse and didn't want to. Not when the end result would only be her own humil-iation. Even if he didn't know what she was thinking, entertaining the notion that Luca might want her had always seemed horrific, even if no one ever found out.

It was so surreal a thought that she was still asking

it even as those firm, powerful lips thrust hers apart, his tongue invading her mouth.

She had never been kissed like this before. Had never received anything beyond polite kisses that had seemed to be a testing of her interest.

Luca, true to form, was not testing her interest. He was *assuming* it. And she imagined that if he found her disinterested, he would work with all that he had to change her mind.

Except, his assumption was correct. And she did not possess the strength to deny that. Not now.

Not when her most cherished fantasy was coming to life, right here in the darkened garden of the palace.

Luca cupped her face, large, hot hands holding her steady as he angled his face and took her deeper.

He kissed exactly like what he was. An autocratic conqueror. A man who had never been denied a single thing in his life.

A man who would not be denied now.

"I cannot watch this," he rasped. "I cannot watch other men dance with you. Put their hands on you."

"You said… You said you had to find me a husband." Her voice was wobbly, tremulous, and she hated that. She wished—very much—that she could be more confident. That she could sound sophisticated. As if this was simply another garden tryst of many in a long line of them. Rather than the first time she had truly, honestly been kissed by a man.

Rather than a girl on the receiving end of something she had desired all of her life.

She didn't want him to know that. She didn't want him to know how she felt.

But then she imagined that she betrayed herself with

each breath, with each moment that passed when she didn't slap his face and call him ten kinds of scoundrel for daring to touch her in that way.

Of course she betrayed herself. Because, though he had been the one to instigate, she had kissed him back.

She had been powerless to do anything else. She had been far too caught up in it, consumed by it. By him.

The story of her life.

Things went well, and then Luca. And it all went to hell. It all belonged to him.

"I am going to find you a husband," he said. "I swore it to my father." He dragged his thumb along the edge of her lip. "But I cannot pretend I don't want you. Not any longer."

"You... You want me?"

"It is like a disease," he ground out. "To want my *sister* as I do."

"I'm not your sister," she said, her lips numb. "We don't have the same parents. We don't share blood at all."

"But don't you see? To my father you were. And you would be to the nation. An affair between the two of us would have disastrous consequences."

She closed her eyes, swallowing hard. "How?"

"Think of the headlines. About how our parents were married, and I debauched you likely from the moment you were beneath my roof. As a child. Or, you seduced me to try and hold on to your place. The nation has accepted you as a princess, without a blood relation, but reminding them so starkly that you do not carry royal blood is only a mistake. Can you imagine? An affair between two people who must thereafter remain family? It would be a disaster," he reiterated.

"Then why did you kiss me?"

"Because I no longer possess the power to *not* kiss you. He had his hands on you," he growled, grabbing hold of her hips and drawing her up against his body. "You may have only ever wanted one man before me. But I will make you forget him."

She gasped. She could feel the aggressive jut of his arousal against her stomach, could feel the intensity in the way he held her. His blunt fingertips dug into her skin, and she was certain that he would leave bruises behind. But she didn't care. She would be happy to bear bruises from Luca's touch. Whatever that said about her.

And then, he stopped talking. Then, that infuriating, arrogant mouth was back on hers, kissing, sucking and tasting. He angled his head, dragging his teeth along her tender lower lip before nipping her, growling as he consumed her yet again.

Sophia didn't know this game. She didn't know what to do next. Didn't know how to use her lips and tongue just so as Luca seemed to do.

So she battled against inexperience with enthusiasm, clinging to the front of his jacket with one hand, the other wrapped around his tie as she raised herself up on her toes and kissed him with all the needs she had inside her. She found herself being propelled backward, deeper into the garden. There was a stone bench there, and Luca gripped her hips, sliding his large, warm hands down her thighs, holding on to her hard as he lifted her so that her legs were wrapped around his waist. Then he brought both of them down onto the stone bench, with her sitting on his lap.

Her thighs were spread wide, the quivering, needy

heart of her pressed hard against that telltale ridge that shouted loudly to her that this wasn't a hallucination. That Luca did want her. That no matter it didn't make any sense, that no matter it went against everything she had always believed about him, about herself, about who they were, it was happening.

He moved his hands back to cup her rear, drawing her even more firmly against his arousal. Heat streaked through her veins, lightning shooting through her body. She had never felt anything like this. Like the all-consuming intensity of Luca. That sure and certain mouth tasting her, the friction slick and undeniably intoxicating. Like those big, hot hands all over her curves. His length between her thighs. He was everywhere. All around her. Flooding her senses. It wasn't just his touch. It was his flavor. His scent.

Familiar and so unfamiliar all at the same time. She knew Luca. From a distance. He had been in her life for so many years. Part of so many formative feelings that she'd had. He had most definitely been her very first fantasy. But those fantasies had been muted. They had not come close to the reality of the man himself. Of what it meant to be held by him, kissed by him, consumed by him.

This was no gauzy fantasy. This was something else entirely. It was harsh, and it was far too sharp. She was afraid it was going to slice her in two. The feelings of pleasure that she felt were nothing like the fluttery sensations that had built low in her stomach when he used to look at her across a crowded room. Were nothing compared to the swooping feeling she would get in her stomach when she would allow herself to imagine something half as racy as him kissing her on the mouth.

No. This was pain. Sharp between her legs. A hollow sensation at her core that terrified her, because she didn't feel as though he had created it just now so much as uncovered it. That she was hollow until she could be filled by him. That if he didn't, she would always remain this way.

Luca.

This was a raw, savage uncovering of desire. Desire that she had always known was there, but that had been muted, blunted, by her innocence. By the sure certainty that nothing could ever happen between them.

But now he wanted her. And she didn't know if she was strong enough to bear it.

Because it wasn't just what might happen next. No. It was what would happen when it ended. Then it would end. He had said as much.

He might have confessed his desire for her, but there were no other feelings involved. He had spoken of nothing tender. No. It was nothing but anger in Luca's eyes. Anger and lust.

That was what had been on his face when he had chased her down in the corridor days ago. Anger. Rage. And lust. The unidentified emotion in his eyes. The one she had not been brave enough to identify.

He moved his hand up the back of her head, cupping her skull, then he plunged his fingers deep into her locks, curling his hand into a fist and tugging hard, forcing her head backward, pressing his lips to the curve of her throat. And she felt like wounded prey at the mercy of a predator. Her most vulnerable parts exposed to him.

And yet she allowed it. Didn't fight against it. Wanted it.

Needed it.

That was the worst part. This was something more than want. This was part of her essential makeup.

She had been exposed to Luca at such an early age that he had been formative to her. That he was part of her journey to womanhood. So maybe this was apt. Terrifying though it might be, maybe this was something that needed to happen.

This wasn't the Middle Ages. None of those men out in the ballroom had been promised a virgin princess.

She owed them nothing, for now. For now, it was only Luca.

For now.

And that would have to be enough.

"Dear God," he rasped, dragging his tongue along the edge of her collarbone, down lower to where the plump curve of her breasts met the neckline of her dress. "I've lost my mind."

"I..." She was going to say something witty. Something about the fact that she had lost hers right along with him. But she couldn't speak. Instead, she heaved in a sharp breath, bringing that wicked mouth into deeper contact with her breast. He growled, jerking the top of her dress down, exposing her to him.

She had never been naked in front of a man before. She found she wasn't embarrassed. Certainly, the darkness out in the garden helped, but she knew that with the aid of the moonlight he could still see plenty. But it was Luca. The only man that she had ever been prepared to have seen her naked body. The only man she had ever fantasized about. This was terrifying. It went far beyond anything she had imagined. But it was with him.

And that made all the difference. It made every difference.

He said some words in Italian that she didn't understand. She was fluent enough, having lived in San Gennaro for so much of her life, but she didn't know these words. Hot and filthy-sounding, even without the translation. He scraped his cheek along that tender skin, his whiskers abrading her skin. And then he drew one aching, tightened nipple deep into his mouth, sucking hard.

She arched her back, crying out as pleasure pierced her core like an arrow.

He brought one hand up to cup her breast, rough and hot. She wanted to ask him why his hands were so rough. Wanted to ask him what he did to keep his body so finely honed. Why a man who should have the body of any man with a desk job looked as he did.

But she couldn't ask. All of her words, all of her questions, were bottled up in her throat, and the only thing that could escape was one hoarse cry as he moved from one breast to the next with his mouth, sucking the other nipple in deep, teasing her and tormenting her as he did.

For a moment she had the thought that this was too much too soon. She wasn't ready for this. How could she be? She had never even kissed a man before, and now she was in the arms of King Luca, her top pulled down, her breasts exposed. Riding the hard ridge of his arousal. How could that not be too much? How could she possibly withstand such a thing?

But suddenly, perhaps in time with the flex of his hips upward—that iron part of him making contact with the place where she was softest, most pliant and most sensitive—perhaps it was that that crystallized everything for her. It wasn't enough. And she had waited a lifetime for it. It didn't matter what experience or lack of it she'd had before. Not in the least. What mattered was that it was him.

That she had longed for, craved, desired this very thing for what felt like an eternity.

Luca. Her stepbrother. The man who seemed for all the world to find her utterly and completely beneath his notice, was kissing her. And she could not deny him anything that he wanted.

She could not deny herself what she wanted.

Luca's large, warm hands slid down the shape of her body as if he was taking her measurements with those strong fingers. Then they moved down farther, to her thighs, finding the hem of her dress, already pushed up partway, and shoving it up farther, exposing her even more.

He made a low, feral sound. Hungry. Untamed. Perhaps he was like this with all women; that was a possibility. One that she didn't want to think about. At least not too much. She would like to be special. But she had no idea how she could be. Anything between them was impossible, and she knew it. She had always known it. That didn't mean her feelings disappeared.

"I have wanted you," he said, his voice rough, as rough as the scrape of his whiskers against the side of her neck as he dragged a kiss down her throat. "It is a madness. It is like a sickness. And nothing…nothing has ever come close to banishing it from me. You are like a poison in my blood."

The words sounded tortured. Tormented. And for a moment she wondered if he felt even the slightest bit of what she had felt over the past years. And if he did… Then whatever this could be, and she had no illusions that it could be anything remotely close to permanent, she knew it was the right thing.

Madness. Sickness. Poison.

Those words described what she felt for Luca far too closely. They resonated inside her. They were her truth. And if they were his…how could she deny it?

She was no longer content to simply sit on his lap and be kissed. No. She wanted him. She wanted this. And she was going to have him.

She returned volley with a growl of her own, biting his lower lip as she moved her hands to that black tie that held his crisp, white shirt shut. With trembling fingers she undid the knot and pulled it open, then made quick work of the top button of that shirt. Followed by the next. And the next. She pushed the fabric apart, exposing muscles, chest hair and hot, delicious skin to her touch.

She had heard people talk about desire. But they had never said that it was so close to feeling ill. So close to feeling like you might die if you couldn't have what you wanted.

So close to pain.

There was a hollow ache between her legs, running through her entire body, and she felt that if it was not filled by him she wouldn't be able to go on. It was as simple as that.

She traced her fingertips over his chest, across his nipple, gratified by the rough sound of pleasure that exited his mouth as she did so. He wrapped his arms around her tightly, lowering his head again, tasting and teasing her breasts as he did. She had never imagined that insanity could be blissful. But hers certainly was. Magical in a way that she had not imagined it could be,

She had not thought that there could be beauty in torment. But there was. In this moment.

In this world they had created in the rose garden, separate from the concerns happening in the ballroom. The concerns of their lives, real lives, and not this stolen moment.

There were men in there that she was expected to consider seriously as husbands. A whole raft of duties and responsibilities waiting for both of them that had nothing to do with satisfying their pleasure under a starry sky with only the moon as witness.

But she was glad they had found this. This quiet space. The space where only they belonged. Where their parents' marriage didn't matter. Where their titles didn't matter. Where—whatever that could possibly mean to a man like Luca—they simply were Luca and Sophia, with nothing else to concern them.

He kept on saying things. Rough. Broken. Words in Italian and English. Some of which she couldn't understand, not so much because of the language barrier but because of the intensity in his words, the depth of them. The kinds of things he said, talking about doing things she had never imagined, much less spoken about.

But they washed over her in a wave, and she found she wanted them all. That she wanted this.

Him.

Broken, and out of control in a way that she had never imagined it was possible for Luca to be. At all other moments he was the picture of control. Of absolute and total certainty. And in this moment he did not seem as though he had the power to be that man.

It made her feel powerful. Desired.

His hands moved between her thighs, sliding between the waistband of her panties and teasing her where she was wet and ready for him. For a moment she felt a fleeting sense of embarrassment, a scalding heat in her cheeks. Because certainly now he would know how much she wanted him. How much she felt for him. What woman would be like this if she didn't? And there, he found the incontrovertible evidence. But if it bothered him, he didn't show it. Instead, he seemed inflamed by it. Seemed to want her all the more.

"Perhaps later," he rasped, kissing her neck, her cheek, making his way back to her lips. "Perhaps later I will take my time. Will be able to savor you as you should be. But now... I find there is not enough time, and I must have you."

She wanted him to have her. Whatever that might mean. She needed it.

He shifted, undid the closure on his pants and wrapped his arms tightly around her, angling her hips so that she was seated above him, the head of his arousal pressing against the entrance to her body.

And then he thrust up into her, deep and savage, giving no quarter to her innocence at all. It hurt. But Luca didn't seem to notice. Instead, he began to move inside her in hard, decisive thrusts. She couldn't catch her breath. But then, she didn't want to. Even as she felt like she was being invaded, conquered, she didn't want him to stop. Even as it hurt, she didn't want him to stop. Gradually, the pain gave way to pleasure, an overwhelming, gripping sense of it that built inside her until she thought she wouldn't be able to take it much longer.

When it broke over her it was like a wave containing a revelation, pleasure like she had never known bursting through her. If she had looked up to find fireworks in the sky she wouldn't have been surprised. But the only thing above her was stars. The fireworks were in her.

They were the fireworks.

She and Luca together.

She held on to him tightly as she rode out her release, pulsing waves that seemed to go on and on crashing inside her endlessly. Then he gripped her hips hard, driving himself up into her with brute force as he found his own release, a growl vibrating through his chest as he did.

And then somehow, it was over. Nothing but the sound of their breathing, the feel of his heart pounding heavily against her hand, where it rested against his sweat-slicked chest.

The night sky no longer seemed endless. Instead, it pressed down on them, the reality of what had just occurred lowering the blackness but leaving the stars out of reach.

She felt dark. Cold.

She was cold. Because she was naked in a garden.

Luca moved her away from him, beginning to straighten his clothing. "We must go back," he said, his tone remote and stiff.

"How?" she asked. Because she had a feeling he did not just mean to the ball, but to the way things had been before he had touched her. Before that rock wall had broken between them and revealed what they had both desired for so long.

"It doesn't matter how. Only that it must be."

She looked at him, searching his face in the darkness. "I don't know if I can."

"But you must," he said, uncompromising.

The light from the moon cast hollows of his face

into light and shadow, making it look as though he was carved out of the very granite his voice seemed to be made of.

"You will go back into that ballroom and you will dance with the rest of the men you said you would dance with. Then you will choose a husband," he continued.

"Luca," she said, her voice breaking. "I can't do that. Not after I was just…"

"It is only sex, *sorellina*," he said, the endearment landing with a particular sharpness just now. "You will find a way to cope."

Panic attacked her, its sharp, grasping claws digging into her. "I was a virgin, you idiot."

That stopped him. He drew back as though he had been slapped.

"You said…you said you wanted a man."

She looked away, her shame complete now, her face so hot she was sure she was about to burst into flame. "Who do you think I wanted, you fool?"

The silence that fell between them was heavy. As if the velvet sky had fallen over the top of them.

"Not the choice I would have made my first time. But the choice was yours. You had every chance to say no. You did not." Suddenly his tone turned fierce. "Am I to assume you didn't want to? Are you trying to imply that you didn't know what you were doing?"

"No," she said. "I knew what I was doing."

"Then I fail to see what your virginity has to do with any of it. This is hardly Medieval times. No one will expect a virgin princess on their wedding night anyway."

"I suppose not."

"I must go back. I am the host, after all. Take all the time you need to gather yourself."

He said that as though she should be impressed with his softness. With his kindness. She was about to tell him how ludicrous that was, but then he turned and walked away, leaving her there, half-naked on a stone bench, having just lost her virginity to her stepbrother. To her king.

Her lungs were going to cave in on themselves. Collapse completely, along with her heart. It was shattered anyway, so it didn't matter where the pieces landed.

This was her fantasy. That bright little spot of hope that had existed somewhere inside her, a glimmer of what could be that kept her warm on the darkest of nights.

Now it was gone. Snuffed out. As dark as the night around her.

When she went to bed at night, she would no longer wonder. Because she knew. It had been better than she had imagined. Had transformed her. In more ways than the physical. He had been inside her. Joined to her. This man that had held her emotions captive for half of her life.

This man she'd spent nights weaving beautiful, gilded stories about in her head before she fell asleep. If only. If maybe. If someday.

But it had happened. And now there was no more rest in *if only*.

Nothing remained but shattered dreams.

He acted as though they would be able to go back to normal. But Sophia knew she would never be the same again.

CHAPTER SIX

SOPHIA HAD AVOIDED him for the past few weeks. Ever since she had gone back into the ballroom and proceeded to dance with every man he had commanded her to.

She had been pale-faced and angry-looking, but gradually, it had all settled into something serene, though no less upset.

But he did not approach her. Not again. And she moved around the palace as if she were a ghost.

He had failed her. Had failed them both. But there was nothing to be done. There was no use engaging in a postmortem. His control had failed him at the worst possible moment.

He had done the one thing he had purposed he would never do. And it had been all much more a spectacular failure than he had initially imagined it would be.

A *virgin*.

He had not thought she would be that.

She had gone to university. Had moved out in the world for quite some time, and she was beautiful. In his mind, irresistible. Hell, in practice she was irresistible. Had he been able to resist her, then he surely would have.

No man could possibly resist her. If his own ironclad control had failed...

So perhaps that was his pride. Because clearly she had somehow remained untouched all this time.

And he had failed at maintaining that particular status quo.

But that other man had been touching her. Holding her in his arms.

Perversely, he was satisfied by the fact that he had been the first man to touch her. It was wrong. And he should feel a deep sense of regret over it. Part of him did. But another part of him gloried in it.

As with all things Sophia, there was no consensus between desire and morality.

The only contact he'd had with Sophia had been for her to tell him that she wanted to speak with him today. And so he sat in his office, his hands curled into fists, resting on the top of his desk while he waited for her to appear.

The fact that she never failed to put him on edge irked him even now.

There'd never been a more pointless and futile attraction in the history of the world. Or, perhaps there had been, but it had not bedeviled him, and so, it didn't concern him now. No, it was Sophia who had that power over him.

And she was not for him.

There was no way he could reconfigure their fates to make it so. No way that he could switch around their circumstances. Even if she weren't his stepsister...

He was not the man for her.

The door to his office cracked slightly, and she slipped inside, not knocking. Not waiting for an announcement. Because of course she wouldn't. Of course she would break with protocol, even now. Not allowing the blessed formality inherent in royal life to put some distance between them when it was much needed.

"You wished to come and speak to me?"

"Yes," she said. "But I should think that was self-evident. Considering that I made an arrangement to come and speak to you, and now I am here doing it."

"There is no need to be sarcastic, Sophia."

"I'm surprised you recognized it, Luca."

For a moment their eyes caught and held, the sensation of that connection sending a zap of electricity down through his body.

She looked away as though she had felt that same sensation. As though it had burned.

"I recognize it easily enough. What did you wish to speak to me about?"

"I wanted to tell you that I've made my selection. I've decided who I will marry."

That was the last thing he had expected, and her words hit him with the force of a punch squared to the chest. So intense, so hard, he thought it might have stopped his heart from beating altogether.

"You have?"

"Yes. I hope that you value an alliance with Sweden."

He had not been aware that he possessed the ability to feel finer emotions. Until he felt a last remaining piece of himself—one he had not realized existed—turn to stone. "I'm surprised to hear you say that."

"That I selected him specifically? Or that I have selected anyone at all?"

"That you have complied at all. Rather than making this incredibly difficult."

She clasped her hands in front of her, her dark hair falling down into her face. The outfit she was wearing was much more suited to her than her usual fare. Tight, as that ball gown on the night he had first kissed her had been. A tangerine-colored top that shaped exquisitely to her curves, and a skirt with a white and blue pattern.

But the pattern was secondary to the fact that it hugged her body like a second skin. As he wished he could hug her even now. What he wouldn't give to span that glorious waist again, to slide his palms down to those generous hips.

Having her once had done nothing to eradicate the sickness inside him.

But this marriage… Perhaps it would accomplish what he had hoped it would.

And in the end, he would still have been the one to have her first.

Yes. But he will have her second, if he hasn't had her already, and you will have to watch the two of them together.

He had always known that would be his fate. There was no fighting against it.

"I had some very important questions answered the night of the ball," she said, making bold eye contact with him. "I have no reason to fight against this marriage. Not now."

There was an unspoken entreaty in those words, and it was one he could not answer.

He would have to marry, yes, that was certain. But it would never be a woman like her. It would be a woman who understood. One who didn't look at him with hope in her eyes.

One who wouldn't mind that the part of him that could care for another person, the part of him that loved, had been excised with a scalpel long ago.

That he was a man who ruled with his head because he knew a heart was no compass at all. Least of all his.

It felt nothing. Nothing at all.

"Excellent," he said. "I'm glad there's no longer a barrier."

Color flew to her cheeks, and he did nothing to correct her assumption that he had made an intentional double entendre. He had not. But if it made her angry, all the better.

"Let me know how soon you wish for the wedding to be, and I will arrange it."

"In a month," she said quickly. "We are to be married in a month."

"Then I will prepare an announcement."

Sophia's head hurt. Her heart hurt. Everything hurt. The depression that she had fallen under since the ball was pronounced. It made everything she did feel heavy. Weighted down.

The engagement to Erik hadn't helped matters. The courtship in general hadn't helped at all. And she felt like a terrible person. He was solicitous, kind. Their interactions had not been physical at all. The idea of letting him touch her so closely to when she and Luca had…

Though part of her wondered if she should. Like ripping off a Band-Aid.

The mystery was gone from sex anyway.

A tear slid down her cheek and she blinked, shocked, because she hadn't realized she had been so close to crying. She wiped it away and swallowed hard, attempting to gather herself.

She was currently getting a wedding gown fitted. That meant she had to look a little bit less morose. Though, right now, she was sitting in the room alone, wearing nothing but a crinoline.

Both the seamstress and her mother would be in the room soon, and she really needed to find a way to look as if she was engaged in the process.

But then, she felt as if she had not been engaged in the process of her life for the past few weeks, so why should this be any different?

It had been foolish, perhaps, to jump into marrying Erik, simply because she wanted to do something to strike back at Luca. Simply because she wanted there to be something in her life that wasn't that deep, yawning ache to be with him.

They couldn't be together. It was that simple. He didn't want to be with her. Oh, he had certainly revealed that he lusted after her in that moment in the garden, but it wasn't the same as what she felt for him.

And furthermore, he was allowing her to marry another man.

Another tear splashed onto her hand.

Was that why she was doing this? Was that why she was going through with the engagement? Because she wanted him to stop it?

That was so wholly childish and ridiculous.

And yet she had a feeling she might be just that ridiculous and childish.

The door to the dressing room opened, and the designer and her mother breezed inside at the same time.

Her mother was holding the dress, contained in a plastic zip-up bag, and the designer was carrying a kit.

"Let's help you get this on," the woman said briskly.

Sophia's mother unzipped the bag and helped Sophia pull the dress over her head as the designer instructed. There was much pinning and fussing and exclamation, and Sophia tried very hard to match those sounds.

"Are you okay?" her mother asked as the designer was down on her hands and knees pinning the hem of the gown.

"I'm...overwhelmed." She figured she would go for some form of honesty. It was better than pretending everything was fine when it clearly wasn't, and her mom wasn't going to accept that as an answer.

"It is understandable. This wedding has come together very quickly."

"It's what Luca wants."

"I see."

"It's what Father wanted."

"And what do you want, Sophia? Because as much as I loved your stepfather, and as much as I know he had your best interests at heart... I didn't marry him because I wanted to be queen. I didn't marry him for money, or status. I married him because I loved him. And I want nothing less for you. I understand that he did this because it is what he would have done for his biological daughter if he'd had one. You are not from this world. And you don't have to comply to the dictates of it if you don't wish to."

What was the alternative? Living life with Luca glowering down at her. Wanting him. Watching him get married and have children...

Well, it was that or cutting herself off from her family altogether.

For a moment she stood adrift in that fantasy. Blowing in a breeze where she was tied to nothing and no one. It made her feel empty, hollow. Terrified.

But at least it didn't hurt.

"I want this," she said, resolute. "It's the right thing. And he's a very nice man."

Her mother sighed heavily. "I'm sure that he is."

"You know that Luca wouldn't allow this if he wasn't suitable. If he wasn't good."

"Certainly not," she said. "I know Luca would never allow any harm to come to you. Not physical harm, anyway."

Sophia gritted her teeth, wondering, not for the first time, if her mother suspected that there was something between Luca and herself. If she did, she was not saying anything. Resolutely so.

And Sophia certainly wasn't going to say anything.

She looked down and kicked the heavy skirt of her dress out of the way, and then she straightened, looking at herself in the mirror. Suddenly, she felt dizzy, wobbling slightly as she took in the sight of herself wearing a wedding gown. A wedding gown.

She felt ill.

"Excuse me," she said, clamoring down from the stepstool and dashing into the adjoining bathroom, slamming the door behind her as she collapsed onto her knees and cast up her accounts into the toilet.

She braced herself, shaking and sweating, breathing hard. She had never been sick like that. So abruptly.

She felt terrible. Throwing up hadn't helped.

She pushed herself up, afraid that she had damaged the gown, but it looked intact.

There was a heavy, sharp knock on the door. "Sophia?" It was her mother. Worried, obviously.

"I'm fine," she said. "Just a little bit…nauseated."

"Can I come in?"

"Okay."

The door opened and her mother slipped inside, her expression full of concern. "Are you ill?"

"I wasn't," Sophia said.

"You just suddenly started to feel sick?"

"Yes."

"Sophia…" Her mother looked at her speculatively, "forgive me if this is intrusive… Is it possible that you… Are you pregnant?"

The tentative grasp that Sophia had on the ground beneath her gave way. And she found herself crumbling to the floor again.

"Sophia?"

"I…"

"Are you pregnant?" her mother asked.

"It's possible," she said.

"I suppose the good thing is that the wedding is soon," she said, bending down and grabbing hold of Sophia's chin, her matching dark gaze searching Sophia's. "Are you happy?"

"I'm scared," Sophia said.

She couldn't organize her thoughts. She was late. It was true. She hadn't given it much thought because she had been stressed out with planning the wedding. But she was quite late. And she and Luca had not used a condom that night.

One time.

She'd had sex one time.

With the last man on earth she should have ever been with, and she had gotten pregnant. What were the odds of that happening?

Of course, now she was engaged to another man, a man whose baby it couldn't possibly be, because she had never even kissed him.

But there was going to be a wedding. Invitations had been sent out. Announcements had been made. She was being fitted for a dress.

"Of course you are," her mother said. "It's a terrifying thing facing a change like this. But wonderful." She put her hand on Sophia's face. "You're the best thing that ever happened to me, Sophia."

Sophia tried to smile. "I hope I'll be even half as good a mother as you have been to me."

"You will be."

"I wish I had such confidence."

"You will have help from your husband," her mother said. "I didn't have any help. It will be so nice for you to start with more in life than we had."

Sophia's mouth felt dry as chalk. How could she tell her mother that it wasn't her fiancé's baby?

That it was Luca's.

She couldn't. So she didn't. Instead, she let her mother talk excitedly about the wedding, about being a grandmother. Instead, she went outside and finished the fitting.

When it was over, she walked down the empty halls of the palace, back in her simple shift dress she had been wearing earlier. Then she pushed the door to her bedroom open. She looked around. At this beautiful spectacular bedroom that it was still difficult to believe belonged to her.

She stumbled over to her bed, a glorious, canopied creation with frothy netting and an excess of pillows.

Then she lay across that bed and she wept. She wept like her heart was breaking.

Because it was.

And she had no idea what to do about it.

CHAPTER SEVEN

ULTIMATELY, SOPHIA FELT it was wisest to procure a test through the official palace physician. The princess was hardly going to go to a drugstore to acquire a pregnancy test. It would be foolish. Things like that could never stay secret, not for long. Not in a media-hungry society, always looking for scandal.

One of the many things she'd had to learn, because it wasn't ingrained. That anyone would be interested in the life and times of a girl like her. But they were now. Because of who her mother had married.

Because of who she was, all thanks to a piece of paper. Nothing more.

Oftentimes, she appreciated what had come from that marriage.

This was one of the times she appreciated it less.

Fortunately, she trusted the woman that she had seen for years, recommended to her by palace staff. And she knew that her confidentiality was in fact one of the most important parts of her role as the physician to all members of the royal family, and palace staff.

Unfortunately, no matter how good the doctor was, she could not change the test results with skill.

Sophia paced back and forth while she waited. She

knew pregnancy tests didn't take *that* long. Still, the doctor was certainly taking her time in the makeshift lab, AKA, Sophia's en-suite bathroom.

When the door finally did open, the doctor looked blank. Sophia couldn't read a plus or negative sign on the woman's face. "The test is positive," she said. "Congratulations."

Sophia didn't want to be congratulated. Why should she be? She'd made a massive mistake and put everything Luca believed in in jeopardy. She was risking public embarrassment, wasted money on a wedding…she… she deserved something. But it wasn't congratulations.

"Thank you," Sophia said, instead of any of the things she was thinking. "The wedding is soon at least, so all will be sorted."

Except, she had no idea how to sort it out. This wedding was happening. All of the moving parts were at critical mass.

Tomorrow. The wedding was tomorrow. People were coming from all over to attend.

She was going to have to go to him. She was going to have to see Erik and let him know exactly what transpired. Likely, he would want to break it off. But it was entirely possible that…

She had no idea what she was supposed to do. Was she going to hide Luca's child from him? And what would he think? There was no way he would believe that she had immediately gone to bed with another man. He would know the child was his.

Would he?

It was entirely possible she could convince him she had played the role of harlot. That she had gone straight from Luca, on a garden bench, to Erik's bed.

But Erik was blond, while Luca was dark, darker than she was. The child would not look like Erik.

"I just need some time alone," Sophia said finally. "That's all I need."

The doctor nodded, collecting things and leaving Sophia in her bedroom. Leading her to solve a problem that might well be utterly and completely unsolvable.

She walked over to the closet and opened it up, letting her hands drift over the silk fabric of the wedding gown that was hanging there.

She was carrying Luca's baby. And she was supposed to walk toward another man tomorrow and say vows to him. Promise to love him, stay with him forever. She was supposed to have her wedding night with him.

A violent wave of nausea rolled over her.

She had been lying to herself this entire time. Thinking that she could do this. Thinking that she could be with another man. That she could make all of her feelings for Luca go away if she only tried hard enough. That if she replaced him in her bed she could replace him in her heart, but she didn't know how that could possibly be.

She swallowed hard, her throat dry. There was no going back. Not now.

There couldn't be. There was so much riding on this. Luca was right. Deals had already been made with Erik regarding his holdings, based on this marriage. Luca's reputation…in the eyes of the people, of the world, it mattered.

San Gennaro's reputation depended on Luca's. And…this could potentially compromise that.

And she had to think of that.

It had nothing to do with her being afraid. With her

feeling raw and wounded. Nothing at all. It was the greater good. Not…not the fact that thinking of Luca hurt.

Yes, Erik she was going to have to talk to. Because she owed her future husband honesty if nothing else.

Luca…

She had a feeling it would not be a kindness to give him honesty.

Her head throbbed, her entire body feeling wrung out. She knew that her logic was fallible at best. She knew that she was wrong in so many ways, but she couldn't untangle it all to figure it out.

She picked up the phone, and she dialed the number she needed to call most.

"Hello?"

"Erik," she said, not sure if she was relieved or terrified that he'd answered. "There's something I need to tell you."

"You are not running out on the wedding, are you?"

"*You* might. When you hear what I have to say." She swallowed. "I'm pregnant."

There was nothing but silence for a moment.

"Well," he said, his tone grim. "We both know it isn't mine."

"Yes. We do. But…no one else has to know that. It would be for the best if the baby's father didn't know. And I can't have anyone… I can't have anyone knowing." She tightened her hold on her phone, her heart hammering so hard she could scarcely hear herself speak. "But only if that… If it doesn't offend you in some way."

"I cannot say I'm pleased about it. Though I appreciate the fact that you did not try to pass it off as mine."

"I wouldn't have done that," she said quickly. "Before we get married, you have to know the truth."

"Whose is it?" he asked.

She hesitated. "I cannot give you *that* truth. That's the one thing I can't tell. Trust me on this one thing. I know I made a mistake, but I told you this much. I'm not trying to trick you."

"I see," he said, his tone brave. "You didn't know you were pregnant before now?"

"I swear I didn't."

There was a long pause, silence settling over her, over the room, the furniture groaning beneath its weight.

"It is too late to turn back," he said at last. "I require this union with your country. The alliance and the agreements that were promised to me... I want to see them honored. And if we were to cancel the wedding at such a late date the resulting scandal would be a serious issue."

"Yes," she replied, her lips numb. "That is my feeling on it, as well."

"Then we will go ahead with the wedding."

She must have agreed, but she couldn't remember what she said the moment after she'd spoken the words.

Sophia hung up the phone, not feeling any sense of relief at all. She curled up into a ball on the bed as hopelessness washed through her. Tomorrow it would be finished. It would finally be over.

Except, it never would be. Because whatever the world believed, whatever anyone knew...

The child in her womb was Luca's. A part of him. A part of her. The evidence of their passion, of her love. A bright and shining thing that she would never be able to ignore.

But Luca had been clear. There can be no scandal. She would not subject their child to that. She would not subject him to it.

And so she would have to subject herself to this.

For the second night in a row, Sophia cried herself to sleep.

The morning of the wedding dawned bright and clear, and Sophia awoke feeling damaged. Empty.

Except she wasn't empty. She was carrying Luca's child.

That fact kept rolling through her mind on a reel all while her hair was fixed, her makeup done, her gown given its final fittings.

Her mother looked at her with shining eyes, pride in them. Misplaced.

So badly misplaced.

"Are you all right?" she asked.

"Nervous," she said honestly.

It echoed the exchange they'd had during the fitting. But it was all the more real now. Her tongue tasted like metal, her whole body like a leaden weight.

"Did you take a test?" her mother asked.

"Yes," Sophia said.

"And?"

"It's positive," Sophia returned. "I'm having a baby."

Her mother held her for a long time before letting her go finally. "Have you told Erik?"

"Yes."

If her mother thought something was amiss—and Sophia thought she might—the other woman said nothing. Instead, they continued readying themselves for the ceremony. Then, a half hour before everything was set to begin, Sophia was ushered into a private room where no one could see her. Where the big reveal of the bride would be preserved.

It was dark in there. Quiet. The first moment of reflection she'd had all day. Her veil added an extra layer of insulation against reality. And gave her too much time to think.

She resented it. She didn't want to reflect on anything. She wanted all of this to be over.

She wanted it done, so that there was no going back. She wanted her wedding night done.

Wanted that moment to pass so that Luca would no longer be the only one who'd had claim on her body. So that perhaps she could start building some sort of bond with Erik.

As if you believe that will work.

She had to. What other choice did she have? Tell her *stepbrother* she was having his baby? A stepbrother who didn't seem to want her as more than a physical diversion? Even if it wasn't for the potential scandal…

Luca had been more than willing to send her straight to the arms of another man out of his sense of duty, after taking her virginity in an open space where anyone could have caught them.

Yes, on some deep level she felt this was a betrayal of Luca, but she felt as if he had betrayed her first.

He had made no move to stop this wedding. None at all. He was truly going to let her marry another man.

Then she realized that all this time she had been hoping he would stop it. That he would step in. He said he could not stand to have another man touch her, as he had done the night of the ball.

In the end she had hoped, beyond reason, beyond anything, that he would make this stop.

But he had not.

The realization was like a hot iron through her chest. What a fool she was. She'd been clinging to hope, even now. Hope was why she was here. Because she kept imagining…

She squeezed her eyes shut, a tear streaming down her cheek.

She would be damned if she would go crawling to him. Confess to him she was pregnant with his child when he had already made it clear he did not want her.

And perhaps it was wrong. Perhaps she had no right to those feelings.

Perhaps, as the father, regardless of the fallout, he should be made aware of the baby.

But she couldn't.

Because what if he stopped it all then? What if that was the only reason?

How could she live with herself after that? How could she live with him?

Suddenly, the door to her little sanctuary burst open. His hands clenched into fists, his expression unreadable.

Luca.

CHAPTER EIGHT

RAGE ROLLED THROUGH Luca like a thunderstorm. There she was. His duplicitous stepsister. Her expression obscured by a veil, her figure a stunning tease in that virginal-looking gown.

They both knew she wasn't a virgin.

He had been the one to ruin that, to ruin her. He was well aware.

And then there was the other bit of evidence that she was not as innocent as she currently appeared to be.

"Are you here to give me away?" she asked, her tone maddeningly calm.

"Is that what you want? You want me to march you out of here and pass you off from my arm to his? Fair enough, as you seem to have gone from my bed and straight into his."

He waited for her to correct him on that. But she did not.

"It's a bit late to be acting possessive, *fratello*."

The word *brother* stabbed into him. Sharp. Enraging. The reason she was here prepared to marry another man in the first place.

"Is it now?" It did not feel too late. It felt altogether like just the right time.

She took a step back, stammering. Wondering if she had overplayed her hand. "I'm in a wedding gown. The guests have all arrived. I assume there is a priest."

"You know as well as I do that there is."

"Then unless you intend to give me to my groom, symbolically, of course, I suggest you step aside."

He crossed his arms, standing between Sophia and the door. "Absolutely not."

"I need to go, Luca," she said, her tone pleading with him.

"Answer me one question first," he said, taking a step toward her. His heart was pushing the limits of what a man could endure, he was certain, his stomach twisted.

"What question?" she asked.

"Have you slept with him?" He asked the question through gritted teeth, his entire body tense.

She turned to the side, the veil a cascade of white and bland separation, concealing her expression from him. "I don't see how that's any concern of yours."

"It is my concern if I say it is," Luca returned. "Answer the question, Sophia. And if you lie to me, I will find out."

Suddenly, her posture changed. She came alive. As though she'd been shocked with a live wire.

"Oh, no," she said, delicate hands balled into fists. "I haven't slept with him. But I intend to do so tonight. I would show you the lingerie I selected, but that would be a bit embarrassing. After all, you are only my very concerned stepbrother."

A red haze lowered itself over Luca's vision.

Anger was like a living thing inside him, roaring, tearing him to pieces. He had no idea what answer he would have preferred. One that proved she had been touched by another man, but might not be attempting to deceive them both…or this.

She was doing exactly what he had suspected. And by admitting that, she had also confirmed what he had suspected, his heart raging, when those lab results had come across his desk only an hour ago.

He had imagined…

He had imagined that she would come to him if the news was relevant to him.

She had not. But there was a chance. He had known that. Even if she had slept with Erik the day after she had been with him, there would be a chance.

And here, she had made it very clear, that there was only one possibility.

Still, she hadn't come to him. As if on some level she knew. Knew she should not bind herself to him. As if she could see the cracks in his soul.

If he were a good man, if any of his outward demonstrations of royal piety were deeper than skin, he would let her be.

Would let her go off and marry Erik.

But he had reached an end. An end to the show he had lived for the past two decades.

An end to anything remotely resembling *good*.

"We will have to send our regards to Erik," he said, taking a step forward.

"Why is that?"

"Because I…" He reached forward, grabbing the end of her veil, lifting it and drawing it over her head, revealing that impossibly lovely face that had called to him for years now. That was his constant torment. His constant desire. "I am about to kiss his bride for him."

Luca drew her into his arms; she was his now. There was no denying it. There was no other alternative.

When they parted, she was staring at him, wide eyed.

"And he," Luca continued, his voice rough, "is about to find himself without a wife."

Then he lifted her up and threw her over his shoulder, ignoring the indignant squeak that exited her lips.

"What are you doing?" She pounded a fist against his back.

They were turning into a bad farce of a classic film. And he didn't care. Not one bit.

"Well," he said, continuing to hold her fast. "It seems that we have skipped a few steps. Here you are, in a wedding dress, but our relationship has already been consummated. And it appears that you are pregnant with my child."

"Luca!"

"Did you think I wouldn't find out?" He carried her out of the chapel and across the lawn. It was private back here; paparazzi and guests both barred from coming into this section of the grounds, where the bride might be disturbed. And here, Luca had a private plane waiting.

Just in case.

Just in case of this exact moment.

It felt like madness. Like something that had overcome him in the moment. Strong enough he'd had to pick her up and haul her off.

But obviously some of his madness was premeditated.

Though he had not envisioned this exact scenario, it was clear to him now there had never been another possible outcome.

"Forgive me," he said, not meaning at all. "But I feel as though at this moment in time a wedding ceremony is a bit redundant. We are headed off on our honeymoon."

"We can't," she protested, beating against him again with one closed, impotent fist.

A rather limp, ineffective protest, all in all. When the poor creature could scarcely move.

"I am the king, *sorellina*. And I can do whatever I want."

Yes. He was king. And he could do whatever the hell he wanted. He had been far too caught up in being honorable. In being dutiful to his country. In doing as his father had asked. In doing as his country expected.

In protecting Sophia. Making sure she had the life that would best suit her, not the one that would best please him.

What the hell was the point of being king if you didn't take everything that you desired?

And he desired his stepsister. She was also carrying his heir.

That meant that she would be his.

Regardless of what anyone thought.

It was all clear and bright now. As if the sun had come out from behind the clouds.

"What if I refuse?" she asked.

He carried her up the steps, onto the plane, holding her still while his staff secured the cabin. None of them daring to question him. "You're not in a position to refuse," he said as he placed her in one of the leather seats and solicitously fastened her seat belt. "You are only in a position to obey."

She didn't speak to him for the entirety of the flight. He supposed on some level that was understandable.

She simply sat there and looked at him, radiating rage and tulle, resembling an indignant cake topper. Disheveled, from his carrying her out across the lawn and onto the plane, her hot eyes bright and angry, that lovely lace wedding gown making her look the perfect picture of a bride.

She would need a new wedding gown for when they married. As beautiful as she looked now he would be damned if she walked down the aisle toward him in a dress she had meant for someone else.

That was not something he could endure. He found that he was quickly getting to the end of his endurance where she was concerned.

Scandal was something to be avoided at all costs. It was something his mother had drilled into his head even after she had known...

She had protected the reputation of the family.

And now he was about to destroy that. Then it called into question a great many things.

But here was the point where he had to break from his desire to prevent scandal.

Because if there was one thing, one bitter shard of anger that existed in his chest that cut deeper than all the others, it was the fact that his mother had prized reputation over protecting her son.

Over pursuing retribution for him.

She had cared more for her marriage. More for her paramour.

He would not care more for a clean slate than for this child that Sophia carried. He had needed to marry. Had needed to produce an heir, and it seemed that he was halfway there already. Why should he preserve the nation, their sensibilities, and ignore the fact that this was a moment to seize on something that would be an important asset. Truly, he could not have planned this better.

Because there was only one way that he would be able to justify claiming Sophia as his own. Only one way he would be able to justify having her in his bed for life.

The child.

That, no one would be able to argue with. And yes, it would come at the cost of an ugly scandal. The things that would be written about them…

They would not be kind.

Those headlines would exist, and it was something that their child would have to contend with. Something they would have to contend with.

But in the end, the memory would fade, and they would be husband and wife longer than they had ever been stepbrother and stepsister.

In the end, it would work.

Because it had to.

He was not in the mood to allow the world to defy him. He was not in the mood to think in terms of limits.

He had, for far too long.

He was a king, after all.

And for too long he had allowed that to limit him.

No more.

"Do you want to know where we're going?" he asked, leaning back in his seat and eyeing the bar that sat across the cabin.

"I don't wish to know anything," she said, pale of face and tight-lipped with rage.

"Did you love him so much that this is an affront to you?"

"I tried," she said, whipping around to face him, her dark curls following the motion.

"I tried to do the right thing. I tried to do what you asked of me. I was willing to—"

He could not hear her lies. He held up a hand and stopped her speaking. "You were willing to try to pass my child off as another man's. For that, I cannot forgive you."

"You were willing to let me marry another man," she said. "Only when you found out that I was carrying your child did you try and stop it. You took my virginity in a garden. You gave no thought to protecting me. You took advantage of my innocence. You were going to let another man have me. For that, I cannot forgive *you*." She looked away from him again, pressing one hand to her stomach. "He knew it was not his child, Luca. Whatever you think of me, I would not try and convince another man that this baby was his."

"Does he know it's mine?"

She looked toward him, her dark eyes flashing. "I told him it was the one thing we could never speak of."

"I know you only found out yesterday," he said.

"How did *you* find out?" she asked.

"The palace physician reports directly to me, Sophia. In these matters, there is no privacy."

Her face drained of the rest of its color, her entire frame shaking with rage. And perversely, even in the moment, he found his eyes drawn, outlined to perfection by the sweetheart neckline of the gown, to the delicate swell of her breasts.

A sickness. Sophia would always be his sickness.

"How dare you?"

"I dare *everything*," he said, his voice like granite

even to his own ears. "I am the King of San Gennaro. You are pregnant with my heir. You would have me leave that to chance?"

"I was trying to prevent a scandal. And I don't want your obligation, Luca."

"You have it," he bit out. "Endlessly, *sorellina*, and there is no way around that."

"Would you have let me marry him?"

His throat tightened, adrenaline working its way through his veins. He closed his hands into fists and squeezed them. "Of course," he said. "Because when it comes to matters of the flesh, you can hardly allow them to dictate the course of a country."

"Except, apparently, when that flesh takes shape as a child."

"Naturally," he bit out. "I will hardly allow another man to raise my child. I will hardly sacrifice my son's birthright on the altar of my reputation. On this you are correct, Sophia. I was careless with you. And that carelessness should not come back on our child."

"It might not be a son. It might be a daughter. In which case, you might wish you had allowed me to marry someone else."

"Never," he said, his voice rough.

"You don't seem overly happy."

"Happiness is not essential here. What is essential is duty. What is essential is that I do what is right by my child."

"Yes, I suppose it is what your father tried to do for me. Bundle me up and sell me off to the most worthy of men."

"Yes, and sadly you seem to be stuck with me."

She said nothing to that. He imagined she didn't think he meant it. He did.

He had his darkness. He had his trauma, and he would never have chosen to lock Sophia into a union with him. But the fact remained, it was unavoidable now.

And if that meant he got to sate his desire in her lovely body, then so be it.

"You will be my wife now, Sophia," he said.

"When?" She said it like a challenge. As if she didn't believe him.

"Oh, as soon as we can arrange it. We're going to San Paolo."

Her expression went strangely…soft. Very odd in the context of the moment, when before she'd been looking nearly feral. "Your father's island?"

"It is *my* island now." A soft, firm reminder that his father was gone.

That, though he would have strongly disapproved of this, he was not here to see it. No one was. Not now.

How easy it would be to lay her back on that chair, to push up that wedding dress and lose himself inside her. Talking was a pointless exercise when it was not what he wanted.

Heat lashed through him. He wanted her. Even in this moment, when all should be reduced to the gravity of the situation, he wanted her.

"This will not be easy," she said, her voice shaking.

"Denying me my child would have been simple, Sophia?"

"That isn't what I mean. Don't be dense, Luca. The world will be watching us. Will be watching and judging and we will be bringing a baby into that. It seemed kinder in some ways to try and avoid all of that."

Rage was like a storm inside him. By God, he couldn't cope with not having power. With having his choices taken from him. "You don't have a biological father of your own. The man couldn't be bothered to raise you. How dare you visit the same fate upon your child?"

"Biology doesn't matter," she snapped. "All that matters is that a man is good. Your father was the best father I could have ever asked for. My own father… He didn't want me. He didn't care for me. He didn't matter. Not when I had your father to call my own. He *earned* that place. He wasn't born with some magical right given to him by blood you can't even see. That's how I thought I could do it. Because I know full well that it's not genetics that make a parent."

"And what about me? You think so little of me that you think I am like the man who sired you? That I am like a man who could walk away from his child and never think of her again?"

"I figured what you didn't know couldn't hurt you. Or your goals. Or the country."

"How cavalierly you played with our fates," he bit out.

"How cavalierly you played with my privacy," she shot back.

"You don't deserve privacy," he returned. "You proved that with your betrayal."

Silence descended on the plane. Luca stood up and made his way across the space, heading over to the bar and pouring himself a measure of scotch.

"None for you," he said, his tone unkind. He was well aware of it. He didn't care. She did not deserve his kindness at the moment.

"You hate me," she said softly. "You always have. Or, if you don't hate me, it's a kind of malevolent indifference the likes of which I have never experienced. I would have said it was impossible. To dislike and not care at the same time. But you seem to manage it."

He shook his head, laughter escaping in spite of himself. Then he took a drink of scotch. "Is that what you think?"

"It is what I *know*, Luca."

"You are a fool," he said, knocking back his drink, relishing the burn all the way down to his gut. At least that burn was expected. Acceptable.

Then he stopped over to where she was seated, leaned forward, bracing his hands on the arms of the seat, bracketing her in. His eyes met hers, electricity arcing between them. His skin tingled with her being this near, his entire body on high alert. His heart was pounding heavily, his blood flowing south, preparing his body to enter hers.

He wondered if every time he was near her it would be thus. And concluded just as quickly that as it had been this way for nearly a decade it was likely not to change anytime soon.

"You think I hate you? You think I am indifferent to you? If I behaved that way, Sophia, it was only because I was attempting to protect your innocence. Attempting to protect you from my lust."

"Luca…"

He stood up, running his hands through his hair. "I have always known there was something wrong with me," he said. "That I could not trust my own desires. I proved it to be so the other night. But I quite admirably steered clear of that destruction for a very long time."

"You want me?" she asked, her voice small.

"Did I *want you*? I wanted no one else. Do you have any idea how many delightfully curvy brunettes I have taken to my bed and attempted not to make them you in my mind as I made love to them?"

Her face was white now, her lips a matching shade. "Am I supposed to be flattered by that? That you used other women and thought of me?"

"No one should be flattered by it," he said darkly. "But I feel strongly that no one should be flattered by my attentions, either."

"Why?"

The question was simple, and he supposed it was the logical one, and yet, it surprised him. He had not expected her to come back at him with the simplest and most reasonable question.

"It is not important."

"I think that it might be," she said.

"Truly it is not. All you need to know is that you will marry me. It is nonnegotiable. You will be my queen, and our child will be the heir. If you feel regret over it, you should've thought of that before you climbed on my lap in the garden."

"If you feel regret then perhaps you should've thought of that before you took me without a condom," she shot back.

Heat, white and sharp, streaked through him like a lightning bolt, and he had to grit his teeth, plant his feet firmly on the floor and tighten his hands into fists to keep from moving toward her. To keep from claiming her. To keep from doing just what she described now again.

"I have no regrets," he said. "I'm not so certain you'll feel the same in the fullness of time."

Sophia felt drained, utterly bedraggled by the time the plane landed, and she trudged off and onto the blaring heat of the tarmac. Her gown was beginning to feel impossibly heavy, but Luca had not offered her anything to change into.

Had she not just spent an extremely cool three hours on the plane with Luca, alternating between stony silence and recrimination, she would have thought she was in some kind of a dream.

An extremely twisted one.

It was far too hot on San Paolo for layers and layers of lace and chiffon. For the crinoline she had on beneath the gown.

The sky was jewel bright, reflected in the clear waters that stretched out around them, like an impassible moat, cutting them off from the world. The beach was bleached white by the sun, shrubby green grass and broken shells the only intrusion of color along the shoreline. And beyond that was the magnificent palatial estate that Luca's father had built just for their family. She had spent part of her childhood here on this island, and she had always thought it to be like heaven on earth.

Right now she did not feel so enamored with it.

But then, right now she did not feel so enamored with anything.

On the one hand…she had never been so relieved in her life. To have been carried out of that wedding before it had a chance to take place. Because truthfully, she did not want to marry Erik.

But it was difficult to think about marrying Luca. When she knew that he was only doing it for the child. When she knew that he would have let her walk down the aisle toward another man, that he would have done nothing to stop Erik from claiming her. Touching her. Kissing her. Joining his body to hers.

It was almost unimaginably painful. That full realization. That on her own she had not been enough.

It was that feeling of fantasy, of being in another time and space, that carried her through. That allowed her to breathe while they were driven from the landing base to the villa.

It was all white stucco and red clay roofing, brilliant and clean construction amidst the spiky green plants that surrounded the house.

The home itself was three floors, making the most of the fact it was built into the side of the mountain, that it overlooked the sea. She knew there was a large outdoor bathtub that faced out over the water, made of glass, as if to flaunt the exclusivity of the location.

She could not understand this as a child. It made no sense to her why someone would take their clothes off outdoors. Or why one person would get into a bath that size when there was a pool to swim in.

As an adult, she more than understood.

Because she could well imagine the hours she and Luca could spend in there, naked and slick, with nothing but the sea as witness to their time spent there.

She ached for it, shamefully. Even knowing that he did not want her. Not like this. Not forever.

They stepped inside the cool, extensive foyer, and Sophia looked around, nostalgia crashing into the present moment like a tidal wave. It was so strange. She could remember walking into this place as a girl. With her stepfather and her mother holding hands as a couple, with Luca the stormy and electric presence that made her feel strange and out of sorts. One that she wanted to run away from as much as she wanted to linger here.

That, at least, was the same.

She wanted to run from them as much as she wanted to run to heaven. Wanted his hands on her body, and wanted to shout and scream at him about how he was never permitted to touch her again.

He had devastated her.

And the worst part was, even as he had fulfilled the fantasy of rescuing her from the wedding she had not wanted, he had shattered her completely by doing so. Because of the reasons surrounding it.

She supposed it would be a wonderful thing if she could simply be happy to have Luca. If she could simply be grateful that he had come for her, regardless of the circumstances.

But she couldn't be.

Was it so much to ask that something be about her, and not someone else?

The fact of the matter was she hadn't been enough for her biological father. He hadn't wanted her. Not in the least. She loved her stepfather dearly, but she had been more of an impediment to his marrying her mother than she had been an attraction. He had certainly come to love her, and she didn't doubt that. But still…

She was loved circumstantially.

With Luca, she wasn't even loved.

How much more romantic that had seemed when he was out of reach.

"It seems my phone has… I believe they say blown

up?" Luca said, the words hard and crisp as he looked down at his mobile phone.

That felt strange. Wrong. Because she had been lost somewhere in the veil of fantasy and memory. And neither of those contained cell phones.

"Why?"

"Really?" he returned.

He had one dark brow raised, his handsome face imbued with a quizzical expression. And then suddenly it hit her. She had been so lost in her present pain that she had forgotten. Had forgotten that of course Luca's phone would be lit up with phone calls and text messages. With emails from members of the press, trying to find out what had happened.

By now, everyone knew that the wedding hadn't happened.

Suddenly, her arms felt empty, and she looked around. Realizing then that she had no purse, that she had not taken her phone. She had nothing. Nothing but this wedding dress for a wedding that hadn't happened.

"Luca," she said. "My mother is going to be frantic."

"Yes," he said, scrolling through his phone. "She is. She is deeply concerned that you've been kidnapped."

"I *have* been," she all but shouted.

"By me," he said simply.

"As if that doesn't make it kidnap?"

"I am the king of the nation," he said. "No one is going to arrest me over it."

"That is an extremely low standard to hold yourself to."

"I find at the moment I don't care overmuch."

"Are you going to tell her?" Sophia asked.

"Well, eventually we're going to tell everyone."

"Let me call my mother," she said.

Luca arched a brow. "I do not want your mother on the next flight here."

"You've kidnapped her daughter, what do you expect?"

"I don't want company."

"Why?"

Suddenly, she found herself being swept up off the ground once again. "You have made a bad habit of this."

"I don't find it a bad habit."

He began marching up the stairs, her wedding gown trailing dramatically behind her as they went.

"What are you doing?"

"Claiming your wedding night."

"There was no wedding. And anyway, it wasn't supposed to be *your* wedding night."

"It is about to be." He growled, and he leaned down, claiming her lips with his own.

The moment his mouth made contact with hers it was like the tide had washed over her. And she and her objections were left clinging to the rocks. With each brush that swept over her, she lost her hold on one of them. Her anger washed away. Her doubt. Her resilience. Her resolve.

Whatever Luca felt for her—and she didn't think it was anything tender at all—he wanted her. There was no denying that. He had said as much on the plane, hadn't he?

She had been so lost in her head over the fact that the baby was what had stopped him from letting the wedding go forward, that she hadn't fully taken that part on board. But it was real. It was true.

This was honest. If nothing else between them was. It was real, if the rest could not be.

This was why they were here. The electric, undeniable chemistry that existed between them, in defiance of absolutely everything that was good and right in the world.

She did not taste love on his tongue as it swept over hers. But she tasted need. And that, perhaps, could be enough.

His hold tight on her, he carried her all the way to the top of the stairs and down the landing toward the master bedroom, a room that they had certainly not stayed in before. Well, perhaps Luca had, but she had not. He all but kicked open the double doors, sweeping them inside and depositing her down at the foot of the bed.

"Where is… Where is everyone?" she asked, feeling like she was in a daze. She had only just realized that there seemed to be no servants present.

"I had everyone vacate. Supplies were left, including clothing for you, so you won't need for much. But we need privacy."

"Why?" Tears stung her eyes, an aching pain tightening her throat. She could not understand why he needed this.

This was all too much. She hadn't appreciated fully the protection that had been built into wanting a man she could never have. For her heart. For her body.

Now he was here. Looming large and powerful, so very beautiful.

It all felt too much. Like she would be consumed. Destroyed. Nothing at all of Sophia remaining.

"Because that bastard was going to put his hands on

you tonight," he said, his voice rough. "He was going to touch you. He was going to kiss you. Perhaps you were even fantasizing about it. But I will not have that. I will be the only man to touch you. No other. I will be the only man you want. The only desire in your body will be for me. I will be what you crave. Your body is mine."

"You didn't want me," she said, choked.

"No," he said. "I wanted… I prayed…to not want you. There is nothing that will take it from me. And so there is nothing but this. To take you in any way that I can. To have you. Fate is sealed where we are concerned. There is no reason now not to glory in it."

He reached behind her and grabbed hold of either side of the wedding gown, and he wrenched the corset top open. She gasped as it loosened, felt free as the fine stitching that had been so carefully conformed to her body came loose, and her breasts were left bare to him.

"So beautiful," he said, his dark head swooping down, his tongue like fire over one distended nipple.

How she ached for him. For this. Even as she hurt. Even as her desire threatened to destroy her, she wanted nothing more than to give in to it.

She breathed his name, lacing her fingers through his hair as he sucked her indeed. As he moved his attentions to her other breast, tracing a circle around one tight bud with the tip of his tongue.

"You're right," she said, her voice trembling. "This is madness."

"I knew it would destroy us, Sophia. I knew it could bring down an entire kingdom. But now here we are. There is nothing on earth I have wanted to be rid of more than this desire for you," he said, his voice low, tortured. "And good God I want to burn."

It was like fire. His touch branding her as he removed the layers of clothing from her body. As he left her completely naked except for her high heels, as he pushed her down onto the bed and spread her thighs wide, exposing the most intimate part of her body to his gaze.

He got down on his knees then, grabbing hold of her hips and forcing her toward his mouth.

"Luca," she said, shocked, appalled that he would do such a thing.

"This has been my greatest desire," he said. "Even more than sinking into your tight, wet body, I have wanted to taste you. I have wanted you coating my tongue, my lips. Sophia…"

He dipped his head then, that wicked, electric tongue swirling over the bundle of nerves at the apex of her thighs, tracing a line down to the entrance of her body and drawing the evidence of her desire from her. He added his fingers then, penetrating her, coaxing pleasure from deep inside her. It was too much. It was not enough. It was like a sharp pain that ran deep inside her. That could only be satisfied by him. Only him.

He pressed two fingers into her while he continued to lave her with the flat of his tongue, and she shattered completely. There were no thoughts in her head. Not about a wedding that might have been, not about the man who was supposed to strip this down off her tonight, not about scandal, not about anything. Nothing but this. The extreme heat bursting through her like light in the darkness.

He moved away from her then, his gaze predatory as he unbuttoned the crisp white shirt he wore, as he pushed his jacket from his shoulders and the shirt followed suit.

She could only stare at him. At the beautiful, perfect delineation of his muscles, the dark hair sprinkled there. Could only watch as his clever, masculine fingers made quick work of his belt, of his pants, as he left every last inch of his clothing on the floor, revealing powerful, muscular thighs and the thick, hard part of him that made him a man.

She'd had him inside her once. She would again. Even now, it seemed impossible.

If she had been able to see him the night she had been a virgin she would've been much more apprehensive.

At least now she knew that such fullness in size brought pleasure.

He growled, moving toward her with the liquid grace of a panther. Then he grabbed hold of her hips again, lifting her completely off the bed and throwing her back, coming to settle himself between her legs and thrusting into her with one quick, decisive movement.

Their coupling washed away everything. Like a cleansing fire, destroying the hay and the stubble, all of the temporary things, and leaving behind what was real.

This.

This connection between them that existed for no reason she could see other than to torture them. That remained.

Because whatever it was, it was real.

Each thrust of his powerful body within hers brought her to new heights, and she met each and every movement. With one of her own.

Until he shattered. Until, on a harsh growl, he spent himself deeply within her, and she was powerless to do anything but follow him over that precipice. When it was over, she held him. Because holding on to him was the only way to hold things together.

And she feared very much that the moment she let go, everything was going to fall apart.

Including her.

CHAPTER NINE

HE LEFT HER there in the expansive bed all by herself. Her dress was torn, past the point of fixing, and though he had mentioned there would be a new wardrobe supply for her here, she had no idea where said wardrobe was. Not that she had gone poking around.

She felt too...something. Sad. Bereft, almost, but also boneless and satisfied in a way she never had been before. Or, if she could compare it to anything, it was the way she had felt after their first time. Not happy, no. There was no room between them for something so simple as happy.

It was more like she was lying in the rubble of a building that had needed demolition.

That didn't make it easy. It didn't make it less of a pile of rubble. But there was something inevitable about all of it that made something in this a relief.

Even as it was a sharp pain, like being stabbed in the center of her chest.

She needed to call her mother. She knew full well that Luca did not want her to divulge their location. But he had left her. And there was a phone on the desk. Unless he had done something truly diabolical and cut the line, there was nothing stopping her from getting in touch with the one person who truly needed to know that she was okay.

She wrapped herself several times in the feather-soft white sheet, making sure it was secure at her breasts, before going to the phone and with trembling hands picking up the receiver and listening for the dial tone.

It had one. So, provided she could dial off the island, she should be able to get in touch with her mother.

"Let's see," she mumbled as she typed in the country code for San Gennaro followed by her mother's number.

The phone rang just once before her mother answered. "Hello?"

"Mom," Sophia said.

"Where are you?" her mother asked, panic lacing each word. "Are you safe?"

"Yes," she said.

It was true that she was physically safe. Emotionally was another matter.

"What happened? You were at the chapel and ready, and Luca went in to fetch you and… Is Luca with you?" her mother asked.

"Luca…" The rest of the sentence died.

"What is it?"

"Luca is the reason that I've gone missing," Sophia finished.

The silence on the other end was brittle, like a thin pane of glass that she was certain would splinter into a million pieces and shatter if she breathed too deeply.

"Is he?" her mother asked finally.

"There's something I have to tell you…"

"Oh, Sophia," her mother said, the words mournful. "I had hoped… I had hoped that you had put your feelings for him behind you."

"It's his baby, Mother," she said, the words coming out raw and painful.

More silence. But this one was full. Of emotion. Of words left unspoken. Sophia couldn't breathe.

"I see," the queen finally responded.

"We didn't mean for... I tried... He tried." She closed her eyes, swallowing hard. "We did try."

"Just tell me he never took advantage of you when you were younger." There was an underlying venom in her words that left Sophia in no doubt her mother would castrate Luca if the answer was yes.

Sophia shook her head, then realized her mother couldn't see. "No. Never. It was just... This time was the first time. The time that we...the pregnancy, I mean. That was the first time"

"I knew," her mother whispered. "But I hoped that it would pass. For both of you."

"You knew that he... That he had feelings for me?"

"I knew that he *desired* you. Far sooner than he should have. And I told his father to keep him away from you. There was no future for the two of you, Sophia. You have to understand that."

"I do," she said. "Why do you think I was prepared to marry another man?"

"Yes, well, that has created quite a scandal."

"Just wait until they find out what actually happened. I imagine my running off before the wedding is not half as salacious as the fact that I have run off with my stepbrother because I'm having his baby."

Her mother groaned, a long, drawn-out sound. "Sophia... The scandal this will cause."

Sophia cringed, feeling desperately sad to hear such

distress in her mother's voice. "I'm so sorry. So very sorry I disappointed you."

Her mother's voice softened. "I'm not disappointed. But it's a hard road, Sophia. Being married to a king. And that's simply when you're a commoner. I cannot imagine how difficult things will be for you and Luca. All things considered. I had hoped that you could avoid it."

"We did. Until we couldn't."

She was embarrassed to be talking with her mother in this frank fashion. Until only recently she had been a virgin, after all, and now she was confessing that she had been overwhelmed by a state of desire. Her mother knew full well what that meant.

"If it was love…" Her mother trailed off.

Sophia's shoulders stiffened, her back going straight, a pain hitting her in the stomach. "If it was love, I never would have pretended I might be able to marry Erik. Luca does not love me."

But she did wonder if perhaps marrying Erik had been about running away. Not from scandal, not even from this conversation with her mother.

From all that Luca made her feel. All he made her want.

"He is a good man," her mother said as if trying to offer her some consolation.

"I know he is. Too good for such a scandal."

"But too good to turn away from his responsibility. Still… I have to wonder if it would've been better if he would have allowed you to marry Erik."

Those words went through her like a lance. "Why?"

"If he can't love you…"

Her mother's choice of words there was interesting.

If he couldn't love her. Did that mean that her mother thought she was difficult to love, too? Or did she believe that Luca had a difficult time loving?

In many ways Sophia wondered if they were both true.

She didn't want to love him. That much was certain. Whatever she felt was far too bright and painful all on its own.

"I'm not sure I love him," she said truthfully. "I only know that whatever this is between us is undeniable. And he has chosen to make a scandal. I will only go so far to protect him. I'm not going to force him to disavow his child."

"Of course not. But, Sophia, it's going to be such a difficult life. Where are you? I feel like I should come and get you."

"I—"

The door opened and she turned sharply. Luca was standing there, regarding her with dark eyes. His expression was like a storm, his mouth set into a firm line.

"I have to go."

She hung up the phone, much to her mother's protests. And then Luca walked over to the phone and unplugged the power cord from the base. "I do not wish to be disturbed," he said. "How much did you tell your mother?"

"I told her that I'm having your baby."

He chuckled, bitter and hard. "I imagine her faith in me is greatly reduced by this news."

Sophia wrapped her arms around herself. "She said that she always knew. That you wanted me. That I wanted you."

"Fascinating," he said, not sounding at all fascinated. "But you had no idea, did you?"

"I didn't," she said truthfully. "I thought you despised me."

"You refused to be any less attractive to me, no matter how the years went on. You refused to shrink. You refused to be invisible. I certainly despised you, Sophia, but my desire for you is not exclusive from that."

"That's beautiful, Luca. Perhaps you should take up poetry."

"How's this for poetry? You're mine now." He took a step toward her, grabbing hold of the sheet that she had resolutely wrapped around her curves, and he pulled her to him, wrenching the soft, exquisite cotton from her body. "There is to be no doubt of that."

She stood there, naked and trembling, feeling hideously exposed in ways that went well beyond her skin.

"Then that makes you mine," she shot back, feeling run out and fragile after the day she had had. "Doesn't it?"

His dark eyes sharpened. "I'm not sure I get your meaning."

"If I belong to you, then I require nothing less. If we are to be married, Luca, I will be the only woman in your bed. You have all of me or you have none of me."

"I was never going to be unfaithful to whatever wife I took. I would hardly be unfaithful to you."

Electricity crackled between them, and neither spoke what was so patently obvious. So obvious that it lit the air between them with electricity.

That at least for now, there was no chance either of them would take another to their beds. They would have to exhaust the intense desire between the two of them first, and at the moment Sophia could not imagine it. Granted, she was new to sex, but she had a feeling that what existed between herself and Luca was uncommon in every way.

"What are you going to do?" she asked, her voice small, taking a step away from him.

"Tonight? Tonight I intend to take you back to my bed, spread you out before me and feast on you until you're crying out my name. Until my name is synonymous with *lover*, not *brother*."

His words set a rash of heat over her body. "I mean, about us. About telling the world about us. About our upcoming marriage. About…what we are going to do next."

"I'm going to make a press release to go out tomorrow morning. And you and I will stay here incommunicado until some of the furor dies down. Then I will marry you. Not in that dress," he said, looking at the scrap of white on the floor.

"I think that dress is beyond saving now," she mused.

He looked at her, his dark eyes suddenly bleak. "Who knew I would have something in common with a gown."

But before she had a chance to question such an odd statement, she was back in his arms, and he was kissing her again. And she had a feeling that there would be no more talking tonight.

The next morning Luca was full of purpose when he awoke. Sophia was naked, soft and warm, pressed up against his body, one breast resting at his biceps. She was sleeping peacefully, her dark hair a halo of curls on the pillow around her head. He had done it. He had destroyed everything.

It was strangely satisfying. A perfect and sustained string of curses directed to his mother even if it was going to have to make its way into the beyond.

A scandal she would not be able to squash.

He supposed it was unkind to think poorly of one's dead mother. But he could not find a kind thought for his own.

Strange, how he spent very little time thinking about her. He had already made decisions about himself, about his life, based on the events that had occurred in his childhood. He didn't have to think about them every day.

Truthfully, he didn't even have to think about them yearly. He spent a great deal of time not pondering the ways in which he was damaged, and even when he didn't think of it, typically in reference to why he had to keep his hands off Sophia—a horse that had well and truly left the barn now—it was only in terms of his scarred soul, not in terms of actual events.

This forced him to think of it. The fact that his responsible, pristine image was about to be destroyed, made him think of it.

No one can ever know about this. If your father knew about Giovanni our marriage would be over. And can you imagine what people would think of you? They would never forget, Luca. It is all you would ever be.

He gritted his teeth and got out of bed, staring out the window at the ocean below.

He had a press release to prepare.

He set about to doing just that, contacting his palace staff and letting his majordomo know exactly what had transpired. Exactly what would be happening from here on out. If the other man was shocked, he did not let on. But then, he supposed it was in the other man's job description to remain impassive about such things.

Luca also left instruction to keep his and Sophia's location secret.

With that taken care of, Luca decided that he needed to figure out what he was going to do with his fiancée. That was how he would think of her from now on. Until, that was, he was able to think of her as his wife. She was no longer first and foremost his stepsister.

In his mind, she never had been.

And that meant that he had to get to know her.

He had avoided that. For years he had avoided that. Of course he had. He had not wanted to foster any kind of attraction between them.

It had turned out that was futile anyway, because the attraction between them had been hell-bent on growing no matter what either of them did.

Now the fact remained, he was going to marry her, and he didn't know her at all.

That was not actually a point of contention for him, but he would have to be able to make conversation about her. They would have to be able to come to an accord on how they talked about their relationship.

And he had a feeling that Sophia would want to feel as if she knew him.

He had done what he had intended to do by bringing her here to the island. He had isolated her. And he had managed to get her into proximity with him. To keep her from marrying Erik. But he would not be able to keep her here forever. That meant that something other than kidnap was going to have to bind them. Eventually. Something other than sex would help, as well.

Although at the moment the sex was enough for him.

His staff had generously stocked the kitchen with a basket of croissants. Opening the fridge, he found a tray of fruit, figs and dates. Cheeses. Then, there was a pot of local honey in a small jar on the counter. He cobbled those things together, along with herbal tea, and brought them up to the bedroom. When he opened the door, Sophia shifted, making a sleepy sound.

She opened her eyes, and he could see the exact moment her vision came into focus.

She frowned. "Is that for me?"

"Yes," he said, sitting down on the edge of the bed.

He was gratified to see that her gaze drifted away from the food and onto his chest, which was still currently fair. Her cheeks flushed, and she looked away.

It pleased him to see that she was not immune to him.

That someone so soft and lovely could be so affected by him.

He shoved that thought to the side.

"That's…kind of you." She shifted, pushing herself into a sitting position, holding her sheets against her breasts modestly. "What is this?" She opened up the pot sitting on the tray and frowned deeply. "This isn't coffee."

"You're pregnant," he pointed out. "I believe I recall hearing that pregnant women should not drink caffeine."

"Not *too much* caffeine." She sounded truly distressed. "That doesn't mean I have to drink…herbs."

"I was only doing the best I could. I'm not an expert."

"That might be a first," she said.

"What?"

She treated him to a smile that was almost impish.

Something he wasn't used to having directed at him. "You admitting that you don't know everything."

"Sophia…" he said, his tone full of warning.

"You can't tell me it isn't true."

"I was raised to be arrogant. It's part and parcel to being in charge."

"Really?" she asked.

"Nobody wants an uncertain king."

"Perhaps. But no one wants an insufferable husband, either."

Neither of them spoke for a moment. Sophia reached into the basket and procured herself a croissant.

"You like coffee," he said.

She lifted a shoulder. It was gloriously bare and he knew now from experience that her skin was as soft as it looked. He wished to lick her. If only because he had spent so many years not licking her. "Yes."

"I didn't know that."

"Almost everyone likes coffee. Or needs it, if it comes down to it."

"But we have never discussed what you like. Or what you don't like."

She looked thoughtful for a moment, and that should've been an indicator that this was not going according to plan, as he really should have guessed that Sophia was never going to be anything like compliant.

"Well," she said, "I like coffee, as established. My hobbies include getting fitted for wedding gowns that will eventually be torn off my body, and being kidnapped and spirited away to a private island."

Luca cast her a hard look. "Much more exotic than stamp collecting, you have to admit."

"Indeed. Although, my wretched dress is not going to increase in value. A stamp collection might."

"I beg to differ. By the time news of our union hits global media I imagine that torn gown will be worth quite a bit."

Sophia frowned, grabbing a strawberry from the fruit tray and biting into it angrily. "Global media," she muttered around the succulent fruit.

"There is no way around it. We are a headline, I think you will find."

"I tried *not* to find."

"Sophia," he said, suddenly weary of games. "There was no other alternative. No other outcome, and you know that. It was always going to be this."

He meant because of the baby. And yet, he couldn't escape feeling that there was something else in those words. Some other, deeper truths being hinted at.

"We tried," she said, sounding desolate.

"Not that night. Not the night of the ball."

She looked up at him, her expression quizzical. "Really?"

"You know it's true," he said. "Had I tried, I would never have touched you. But I didn't. It was simply that what I wanted became so much more powerful than what I should do. And I could not... Could not allow him to touch you."

"We would have allowed him to touch me last night," she said quietly, picking at a fig.

"He didn't," Luca said. "That's all that matters."

"Luca," she said, looking up at him, her expression incisive. "Why is reputation so important to you? I mean, beyond the typical reasons. Beyond the reasons that most rulers have. You have never been... I knew your father.

I loved him. As my own father. He was the only father I ever knew. He was serious, and he treated his position with much gravity. But it's not like you. You do everything with such gravity. And I… Truthfully, whether you believe me or not, part of the reason I didn't tell you is that I didn't want to put this on you. I know how much your country means to you…"

"Not more than my child," he said, fire rising up in his chest, bile in his throat. "Nothing matters more than my child, Sophia, you must know that. The moment those test results came across my desk I had to know. I will not sacrifice my child on an altar with my country's name stamped onto it. With my reputation on it. My name is only a name. The baby you carry is my blood." He took a deep breath. "What good is a legacy if you don't defend the ones who are supposed to carry it out when you die?"

"I'm sorry," she said, and she sounded it. "You're right. For all that we…" She squeezed her eyes shut. "For all that I have carried a certain fascination for you for a great number of years, I don't know you." She opened her eyes, tears glistening in them. "If I could guess at this so wrong, then it is apparent there are things I don't know."

"You're not wrong," he said, the word scraping his throat. "On any score with this, I would have protected the name. But not at the expense of a child."

It was the breaking point. Because if the name didn't matter, then what he had endured, then the lack of action his mother had taken to defend him, would be null and void, and that was unfathomable to him in many ways. This was where the corner turned. Where it became far too close to what had been done to him. And that, he could not allow.

"What are we going to do today?" The question was open, honest, and it made him feel strange.

"I had not given it much thought."

That was a lie. What he wanted, what he wanted more than anything, was to strip her completely naked, rip that sheet right off her as he had done last night, and keep her that way for the entire day.

"Your wardrobe should arrive soon," he said instead of that. "And then of course, there is the beach, and the pool."

"Badminton," she pointed out. "We used to play badminton."

"You cannot be serious."

"We're rather cut off here, Luca," she said. "I was thinking of all the things we used to do to entertain ourselves."

He treated her to a scorching look, and he watched as her face turned scarlet all the way up to the roots of her hair.

"We can't do that the entire time," she protested, her hand flinging out wide like an indignant windmill.

He leaned forward, gripping her chin with his thumb and forefinger. "Why not?"

Her eyes widened. "Because… Because… We can't." Her protest was beginning to sound weak.

"I'm going to need a better reason than that, Sophia. As we have spent years not doing it, and I feel that we have much time to make up for."

"Well," she said, sniffing piously. "It's not done."

"I assure you, *cara*, that it is done quite frequently."

"You would *die*." She sounded entirely certain of this assessment.

He couldn't help himself. He laughed. "That's a bit overdramatic, don't you think?"

"No," she protested. "There is nothing dramatic about it. You've been there both times we've, well, you know. I can't breathe for nearly an hour afterward. If we did it all day…"

"It would be different," he said. "But no less impacting."

"Is it always like this, then? Does it just naturally shatter you less and less each time? Is this how it's been with all your lovers?"

He could lie to her. But then, a lie would neither bring him joy nor accomplish anything. Truth was the best option.

"It has never been like this with any of my previous lovers," he said. "I already told you that you have been my obsession for far too long. And there has been nothing that I could do to put a dent in that hunger. And before you… I didn't know such hunger at all."

"Oh," she said, sounding subdued.

"I wished often that it was simple enough to just want another woman," he said. "But it is not."

He shook his head. "There is no way around it. We must go through."

"Perhaps after badminton."

"If you get out a badminton racket, I will break it over my knee." Possibly, he could break it over another part of his body, given how hard he was at the moment.

It didn't take much. He was held in thrall, just for a moment, as the sunlight broke through a crack in the curtains, streamed onto Sophia's lovely upturned face, catching the light behind her wild curls. Sophia was naked in his bed. After so many years of lust.

She was his. There was triumph in that, to be certain.

He was Nero. Fiddling while Rome burned, he supposed. But Rome was going to burn no matter what at this point. He supposed he might as well play away.

"There is one thing I'm curious about."

"Whether or not I take cream in my coffee?"

"No. Why were you a virgin, Sophia?"

She drew back, pressing her hand to the center of her chest, the expression almost comically missish. "Does it matter?"

"The very fact that you would ask that question says to me that it must."

"I never found anyone that I felt… Luca, if no other man could make me feel what I felt just looking at you, if he kissed me, if he touched me, what was the point of going to bed with him? I would be thinking of you."

He was humbled by that. Shame. A familiar, black fog rolling over his shoulders and down his spine. Yes, shame was his constant companion. And sex was…

It never occurred to him to deprive himself of sex. His introduction to it—such as it was—had not been his choice. And he had set out to make a choice after that, and every time thereafter.

It had become a way of putting distance and bodies between that first encounter.

To prove to himself that in truth, the two experiences were not even the same. But what had been done to him against his will that night was something dark. Something ugly.

Control. A deep contempt for another person's autonomy.

"I was with other people and thought of you," he pointed out. "Unless I made it a point not to. And then,

I made sure it was someone who was quite different to you."

"I suppose that's the difference between men and women, then," she said.

"Or simply the difference between you and me," he responded. "Sophia… There are many reasons that I never allowed myself to touch you for all that time."

"Your reputation."

"My reputation, the reputation of San Gennaro, is only a piece of the puzzle."

"Then tell me what the puzzle is, Luca. I feel like I should understand since we are supposed to be married. I feel like I need to understand you."

"We have a history," he said slowly. "One that has been difficult. I cannot… I cannot adequately express to you the way it was when I first noticed you as a woman. The way that it hit me. You were always…reckless and wild in a way that I could not fathom, Sophia, and yet the fact that it bothered me as it did never made any sense. Until you turned seventeen. And suddenly…everything that you were, this vivacious, irrepressible girl, crashed into what you had become. I knew I couldn't have you. I knew that it was impossible. And so, as much as there was never closeness between us, I pushed you away. I don't regret that. It was my attempt at doing what was right. I failed, in the end. And so, those years, that history, is useless to us. Let us forget who we were in the past and why. We have to make a way forward, and I don't think there are answers lurking behind."

She narrowed her eyes, looking at him with total skepticism. He could see that she did not agree with him, not remotely.

But there was no point talking about the shadows

in the past. He didn't want her to know him. He didn't want anyone to know him. They could have a life, like this. One where they made love and she teased him. Frankly, it was a better life than he had ever imagined for himself.

He had not ever fathomed that his duty could be quite so pleasurable.

He had resolved himself to a life without the woman that he wanted most. Now he had her. There was no point dragging skeletons out of the closet.

"You have an objection, *cara*?"

"You want to act as though we haven't known each other for most of our lives? You don't want to go back and try to understand who I was?"

"Isn't it most important that we understand who each other is now?"

"Can we do that? Can it be accomplished if we don't actually know what each other was built with?"

"There are no surprises in my story. I was born into royalty." He shrugged his shoulders. "Here I remain."

"You lost your mother when you were sixteen. I suppose that was very painful for you."

"Yes," he responded, the word sharp like a blade.

It was painful. But perhaps not in the way she meant. Not in any way he could put into words.

Losing someone you were meant to love, someone you had grown to hate, was its own particular kind of pain. There had been guilt. Such guilt. As if it were the hatred in his heart that had poisoned her to death. As if he had somehow caused her car to go off the road that day.

He knew better than that now.

But that, too, was a discussion they would not have.

"Today I thought we might have a walk on the beach," he said. "What do you think of that?"

She nodded slowly. "That sounds nice."

Though she still didn't sound convinced.

She would see. It would be better his way.

And if Sophia wanted to share herself with him, he was more than happy to allow it. In fact, he found he was quite hungry for it.

But he would not poison her with the stories of his past.

The poison in his own veins was quite enough. He refused to spread it.

On the score of protecting the family reputation, of protecting her from a life with him, he had failed.

He did not have to fail when it came to everything else.

Sophia was hot and sweaty after spending an afternoon combing through the white sand beaches, finding seashells and taking breaks from the sun to soak her feet in the water.

True to his word, her clothing had eventually arrived, and she had found a lovely white dress that seemed suited to the surroundings. They had walked together, and he hadn't touched her.

It occurred to her that Luca had *never* touched her without sexual intent. Nothing intentional anyway.

There had been no casual handholding. He'd never moved to touch her with affection, only to strip her of her clothes.

Which was why when they had been on their return trip to the estate she had looped her fingers through his and taken control of that situation.

She had almost immediately wished that she hadn't. It had been so impacting. So very strange. To hold Luca's hand. Like they were a couple. Not just secret, torrid lovers, but something much gentler and sweeter, too.

Strange, because there was no real gentleness in their interaction.

Although, it had been quite a nice thing he'd done this morning with the fruit. The herbal tea notwithstanding.

When they returned to the villa, dinner had been laid out for them on the deck that overlooked the sea. A lovely spread of fresh seafood and crisp, bright vegetables.

All a little bit healthy for her taste. Though that concern was answered at the end of the meal when Luca went into the kitchen and returned a moment later with the truly sinful-looking dessert made of layers of cream, meringue and raspberry.

Sophia took a bite of the decadent dessert and closed her eyes, listening to the sound of the ocean below, the sun still creating warmth, even as it sank down into the sea. A breeze blew gently through her hair, lifting the heavy curls off the back of her neck, cooling her.

For a moment she had the horrible feeling that if she opened her eyes she would find that Luca wasn't really there. That she had somehow hallucinated all of this in order to survive the wedding.

That in reality she was on her honeymoon with Erik. Because of course it had to be a fantasy that Luca had come to claim her. That he had whisked her out of that waiting room in the back of the chapel and spirited her off to a private island.

But no. When she opened her eyes there he was. Regarding her closely, his dark, unfathomable eyes assessing her. The remaining light of the sun shone brilliantly on his razor-sharp cheekbones, highlighting the rough, dark whiskers that had grown over his square jaw. She did not think he had shaved since they had arrived.

She suddenly had the urge to watch him shave. To watch him brush his teeth.

To claim all those little intimate moments for herself. Those routine things that were so easy to take for granted. She wanted to be close to him.

That was the sad thing. She had made love to him a few times now, and still, she didn't feel…like they were close.

Physically, they had been as close as two people could be. But there was still a gulf between them. She wanted to know what had created him. This good, hard man who clung to his principles like a mountain climber holding on to the face of a rock.

He fascinated her, this man. Who only ever let his passion unleash itself in the bedroom. Who was otherwise all things reserved and restrained.

That he had been hiding his desire for her for so many years was a revelation.

But he didn't *want* her to know him. He had made that clear.

She understood now why her mother had sounded so upset on the phone. It wasn't simply the issues that they would have with the press. But the pain she would experience, having feelings for her husband that far outweighed the feelings he had for her. Of wanting more of him than he would ever share. Luca desired her. He wanted her body. He'd had it. But sex and intimacy were not the same things.

That fact had become clear when they held hands on the beach and it had rocked her world in a wholly different fashion than being naked with him had.

One thing was clear: sex was certainly the way to reach him.

Because it was the only time when his guard was down. Of course, hers was equally reduced when they were making love. He did things to her... Made her feel things... Things she had not imagined were possible. And she wanted more. She had never thought of herself as greedy, not really.

How could a woman who had been born into poverty and become a princess overnight ever ask for more out of life? And yet...she wanted more. Being with him, finally having what she had held herself back from for all that time, had only made her more greedy.

There was something about today, about the beautiful afternoon spent walking on the beach that ended with holding hands, and this magical dinner, that made her feel a sense of urgency. Or maybe it wasn't the dinner, or the handholding. Maybe it was simply the fact that they were to be married. And if they were going to get married then it meant this was forever. And if this was going to be her forever...

It had been a certain kind of torture, wanting Luca and not having him. But having him in some ways, but never in others, was worse.

Or if not worse, it was simply that it was closer. She couldn't pretend that there was nothing between them, not when she was sharing his bed.

He was beautiful. And physically, he made her feel so very much. It wasn't enough.

And maybe she was so perfectly aware of how not

enough it was in part because she knew full well that it could be more.

She had seen that passion. She had felt it. Had been over him, beneath him, as he had cried out her name and lost himself completely in their lovemaking.

She wanted *that* man out of bed, too.

But in order to reach him, she imagined she had to appeal to him first in bed.

Not a hardship as far as she was concerned.

But it would perhaps require her to be a bit more bold than she had been previously.

After all, she had been a virgin until only recently. But the fact remained that what she had told Luca earlier was true. She had been a virgin because of him. Because of the way he had made her feel.

That meant he could have any of her. All of her. Because he was the one her body had been waiting for, so truly, there was no reason for her to be timid. Not where he was concerned.

"Just have some business to attend to," Luca said, rising from his chair. "I will meet you in our room."

The meaning behind his words was clear. But if Luca thought he was going to be in control of every interaction between them…well, she was about to prove to him otherwise.

CHAPTER TEN

LUCA WAS QUESTIONING the wisdom of checking the way their story was being played out in the headlines before he and Sophia left the island. What was the point? He could have simply left it all a mystery. Could have spent this time focused on her.

But no, the ugly weight of reality had pulled on him, and he had answered. So he had done some cursory searches to see if they had been splashed all over the tabloids yet.

He had underestimated the intensity of the reaction.

The headlines were lurid. Bold. Scandal in the palace. A borderline incestuous love affair between stepsiblings that had been going on for… God knew how long.

A good and handsome groom had been left at the altar, the King of San Gennaro finally snapping and claiming his illicit lover before she could marry someone else.

There were one, maybe two, stories that shed a more romantic light on the situation. Forbidden lovers who had been in crisis. Who had not been able to choose to be together until it had been decided for them by fate. By a pregnancy.

The truth was somewhere in the middle. He and Sophia certainly weren't in love.

He looked out the window, at the clear night sky, the stars punching through the blackness. It reminded him of being with Sophia. Little spots of brightness that managed to bring something into those dark spaces.

There was so much more darkness than light. And it was amazing that the blackness did not consume it.

For a brief moment he felt something like hope. Like perhaps it would be the same with her. That *his* blackness would not cover her light, but that her light would do something to brighten that darkness.

But no.

It could not be. Not really. He was not fool enough to believe it. Hope, in his experience, was a twisted thing.

Was for better men than him.

Suddenly, he was acutely aware of the pitch-dark. Of the way that it stretched out inside him. Yawning endlessly.

He needed to get back to her. Needed to have her hold him in her arms.

A wretched thing. Because he should be the one carrying her.

It was amazing, but somewhere, amidst all the granite inside his chest, there was softness for her. A softness he had never allowed himself to truly focus on before. He had been too obsessed with pushing her away. With keeping his feelings for her limited.

It was over now.

He had her. So he supposed…

The headlines once again crowded his head. It wasn't fair. That Sophia should be subjected to such a thing. Already, there had been many unkind things written about her mother and about her when she was young. And yes, gradually, the tide had turned in their favor. And even then, most had seen it as a fairy tale. He doubted very much that people would ever see this as any kind of fairy tale.

In that world stepsiblings were always wicked. And they certainly didn't get a happy ending.

Least of all with the princess in the story.

No. Theirs was not a fairy tale.

Theirs was something dark and frightening, obsession and lust creating a cautionary tale.

One he certainly wasn't going to heed. It was far too late for that.

He turned and walked out of the office, heading down the long hallway toward the room he was sharing with Sophia.

She might be asleep. She might not have waited up for him.

He pushed the door open without knocking, and did not see her in bed. In fact, he did not see her anywhere.

He frowned. And then he looked up and saw her standing in the doorway of the balcony that contained the large bathtub he had built several fantasies around.

She was wearing nothing more than a white gown, diaphanous and insubstantial. He was certain that— even in the dim light—he could make out the shadow at the apex of her thighs. Of her nipples.

"What are you doing?" he asked.

Her dark brown hair was a riot of curls, those generous curves calling to him.

Every time they'd been together it had been frantic as if they were both afraid one or both of them might come to their senses and put a stop to everything. This was different. There was a look in her eye that spoke of seduction. Seduction certainly hadn't been involved in any of their previous couplings.

He swore, beginning to undo the buttons on his shirt, until Sophia held up a delicate hand. "Not so fast."

"You will not tease me," he growled, taking a step toward her.

"I don't want to tease you."

"Then why are you stopping me from ravishing you? Because you know all I can think of is ripping that dress off you."

"You keep doing that to me," she scolded.

"Perhaps I think white isn't your color. Or perhaps I think the clothing doesn't suit you. But then, the conclusion could be drawn that I simply don't think clothes in general suit you. I've often wondered why I never cared for the image that the palace stylist had cultivated for you. And obviously the new one has done better. But I think the real reason is quite simple. I like you better naked. And part of me always knew that I would."

She looked down for a beat, those long, dark lashes fanning over her cheekbones. The only sign that she was perhaps not as confident as she appeared.

But then she looked up at him, those brilliant, defiant eyes meeting his. Sophia. Always there to challenge him.

"I'm happy to get naked for you, Luca," she said, the way her lips formed the sounds of his name sending an illicit shiver down to his manhood, making him feel as though she had licked him there.

"But what?"

"I require a forfeit."

"A forfeit?" He paused for a moment, the only sound

coming from the distant waves crashing on the rocks below, and the thundering of his heart in his ears. "Well, now, that is very interesting. Do you wish me to get down on my knees and worship at the cleft of your thighs? Because I'm more than happy to spend an evening there."

"No. That would be too easy. For both of us. I will take off this gown in exchange for one thing."

"What is that?"

"You have to tell me one thing you have never told another soul. It might be enough for you to pretend that we only just met, Luca, but it is not enough for me."

His stomach curdled. Going sour at the thought. Because there was only one thing that sprung readily to his mind. There was no other living soul who knew what had happened to him, even though at one time someone certainly had known.

Well, perhaps there was another living soul who knew. Whether or not Giovanni was dead or alive wasn't something Luca was privy to. He didn't want to find out. He hoped the man was dead. If he wasn't, Luca would be far too tempted to see to his demise himself.

Though, considering the scandal that had just erupted, perhaps murder would be surmountable. Or at least not so glaring in the face of all this.

Still. He was not going to tell Sophia.

He gritted his teeth, casting his mind back to something… Anything that he might be able to tell her. So desperate was he to have her naked.

"I was rejected by the first girl I ever cared for," he said. "Though I use the words *cared for* euphemistically here, considering I didn't know her at all."

That wasn't something he often thought about. What

had happened the night of the ball. Before he had been violated. When everything had been simple and he had been innocent in many ways.

"What?"

"There was a girl who came to a ball that my father threw. There were dignitaries from all around the world." Which was what had allowed his mother to sneak her lover into the palace.

A man that Luca had met on a few occasions and had gotten a terrible, sick feeling in his stomach whenever he spoke. He had sensed that he knew the relationship between Giovanni and his mother. But then later he wondered if really that disquiet that he felt had to do with the fact that Giovanni was a predator. A predator who had set his sights on Luca.

"There was a girl called Annalise. She was beautiful. Her father was a dignitary in Morocco and they were visiting the palace for our grand party. I was entranced by her. She refused to dance with me. But then we spoke for a while. I led her out to the garden, and I tried to kiss her. She dodged me, and I ended up kissing a rosebush instead."

Sophia laughed, clearly not expecting the story. "You were a prince."

"And she was unimpressed with me."

"How old were you?"

"Sixteen. I believe she was eighteen."

"Oh, no," Sophia said, laughing. "You were punching above your weight."

"I had imagined that being the prince in the palace in which her family was staying might lend me an edge."

Sophia giggled, ducking her head, the expression making her look young. Making him feel young. As if perhaps he were that boy he had been that night. Innocent. Full of possibilities. To love, to be loved.

Living a life that would not ultimately culminate in the moment when his mother proved her lack of care for him.

But perhaps living the life that his head appeared to be at that point in time. Golden. Glittering. One of a privileged, infinitely fortunate prince who had the world at his feet.

Though, in this moment, he would give the world in place of Sophia.

"I like her," Sophia said. "A woman who was not impressed with you just because of your title."

"The same can be said for you, I think," he said, taking a step toward her. She took a step back.

"If anything," Sophia said, "I have always found your status to be a hindrance. Imagine what it would have been like if we would have met under different circumstances."

"You would still be younger than me," he said. "So it would still take time for me to see you differently."

"All right. What if you met me at seventeen, instead of at twelve?"

"Perhaps I would have asked you for your phone number."

She laughed. "That's so startlingly benign. You and I have never been afforded anything quite so dull."

"No, indeed."

"I must warn you," she said. "I don't intend for tonight to be dull, either."

"I believe we have started as we mean to go on."

"I suppose so."

"Your dress," he said. "I have given you my forfeit. You owe me mine."

She said nothing. Instead, she raised her hand, brushing the thin strap of her dress down so that it hung loosely over her shoulder. And then she did the same to the other side. The diaphanous fabric barely clung to her body, held up by those generous breasts of hers. He wanted to wrench it down, expose her body to his hungry gaze.

But this was her game. And he was held captive by it. Desperate to see what her rules might be.

He had grown into a man that most would never dream of defying. That was by design. But Sophia… She dared. And he wanted to see what else she might dare.

"I believe it was for the entire dress," he pressed. He stood, curling his hands into fists, his heart thundering so hard he thought it might burst through a hole in his chest.

She made him…

She made him wild. And he had not been wild for a very long time.

"I suppose it was," she returned. "Though I see that you are standing there fully clothed. And it doesn't escape my notice that the first time we were together you were also mostly clothed, while I…"

"Your dress was still on. Technically."

"I was exposed."

"All the better to enjoy you, *cara.*"

She shivered, and he was gratified by that response. "Well, I want to enjoy you. I want you naked."

She lifted her chin, her expression one of utter defiance. Defiance he wished to answer. Though he had a feeling that his little beauty's boldness might end if he actually complied with her request.

For all that she was playing at being in charge here, for all that she was a responsive and generous lover, she was still inexperienced.

He wondered how long it would take for that to not be the case. How many times. How many kisses. The number of moments he would have to spend in her bed in order to strip that inexperience from her. That innocence. Until she would look at him boldly when he removed his clothes, until she would no longer blush when he whispered erotic things in her ear.

He looked forward to the progression, but he was not in a hurry. For now, he would enjoy this.

More than anything, he looked forward to the fact that there would be a progression, rather than a one-off and a garden alcove, like he had imagined it would be.

He gripped the hem of the black T-shirt he was wearing and dragged it over his head, casting it to the floor, making similar and quick work of the rest of his clothes. Until he stood before her with nothing on.

She did shrink back, only slightly. He had been correct in his theory that she might still find the sight of him without clothes to be a bit confronting.

He spread his arms wide. "And here I am for you, *cara mia*. Where is my reward?"

She turned around quickly, and if it wasn't for the heavy rise and fall of her shoulders, he might have thought it an extension of the game, rather than a moment where nerves had taken over.

But then she lifted her arms, taking a slow, indrawn breath, the fabric of the gown slipping, falling to her waist. Exposing the elegant line of her back, the twin dimples just below the plump curve of her ass. Still covered by that flowing dress.

He gritted his teeth, holding himself back. He wanted nothing more than to move to her. Than to take control. He ached with it.

But he waited. Still, he waited.

She placed her hands at her hips, pushing the fabric down her slender legs, revealing the rest of that tempting skin.

And then, his control was lost.

He walked up behind her quietly, careful not to give her any indication of what he planned to do next.

Slowly, very slowly, he reached out and swept her dark hair to the side, exposing her neck. And he kissed her. His lips pressed firmly against the center of the back of her neck, careful not to touch her anywhere else.

She gasped, a sharp sound of need winding its way through the breath.

He drew back, pressing the back of his knuckles to that spot between her shoulder blades, following the indent of her spine down low. She squirmed, wiggling her hips, and he gripped her left side with his hand, holding her still as he followed his journey down all the way until his fingers pressed between her thighs, finding that place where she was soft and wet just for him.

He moved his hand back upward to cup one rounded cheek, squeezing her hard as he slid the hand that gripped her hip around her stomach, pulling her up against him so that she could feel the evidence of his arousal pressing against her lower back.

"I'm growing impatient of games," he whispered into her ear, capturing her lobe between his teeth and biting her gently.

She arched against him, her lovely ass pressing into him.

She wiggled.

"If you keep doing that, Sophia," he said, "you're going to push me to my limit."

"Perhaps I want to find it."

"I'm not sure you do."

"I don't want your control," she said softly. "I don't want you to be solicitous and careful. I know that you are a man of honor, Luca. But I feel that there is no place for honor between us just now." She arched even farther into him. "Indeed, there's not much room for anything between us. It's just our skin, our bodies, pressed against each other."

He pushed his hand down toward the apex of her thighs, those downy curls beneath his fingers the filthiest pleasure he'd ever experienced in his life.

He pushed down farther, brushing his fingers over that sensitive bundle of nerves, through her folds, finding the entrance to her body and pressing his fingers inside her. She let her head fall back against his shoulder, relaxing on an indrawn breath.

"Is this what you wanted?" he asked. "You want me uncontained? You want me out of control? As if it has not been so from the moment I first laid my hands on you in that garden?"

"You are far more controlled than I would like," she gasped.

"Control is a good thing," he said. "I think you will find."

He swept his free hand up to cup her breast, teasing her nipple with his thumb. "You will benefit from my control," he rasped, drawing his cheek down the side of her neck, over her shoulder, well aware that his whiskers were scraping delicate skin. She moaned. A clear sign that she quite liked his control in the right venue.

"But I don't have any," she whispered.

"Is that what you think? Sophia, you have had control of me for far too long. My thoughts turn on the sway of your hips, my focus shifting with each breath you take in my presence. How can you not know this?"

"You said I was your sickness," she breathed.

"And indeed it is true." He kissed her shoulder. "There is no cure. I am a terminal case. But I have accepted this."

"I'm not sure how I'm supposed to—" she gasped, her breath hitching as he pressed his fingers deeper inside her "—feel about that."

"Feel this," he said, thrusting his hips against her backside again. "And feel the pleasure that I give you."

She reached up, grabbing hold of the hand that was resting on her breasts, as though she was trying to get him to ease his pleasuring of her. As though it was too much. He collected that wrist, holding it in his hand like an iron manacle, and then he took hold of her other hand, bringing them around behind her and holding them fast, pinning them to her lower back as he continued to toy with her between her legs with his free hand.

She shifted her hips. "You're holding me prisoner now?"

"It seems fair. I've been held captive by you for years now."

"Luca," she breathed his name, total capitulation to what was happening between them. He worked his fingers between her legs faster, stroking her slickness over her clit before bringing his fingers down to the entrance of her body again, delving deep. The waves of her release seemed to come from deep within her, her internal muscles pulsing hard around his fingers as she found her pleasure.

He propelled her out onto the balcony, up to the edge of the bath. He tightened his grip on her stomach, lifting them both down into the water, prepared by her already. And there they were calm out under the stars again, only this time, there were no people. Nobody in a nearby ballroom to come out and discover them. No one at all.

He sat on the edge of the tub, whirling her around to face him, wrapping her legs around his waist, the slick heart of her coming into contact with his arousal.

"Out here," he said, "if you scream no one will hear you. Only the stars."

Those stars. That brightness. Her brightness.

"Then I suggest you do your part to make me scream."

He moved both hands down to cup her butt, freeing her wrists as he did. She moved her hands to his shoulders, gripping him tightly as he moved them both across the tub, the slick glide of the water over their skin adding a sharpness to the sensuality of the moment.

"You want to scream?" He moved them over to the glass edge of the tub that overlooked the sea and turned her, maneuvering her so that she was in front of him, facing the water, the reflection of the silvery moon over the waves.

"Hold on to the edge," he commanded.

She did so without arguing, though there was a hesitancy to her movements that spoke of confusion. She would not be confused for long.

He pressed one hand to her hip, and with the other, guided his erection to the entrance of her body. He pushed into her in one decisive thrust, grabbing both hips and pulling her back against him, the motion creating ripples in the water.

She gasped, leaning forward, her breasts pressed against the glass, her hands curved around the edge like claws. She bowed her head over the tub. He reached forward, grabbing hold of her dark curls and drawing her head back, none too gently, as he found her throat with his lips, kissing her, then scraping it with the edge of his teeth.

He rode her like that, one hand gripping her hip tightly, his blunt fingers digging into her skin, the other holding her hair as he thrust into her in an endless rhythm that pushed fire down his spine and sent pleasure through him like a river of molten flame.

He felt when her thighs began to quiver, when she got close to release. And he slipped his hand to her furrow again, brushing his fingers over where she was most sensitive, not stopping even as he felt her release break over her. Not stopping until she was screaming herself hoarse into the night, out over that endless ocean, up to the stars.

Into the darkness.

Into his darkness.

And when his own control reached its end he grabbed hold of her with both hands, holding her steady while he poured himself into her. His despair, his need, his release, nothing like a simple achievement of pleasure, but the sharp edge of a knife, cutting into him, making him bleed.

Reducing him. Right there in front of her. And there

was nothing that could be done about that. Nothing he could do to fight it.

He reached out, holding on to the edge of the tub, bracing himself for a moment while he caught his breath. She looked over her shoulder, those eyes connecting with his. She looked… She looked as undone as he felt, and he could not ignore the question in them. The need. To be held.

He gathered her up in his arms and carried her across the tub and they stepped out onto the balcony. There was a large, fluffy towel folded up on a shelf adjacent to the tub and he grabbed hold of it, wrapping it around her and holding her against him as he brought her back into the bedroom, depositing her onto the center of the bed.

He didn't bother to dry himself, coming down beside her completely naked as she wrapped the edges of the towel more firmly around her body.

She rolled onto her back, letting out a long, slow sigh. She had the towel pulled over her breasts, but it parted just above her belly button, revealing that delicious triangle at the apex of her thighs. He was not going to disabuse her of her illusion that she might be covered.

"Luca," she whispered. "Why do I get the feeling that it isn't the secret of Annalise that stands between us?"

CHAPTER ELEVEN

"I DON'T FOLLOW YOU."

"That's not your secret. You may not have ever told anyone about it, but I think you never told anyone because it wasn't important. I think there's something important. Something you don't talk about because of the heaviness."

She rolled to her side, looking at him, her dark gaze much more insightful than he would like. He felt... Well, he felt naked. A ridiculous thing, because he had been naked this entire time. But suddenly, he felt as though she had cut into him and peeled his skin from his bones, giving her a deep look into places that he had been so certain were hidden. And yet, she had seen. Easily and with accuracy.

"I'm not talking about this now."

"Then when? It's a wonderful thing, a beautiful thing, to have you out of control when we are together like this. But what about the rest of the time? What about what comes after? When we have to live a life together."

He growled, rolling over, pinning her to the bed, pressing his palms into her shoulders. "The dark things that live in me... It will do you no good to know about them." He felt a sick kind of shame roll over his skin like an oily film, as if he had not just been made clean by the water in the bathtub. As if he had not just been made clean by joining to her.

He realized, with a sharp sort of shock, that there was an element of fear buried in his deep reluctance to never speak of his past. Luca was an attractive man, and he well knew it. Not just physically; the women responded to his looks, to his expertly sculpted body and to his sexual prowess. But also, he was a man with money, a man with a title. It would be disingenuous for him to pretend he presented absolutely no attraction to women.

But he realized that the words his mother had spoken to him after that night had taken root deeper than he had imagined. That it would make people think things about him. That it would repulse and appall Sophia if she knew the truth. If she knew the things that had been done to his body, would she want him at all? Or would she find him damaged in some way?

It was an unacceptable weakness. To worry about these things. To care at all.

And that was the real problem. He wanted to pretend that it didn't matter. That he didn't think about it. That it only shaped him in good ways. In ways that he had chosen. But these feelings, this moment, made it impossible. An illusion he could no longer cling to. If he resented Sophia for anything, it was this, most of all.

"Do you want to know why reputation is so important to me?" The words scraped his throat raw on their exit. He didn't want to speak of this, but the very fact that it had become such a leaden weight inside him that it had become something insurmountable, meant it was time for him to speak of it. Because if there was one thing he couldn't stand more than the memory, it was giving it power.

It was acknowledging all that it meant to him.

He wanted it to be nothing. Which meant speaking of it should be nothing. But the ugly turn of that was if it meant something to Sophia… If he had to see disgust or pity in her eyes…

But suddenly, that luminous gaze of hers was far too much for him to withstand. And he thought that perhaps, as long as she wanted him in the end, a little bit of distance was not the worst thing.

"My mother had lovers," he said. "I imagine you didn't know that."

Sophia frowned. "I've never heard my mother or your father speak of his first wife."

"Yes. Well. It is not because he was mired in grief. Though I think he felt some measure of it, they were no longer in love by the time she died, if they ever were. I think…" Suddenly, a thought occurred to him that never had before. "I think your mother was his first experience of love. I think perhaps that is why the connection was so powerful there was no care given to propriety. Not when he already knew what could happen when you married someone who was supposed to be suitable."

"You… You knew that she had lovers. But you must have been…a boy."

"I was. Very young. At first, I did not question the presence of men in the palace and my father's absence. We had many people stay there at many different times. But it was clear, after a fashion, that they were…special to my mother. It could not be ignored. Mostly, they ignored me. But there was one… He often tried to speak to me. Attempted to cultivate a relationship with me. I was sixteen."

"That was just before she died," Sophia said softly.

"Yes. Giovanni was the last one. It was as if everything came to a head at that point." He hesitated. "Remember that ball I told you about?"

"The one with Annalise."

"Yes. I think perhaps the reason that my memory of her is so sharp is because... Sometimes my life feels as if it's divided into before and after. I know that many people would think I mean my mother's death. But that is not the case. Before and after the night of that ball. I was a different person then. A boy. Protected from the world. That is the function of palace walls, after all. They keep you insulated. And I was, for certain."

He didn't want Sophia to touch him while he spoke of this. Didn't want there to have been any contact between them. He rolled to the side, putting a solid expanse of bedspread between them. She seemed to understand. Because she didn't move. She stayed rooted to the spot he had pinned her in a moment ago.

"That night, after the ball ended... Giovanni had gotten me a drink. It was slightly unusual as he took pains in public to pretend he didn't know me. Why hint at a relationship with my mother? But still. I took the drink. I felt...very tired. And I remember I left early. I assume he then took advantage of the fact that people were moving around. The fact that people were walking through the halls... It was all normal. And anyone who was in attendance had certainly been vetted and approved by the royal family."

"Luca," she whispered, "what happened?" He could hear both confusion and dawning horror in her voice.

And he knew that she had not guessed, but that she felt a strong sense of disquiet. Of fear.

He took a breath, closed his eyes. "He violated me."

The words were metallic on his tongue. There were uglier words for what had happened to him. More apparent. But they were still too difficult to speak, because *victim* lay on the other side of them, and that was something he could not admit. Something he could not speak.

"He…"

He did not allow her to speak. "I think you know the answer."

She said nothing for a moment, silence settling heavy around them as flashes of memory replayed themselves in his mind. Flashes were all he had. A blessing of sorts, he supposed. A strange, surreal state brought about by whatever drug he'd been given.

"Why wasn't he arrested? Why weren't you protected?"

"It never happened again," he said gravely. No. He had gone straight to his mother. Because there had been no one else to speak to about it. How could he tell his father what had happened, at the hands of his mother's lover? To do so would mean to uncover her. But surely, she would protect her son.

She had not.

Not really.

Her version of protection had been to ensure that Giovanni didn't come to the palace anymore. She had cut off her association with him, but she did not, would not, push punishing him. For her own reputation.

"The reputation of the nation," he said, his throat tightening. "It was the most important thing."

"How can you say that? Of course it wasn't. Your

safety was the most important thing. Justice for what had been done to you."

Her lip was curled upward, an expression of disgust. Likely directed at what had been done to him, and not at him. But still, somehow it felt all the same.

"What does that mean in context with an entire nation of people?"

"You were raped," she said.

The words hit him like the lash of a whip. "And how is a nation supposed to contend with that? A future king who has been...victimized. Who was held down in his own bedchamber... It could not be. My mother explained why."

"Your mother?"

"There is no point having this discussion. She was correct. It would follow me, Sophia. It would be the story of who I was. Something like that cannot be forgotten. Admitting a weakness on that score..."

"You are not weak," she protested. "There is nothing weak about... You were drugged."

"So easy it would be to destroy the throne then. To attack the kingdom. See how vulnerable I am?"

"No," she protested.

"I don't believe that," he said. "To be clear. I was there, and I'm well aware of what I would have been able to fight and what I could not. But that would be the speculation, Sophia. And there is a reason that this does not get spoken of."

"Luca..."

"I have trusted you with it. You asked for this. You pushed for it. Don't you dare betray me."

He felt some guilt at saying that. As if she would. Of course she wouldn't. She was looking at him with the truest emotion he had ever seen. His mother certainly hadn't looked at him like that. She had been horrified, too. But not about what had been done to him half as much as what the fallout could be. The fallout for her.

He hated this. He hated thinking of it. It was best left buried deep, with the lesson carried forward. There was no point to this. Because there was nothing that could be done. It was dragging out dead bodies and beating them. And there was simply no reason for that.

You could not spend your life punching at ghosts. That much he knew.

"Am I a strong king, Sophia?"

"Yes," she said softly.

"Would I be so strong in the eyes of the people if they knew?"

"You should be," she said.

"But *would I be*? We cannot deal in what should be. If what should have happened had happened I would not have been violated. But I was. I can only deal in reality as it is. And I cannot take chances. Why do you think I did my very best to stay away from you? I have a reputation. Our country has a reputation. And what exists now? It has been built on the back of my silence. And now I've blown it all to hell."

"Luca, you cannot carry all of that. You're a man. You cannot control what people think of you. You're a good man, that's what matters. Not what people think. But what you do for the country."

"So you say. But our standing in the world would greatly be affected by the way the people perceived me. By the headlines. And when it came to my child… There was no choice. In that I would choose him."

"You should have chosen yourself," she said softly.

He bit back the fact that it was his mother who hadn't chosen him. So why the hell should he?

He had already stripped his soul bare, had already confessed to the kind of weakness and shame that made his skin crawl to even consider. The last thing he was going to do was go further into mommy issues.

"I chose San Gennaro," he said instead.

"Luca…"

He got out of bed. "I have some more work to see to."

"It's late."

"Yes," he said. "But it will not wait."

There was no work. But he needed distance. Feeling like he did, he could not allow her to touch him. He needed a chance to get distance from this moment. To forget this conversation had ever happened.

He had expected… He had expected her to pull back, and she wouldn't. Damn her. She surprised him at every turn.

He collected his clothing and pulled it on, walking out of the bedroom, ignoring Sophia's protests. He pushed his hands through his hair and paused for a moment, only just now realizing how quickly his heart was beating. But he had done it. He had spoken the words. Maybe now… Maybe now it wouldn't matter.

He walked down the hall toward his office, and when he entered the room his phone was lighting up, vibrating on his desk.

It was his stepmother. He picked up the phone. "It's late," he said.

"You need to come home," she said.

"I'm busy at the moment."

"Luca," she said, "I would not tell you to come home if it wasn't absolutely necessary. This is all getting out of hand. And you cannot simply leave the country to take care of itself."

"What about Sophia? This is for her benefit, not mine."

"Then leave her there alone. Wherever you've spirited her off to, leave her in peace while you come here to deal with the fallout of your actions."

"I assure you that your daughter has culpability in the situation."

"Oh, I have no doubt, but if your only view is to protect her, then leave her behind and come back and address your people."

"You know I can't do that. If we step out, we must do so together."

"That is likely true. But… Luca, I beg you, don't hurt Sophia. She is not from your world. No matter how long she has lived in it… It is not ingrained in her the way that it is in you. That duty must come first. For her, love will always come first."

Yes, and he knew that. Because for her, what his mother had done was unfathomable. While to him… He might resent it, but… In the end, could he truly be angry about it? What he had said to her was true. He would be defined by that experience if the world knew of it. It was difficult to be angry about the fact that he was not.

"I won't," he said.

"I wish I believed you."

"I will marry her. I will not abandon her."

"That's my concern. But you seem to think that is all that is required of you. There is so much more, Luca."

"What else is there?"

She said nothing for a moment. "Come home."

"I will ready a plane for an early morning departure."

CHAPTER TWELVE

WHEN SOPHIA AWOKE to see Luca standing at the side of the bed, wearing nothing but a pair of dark slacks, his arms crossed over his bare chest, his expression forbidding, she knew something was wrong.

"What?" She scrambled into a sitting position and pulled her sheet up to her chest.

Suddenly, last night came flooding back to her. His confession. What had happened to him at the hands of his mother's lover. He had left after that. And it had hurt that he had pulled away, but she had understood that it had been required.

Still. She wanted to hold him. She wanted to…offer him something.

She knew that he wouldn't let her.

"We need to leave," he said, his voice stern.

He walked over to the closet and took out a crisp white shirt, pulling it over his broad shoulders and beginning to button it slowly.

"Why?" She shook her head, trying to clear the webs of cotton from her brain. "I thought we were going to stay here until everything died down."

"We were. But your mother called. She convinced me otherwise." His jaw firmed, his expression like iron.

"It is not going to be easy. But she is correct. I have left the country to burn in my absence, and I cannot do that. She suggested…that I leave you here."

"I don't want to stay here. I want to go with you."

He seemed to relax slightly at that. But only slightly. "I feel it would be best for you to come with me. It would be good for us to present a united front. However…"

"There is no however," she said, pushing herself up so that she was sitting straighter. "You're right. If you return without me the rumors will only get worse. Whatever you say. I need to be there. I need to be there, speaking for myself. There is no other alternative that is acceptable."

"You are very brave, Sophia."

Was she? She had never felt particularly brave. A girl who had tried once to gain the attention of her father, only to fail. Who had then spent a life infatuated with a stepbrother who didn't even like her.

Suddenly, it all became clear, as if the clouds had rolled back, revealing a clear sky and full sun. She had spent those years infatuated with Luca to protect herself. If she had ever fancied herself in love with him, she had been wrong. Because she had not known him.

He had never even been kind to her. Had never demonstrated any softness toward her. Had taken no pains to make her feel welcome in the palace.

He had been the safest.

Until the moment he had touched her in the garden, and it all became painfully real.

But until last night, she had never really known him.

She had been attracted to the untouchable quality he had. To the safety that represented. And more than that, to his strength. The integrity that he exuded.

She had admired that, because she had known men without it. Her own father being one of them.

But that wasn't enough to be love.

Suddenly, as he stood there, putting himself back together, after making himself so vulnerable the night before, putting the king back on over the top of the wounded boy, she fully appreciated what that integrity meant. What that strength cost.

That the granite in his voice, the hardness in his eyes, the straightness in his stance, the way he held his head high, had all come with great difficulty.

Anyone who knew his public story would think he was a man who was exactly as he had been raised to be. A man who had never faced any real adversity, beyond the loss of his mother. And what famous, handsome prince these days had not experienced such a thing?

But they didn't know. Not really.

Until last night she hadn't, either.

Suddenly, it felt as if someone had reached inside her chest and grabbed hold of her heart, squeezing it hard. Feeling overwhelmed her. There was no safety here. There was no careful divide created by his disdain, no distance at all. This wasn't simple attraction, wasn't fascination. It was more. It was deeper.

It was something she had not imagined possible. Something she hadn't wanted.

Love, for her, apart from her family, had always been a simple word.

This was more. It created a seismic shift inside her, incited her to action. To open herself up and expose herself to hurt.

The very last thing that love was was a feeling. It was so many other things first.

She understood that then.

Because until then, she had not loved Luca.

But she did now. Deeply.

"I must get myself presentable," she said. And then she rose out of the bed, not covering herself at all, and walked over to the closet, where, at the moment their clothes were mingled. Would it always be like this? With their lives tangled together?

She imagined that Luca fancied a royal marriage to be something based on tradition. That they would carry out their separate lives, in their separate quarters.

But their parents hadn't done that. His father, and her mother, had shared everything. Space. Life. Breath.

That was what she wanted. She didn't want to be the wife of his duty. She wanted to be the wife of his heart.

She turned to face him, whatever words on her lips there had been dying the moment that her gaze connected with his. With the heat there. He was looking at her with a deep, ferocious hunger that made her feel... both happy and sad all at once.

Luca wanted her. There was no denying that.

But whatever else he felt...

He was perfect. A man perfectly formed, with a wonderfully symmetrical face, classically handsome features that his aristocratic air pushed over into being devastating. His physique was well muscled, his hands large and capable. So wonderful to be held by.

But he was scarred. Inside, he was destroyed.

And no one looking at him would have any clue.

She wondered...

She wondered if there was any way to reach past those scars.

Any way to touch his heart.

She turned away from him again, concentrating on dressing herself. She selected a rather somber black sheath dress, not one that would be approved by the new stylist, but one that would best suit their return back to the country. She had a feeling they would be trying to strike a tone that landed somewhere between defiance and contrition. Not an easy thing to do. But they would have to be resolute in what they had chosen, while being mindful of the position the nation was put in due to the scandal.

He was distant the entire plane ride back to San Gennaro, but she wasn't overly surprised by that. He was trying to rebuild that wall. Brick by brick. Oh, not to keep out that physical lust. Not anymore.

But that new emotional connection that had been forged last night...

He wanted badly to turn away from that. And she didn't know how to press it. She had always imagined she had lived the harder life. She was from poverty, after all. She had a father who didn't want her. She knew what it was to go to bed hungry. She'd been fortunate enough to come into a wonderful life at the palace, but it had been foreign to her. Filled with traditions and silverware that were completely unfamiliar to her.

But now she knew different.

Now she knew that incredible strength could mask unfathomable pain. The walls of a palace could not keep out predators when they had simply been let in.

When the plane descended it felt like a heavyweight was pushing them down toward the ground. Or perhaps that was just the feeling inside her chest. Heaviness.

She wished they could stay on the island. That they could stay in a world where rigorous walks on the beach and lazy lovemaking sessions in a tub were the most pressing things between them.

She had to wonder… If they had not spoken last night…would he be ready to fly back today? Would he be so dead set on their need to return home?

She wondered if he wasn't facing his duty so much as running from her.

No, that wasn't fair.

If there was one thing Luca was not, it was a coward. He would forcefully tell her he didn't want to speak of something, that was certain, but he would not run.

"Prepare yourself," he said, the first words he had spoken to her in hours as the plane door opened.

And indeed, his words were not misplaced. Their car was down there waiting for them, but it was surrounded. Bodyguards were doing their best to keep the horde at bay, but camera flashes were going off, blinding Sophia as they made their way down the stairs and toward the limousine.

Luca wrapped his arm tightly around her and guided her into the car, speaking firmly in Italian before closing the door behind them.

"We will have to speak to them, won't we?" she asked as the car attempted to maneuver its way through the throng.

"Eventually," he said. "But I will do it on my own terms. I am the king of this nation, and I will not be led around by the dictates of the press. Yes, we have answers to give. Yes, we must return and create a solid front for the country. But I will not stand on the tarmac and give an interview like some fame whore reality TV star."

She examined the hard line of his profile, shiver working its way down her spine.

Everything he believed in was crumbling in front of him, and still, he was like granite. Protecting his image had been everything, because if it wasn't...

She felt like she'd been stabbed in the chest as she realized, fully, deeply, the cost of all this to him. How it linked to the pain of his past, and the decisions that had been made then.

It made her want to fix it. To fix him. Because she had been part of this destruction. But she hadn't understood.

"Luca," she said softly.

"We don't need to talk," he said, firm and rigid. "There will be time later."

"Will there?"

"We will have to prepare a statement."

Preparing a statement was not the same as the two of them talking. But she wasn't going to correct him on that score right now.

Later, when she was installed back in her normal bedroom, alone, she wished she had pressed the issue.

But Luca had been forceful and autocratic like he could be, and he had determined that the two of them should not do anything wildly different from normal until they figured out how they were going to handle the public fallout.

She wished that she was in bed with him.

But then, maybe it was good for her to have some time alone.

She tossed and turned for a few moments, and then got out of bed. She crossed the large room, wearing only her nightgown, and padded out to the balcony. She leaned over the edge, staring out at the familiar grounds below, illuminated by the moonlight. She looked in the direction of the garden. Where all of this had started.

She wouldn't take it back. She simply wouldn't.

Not when being with him had opened the door to learning so much about herself.

To learning about love.

The discovery that she had been protecting herself all those years was a startling one, and yet, not surprising at the same time.

The breeze kicked up, and she could smell the roses coming in on the wind, tangling through her hair. She closed her eyes. And for a moment she thought she might be able to smell Luca's aftershave. His skin. That scent that had become so beloved, and so familiar.

"Here you are."

She whirled around at the sound of his voice, only to see him standing in the doorway of the balcony, looking out.

"Did you think I had jumped?"

"I rather hoped you hadn't."

"I thought we weren't going to talk tonight."

"I couldn't sleep," he said.

He pushed away from the door frame, and came out onto the balcony. He was wearing the same white button-up he'd had on earlier, the top three buttons undone. She could imagine, so easily, what his muscular chest would look like. What it would feel like if she were to push her hand beneath the edge of the shirt and touch him. His hair was disheveled as though he had been running his hands through it. Her eye was drawn to the gold wristwatch he was wearing. She didn't know why. But it was sexy. Maybe it was just because to her, he was sexy.

"I couldn't sleep, either." She frowned. "But I suppose that's self-evident."

"Perhaps."

"It's dark out here," she said, lifting her shoulder.

"What does that mean?"

"We can talk in the dark." She hadn't meant to say that. But she wondered if it was true. If this balcony could act as a confessional, like their bed had done last night.

"We can talk in the light just as well," he said, his tone stiff.

"No," she said, weary. "I'm not sure we can. At least, I think it doesn't make things easier."

"What is it you have to say?"

"I hope that you have some things to say to me. But…"

She wasn't quite in a space where she wanted to confess her undying love. But she did want him to know… She wanted him to know something. "You know," she said slowly. "After our parents were married… I saw my father. He found me. Actually, all of the press made it easy."

Luca frowned. "You were protected by guards."

"Yes. But they were hardly going to stop me from meeting with my father."

"I didn't know about it."

"Well, you wouldn't have. You were away at university by then. We saw each other for a while… Until your father refused to give him a substantial sum of money. I was so angry, Luca. I thought that your father was being cruel. Because after that my father took himself away from me. He didn't want me. He never did. But I couldn't see that. Not then. I was only thirteen, and it felt immeasurably awful to have my father taken from me simply because yours wouldn't give him what he needed."

"What a terrible thing," Luca said, his voice rough. "To be so badly used by a parent."

"But you know about that, don't you? I didn't think you did. I thought… I thought for you things were so easy. I admired you. Even when you weren't nice to me. I admired how certain you were. How steady. You were all of these things that I could never be, wearing this position like a second skin. But now I know. I know what it costs you to stand up tall. And it only makes me admire you all the more."

He ignored her, walking over to the balcony, standing beside her. He gripped the railing, and she followed suit, their hands parallel to each other but not touching. Still, she could feel him. With every breath.

"How did you come to be close with my father? After all that anger you had toward him?" Luca asked. He quite neatly changed the subject.

But she didn't mind talking about this. She wanted to tell him. She wanted to… Well, she wanted to give no less than she took.

Or, what she hoped to take.

"He proved to be the better man," she said.

"How?" He seemed hungry for that answer.

"My father quit seeing me after your father refused to pay him off. Meanwhile, I was a wretch to your father. I was rude. I was insufferable. And he never once threatened to remove himself from my life. No. He only became more determined to forge a relationship with me. He refused to quit on me. Even when I was a monster. He could have… He could have simply let us exist in the same space. There was no reason that he had to try to have a relationship with me. But he did. He proved what manner of man he was through his actions. He showed me what strength was. What loyalty was." She swallowed hard, her throat dry like sandpaper. "He demonstrated love to me. And I had certainly seen it coming from my mother. But not from anyone else. He made me feel like I was worth something."

Yes, the king had pursued her. Her affection. He had made that relationship absolutely safe for her before she had decided to give of herself. But when it came to Luca…it wasn't the same.

When it came to him, she might have to put herself out there first. And she…

That was terrifying. She wasn't sure she could.

It wasn't something she was sure she could do.

If only he would…

She bit her lip. "I was very grateful to have your father. He did a lot to repair the damage that my own father created."

"I can only hope to be half the father he was."

"Well, I hope to be as good of a mother as my own."

It was the first time they had really talked about the baby in those terms. It had all been about blood, and errors and duty. But it had been real. It had not been about being a mother and a father.

"Your mother has always been good to me," he said. "She never had a thing to prove, you know. Not a thing to hide. Not like my own mother did. She is a truly kind woman, who had many things said about her by the media. Cruel, unfair. But she held her head high. You are the same, Sophia. I know you are. You will show our child—son or daughter—how to do the same."

She ducked her head, her heart swelling. "I hope so."

"If it had to be that our child was born in scandal, there is no one I would trust better to teach him to withstand."

Suddenly, Luca released his hold on the railing and turned away from her. She felt the abandonment keenly. As if the air had grown colder. Darker.

"Wait." She held up her hand, even though he couldn't see her. But he stopped, his shoulders held rigid. "I don't... I'm not sorry. So you know. I don't regret this."

Only the slight incline of his head indicated her words had meant something to him. The pause he took.

"Good night, Sophia," he said.

She wanted to say more. The words gathered in her chest, climbed up her throat, tight in a ball like a fist. But she couldn't speak them. So instead, she issued a request. "Stay with me. Tonight."

Then he took her by the hand, and led her to bed. And he did stay, all through the night.

It was surprising how quickly a royal wedding could be put together. Certainly, the wedding that they had assembled for Erik and Sophia had come together quickly enough, but this had been accomplished in lightning speed. They had handled the press a few days earlier, making a joint statement from the grounds of the palace, that had been streamed live over the internet and television. They had spoken about their commitment to San Gennaro, and to each other. And unsurprisingly it had been met with somewhat mixed reviews. But he had expected nothing less.

There was no way they were going to have a universal buy-in from the public. Not given the state of things.

They would have to win them over through the course of time. He had a feeling the baby would help.

Babies often did.

They were to be married in two days' time, and truly, he couldn't ask for things to be going much better than they were. He had Sophia in his bed every night, in spite of his determination that they would not carry on in that regard once they were back at the palace, and everything was going as smoothly as it possibly could. In terms of his lack of control when it came to bedding her...

She was his weakness. That was the simple truth.

He was a man who hadn't afforded himself a weakness as long as he'd been a grown man. Sophia had always challenged him. Had always slipped beneath his resolve and made him question all that he knew about himself.

He didn't like it. But he rather did like sleeping skin to skin with her.

Sacrifices had to be made.

There would be a small gathering tonight, of the guests arriving for the upcoming union. Nothing large, like it would have been with more time. Like it would have been if there wasn't a cloud hanging over the top of them.

It would fade. Surely, it would fade.

And if it didn't? An interesting thought to have. He had been so wedded to his reputation, to guarding what everyone thought, the idea that he had no more control over it was...

He frowned. He wasn't even certain he cared.

Sophia was the mother of his child. She was to be his wife. There was no arguing with that. And as she had said to him just the other night…whatever people thought of him, he could rule. And he could do it well.

The rest didn't matter.

"How are you finding things?" he asked as Sophia was ushered toward him at the entrance of the dining hall.

She was wearing a dress of such a pale color that the sequins over the top of it looked as though they had been somehow fastened directly to her pale, smooth skin. It glittered with each step she took, and the top came to an artful V at her breasts, showing off those delicate curves in exquisite fashion.

She took hold of his arm, looked up at him. "Entertaining dignitaries' wives is a strange experience."

"But it is your life now," he pointed out.

She wilted somewhat at that.

"I am sorry, *cara mia,*" he said, "but it cannot be ignored that being queen does carry its share of burdens. Your mother, I'm certain, knows all about that."

"Yes," she said, though somewhat hesitant.

He wondered what the caveat was, because there was one. He could hear it. Unspoken, deep down her throat. But they were walking into a dining room crowded full of people, half of whom were hoping they would be witnessing some sort of glorious meltdown, he was certain, so he was hardly going to broach the topic now.

He sat at the head of the table, and Sophia had departed from him and made her way down to the foot.

Tradition, he mused, was such a fascinating thing. Things like this… They formed from somewhere, and that demonstrated that humans could clearly create them out of thin air. On a whim. But there were certain points in history where tradition had simply been followed, and not created. As though someone else had made those rules, and human beings were bound to them. As though they could not be broken.

Tradition. Appearances.

Those things had been paramount to his mother, even while she had lived in exactly the fashion she had wanted. And he… He clung to it because it gave him a sense of purpose. Because it made him feel as if what had happened to him—and the lack of fallout after—had been unavoidable.

It was the reason that he was seated across the room from Sophia now, when he would like her at his side.

All of these fake rules.

He was a damned king, and yet there were all these rules.

The rules that kept him from receiving any sort of justice. The rules that prevented him from acting on his attraction to Sophia in the first place.

And the rules that kept him from sitting beside her now. The rules that had kept them from spending the day together.

A strange thing. All of it.

Those seated around him directly had been artfully chosen people. Selected carefully by members of his cabinet. People who would only speak highly of him, and certainly not call into question his union with his stepsister. He was certain the same could be said for those who had been seated directly around Sophia, and those in the middle could fling poison back and forth across the table to their hearts' content, for he and his bride could not hear it.

When the meal was finished he rose, nodding his head once and signaling Sophia to follow suit.

She looked up at him with slightly cautious eyes, but she followed his lead. She had watched his father and her mother do this many times. She knew that she was simply to follow his lead.

They met at the center of the table and he took her arm again, then they turned toward the doors and made their exit.

The guests would follow shortly, but they had a moment, a quiet moment there in the antechamber.

"Are you all right?"

"Yes," she said. "I do understand how these things work."

"But it's only just dawning on you that your role in them has changed. Am I correct in assuming that?"

"It's a lot of things. Marrying you. Becoming a mother. The fact that I was going to be queen was low on my list of things to deal with."

"And yet, you will be my queen. Tomorrow."

Her skin looked a bit waxen, pale, her gown and her necklace glittering in the dim light, which was helpful to her, as she herself did not glitter at all at the moment.

"It's too late to go back," he said.

She jerked her focus toward him. "I didn't say that I wanted to."

"You don't seem happy."

"I'm overwhelmed. I have been overwhelmed from the moment that you kissed me in the garden all those weeks ago. I don't know how you can expect me to feel any differently than that."

"Well, I suggest that by the time we are in the chapel tomorrow you find a way to feel slightly less over-whelmed."

She lifted a brow, her expression going totally flat. "As you command, sire."

He had no opportunity to respond to that because their guests began to depart the dining room and fill the antechamber.

"With regrets," Luca said, "I must bid you all good-night. As must my fiancée. With the wedding tomorrow we do not wish to overextend her."

He wrapped his arm around her waist, breaking with propriety completely by engaging in such an intimate hold in public, and propelled her from the room. She was all but hissing by the time they arrived in her bedroom.

"Luca," she said. "We have guests, and I spent the entire day on my best behavior, not so that you could ruin it now."

"My apologies," he said, his tone hard. "I am ever ruining the reputations of others."

She looked ashamed at that. And he felt guilty. Because he knew that wasn't what she meant.

"Luca, I didn't mean..."

"I'm aware. I apologize for using that against you."

She didn't seem to know what to say to that. "Don't apologize to me," she said finally. "We're going to have to learn how to make this work."

She looked thoughtful at that.

"We don't have a lot of practice getting along. Not outside of bed anyway," he said.

"That is very true." She clasped her hands and folded them in front of her body. Then she let out a long, slow breath and lifted one leg slightly, towing her high heel off, before working on the other. It reduced her height by three inches, leaving her looking a small, shimmering fairy standing in the bedchamber.

"I know how they made it work," she said slowly. "I know why it was easy for them."

"Why is that?"

"They loved each other. They loved each other so very much, Luca. It wasn't a child, or the need for marriage or money that brought them together. They risked everything to be together. Not because they had to, but because they wanted to."

Her words were soft, and yet they landed in his soul like a blow. "I don't understand what you want me to do with that. I don't understand what you want me to say. You're pregnant. Your mother was not pregnant. I cannot change the circumstances of why we are marrying."

"I know," she said. "But I've found that over the past weeks my reasons for marrying you have changed." She looked up at him, her dark eyes luminous. "Luca, I imagined myself half in love with you for most of my life but it wasn't until after that night in San Paolo that I realized that wasn't true."

His stomach crawled like acid. Of course. She had realized she didn't love him after she found out that he had been such a weak victim of such a disgusting crime. That his body had been used in such a fashion. Of course she was repulsed by him. Who wouldn't be? He was repulsed by himself most of the time. Questioning a great many things about him. Questioning his attraction to Sophia herself. If it was something inside him that had been twisted and broken off beyond repair. Something that had caused him to want a thing that was forbidden to him.

"I am sorry to have destroyed your vision of me."

"No," she said. "That was when my vision of you became whole. Luca, you were a safe thing to love. I couldn't be with you. You were my stepbrother. How could it ever happen? You could never hurt me, not the way my father had done. And all the better, as long as I was obsessed with you, no one else could hurt me, either. You were a wall that I could build around myself. A thing to distract my heart with. The minute that you touched me that wall was destroyed. I didn't know you. How could I love you if I didn't know you? I admired things about you. I admired your strength. I admired what an honest man you were. But I didn't know the cost of those things, Luca, and knowing that… That was when I began to love you for real. I love you, Luca. I didn't want to say it. Because I wanted so badly to protect myself. I have been rejected before. I loved my father, and he only wanted to use what money your father could give him. I could not face being the one who tore themselves open and revealed their whole heart, only to be met with nothing. And I almost did… The other night I almost did. But I was afraid. I'm not going to be afraid anymore. I don't want to be. You deserve more than someone hiding and protecting themselves." She swallowed hard. "I love you."

Everything inside him rebelled at her claim. Utterly. Completely. There was no way it could be true. No way in heaven or hell.

"You don't love me," he said, his voice hard. "You want to make all of this a bit more palatable for you. You want to make it easier. But you don't love me."

"I do."

"Fine. Think what you wish, but that doesn't mean it's going to change anything."

"Why not? Why can't it change anything?"

"Because I don't love anything," he said. "Nothing at all."

"That can't be true, Luca. You loved your father. You care a great deal for my mother…"

"Family. Is different."

"How? Your mother was family…"

"I'm going to marry you, Sophia," he said. "I don't see why we need to get involved in an argument regarding feelings. I have committed to you. Why should you want anything else?"

"Because it's not just something else. It's everything else. Love is vital, Luca, and without it… It's the glue. It's not about lust. It's not blood. It's love."

"There we disagree. Because some days it's the promises that will be all that hold us together. That is how life works. Sometimes it's simply the things you have decided that keep you going. You cannot make decisions in desperation. You must make them with a cool head, and only then can you be certain you will act with a level of integrity."

"Fine. I can accept that you feel that way. In fact, it's one of the things I admire about you. You're a good man. You always have been. There is no doubt about that. But there has to be more. We cannot have one without the other. I don't want commitment without love, Luca. I can't."

"Why not?"

He could not understand why she couldn't let this go. Love was nothing. Love was…

Love failed. It left you bleeding on the ground. He had heard it said many times that love did not seek its own, but that was not his experience.

His mother cared only for herself.

He had been a casualty in her pursuit of pleasure, in her pursuit of protecting her own comfort.

He hadn't mattered.

Why should Sophia feel that he did? And why should she try to demand that he...?

It didn't matter. It didn't matter as long as he promised to stay with her.

"Because don't I deserve to be loved? Don't I deserve to be at the forefront of whatever action is being taken? I have been loved, richly so in my life. But... I've never been chosen. My mother loved me in spite of the fact that having me plunged her into poverty. Your father loved me because he loved my mother. My own father didn't care at all. He wanted money. And you want the baby. Is it so much to ask, Luca, that I be wanted for who I am? That I be loved for who I am?"

"I have told you a great many times that you are a sickness in my blood. If I didn't want you then we wouldn't be here at all. There would be no baby."

"Being your sickness isn't the same as being your love, Luca, and if you can't sort that out, then I'm not sure we have anything left to say to each other."

"So you'll just storm away from me?" he asked, anger rising up unreasonably inside him. "If you can't have exactly what you want the moment you want you're going to leave?" Of course she would. Why would she stay with him? That was the fundamental issue with all of this. She could profess to love him, and she might even believe it. But when it all came down, that would not be so. It couldn't be.

Because he was a man who had been used and discarded. The violation he had experienced at the hands

of his mother's paramour not remotely as invasive as
the one he had experienced when his mother had chosen
to maintain her reputation over protecting him. Seeking justice for him.

And he had no idea how to feel about it. Because she
was dead. Because he wasn't entirely certain he wanted
his pain splashed all over the headlines, and had they
sought legal action against the man who had harmed
him, he certainly would have been in the headlines.

He didn't know what he wanted. He didn't know
what he was worth.

But he knew he wasn't worth Sophia and all of the
feelings she professed to have for him now.

She had tried to explain to him how her feelings for
him had shifted, but she didn't truly understand. She
couldn't.

"I told my mother what was done to me," he said,
his voice low. "I went to her. Trusted her. I had been
drugged. I had been violated. Abused. And I told her as
much. That she had let that man into the palace, and that
he had sought me out and harmed me in such a way. She
was upset. And she was fearful. But it was not for me. It
was for her own self. She could not have my father finding out she had been conducting affairs. She could not
have the public finding out that she had been engaged
in such a thing. And if we were to bring him before the
law, then of course he would expose my mother for what
she was. She couldn't have that. She didn't care for me,
Sophia. Not one bit. My own mother."

"She was broken," Sophia said. "As my father is broken. You cannot possibly think that I deserve the way
my father treated me, can you?"

"That's different."

"It isn't. You're just too afraid to step out from beneath this."

"Because on the other side is nothing. Nothing but the harsh, unending truth that I was nothing more than an incidental to the person who should have loved me simply because of the connection that we shared."

"Luca," she said. "I love you."

Suddenly, the emotion in his chest was like panic. Because she kept persisting even though he had told her to stop. And the monster inside him was growling louder, and he couldn't drown it out with platitudes. Nothing about promises or duty, or about standing tall in the face of an unfriendly press. About being a king and therefore being above these kinds of emotions, needing to rule with a cool head and a steady heart, rather than one given to things such as this. But he could not speak those words. He could not even feel them.

"You cannot love me," he said. "You cannot love me because I do not love myself." He gritted his teeth, despising the weakness inside him. "The man I could've been was stolen from me. I had to rebuild myself out of something, because God knows nobody was going to do it for me. I was broken open. All that I might have been poured out. And when I put myself together I did not make an effort to replace those things within me that were weak. Those things within me that had… That made me seem as though I might make a good victim."

"No," she said. "That's not fair."

"There is no fair in this. I was chosen for a reason. The boldness that it takes to do to me what that man did. Did you ever think of it that way? I was the future King of San Gennaro, and he felt as though he could take advantage of me, and he knew that he would not be punished. He knew that my mother would protect him. He knew that I would not be able to come forward and speak out against him. My hands would be tied. I refused… I refused to be remade in the same fashion that I had been born. I despise what I was, but I like the man I am now a little more. You cannot…"

He turned away from her, closing his eyes and gathering his control once again. "You cannot."

"Luca," she said, sounding broken, and he hated that, too. She deserved something else. Something different. A chance to be with a man, to want a man, to care for a man, who was not…broken in this way.

"Do you know," he said. "I have often wondered if there was something inherently sick inside me."

"You keep saying that word."

"I know. Because I wonder if it's why I've wanted you so badly for so long. Because there was something in me…"

"No. Stop trying to push me away."

"I'm not trying to push you away. I'll marry you. But I'm never going to love you in the way that you want me to. I can't. That part of myself is gone. It's dead. I had to cut it out of me so that I can survive all that I went through." He shook his head. "I will not change it for you. I cannot."

To change now would be to open himself back up to the kind of pain that he wanted gone from him forever, and he wouldn't do it.

"But you are pushing me away," she said.

"Sophia…"

She took a step away from him. "I'm sorry, Luca. I love you. And I'm not going to marry you simply because of duty. I would marry you because I loved you but I want you to marry me for the same reason. It would be so easy…" Her words came out choked, her brown eyes filling with tears. "It would be so easy to simply let this be. To take what you're offering, and be content with that. But I… I cannot. Luca, I can't. Because I think we could both have more. It doesn't have to be a sickness. It can be the cure. But only if you let it. And if I stay, and I allow you to have me without risking anything…"

His stomach tightened, turned over, and he ceased hearing her. Stopped listening. "If you don't want a man who's been raped, *cara mia*, all you have to do is say so."

"*Don't.* Don't make it about me being scared. I am scared, but I'm doing the brave thing. The hard thing. I refuse to let us live our lives as broken pieces when we can be whole together."

"What are you saying?"

"That for the second time, Princess Sophia is not going to show up to her wedding."

And with that, Sophia turned and walked out of the room, not bothering to gather her shoes. And he simply stood there, looking at them. Thinking this was the strangest interpretation of a Cinderella story he had ever heard of.

But after that came a strange pain in his chest like he couldn't remember feeling before. And he didn't even try to stop it from dropping him to his knees.

CHAPTER THIRTEEN

SOPHIA RAN UNTIL her mind was blank. Until there was nothing but her bare feet pounding down on the damp grass, the blades sticking between her toes, mud giving way and creating a slick foothold as she prayed her legs wouldn't fail her. Prayed they would carry her far away from Luca. From heartbreak.

She was still on the palace grounds, for they extended vastly, and she knew that she was going to have to stop running and get in a car. Get on a plane, to truly escape Luca. But for now she couldn't stop. For now she could do nothing but run.

She stopped when she came to the edge of the woods, and then she took a cautious step forward, the texture of the grounds changing to loose dirt and pine needles, the heavy tree cover protecting her from the pale moonlight. It was cool, almost frigid, there beneath the dark trees.

She shivered. She wrapped her arms around herself, trying to catch her breath. She took another step forward, and another, her dress shimmering in front of her, catching stolen beams of moonlight, flashing in the darkness.

She didn't know what she had just done. Didn't know what her plan was.

To walk into the forest and die?

No.

That was hardly the solution to dealing with a man not returning your affection.

She had been right, in what she had said to him. She couldn't go through with a marriage to a man who didn't love her. Not just for her own sake, but for his.

She had the feeling that many people—herself included until recently—thought love to be a beautiful, quiet thing. A force that allowed you to be yourself. And while that was true…it didn't mean the self that you projected to the world.

Real love, she fully understood now, challenged that identity. It forced you to reach down deep to your essence, and ask yourself who you were *there*. Real love was not about being comfortable. Not about being protected. Real love was about being stripped bare. Was about revealing yourself, unprotected to the other person, trusting that they would not use your tender and vulnerable places against you. That they would protect them for you, so that you didn't have to.

Real love was the difference between hiding in a darkened forest, or standing in the light.

Right now she was hiding in a forest.

She closed her eyes, a tear tracking down her face.

And it was then she realized where her feet were carrying her. She pressed on through the forest. Through and through. Until she found the paved drive that wound through the trees.

Her mother had moved into the dower house some time ago. It was an outmoded sort of thing, surely, as the palace was so large, but her mother seemed to like it. Liked having her own house rather than standing on ceremony in the massive palace.

It gave her a sense of peace. Gave her a small slice of her simple life back. Although the cottage, with its impeccably tended garden, bright pink roses climbing up the sides of the walls and exquisite furnishings was far grander than anything possessed by Sophia or her mother in their former lives.

It was dark now, the white stucco of the cottage shining a pale beacon through the dimness, the roses fluttering slightly against the wall as the breeze kicked up.

The gravel in the driveway cut into her feet, but she didn't care.

She walked up to the door and knocked.

It opened slowly, and then more quickly when her mother realized it was her.

"Sophia," she said. "What are you doing here?"

"I…" She swallowed hard. "I didn't know where else to go. I didn't even know I was coming here until… Until I realized where I was."

"What happened?"

"Luca and I fought. I… I called off the wedding."

"Come inside," her mother said, ushering her in.

There, Sophia found herself quickly wrapped in a blanket and settled on the couch, and before she knew it, a cup of tea was being firmly placed into her hand.

"Tell me."

"He doesn't wish to love me," Sophia said. "Which I feel is very different to not loving me at all. He doesn't want love. It… It frightens him." She would not reveal Luca's secrets to her mother. Because though she trusted her mother to keep confidences, they were Luca's secrets to tell. "He is very wounded by some things in his past, and he doesn't want…"

"He doesn't want to be healed?"

"Yes. Was his father like that?"

"No." Her mother shook her head. "I was. Your father hurt me deeply. Years of being shunned for being a single mother. The casual judgment I faced every day leaving the house. Collecting assistance so that I could feed you. It all left me scarred and hardened. And then I met Magnus. He charmed me. And yes, when we met, seduced me. I'm not going to dance around that, Sophia, since I know you know full well about those things."

Sophia felt her face heat. "Indeed."

"It was easy for him to tempt me into his bed, but into his life was another thing entirely. And I did my best. To work my job, to keep my liaisons with a king private. To continue to be a good mother to you. I thought I could keep all those things separate. That all of those parts of myself didn't have to be contained in one woman. That I could put walls up." She smiled softly. "But I couldn't. Not in the end. But I was hanging on very tightly to my pain. And I realized I was going to have to open my hands up and drop that pain if I was going to grab hold of what he was offering me. But when your pain has been fuel for so long, it is a difficult thing to do."

"I think that's how it is for him. I think his pain has kept him going, because without it…"

"Without it there's only despair. Anger is much easier. Do you know what else anger is preferable to?"

"What?"

"Hope. Learning to hope again is a terrifying thing. And when you have been harmed, you don't want it.

You resist it. Those little bits of light creeping back into the darkness are the most terrifying thing. You cannot hide in the light, Sophia. Darkness is a wonderful concealment. But it conceals everything. The beauty of the world. All that we can have around us. But it reveals us, too. The light. I suspect that is what Luca is resisting."

"What should I do? Should I go back to him? Love him even though he doesn't love me?"

"I can't tell you what to do. I don't want you trapped in a loveless marriage. But..."

"If I love him it isn't loveless," she said softly.

"No. It isn't." Her mother sat down on the couch next to her, clasping her hands in her lap. "The king loved me all the while when I could not love him. But he also didn't compromise. He did not want a mistress. He wanted a wife. And as far as he was concerned, if I didn't love him, even if we took vows, I might as well be a mistress."

"So he gave you an ultimatum."

"No. He just made it known he could not fully bring me into his life without love."

"Well. Luca and I can't exactly have that sort of arrangement. We are going to have a child together. And I live in the palace half the time."

Her mother laughed softly. "I'm not telling you what to do, Sophia. I feel there is the potential for heartbreak at every turn with this situation."

"That's not very encouraging."

"It isn't supposed to be encouraging. It's just the truth. I guess the question is... If he's going to break your heart either way... Would you rather be with him or be without him?"

"I don't know."

Except she did know. She wanted him. She wanted to be in his life, in his bed, but it felt like a potentially dangerous thing to do. The wrong thing. Like it would damage...

Her pride. Her defenses.

Perhaps she was more like her mother than she imagined.

Claims of love were bold, but quite empty when the action was withheld until the other person performed to your specifications.

His mother had given up on him. Had put herself before him.

Sophia realized she could not do the same.

Luca was not a man given to drink. He was not a man who indulged in anything, particularly. But he was drunk now. There was nothing else that was going to calm the pounding ache in his head. In his chest. He had sat there, for hours, on the floor of Sophia's bedroom, pain biting into him like rabid wolves. And then he had gotten up and gone back to his own quarters, and proceeded to drink the contents of his personal bar.

Now the pain was just swimming back and forth inside him, hazy and dull and no less present.

And he had even less control of his thoughts now. Chasing through his mind like rabid foxes after their own tails.

He was worthless. Worthless. A king of an entire country, worth absolutely nothing.

He did not allow himself those thoughts. He never did. But in this moment, he not only allowed them, he fed them. Like they were his pets. He allowed them to rain down on him, a black misery that coated him completely.

He embraced, wholly, his misery. His self-pity.

Sophia had spoken of how he stood tall in spite of everything. But here he was, on the floor. Prostrate to the sins that had been committed against him, and to what remained of his own soul. Black and bruised like the rest of him.

Dark.

He was a night without stars.

Sophia was the stars.

He rolled onto his back, the earth spinning on its axis.

He was worthless because he had been treated like an object. Worthless because his own mother had not cared to seek justice for him.

And yet, in the midst of those thoughts, in the midst of that darkness, there came a glimmer.

Sophia did not see him as worthless. Sophia thought he was strong.

Sophia thought he was worthy of love.

And in an instant, as though the sun had broken through storm clouds, he felt bathed in light.

Why should his mother, Giovanni, be the ones who formed his life? Why should they decide what he was?

Perhaps, in withholding what had happened to him from the media, his mother had protected him from having the public form an opinion on who he was, but within that, he had allowed her to form his opinion of his life. Of what he could be. Of what he could have.

He had escaped the press defining him by that night, but he defined himself by it. By his mother's response.

Had trained himself to believe that if he did not act

above reproach in every way at all times, that he would be as useless as he had long feared.

Sophia saw more than that. Sophia saw through to the man he might have been. She made him think that perhaps he could be that man again.

And he had sent her away, because he didn't feel worthy of that.

But she thought he was. She mattered more. She mattered more than Giovanni. She mattered more than his mother.

She mattered more than all the stars in the sky.

If Sophia could love him...

Pain burst through him, as brilliant and blinding as the light from only a moment before.

He loved her. He loved her. And he had hurt her. He had sent her away to protect himself. Which was truly no different than what his mother had done, in many ways.

Putting himself before her.

He would not.

He didn't want to marry Sophia because of the baby. He didn't want her because he was sick.

He wanted her because she was her.

Undeniably, beautifully her.

When he closed his eyes, it was her face he saw.

And then, he knew nothing else.

CHAPTER FOURTEEN

THE DAY OF the wedding, Sophia stayed in her mother's house until clothing could be sent. Then she was bundled up and whisked off to the palace, where she checked to see if anything had been canceled.

It had not been.

Perhaps it was Luca's ferocious pride not able to come to grips with the fact that she was going to defy him.

Perhaps he had a plan to try and win her back.

Or perhaps, he had simply known that in the end she wouldn't leave him to be humiliated.

Whatever the reasoning, she would find out later. With the help of her stylist, she got dressed in her wedding gown far earlier than was necessary. And then she began to make inquiries of the staff.

"Where is he?" she asked.

"The king?"

"Yes."

"In his rooms. But you know it is bad luck for the groom…"

"I already had the bad luck to fall in love with my stepbrother. I think I have reached my limit." She picked up the front of her dress and dashed across the palace, making her way to Luca's chamber.

But he wasn't there. Dejected, she began to make the journey back to her own. The halls were remarkably empty, the staff all seeing to preparations for the wedding that might not happen, it seemed to Sophia.

So she was surprised when she heard another set of footsteps in the corridor.

She looked up and saw Luca standing there. He was wearing black slacks and a white shirt that was unbuttoned at the throat. For one blinding second she could hardly fight the impulse to fling herself across the empty space between them and kiss him there. Right at his neck, right where his heart beat, strong and steady.

But she remained rooted to where she was, her breathing shallow.

"Luca," she said.

"I was searching for you," he said.

"Here I am."

He frowned. "You're wearing a wedding gown."

She swished her hips back and forth, the dress swirling around her legs. "Yes."

"You said you wouldn't marry me."

"I changed my mind."

"Well. I have decided that I changed my mind, as well."

"What?"

"I do not wish to marry you simply because you're having a baby, Sophia. You're right. That would be a terrible thing. A terrible mistake."

Sophia felt crushed. As if he had brought those strong hands down over her heart and ground it into powder.

"You don't want to marry me?" she asked.

"I do want to marry you," he said. "But I'm happy to not marry you. We can live in sin. We can have a bastard. We could create scandal the world over and forget everyone else."

Sophia was stunned. She blinked. "No. Luca, your reputation... The reputation of San Gennaro..."

"It doesn't matter. If I must court scandal to prove my feelings for you, then I will do so. It is nothing in the face of my feelings for you. My love for you. And if I have to burn all of it to the ground to prove to you that what I feel is real, believe me, Sophia. My reputation is nothing, my throne is nothing, if I don't have you. I would give all of it up. For you. That was the real sickness in my blood, my darling girl. That I wanted so badly to hold on to this thing that I believed was more important than anything. Was the only thing that gave me value. While I fought with what I really wanted on the inside. You. It was always you. But I knew that I was going to have to give up that facade of perfection that felt as if it defined my very existence if I was going to have you. Please believe me, *cara mia*, I would gladly leave it all behind for you. For this. For us."

Then Sophia did cross the space between them. She did fling her arms around his neck. And she kissed him there, where his pulse was throbbing at the base of his throat. "Luca," she whispered. "Luca, I believe you. And I want to be married to you. Because I want it to be real. I want it to be forever. We could make vows in a forest, and I know it would be just as real, but we might as well give our child legitimacy, don't you think?"

"I mean, I suppose it would make things easier. With succession and everything."

"You're a king. We could bend the rules. But I feel like perhaps we should just get married."

"I kept thinking there were more rules for me because I was a king. But all those chains were inside me. And all the darkness… It's because I refused to let the light in. I stood there, on the island, and looked up at the stars. And I marveled at them. And wished very much that I could… That I could be more than darkness. That you could be my light. The only one stopping that was me. All along. The only thing stopping it was…"

"Fear. I understand that… That hope is the most frightening thing there is."

"It is," Luca agreed. "Truly terrifying to want for more when you simply accepted all the things you would never have. When you've told yourself you don't need it."

"Luca," she said softly. "You're not broken. You are not damaged. The people who hurt you… They are the ones who are broken."

"I was broken," he whispered. He grabbed hold of her hands and lifted them, kissing her fingertips. "I was broken for a time. But not now. You put me back together."

"We put each other back together."

"I love you," he said.

"I love you, too."

"I did not think I would get my happy ending."

"You didn't?"

He shook his head. "Stepsiblings of any stripe are always evil."

"Well, then I could just as easily have been evil, too."

"Of course not," he said. "You're the princess."

"And you happen to be my Prince Charming, Luca. Stepbrother or not."

"Am I very charming?" He grinned at her, and the expression on his face made her light up inside.

"Not always," she said, smiling slightly. "But you're mine. And that's all that matters."

"That makes you mine, too."

"I choose you. I choose you over everything," she said. She pressed a kiss to his lips, and he held her for a moment.

"I choose you, too," he said. "Over everything."

And though they spoke their vows later that day, it was those vows that she knew would carry them through for the rest of their lives.

EPILOGUE

SHE WAS ABOVE him in absolutely every way. A radiant angel of light, his wife. And never had he been more certain of that than when he looked at her, holding their daughter in her arms.

He had been right about one thing, the scandal of their union had settled quickly enough once the excitement over the royal baby had overshadowed it all. A new little princess was much more interesting to the world over than how Sophia and Luca had gotten their start.

Luca knelt down by his wife's hospital bed, gazing in awe at the two most important women in his life.

"What do you think, Your Majesty?" she asked.

"I think…" He swallowed hard. "I think that with two such brilliant lights in my life I will never have to be lost in darkness again."

* * * * *

COMING SOON!

We really hope you enjoyed reading this book. If you're looking for more romance, be sure to head to the shops when new books are available on

Thursday 3rd October

To see which titles are coming soon, please visit

millsandboon.co.uk/nextmonth

MILLS & BOON

Coming next month

A PASSIONATE REUNION IN FIJI
Michelle Smart

'Hiding away?' Livia asked.

'Taking a breather.'

Dark brown eyes studied him, a combination of sympathy and amusement in them. Livia knew well how social situations made him feel.

She caught the barman's attention and ordered herself a bourbon too. 'This is a great party.'

'People are enjoying it?'

'Very much.' She nudged him with her elbow and pointed at one of the sofas. Two of the small children he'd almost tripped over earlier were fast asleep on it. A third, who'd gone a pale green colour, was eating a large scoop of ice cream, utter determination etched on her face. 'Someone needs to get that girl a sick bag.'

He laughed and was immediately thrown back to his sister's wedding again.

He'd approached Livia at the bar. She'd said something inane that had made him laugh. He wished he could remember what it was but it had slipped away the moment she'd said it, his attention too transfixed on her for words to stick.

She'd blown him away.

Those same feelings…

Had they ever really left him?

The music had slowed in tempo. The dance floor had filled, the children making way for the adults.

'We should dance,' he murmured.

Her chest rose, head tilted, teeth grazing over her bottom lip. 'I suppose we should…for appearances' sake.'

He breathed deeply and slowly held his hand out.

Equally slowly, she stretched hers out to meet his. The pads of her fingers pressed into his palm. Tingles shot through his skin. His fingers closed over them.

On the crowded dance floor, he placed his hands loosely on her hips. Her hands rested lightly on his shoulders. A delicate waft of her perfume filtered through his airwaves.

He clenched his jaw and purposely kept his gaze focused above her head.

They moved slowly in tempo with the music, their bodies a whisper away from touching…

'When did you take your tie off?' Livia murmured when she couldn't take the tension that had sprung between them any longer.

She'd been trying very hard not to breathe. Every inhalation sent Massimo's familiar musky heat and the citrus undertones of his cologne darting into her airwaves. Her skin vibrated with awareness, her senses uncoiling, tiny springs straining towards the man whose hands hardly touched her hips. She could feel the weight in them though, piercing through her skin.

Caramel eyes slowly drifted down to meet her gaze.

The music beating around them reduced to a burr.

The breath of space between them closed. The tips of her breasts brushed against the top of his flat stomach. The weight of his hands increased in pressure.

Heat pulsed deep in her pelvis.

Her hands crept without conscious thought over his shoulder blades. Heart beating hard, her fingers found his neck…her palms pressed against it.

His right hand caressed slowly up her back. She shivered at the darts of sensation rippling through her.

Distantly, she was aware the song they were dancing to had finished.

His left hand drew across her lower back and gradually pulled her so close their bodies became flush.

Her cheek pressed into his shoulder. She could feel the heavy thuds of his heart. They matched the beats of hers.

His mouth pressed into the top of her head. The warmth of his ragged breath whispered in the strands of her hair. Her lungs had stopped functioning. Not a hitch of air went into them.

A finger brushed a lock of her hair.

She closed her eyes.

The lock was caught and wound in his fingers.

She turned her cheek and pressed her mouth to his throat…

A body slammed into them. Words, foreign to her drumming ears but unmistakably words of apology, were gabbled.

They pulled apart.

There was a flash of bewilderment in Massimo's eyes she knew must be mirrored in hers before he blinked it away.

A song famous at parties all around the world was now playing. The floor was packed with bodies all joining in with the accompanying dance. Even the passed-out children had woken up to join in with it.

And she'd been oblivious. They both had.

Continue reading
A PASSIONATE REUNION IN FIJI
Michelle Smart

Available next month
www.millsandboon.co.uk

LET'S TALK

Romance

For exclusive extracts, competitions
and special offers, find us online:

Want even more
ROMANCE?

Join our bookclub today!

Visit millsandbook.co.uk/Bookclub
and save on brand new books.

MILLS & BOON